THE BALL AND THE CROSS

G. K. Chesterton

With a New Introduction by
Martin Gardner

DOVER PUBLICATIONS, INC.
NEW YORK

Copyright

Introduction copyright © 1995 by Dover Publications, Inc.
All rights reserved under Pan American and International Copyright Conventions.

Published in Canada by General Publishing Company, Ltd., 30 Lesmill Road, Don Mills, Toronto, Ontario.
Published in the United Kingdom by Constable and Company, Ltd., 3 The Lanchesters, 162–164 Fulham Palace Road, London W6 9ER.

Bibliographical Note

This Dover edition, first published in 1995, is an unabridged republication of the edition published by Wells Gardner, Darton & Co., Ltd., London, 1910 (it had been published in book form in New York the previous year by the John Lane Company, and had been serialized in 1905 and 1906 in *The Commonwealth*, London). Martin Gardner has written a new Introduction specially for this edition.

Library of Congress Cataloging-in-Publication Data

Chesterton, G. K. (Gilbert Keith), 1874–1936.
  The ball and the cross / G.K. Chesterton ; with a new introduction by Martin Gardner.
    p.   cm.
  ISBN 0-486-28805-6 (pbk.)
  1. Friendship—Scotland—Fiction.   2. Catholics—Scotland—Fiction.   3. Atheists—Scotland—Fiction.   4. Men—Scotland—Fiction.   I. Title.
PR4453.C4B143   1995
823'.912—dc20   95-11742
                                                                                    CIP

Manufactured in the United States of America
Dover Publications, Inc., 31 East 2nd Street, Mineola, N.Y. 11501

Introduction to the Dover Edition

"Think not that I am come to send peace on earth:
I came not to send peace, but a sword."
— MATTHEW 10:34

The Ball and the Cross was Chesterton's second novel and like all his novels is a mixture of fantasy, farce and theology. The basic plot is easily summarized. Evan MacIan is a tall, dark-haired, blue-eyed Scottish Highlander and a devout but naive Roman Catholic. He is so politically conservative that he is a Jacobite who longs for a restoration of the Stuart monarchy. James Turnbull is a short, red-haired, gray-eyed Scottish Lowlander and a devout but naive atheist. Politically he is a romantic socialist. (In his previous novel, *The Napoleon of Notting Hill*, G. K. gave the name Turnbull to the owner of a curiosity shop who is also a military genius.) Both men are fanatical in their opinions.

The two meet when MacIan smashes the window of the street office where Turnbull publishes an atheist journal. This act of rage occurs when MacIan sees posted on the shop's window a sheet that blasphemes the Virgin Mary, presumably implying she was an adulteress who gave birth to an illegitimate Jesus. When MacIan challenges Turnbull to a duel to the death, Turnbull is overjoyed. For twenty years no one had paid the slightest attention to his Bible bashing. Now at last someone is taking him seriously! Most of the rest of the story is a series of comic events in which the two enemies wander about seeking a spot for their duel, only to be forever prevented from fighting by the police and other civil authorities.

Two asymmetrical romances enter the narrative. MacIan, the believer, falls in love with Beatrice, an Englishwoman who is an agnostic. Turnbull, the skeptic, is smitten with Madeleine, a Frenchwoman who is a practicing Catholic. At the end, each man comes to admire the other for the courage of his convictions, and they become good friends even as they continue their efforts to fight. At one point MacIan saves Turnbull from drowning.

iii

On the lowest level of allegory Chesterton is celebrating in this story a vigorous verbal duel that he had fought with Robert Peel Glanville Blatchford, a now-forgotten but then widely read journalist who was an archenemy of Christianity. In book after book, article after article, Blatchford exalted atheism, blasted the Bible and trumpeted socialism. Chesterton considered him a worthy opponent, and for two years the two men, as G. K. put it in a letter, crossed "intellectual swords."

Blatchford attacked Chesterton in his own socialist weekly, *The Clarion*, and G. K. slashed back in his column in *The Daily News*, in the Christian socialist periodical *The Commonwealth*, and in three articles for *The Clarion* that you will find reprinted in *Collected Works of G. K. Chesterton*, Vol. I (Ignatius Press, 1986). Dozens of the arguments Chesterton used with gusto in *The Clarion* are later repeated by MacIan and in Chesterton's *Orthodoxy*.

Chesterton of course bore no outward resemblance to MacIan, who was tall and thin, and totally lacking G. K.'s sense of humor. Nor did Blatchford have any physical resemblance to Turnbull. In his autobiography Chesterton describes Blatchford as "an old soldier with brown Italian eyes and a wondrous mustache." There is no doubt, however, that *The Ball and the Cross*, which G. K. wrote only a year after his battle with Blatchford, is a comic portrayal of that battle with real swords taking the place of verbal thrusts.

Just as almost no one in Chesterton's novel takes seriously the duel between MacIan and Turnbull, so almost no one in England paid serious attention to the Blatchford–Chesterton debate. Amusing, yes; significant, no. Even Blatchford said he thought G. K. was a mere actor pretending to be a Christian. In his memoirs Chesterton tells of attending a dinner sponsored by the *Clarion* staff at the time he and the editor were fighting. G. K. found himself sitting next to a man who wanted to know if he really believed all the things he had been saying.

> I informed him with adamantine gravity that I did most definitely believe in those things I was defending against Blatchford. His cold and refined face did not move a visible muscle; and yet I knew in some fashion it had completely altered. "Oh, you *do*," he said, "I beg your pardon. Thank you. That's all I wanted to know." And he went on eating his (probably vegetarian) meal. But I was sure that for the rest of the evening, despite his calm, he felt as if he were sitting next to a fabulous griffin.

Chesterton goes on to say that one central point in his dispute with Blatchford was over free will. Blatchford was a strict determinist. Chesterton sensibly argued that if you didn't believe the will was free, it would be unreasonable to thank someone for passing you the mustard.

And yet the two men remained friends. In *Heretics* Chesterton calls Blatchford "a very able and honest journalist." Indeed, G. K. had more respect for him than Blatchford had for G. K. I have no doubt that Chesterton was thinking of Blatchford when he has MacIan call Turnbull a "good atheist . . . you clean, courteous, reverent, pious old blasphemer." It is surely a coincidence, but I discovered (with the help of my numerologist friend Dr. Irving Joshua Matrix) that if you take JT, the initials of James Turnbull, and shift each letter ahead eight steps in the alphabet (assume Z is followed by A) you arrive at RB, the initials of Robert Blatchford. Moreover, if you shift GKC back two steps you get EIA, which might stand for Evan and Ian. (And GC shifted back one step produces the FB of Father Brown.)

What finally happened to Blatchford? Fasten your seat belt! After his wife Sally died in 1921, a British medium put him in touch with her spirit and in 1923 he became a Spiritualist! "I am quite satisfied that I was with Sally," he wrote to a friend, "and I feel very happy about it." His little book *More Things in Heaven and Earth* (1926) is about his newfound faith.

I do not know whether Chesterton, who died in 1936, ever expressed relish over this conversion of his friendly enemy to miracles and a strong belief in an afterlife. It surely would have reminded him of his oftenquoted aphorism, that when people stop believing in God they do not believe in nothing but in anything. Conan Doyle, too, turned to Spiritualism after abandoning Catholicism. In his history of Spiritualism, Doyle proudly lists Blatchford among prominent "materialists" who converted to spookery.

On a second level of allegory, *The Ball and the Cross* is clearly intended to mirror the conflict between Augustine's City of God, which for Chesterton was the Catholic Church, and the City of Man, which is under the control of Satan. If you are a conservative Catholic you can interpret the novel as about the conflict between the Church and Satan — a conflict destined to last until the end of the world. William F. Buckley, in the introduction to a reprinting of his first book, *God and Man at Yale*, must have had Chesterton's novel in mind when he wrote: "The duel between Christianity and atheism is the most important in the world. I further believe that the struggle between individualism and collectivism is the same struggle reproduced on a higher level."

Readers who are non-Catholic Christians can take the novel more broadly as a conflict between Christian faith and atheism, and orthodox Jews and Muslims can similarly see the novel as a conflict between their faith and its enemies. This brings us to the third and highest level of allegory. On this level MacIan does not symbolize any particular faith, but only a faith in God. No chasm in the history of thought is deeper than that between those who believe in a God who cares for humanity and those who see no purpose or morality in the universe apart from the purposes and morals of the human species.

On this nonsectarian level, *The Ball and the Cross* is an indictment of modern culture for being essentially Laodicean. In Revelation 3:16 John attacks the church at Laodicea for being neither cold nor hot: "So then because thou art lukewarm, and neither cold nor hot, I will spue thee out of my mouth." Contrast this (as I learned from Donald E. Knuth's book *3:16*) with John 3:16, a verse that draws a sharp line between the saved and unsaved. In past centuries great thinkers were proud to let everyone know where they stood on religious questions. Today they couldn't care less. A philosopher willing to stand up and fight for either atheism or theism is considered eccentric and slightly mad. Has any philosopher of worldwide eminence since Bertrand Russell openly called himself an atheist?

Laodicean lukewarmness extends even to those who profess a religion. We still insist that our presidents call themselves Christian, but exactly what they believe is deemed irrelevant. Catholic admirers of John Kennedy seem not in the least disturbed to learn that he lost his faith early in life. All that matters is that he went to Mass and pretended to be a Catholic. Who knows or cares what dogmas Ronald Reagan, who professes to be a born-again Protestant, really believes? Who knows what Episcopalian doctrines George Bush believes? We know he was a good pal of Billy Graham and Jerry Falwell, but were these friendships genuine, or were they carefully calculated to win political support from the ever increasing ranks of fundamentalist voters? Bill Clinton is a Baptist and Hillary is a Methodist. Does either of them believe that the tomb of Jesus became miraculously empty? A reporter is free these days to ask a politician if he or she has committed adultery, but to ask about a basic religious belief would be considered the height of bad taste.

MacIan wanted to kill a man because he made unkind remarks about Mary. Indeed, a Catholic who denies the Virgin Birth, the Immaculate Conception and the Annunciation of Mary runs the risk, if not of excommunication, of damnation. In past centuries Catholics and Protestants alike were tortured and killed for expressing skepticism about much less fundamental doctrines.

Today, you will have a difficult time discovering what any prominent Christian actually believes. Does Father Greeley, for example, who has written an article about Mary for *The New York Times Magazine*, believe in the Virgin Birth? Do such Catholic politicians as Mario Cuomo, Jerry Brown, Eugene McCarthy, Edward Kennedy and Geraldine Ferraro? What about such Catholic writers as Pat Buchanan, Garry Wills and Peggy Noonan? John McLaughlin, who presides over the McLaughlin Group on TV, is an ex-priest. What doctrines does he now believe? Who cares? It is not so much that the public is irreligious, but that it is lukewarm, indifferent to dogmas. It is embarrassed when religious views are debated in public.

Millions of Catholics and Protestants around the world now attend liberal churches where they listen to music and Laodicean sermons, and (if Protestant) sing tuneless Laodicean hymns. They may even stand and recite the Apostles' Creed out of force of habit and not believe a word of it. If a pastor or priest dared to preach a sermon on, say, whether Jesus' corpse was actually revivified, the congregation would quickly find a way to get rid of him.

It is a scandal of American Protestantism that no one knows whether Reinhold Niebuhr did or did not believe in the afterlife taught by Jesus. I once tried to find out by writing to his widow, but she replied in a diplomatic letter that she had to let her husband's writings speak for themselves. Alas, nowhere in those writings can one find a clear answer to this question. Either Mrs. Niebuhr herself didn't know, or she wouldn't tell me. *The Ball and the Cross* is about a thick yellow fog that has settled over Christendom. Only Protestant fundamentalists and conservative Catholics, God bless 'em, are willing to take firm stands and say exactly what they believe.

It is this yellow fog that both MacIan and Turnbull detest. Along the way, in their efforts to find a spot where they can fight unmolested, they meet a Tolstoyan pacifist, a purveyor of pornography, a Nietzschean nihilist, a vague Protestant, a good citizen, a wimpish man who loves bloodshed and a pantheist enamored of the "life force." All these men have found mushy substitutes for a robust theism or atheism. When God goes, Chesterton is telling us, half-gods arrive.

Lucifer, with his large cloven chin (the cleft symbolizes his break with God), is of course the Prince of the World. He becomes England's secret ruler, certifying as insane not only MacIan and Turnbull, but all those who have even learned of their desire to fight. Professor Lucifer is the force behind modern science, about which Chesterton unfortunately knew nothing, and especially behind what G. K. considered the false theory of evolution. It is Lucifer who invented his airship's advanced technology, and who runs the asylum in Kent where everything is handled with superb efficiency by invisible machines that keep the walls washed and sterile, and provide mushy food. The asylum, where the doctors are as crazy as the patients, is Chesterton's caricature of a secular world gone mad in its efforts to avoid coming to grips with Christianity.

One must not suppose that Chesterton favored any sort of actual warfare between believers and unbelievers. Both Turnbull and MacIan, after two remarkable dreams, are given visions of the future each has longed for. In Turnbull's dream the cross of St. Paul's is broken, and secular socialism has grown into a police state similar to the Soviet Union under Stalin or Communist China under Mao or its present leaders. In MacIan's dream the ball on St. Paul's has become invisible. The state has become a theocracy, a police state in the grip of Christian fascism. Its spirit is that of the Inquisition, the massacre of St. Bartholomew, the burning of witches, and today's Islamic nations eager for holy wars against infidels.

Note how Chesterton has anticipated the rewriting of history by the Soviet Union when he has England turn the duel into a nonevent by incarcerating everyone who knew about it. Observe how he has anticipated the Soviet Union's use of mental institutions to suppress political dissent. Both MacIan and Turnbull eventually realize that if either of their fanatical views ever captured a nation, the result would be a terrible tyranny and the disappearance of individual freedoms. Only religious tolerance and the freedoms of democracy can prevent the rise of such evil empires.

Would that Chesterton had left it at this, but instead he ends his novel with an improbable climax. At the last moment, when Turnbull witnesses a miracle, he becomes a Christian! The two swords fall to the ground in the pattern of a cross. Chesterton is of course expressing his belief that in some far-off future the entire world will become the City of God, but such an ending certainly turns off any reader who is not a conservative Catholic or a Protestant fundamentalist.

For Chesterton, the arms of the cross stretch into the universe and beyond the universe into infinite realms that transcend the world we know. The ball, in contrast, is finite and self-contained. Rationalism without faith goes round and round in circles, never escaping from the material cosmos. Perhaps H. G. Wells had the ball in mind when, in the parallel world of *Men Like Gods*, he has Jesus killed by torture on a wheel.

Other symbols in the novel are less clear. In the Bible, Michael is an archangel. But the little Bulgarian monk, one of whose names is Michael, is not an angel. I believe that Chesterton intended him to signify the Catholic Church. He is ancient, learned and wise, but when he is persecuted and confined, he takes on the appearance of being childish:

> One talks trivially of a face like parchment, but this old man's face was so wrinkled that it was like a parchment loaded with hieroglyphics. The lines of his face were so deep and complex that one could see five or ten different faces besides the real one, as one can see them in an

elaborate wall-paper. And yet while his face seemed like a scripture older than the gods, his eyes were quite bright, blue, and startled like those of a baby. They looked as if they had only an instant before been fitted into his head.

The monk's final act, when he sings, laughs and performs a miracle, suggests how the Church, in spite of its persecutions, always bursts forth with renewed power, "reeling but erect" as Chesterton put it in *The Everlasting Man*. More than once in the novel Turnbull calls the monk a "thing," and toward the end of Chapter XVII the word is capitalized. It is no coincidence that one of Chesterton's books about the Church is titled *The Thing*.

There is a mystery closely connected to the monk. In each of the cells in which the monk, MacIan and Turnbull are confined, the walls are perfectly smooth except for one iron peg or spike. Turnbull detests it more than the "damned cocoa" he is served daily. (Chesterton hated cocoa. Here its blandness suggests the lukewarm food that the Bible says will be vomited.) So annoyed is MacIan by the spike that he rips it from the wall. "Even now I've got it out," he says, "I can't discover what it was for." And later we learn that "to this day" Turnbull does not know its purpose.

But the monk is not annoyed by the spike, or by anything else about his cell. He likes the cell's long, narrow shape, and he amuses himself by counting the squares on the floor. "But that not the best," he says. "Spike is the best . . . it sticks out." We are not told why he said this. What on earth does it mean?

John Wren-Lewis, writing on "Joy Without a Cause" (*The Chesterton Review*, February 1986), puts forth an interesting conjecture. When the monk is dropped onto the dome of St. Paul's he narrowly escapes death. After reaching the street in safety, he feels like a child again:

> Everything his eye fell on it feasted on, not æsthetically, but with a plain, jolly appetite as of a boy eating buns. He relished the square-ness of the houses; he liked their clean angles as if he had just cut them with a knife. The lit squares of the shop windows excited him as the young are excited by the lit stage of some promising pantomime. He happened to see in one shop which projected with a bulging bravery on to the pavement some square tins of potted meat, and it seemed like a hint of a hundred hilarious high teas in a hundred streets of the world. He was, perhaps, the happiest of all the children of men.

The monk, according to Wren-Lewis, has discovered one of Chesterton's favorite themes — that we are surrounded by "tremendous trifles," little things that ought to give us pleasure and for which we should be grateful. The monk is happy anywhere, even in prison. In his barren cell the spike breaks the smooth monotony of the walls. It is not a flower, or the bird that arouses the gratitude of Byron's "Prisoner of Chillon." Still, it is something, and the monk is thankful for it, taking pleasure in its spikiness. In a later book on Robert Louis Stevenson, Chesterton wrote of Stevenson: "He loved things to stand out; we might say he loved them to stick out; as does the hilt of a sabre or the feather in a cap. He loved the pattern of crossed swords; he almost loved the pattern of the gallows because it is a clear shape like the cross." To Freudians, a spike is a phallic symbol, but Chesterton could not have had that consciously in mind.

I think Wren-Lewis is right about the spike, but it seems to me that Chesterton may also have had in mind a symbolic meaning. The blank walls of the cell represent the blank metaphysics of atheism. They are smooth and continuous like the surface of the ball on St. Paul's. But for Chesterton, history has been repeatedly broken by enormous discontinuities.

The creation of the universe was the first big bang. The fall of Satan and the fall of man were other bangs. The abrupt appearance of life, and the sudden appearance of animals with human souls, are still other discontinuities. Evolution, which Chesterton rejected without understanding, is a gradual process of change that began with the big bang. But for Chesterton, history is a series of things that "stick out." Each person's birth is a spike. Each person's rebirth is a spike. The Incarnation, when God suddenly entered the world, is a colossal peg that for Chesterton was the central turning point of human history. Each arm of the cross is a spike. And the Bible promises an apocalyptic end to history. The big fire that closes *The Ball and the Cross*, forcing Lucifer to leave the earth, is the final conflagration at the end of the world.

If there is no God to give history a transcendent purpose, then the universe and all history are ultimately pointless. But Chesterton, like any theist, believed the universe has a point as sharp as the point of a sword. "For me all good things come to a point," Chesterton writes in Chapter 4 of *Orthodoxy*. Similarly, "Everything is coming to a point," MacIan says in Chapter XIX. Indeed, the conviction that the universe is not pointless is the main point of the novel. Perhaps that is also the basic meaning of the spike.

When we are told that "Above all, he [Turnbull] had a deep hatred, deep as the hell he did not believe in, for the objectless iron peg on the wall," perhaps Chesterton is symbolizing what in *The Everlasting Man* he calls "the halo of hatred around the Church of God." Elsewhere Chesterton liked to symbolize the Church by a key. When MacIan pulls out the spike, it proves to be a key that alters the asylum's machinery and unlocks all the cell doors.

The Ball and the Cross was first published in book form in 1909 by the John Lane Company of New York. Sheets were sent to Wells Gardner, Darton & Co., Ltd., in London, for the first British edition the following year. The novel had previously been serialized in 1905 and 1906 in *The Commonwealth*, the Christian socialist monthly mentioned earlier. It has been translated into French, Italian, Spanish, Czechoslovakian and Polish, perhaps into other languages. Reviews of the book, almost all objecting to the plot's allegorical obscurity, appeared in British journals in 1910.*

A misprint in both American and British first editions is worth mentioning. On page 93, line 6 of these editions, "heal thy working man" should be "healthy-looking man." Also worth noting is that, on page 358, line 18, of the American edition, there is the sentence: "But God blast my soul and body!" The British edition changed this to "But Lord bless us and save us!" And on page 345 we encounter what surely is a mistake of some sort when the monk says: "I am very happy," and the narrator follows this with "said the other, alphabetically." The word "alphabetically" makes no sense. John Peterson, who edits the *Midwest Chesterton News*, has a plausible explanation. Chesterton liked to dictate to stenographers. Did he speak the word "affably," which was either heard as "alphabetically" by the stenographer or later so misinterpreted from her shorthand?

In later years Chesterton expressed dissatisfaction with the novel. Here is a comment from his autobiography:

> I think the story called *The Ball and the Cross* had quite a good plot, about two men perpetually prevented by the police from fighting a duel about the collision of blasphemy and worship, or what all respectable people would call, "a mere difference about religion." I believe that the suggestion that the modern world is organised in relation to the most obvious and urgent of all questions, not so much to answer it wrongly, as to prevent it being answered at all, is a social suggestion that really has a great deal in it; but I am much more doubtful about whether I got a great deal out of it, even in comparison with what could be got out of it.

In a copy of *The Ball and the Cross* owned by Father John O'Connor, the original of Father Brown, Chesterton inscribed a poem that begins:

---

* Here is a partial list, with volume and page numbers: *Atheneum* 1:337; *Catholic World* 91:836; *Independent* 68:417; *Nation* 89:651; *Outlook* 94:504; *Saturday Review* 109:337; *Spectator* 105:285.

> This is a book I do not like,
> Take it away to Heckmondwike,
> A lurid exile, lost and sad
> To punish it for being bad.
> You need not take it from the shelf
> (I tried to read it once myself:
> The speeches jerk, the chapters sprawl,
> The story makes no sense at all)
> Hide it your Yorkshire moors among
> Where no man speaks the English tongue.

Maurice Evans, in a little book of praise for Chesterton, called *The Ball and the Cross* a "confused allegory." Although its central symbolism is obvious, the role of the monk is certainly obscure and unsatisfactory. At the beginning, when he debates Lucifer in the airship, he is a man of vast learning and acute intelligence. Yet at the end he is a helpless, bizarre idiot. Chesterton was probably trying to say that this is how the church appears when pushed down by a secular culture, but even so it is hard to believe that any of Chesterton's readers, or G. K. himself when he was older, could consider his monk a good symbol of the Church.

A philosophical but non-Christian theist such as myself can enjoy the novel on what I have called its third level of allegory. In a sense I admire a Protestant fundamentalist or a conservative Catholic more than someone who either has no religious opinions or, if he or she has, is too timid to talk about them. If you are an atheist or agnostic of the sort that has no interest whatever in the clash between theism and atheism, you will likely find the novel not worth your time. On the other hand, you may still enjoy reading it for its colorful style, with its constant alliteration, amusing puns and clever paradoxes; for its purple passages about sunsets, dawns and silver moonlight; and for the humor and melodrama of its crazy plot.

MARTIN GARDNER

Hendersonville, North Carolina

CONTENTS

CHAPTER I

A Discussion Somewhat
in the Air

THE FLYING SHIP of Professor Lucifer sang through the skies like a silver arrow; the bleak white steel of it, gleaming in the bleak blue emptiness of the evening. That it was far above the earth was no expression for it; to the two men in it, it seemed to be far above the stars. The professor had himself invented the flying machine, and had also invented nearly everything in it. Every sort of tool or apparatus had, in consequence, to the full, that fantastic and distorted look which belongs to the miracles of science. For the world of science and evolution is far more nameless and elusive and like a dream than the world of poetry or religion; since in the latter images and ideas remain themselves eternally, while it is the whole idea of evolution that identities melt into each other as they do in a nightmare.

All the tools of Professor Lucifer were the ancient human tools gone mad, grown into unrecognisable shapes, forgetful of their origin, forgetful of their names. That thing which looked like an enormous key with three wheels was really a patent and very deadly revolver. That object which seemed to be created by the entanglement of two corkscrews was really the key. The thing which might have been mistaken for a tricycle turned upside down was the inexpressibly important instrument to which the corkscrew was the key. All these things, as I say, the professor had invented; he had invented everything in the flying ship, with the exception, perhaps, of himself. This he had been born too late actually to inaugurate, but he believed, at least, that he had considerably improved it.

There was, however, another man on board, so to speak, at the time. Him, also, by a curious coincidence, the professor had not invented, and him he had not even very greatly improved, though he had fished him up with a lasso out of his own back garden, in Western Bulgaria, with the pure object of improving him. He was an exceedingly holy man, almost

1

entirely covered with white hair. You could see nothing but his eyes, and he seemed to talk with them. A monk of immense learning and acute intellect he had made himself happy in a little stone hut and a little stony garden in the Balkans, chiefly by writing the most crushing refutations and exposures of certain heresies, the last professors of which had been burnt (generally by each other) precisely 1,119 years previously. They were really very plausible and thoughtful heresies, and it was really a creditable or even glorious circumstance, that the old monk had been intellectual enough to detect their fallacy; the only misfortune was that nobody in the modern world was intellectual enough even to understand their argument. The old monk, one of whose names was Michael, and the other a name quite impossible to remember or repeat in our Western civilisation, had, however, as I have said, made himself quite happy while he was in a mountain hermitage in the society of wild animals. And now that his luck had lifted him above all the mountains in the society of a wild physicist, he made himself happy still.

"I have no intention, my good Michael," said Professor Lucifer, "of endeavouring to convert you by argument. The imbecility of your traditions can be quite finally exhibited to anybody with mere ordinary knowledge of the world, the same kind of knowledge which teaches us not to sit in draughts or not to encourage friendliness in impecunious people. It is folly to talk of this or that demonstrating the rationalist philosophy. Everything demonstrates it. Rubbing shoulders with men of all kinds —— "

"You will forgive me," said the monk, meekly from under loads of white beard, "but I fear I do not understand; was it in order that I might rub my shoulder against men of all kinds that you put me inside this thing?"

"An entertaining retort, in the narrow and deductive manner of the Middle Ages," replied the Professor, calmly, "but even upon your own basis I will illustrate my point. We are up in the sky. In your religion and all the religions, as far as I know (and I know everything), the sky is made the symbol of everything that is sacred and merciful. Well, now you are in the sky, you know better. Phrase it how you like, twist it how you like, you know that you know better. You know what are a man's real feelings about the heavens, when he finds himself alone in the heavens, surrounded by the heavens. You know the truth, and the truth is this. The heavens are evil, the sky is evil, the stars are evil. This mere space, this mere quantity, terrifies a man more than tigers or the terrible plague. You know that since our science has spoken, the bottom has fallen out of the Universe. Now, heaven is the hopeless thing, more hopeless than any hell. Now, if there be any comfort for all your miserable progeny of morbid apes, it must be in the earth, underneath you, under the roots of the grass, in the place where hell was of old. The fiery crypts, the lurid cellars of the under-world, to which you once condemned the wicked, are hideous enough, but at least they are more homely than the heaven in which we ride. And the time will come when you will all hide in them, to escape the horror of the stars."

"I hope you will excuse my interrupting you," said Michael, with a slight cough, "but I have always noticed — "

"Go on, pray go on," said Professor Lucifer, radiantly, "I really like to draw out your simple ideas."

"Well, the fact is," said the other, "that much as I admire your rhetoric and the rhetoric of your school, from a purely verbal point of view, such little study of you and your school in human history as I have been enabled to make has led me to — er — rather singular conclusion, which I find great difficulty in expressing, especially in a foreign language."

"Come, come," said the Professor, encouragingly, "I'll help you out. How did my view strike you?"

"Well, the truth is, I know I don't express it properly, but somehow it seemed to me that you always convey ideas of that kind with most eloquence, when — er — when — "

"Oh! get on," cried Lucifer, boisterously.

"Well, in point of fact when your flying ship is just going to run into something. I thought you wouldn't mind my mentioning it, but it's running into something now."

Lucifer exploded with an oath and leapt erect, leaning hard upon the handle that acted as a helm to the vessel. For the last ten minutes they had been shooting downwards into great cracks and caverns of cloud. Now, through a sort of purple haze, could be seen comparatively near to them what seemed to be the upper part of a huge, dark orb or sphere, islanded in a sea of cloud. The Professor's eyes were blazing like a maniac's.

"It is a new world," he cried, with a dreadful mirth. "It is a new planet and it shall bear my name. This star and not that other vulgar one shall be 'Lucifer, sun of the morning.' Here we will have no chartered lunacies, here we will have no gods. Here man shall be as innocent as the daisies, as innocent and as cruel — here the intellect — "

"There seems," said Michael, timidly, "to be something sticking up in the middle of it."

"So there is," said the Professor, leaning over the side of the ship, his spectacles shining with intellectual excitement. "What can it be? It might of course be merely a — "

Then a shriek indescribable broke out of him of a sudden, and he flung up his arms like a lost spirit. The monk took the helm in a tired way; he did not seem much astonished for he came from an ignorant part of the world in which it is not uncommon for lost spirits to shriek when they see the curious shape which the Professor had just seen on the top of the mysterious ball, but he took the helm only just in time, and by driving it hard to the left he prevented the flying ship from smashing into St. Paul's Cathedral.

A plain of sad-coloured cloud lay along the level of the top of the Cathedral dome, so that the ball and cross looked like a buoy riding on a leaden sea. As the flying ship swept towards it, this plain of cloud looked as dry and definite and rocky as any grey desert. Hence it gave to the mind and body a sharp and unearthly sensation when the ship cut and sank into the cloud as into any common mist, a thing without resistance. There was, as it were, a deadly shock in the fact that there was no shock. It was as if they had cloven into ancient cliffs like so much butter. But sensations awaited them which were much stranger than those of sinking through the solid earth. For a moment their eyes and nostrils were stopped with darkness and opaque cloud; then the darkness warmed into a kind of brown fog. And far, far below them the brown fog fell until it warmed into fire. Through the dense London atmosphere they could see below them the flaming London lights; lights which lay beneath them in squares and oblongs of fire. The fog and fire were mixed in a passionate vapour; you might say that the fog was drowning the flames; or you might say that the flames had set the fog on fire. Beside the ship and beneath it (for it swung just under the ball), the immeasurable dome itself shot out and down into the dark like a combination of voiceless cataracts. Or it was like some cyclopean sea-beast sitting above London and letting down its tentacles bewilderingly on every side, a monstrosity in that starless heaven. For the clouds that belonged to London had closed over the heads of the voyagers sealing up the entrance of the upper air. They had broken through a roof and come into a temple of twilight.

They were so near to the ball that Lucifer leaned his hand against it, holding the vessel away, as men push a boat off from a bank. Above it the cross already draped in the dark mists of the borderland was shadowy and more awful in shape and size.

Professor Lucifer slapped his hand twice upon the surface of the great orb as if he were caressing some enormous animal. "This is the fellow," he said, "this is the one for my money."

"May I with all respect inquire," asked the old monk, "what on earth you are talking about?"

"Why this," cried Lucifer, smiting the ball again, "here is the only symbol, my boy. So fat. So satisfied. Not like that scraggy individual, stretching his arms in stark weariness." And he pointed up to the cross, his face dark with a grin. "I was telling you just now, Michael, that I can prove the best part of the rationalist case and the Christian humbug from any symbol you liked to give me, from any instance I came across. Here is an instance with a vengeance. What could possibly express your philosophy and my philosophy better than the shape of that cross and the shape of this ball? This globe is reasonable; that cross is unreasonable. It is a four-legged animal, with one leg longer than the others. The globe is inevitable. The cross is arbitrary. Above all the globe is at unity with itself; the cross is primarily and above all things at enmity with itself. The cross is the conflict of two hostile lines, of irreconcilable direction. That silent thing up there is essentially a collision, a crash, a struggle in stone. Pah! that sacred symbol of yours has actually given its name to a description of desperation and muddle. When we speak of men at once ignorant of each other and frustrated by each other, we say they are at cross-purposes. Away with the thing! The very shape of it is a contradiction in terms."

"What you say is perfectly true," said Michael, with serenity. "But we like contradictions in terms. Man is a contradiction in terms; he is a beast whose superiority to other beasts consists in having fallen. That cross is, as you say, an eternal collision; so am I. That is a struggle in stone. Every form of life is a struggle in flesh. The shape of the cross is irrational, just as the shape of the human animal is irrational. You say the cross is a quadruped with one limb longer than the rest. I say man is a quadruped who only uses two of his legs."

The Professor frowned thoughtfully for an instant, and said: "Of course everything is relative, and I would not deny that the element of struggle and self-contradiction, represented by that cross, has a necessary place at a certain evolutionary stage. But surely the cross is the lower development and the sphere the higher. After all it is easy enough to see what is really wrong with Wren's architectural arrangement."

"And what is that, pray?" inquired Michael, meekly.

"The cross is on top of the ball," said Professor Lucifer, simply. "That is surely wrong. The ball should be on top of the cross. The cross is a mere barbaric prop; the ball is perfection. The cross at its best is but the bitter tree of man's history; the ball is the rounded, the ripe and final fruit. And the fruit should be at the top of the tree, not at the bottom of it."

"Oh!" said the monk, a wrinkle coming into his forehead, "so you think that in a rationalistic scheme of symbolism the ball should be on top of the cross?"

"It sums up my whole allegory," said the professor.

"Well, that is really very interesting," resumed Michael, slowly, "because I think in that case you would see a most singular effect, an effect that has generally been achieved by all those able and powerful systems which rationalism, or the religion of the ball, has produced to lead or teach mankind. You would see, I think, that thing happen which is always the ultimate embodiment and logical outcome of your logical scheme."

"What are you talking about?" asked Lucifer. "What would happen?"

"I mean it would fall down," said the monk, looking wistfully into the void.

Lucifer made an angry movement and opened his mouth to speak, but Michael, with all his air of deliberation, was proceeding before he could bring out a word.

"I once knew a man like you, Lucifer," he said, with a maddening monotony and slowness of articulation. "He took this —— "

"There is no man like me," cried Lucifer, with a violence that shook the ship.

"As I was observing," continued Michael, "this man also took the view that the symbol of Christianity was a symbol of savagery and all unreason. His history is rather amusing. It is also a perfect allegory of what happens to rationalists like yourself. He began, of course, by refusing to allow a crucifix in his house, or round his wife's neck, or even in a picture. He said, as you say, that it was an arbitrary and fantastic shape, that it was a monstrosity, loved because it was paradoxical. Then he began to grow fiercer and more eccentric; he would batter the crosses by the roadside; for he lived in a Roman Catholic country. Finally in a height of frenzy he climbed the steeple of the Parish Church and tore down the cross, waving it in the air, and uttering wild soliloquies up there under the stars. Then one still summer evening as he was wending his way homewards, along a lane, the devil of his madness came upon him with a violence and transfiguration which changes the world. He was standing smoking, for a moment, in the front of an interminable line of palings, when his eyes were opened. Not a light shifted, not a leaf stirred, but he saw as if by a sudden change in the eyesight that this paling was an army of innumerable crosses linked together over hill and dale. And he whirled up his heavy stick and went at it as if at an army. Mile after mile along his homeward path he broke it down and tore it up. For he hated the cross and every paling is a wall of crosses. When he returned to his house he was a literal madman. He sat upon a chair and then started up from it for the cross-bars of the carpentry repeated the intolerable image. He flung himself upon a bed only to remember that this, too, like all workmanlike things, was constructed on the accursed plan. He broke his furniture because it was made of crosses. He burnt his house because it was made of crosses. He was found in the river."

Lucifer was looking at him with a bitten lip.

"Is that story really true?" he asked.

"Oh, no," said Michael, airily. "It is a parable. It is a parable of you and all your rationalists. You begin by breaking up the Cross; but you end by breaking up the habitable world. We leave you saying that nobody ought to join the Church against his will. When we meet you again you are saying that no one has any will to join it with. We leave you saying that there is no such place as Eden. We find you saying that there is no such place as Ireland. You start by hating the irrational and you come to hate everything, for everything is irrational and so —— "

Lucifer leapt upon him with a cry like a wild beast's. "Ah," he screamed, "to every man his madness. You are mad on the cross. Let it save you."

And with a herculean energy he forced the monk backwards out of the reeling car on to the upper part of the stone ball. Michael, with as abrupt an agility, caught one of the beams of the cross and saved himself from falling. At the same instant Lucifer drove down a lever and the ship shot up with him in it alone.

"Ha! ha!" he yelled, "what sort of a support do you find it, old fellow?"

"For practical purposes of support," replied Michael, grimly, "it is at any rate a great deal better than the ball. May I ask if you are going to leave me here?"

"Yes, yes. I mount! I mount!" cried the Professor in ungovernable excitement. "Altiora peto. My path is upward."

"How often have you told me, Professor, that there is really no up or down in space?" said the monk. "I shall mount up as much as you will."

"Indeed," said Lucifer, leering over the side of the flying ship. "May I ask what you are going to do?"

The monk pointed downward at Ludgate Hill. "I am going," he said, "to climb up into a star."

Those who look at the matter most superficially regard paradox as something which belongs to jesting and light journalism. Paradox of this kind is to be found in the saying of the dandy, in the decadent comedy, "Life is much too important to be taken seriously." Those who look at the matter a little more deeply or delicately see that paradox is a thing which especially belongs to all religions. Paradox of this kind is to be found in such a saying as "The meek shall inherit the earth." But those who see and feel the fundamental fact of the matter know that paradox is a thing that belongs not to religion only, but to all vivid and violent practical crises of human living. This kind of paradox may be clearly perceived by anybody who happens to be hanging in mid-space, clinging to one arm of the Cross of St. Paul's.

Father Michael in spite of his years, and in spite of his asceticism (or because of it, for all I know), was a very healthy and happy old gentle-man. And as he swung on a bar above the sickening emptiness of air, he realised; with that sort of dead detachment which belongs to the brains of those in peril, the deathless and hopeless contradiction which is involved in the mere idea of courage. He was a happy and healthy old gentleman and therefore he was quite careless about it. And he felt as every man feels in the taut moment of such terror that his chief danger was terror itself; his only possible strength would be a coolness amount-ing to carelessness, a carelessness amounting almost to a suicidal swag-ger. His one wild chance of coming out safely would be in not too desperately desiring to be safe. There might be footholds down that awful façade, if only he could not care whether they were footholds or no. If he were foolhardy he might escape; if he were wise he would stop where he was till he dropped from the cross like a stone. And this antinomy kept on repeating itself in his mind, a contradiction as large and staring as the immense contradiction of the Cross; he remembered having often heard the words, "Whosoever shall lose his life the same shall save it." He remembered with a sort of strange pity that this had always been made to mean that whoever lost his physical life should save his spiritual life. Now he knew the truth that is known to all fighters, and hunters, and climbers of cliffs. He knew that even his animal life could only be saved by a considerable readiness to lose it.

Some will think it improbable that a human soul swinging desper-ately in mid-air should think about philosophical inconsistencies. But such extreme states are dangerous things to dogmatise about. Fre-quently they produce a certain useless and joyless activity of the mere intellect, thought not only divorced from hope but even from desire. And if it is impossible to dogmatise about such states, it is still more impossible to describe them. To this spasm of sanity and clarity in Michael's mind succeeded a spasm of the elemental terror; the terror of the animal in us which regards the whole universe as its enemy; which, when it is victorious, has no pity, and so, when it is defeated has no imaginable hope. Of that ten minutes of terror it is not possible to speak in human words. But then again in that damnable darkness there began to grow a strange dawn as of grey and pale silver. And of this ultimate resignation or certainty it is even less possible to write; it is something stranger than hell itself; it is perhaps the last of the secrets of God. At the highest crisis of some incurable anguish there will suddenly fall upon the man the stillness of an insane contentment. It is not hope, for hope is broken and romantic and concerned with the future; this is complete and of the present. It is not faith, for faith by its very nature is fierce, and as it were at once doubtful and defiant; but this is simply a satisfaction. It is not knowledge, for the intellect seems to have no particular part in it.

Nor is it (as the modern idiots would certainly say it is) a mere numbness or negative paralysis of the powers of grief. It is not negative in the least; it is as positive as good news. In some sense, indeed, it is good news. It seems almost as if there were some equality among things, some balance in all possible contingencies which we are not permitted to know lest we should learn indifference to good and evil, but which is sometimes shown to us for an instant as a last aid in our last agony.

Michael certainly could not have given any sort of rational account of this vast unmeaning satisfaction which soaked through him and filled him to the brim. He felt with a sort of half-witted lucidity that the cross was there, and the ball was there, and the dome was there, that he was going to climb down from them, and that he did not mind in the least whether he was killed or not. This mysterious mood lasted long enough to start him on his dreadful descent and to force him to continue it. But six times before he reached the highest of the outer galleries terror had returned on him like a flying storm of darkness and thunder. By the time he had reached that place of safety he almost felt (as in some impossible fit of drunkenness) that he had two heads; one was calm, careless, and efficient; the other saw the danger like a deadly map, was wise, careful, and useless. He had fancied that he would have to let himself vertically down the face of the whole building. When he dropped into the upper gallery he still felt as far from the terrestrial globe as if he had only dropped from the sun to the moon. He paused a little, panting in the gallery under the ball, and idly kicked his heels, moving a few yards along it. And as he did so a thunderbolt struck his soul. A man, a heavy, ordinary man, with a composed indifferent face, and a prosaic sort of uniform, with a row of buttons, blocked his way. Michael had no mind to wonder whether this solid astonished man, with the brown mustache and the nickel buttons, had also come on a flying ship. He merely let his mind float in an endless felicity about the man. He thought how nice it would be if he had to live up in that gallery with that one man for ever. He thought how he would luxuriate in the nameless shades of this man's soul and then hear with an endless excitement about the nameless shades of the souls of all his aunts and uncles. A moment before he had been dying alone. Now he was living in the same world with a man; an inexhaustible ecstasy. In the gallery below the ball Father Michael had found that man who is the noblest and most divine and most lovable of all men, better than all the saints, greater than all the heroes — man Friday.

In the confused colour and music of his new paradise, Michael heard only in a faint and distant fashion some remarks that this beautiful solid man seemed to be making to him; remarks about something or other being after hours and against orders. He also seemed to be asking how

Michael "got up" there. This beautiful man evidently felt as Michael did that the earth was a star and was set in heaven.

At length Michael sated himself with the mere sensual music of the voice of the man in buttons. He began to listen to what he said, and even to make some attempt at answering a question which appeared to have been put several times and was now put with some excess of emphasis. Michael realised that the image of God in nickel buttons was asking him how he had come there. He said that he had come in Lucifer's ship. On his giving this answer the demeanour of the image of God underwent a remarkable change. From addressing Michael gruffly, as if he were a malefactor, he began suddenly to speak to him with a sort of eager and feverish amiability as if he were a child. He seemed particularly anxious to coax him away from the balustrade. He led him by the arm towards a door leading into the building itself, soothing him all the time. He gave what even Michael (slight as was his knowledge of the world) felt to be an improbable account of the sumptuous pleasures and varied advantages awaiting him downstairs. Michael followed him, however, if only out of politeness, down an apparently interminable spiral of staircase. At one point a door opened. Michael stepped through it, and the unaccountable man in buttons leapt after him and pinioned him where he stood. But he only wished to stand; to stand and stare. He had stepped as it were into another infinity, out under the dome of another heaven. But this was a dome of heaven made by man. The gold and green and crimson of its sunset were not in the shapeless clouds but in shapes of cherubim and seraphim, awful human shapes with a passionate plumage. Its stars were not above but far below, like fallen stars still in unbroken constellations; the dome itself was full of darkness. And far below, lower even than the lights, could be seen creeping or motionless, great black masses of men. The tongue of a terrible organ seemed to shake the very air in the whole void; and through it there came up to Michael the sound of a tongue more terrible; the dreadful everlasting voice of man, calling to his gods from the beginning to the end of the world. Michael felt almost as if he were a god, and all the voices were hurled at him.

"No, the pretty things aren't here," said the demi-god in buttons, caressingly. "The pretty things are downstairs. You come along with me. There's something that will surprise you downstairs; something you want very much to see."

Evidently the man in buttons did not feel like a god, so Michael made no attempt to explain his feelings to him, but followed him meekly enough down the trail of the serpentine staircase. He had no notion where or at what level he was. He was still full of the cold splendour of space, and of what a French writer has brilliantly named the "vertigo of the infinite," when another door opened, and with a shock indescribable he found himself on the familiar level, in a street full of faces, with the houses and even the lamp-posts above his head. He felt suddenly happy and suddenly indescribably small. He fancied he had been changed into a child again; his eyes sought the pavement seriously as children's do, as if it were a thing with which something satisfactory could be done. He felt the full warmth of that pleasure from which the proud shut themselves out; the pleasure which not only goes with humiliation, but which almost is humiliation. Men who have escaped death by a hair have it, and men whose love is returned by a woman unexpectedly, and men whose sins are forgiven them. Everything his eye fell on it feasted on, not æsthetically, but with a plain, jolly appetite as of a boy eating buns. He relished the squareness of the houses; he liked their clean angles as if he had just cut them with a knife. The lit squares of the shop windows excited him as the young are excited by the lit stage of some promising pantomime. He happened to see in one shop which pro- jected with a bulging bravery on to the pavement some square tins of potted meat, and it seemed like a hint of a hundred hilarious high teas in a hundred streets of the world. He was, perhaps, the happiest of all the children of men. For in that unendurable instant when he hung, half slipping, to the ball of St. Paul's, the whole universe had been destroyed and re-created.

Suddenly through all the din of the dark streets came a crash of glass. With that mysterious suddenness of the Cockney mob, a rush was made in the right direction, a dingy office, next to the shop of the potted meat. The pane of glass was lying in splinters about the pavement. And the police already had their hands on a very tall young man, with dark, lank hair and dark, dazed eyes, with a grey plaid over his shoulder, who had just smashed the shop window with a single blow of his stick.

"I'd do it again," said the young man, with a furious white face. "Anybody would have done it. Did you see what it said? I swear I'd do it again." Then his eyes encountered the monkish habit of Michael, and he pulled off his grey tam o'shanter with the gesture of a Catholic.

"Father, did you see what they said?" he cried, trembling. "Did you see what they dared to say? I didn't understand it at first. I read it half through before I broke the window."

Michael felt he knew not how. The whole peace of the world was pent up painfully in his heart. The new and childlike world which he had seen so suddenly, men had not seen at all. Here they were still at their old bewildering, pardonable, useless quarrels, with so much to be said on both sides, and so little that need be said at all. A fierce inspiration fell on him suddenly; he would strike them where they stood with the love of God. They should not move till they saw their own sweet and startling existence. They should not go from that place till they went home embracing like brothers and shouting like men delivered. From the Cross from which he had fallen fell the shadow of its fantastic mercy; and the first three words he spoke in a voice like a silver trumpet, held men as still as stones. Perhaps if he had spoken there for an hour in his illumination he might have founded a religion on Ludgate Hill. But the heavy hand of his guide fell suddenly on his shoulder.

"This poor fellow is dotty," he said good-humouredly to the crowd. "I found him wandering in the Cathedral. Says he came in a flying ship. Is there a constable to spare to take care of him?"

There was a constable to spare. Two other constables attended to the tall young man in grey; a fourth concerned himself with the owner of the shop, who showed some tendency to be turbulent. They took the tall young man away to a magistrate, whither we shall follow him in an ensuing chapter. And they took the happiest man in the world away to an asylum.

CHAPTER II

THE RELIGION OF
THE STIPENDIARY MAGISTRATE

THE EDITORIAL OFFICE of "The Atheist" had for some years past become less and less prominently interesting as a feature of Ludgate Hill. The paper was unsuited to the atmosphere. It showed an interest in the Bible unknown in the district, and a knowledge of that volume to which nobody else on Ludgate Hill could make any conspicuous claim. It was in vain that the editor of "The Atheist" filled his front window with fierce and final demands as to what Noah in the Ark did with the neck of the giraffe. It was in vain that he asked violently, as for the last time, how the statement "God is Spirit" could be reconciled with the statement "The earth is His footstool." It was in vain that he cried with an accusing energy that the Bishop of London was paid £12,000 a year for pretending to believe that the whale swallowed Jonah. It was in vain that he hung in conspicuous places the most thrilling scientific calculations about the width of the throat of a whale. Was it nothing to them all they that passed by? Did his sudden and splendid and truly sincere indignation never stir any of the people pouring down Ludgate Hill? Never. The little man who edited "The Atheist" would rush from his shop on starlit evenings and shake his fist at St. Paul's in the passion of his holy war upon the holy place. He might have spared his emotion. The cross at the top of St. Paul's and "The Atheist" shop at the foot of it were alike remote from the world. The shop and the Cross were equally uplifted and alone in the empty heavens.

To the little man who edited "The Atheist," a fiery little Scotchman, with fiery, red hair and beard, going by the name of Turnbull, all this decline in public importance seemed not so much sad or even mad, but merely bewildering and unaccountable. He had said the worst thing that could be said; and it seemed accepted and ignored like the ordinary second best of the politicians. Every day his blasphemies looked more glaring, and every day the dust lay thicker upon them. It made him feel as if he were moving in a world of idiots. He seemed among a race of men who smiled when told of their own death, or looked vacantly at the Day of Judgment. Year after year went by, and year after year the death of God in a shop in Ludgate became a less and less important occurrence. All the forward men of his age discouraged Turnbull. The socialists said he was cursing priests when he should be cursing capitalists. The artists said that the soul was most spiritual, not when freed from religion, but when freed from morality. Year after year went by, and at last a man came by who treated Mr. Turnbull's secularist shop with a real respect and seriousness. He was a young man in a grey plaid, and he smashed the window.

He was a young man, born in the Bay of Arisaig, opposite Rum and the Isle of Skye. His high, hawklike features and snaky black hair bore the mark of that unknown historic thing which is crudely called Celtic, but which is probably far older than the Celts, whoever they were. He was in name and stock a Highlander of the Macdonalds; but his family took, as was common in such cases, the name of a subordinate sept as a surname, and for all the purposes which could be answered in London, he called himself Evan MacIan. He had been brought up in some loneliness and seclusion as a strict Roman Catholic, in the midst of that little wedge of Roman Catholics which is driven into the Western Highlands. And he had found his way as far as Fleet Street, seeking some half-promised employment, without having properly realised that there were in the world any people who were not Roman Catholics. He had uncovered himself for a few moments before the statue of Queen Anne, in front of St. Paul's Cathedral, under the firm impression that it was a figure of the Virgin Mary. He was somewhat surprised at the lack of deference shown to the figure by the people bustling by. He did not understand that their one essential historical principle, the one law truly graven on their hearts, was the great and comforting statement that Queen Anne is dead. This faith was as fundamental as his faith, that Our Lady was alive. Any persons he had talked to since he had touched the fringe of our fashion or civilisation had been by a coincidence, sympathetic or hypocritical. Or if they had spoken some established blasphemies, he had been unable to understand them merely owing to the preoccupied satisfaction of his mind.

On that fantastic fringe of the Gaelic land where he walked as a boy, the cliffs were as fantastic as the clouds. Heaven seemed to humble itself and come closer to the earth. The common paths of his little village began to climb quite suddenly and seemed resolved to go to heaven. The sky seemed to fall down towards the hills; the hills took hold upon the sky. In the sumptuous sunset of gold and purple and peacock green but for the troublesome and quite unforeseen fact that the innocent Highlander read it stolidly to the end; a thing unknown among the most enthusiastic subscribers to the paper, and calculated in any case to create a new situation.

With a smart journalistic instinct characteristic of all his school, the editor of "The Atheist" had put first in his paper and most prominently in his window an article called "The Mesopotamian Mythology and its Effects on the Syriac Folk Lore." Mr. Evan MacIan began to read this quite idly, as he would have read a public statement beginning with a young girl dying in Brighton and ending with Bile Beans. He received the very considerable amount of information accumulated by the author with that tired clearness of the mind which children have on heavy summer afternoons — that tired clearness which leads them to go on asking questions long after they have lost interest in the subject and are as bored as their nurse. The streets were full of people and empty of adventures. He might as well know about the Gods of Mesopotamia as not; so he flattened his long, lean face against the dim bleak pane of the window and read all there was to read about the Mesopotamian Gods. He read how the Mesopotamians had a God named Sho (sometimes pronounced Ji), and that he was described as being very powerful, a striking similarity to some expressions about Jahveh, who is also described as having power. Evan had never heard of Jahveh in his life, and imagining him to be some other Mesopotamian idol, read on with a dull curiosity. He learnt that the name Sho, under its third form of Psa, occurs in an early legend which describes how the deity, after the manner of Jupiter on so many occasions, seduced a Virgin and begat a hero. This hero, whose name is not essential to our existence, was, it was said, the chief hero and Saviour of the Mesopotamian ethical scheme. Then followed a paragraph giving other examples of such heroes and Saviours being born of some profligate intercourse between God and mortal. Then followed a paragraph — but Evan did not understand it. He read it again and then again. Then he did understand it. The glass fell in ringing fragments on to the pavement, and Evan sprang over the barrier into the shop, brandishing his stick.

"What is this?" cried little Mr. Turnbull, starting up with hair aflame. "How dare you break my window?"

"Because it was the quickest cut to you," cried Evan, stamping. "Stand up and fight, you crapulous coward. You dirty lunatic, stand up, will you? Have you any weapons here?"

"Are you mad?" asked Turnbull, glaring.

"Are you?" cried Evan. "Can you be anything else when you plaster your own house with that God-defying filth? Stand up and fight, I say."

A great light like dawn came into Mr. Turnbull's face. Behind his red

cloudlets and islets were the same. Evan lived like a man wal\
borderland, the borderland between this world and another.
many men and nations who grow up with nature and the cc
things, he understood the supernatural before he understood the
ral. He had looked at dim angels standing knee-deep in the grass l
he had looked at the grass. He knew that Our Lady's robes were
before he knew the wild roses round her feet were red. The deepe\
memory plunged into the dark house of childhood the nearer \
nearer he came to the things that cannot be named. All through his l
he thought of the daylight world as a sort of divine débris, the brokt
remainder of his first vision. The skies and mountains were the splendi\
off-scourings of another place. The stars were lost jewels of the Queen\
Our Lady had gone and left the stars by accident.

His private tradition was equally wild and unworldly. His great-
grandfather had been cut down at Culloden, certain in his last instant
that God would restore the King. His grandfather, then a boy of ten, had
taken the terrible claymore from the hand of the dead and hung it up in
his house, burnishing it and sharpening it for sixty years, to be ready for
the next rebellion. His father, the youngest son and the last left alive, had
refused to attend on Queen Victoria in Scotland. And Evan himself had
been of one piece with his progenitors; and was not dead with them, but
alive in the twentieth century. He was not in the least the pathetic
Jacobite of whom we read, left behind by a final advance of all things.
He was, in his own fancy, a conspirator, fierce and up to date. In the
long, dark afternoons of the Highland winter, he plotted and fumed in
the dark. He drew plans of the capture of London on the desolate sand of
Arisaig.

When he came up to capture London, it was not with an army of
white cockades, but with a stick and a satchel. London overawed him a
little, not because he thought it grand or even terrible, but because it
bewildered him; it was not the Golden City or even hell; it was Limbo.
He had one shock of sentiment, when he turned that wonderful corner
of Fleet Street and saw St. Paul's sitting in the sky.

"Ah," he said, after a long pause, "that sort of thing was built under the
Stuarts!" Then with a sour grin he asked himself what was the corre-
sponding monument of the Brunswicks and the Protestant Constitution.
After some warning, he selected a sky-sign of some pill.

Half an hour afterwards his emotions left him with an emptied mind
on the same spot. And it was in a mood of mere idle investigation that
he happened to come to a standstill opposite the office of "The
Atheist." He did not see the word "atheist," or if he did, it is quite
possible that he did not know the meaning of the word. Even as it was,
the document would not have shocked even the innocent Highlander,

hair and beard he turned deadly pale with pleasure. Here, after twenty
lone years of useless toil, he had his reward. Some one was angry with
the paper. He bounded to his feet like a boy; he saw a new youth opening
before him. And as not unfrequently happens to middle-aged gentlemen when they see a new youth opening before them, he found himself
in the presence of the police.

The policemen, after some ponderous questionings, collared both the
two enthusiasts. They were more respectful, however, to the young man
who had smashed the window, than to the miscreant who had had his
window smashed. There was an air of refined mystery about Evan Mac-
Ian, which did not exist in the irate little shopkeeper, an air of refined
mystery which appealed to the policemen, for policemen, like most
other English types, are at once snobs and poets. MacIan might possibly
be a gentleman, they felt; the editor manifestly was not. And the editor's
fine rational republican appeals to his respect for law, and his ardour to be
tried by his fellow citizens, seemed to the police quite as much gibberish
as Evan's mysticism could have done. The police were not used to
hearing principles, even the principles of their own existence.

The police magistrate, before whom they were hurried and tried, was
a Mr. Cumberland Vane, a cheerful, middle-aged gentleman, honour-
ably celebrated for the lightness of his sentences and the lightness of his
conversation. He occasionally worked himself up into a sort of theoretic
rage about certain particular offenders, such as the men who took
pokers to their wives, talked in a loose, sentimental way about the
desirability of flogging them, and was hopelessly bewildered by the fact
that the wives seemed even more angry with him than with their
husbands. He was a tall, spruce man, with a twist of black moustache
and incomparable morning dress. He looked like a gentleman, and yet,
somehow, like a stage gentleman.

He had often treated serious crimes against mere order or property
with a humane flippancy. Hence, about the mere breaking of an editor's
window, he was almost uproarious.

"Come, Mr. MacIan, come," he said, leaning back in his chair, "do
you generally enter your friends' houses by walking through the glass?"
(Laughter.)

"He is not my friend," said Evan, with the stolidity of a dull child.

"Not your friend, eh?" said the magistrate, sparkling. "Is he your
brother-in-law?" (Loud and prolonged laughter.)

"He is my enemy," said Evan, simply; "he is the enemy of God."

Mr. Vane shifted sharply in his seat, dropping the eye-glass out of his
eye in a momentary and not unmanly embarrassment.

"You mustn't talk like that here," he said, roughly, and in a kind of
hurry, "that has nothing to do with us."

Evan opened his great, blue eyes; "God," he began.

"Be quiet," said the magistrate, angrily, "it is most undesirable that things of that sort should be spoken about — a — in public, and in an ordinary Court of Justice. Religion is — a — too personal a matter to be mentioned in such a place."

"Is it?" answered the Highlander, "then what did those policemen swear by just now?"

"That is no parallel," answered Vane, rather irritably; "of course there is a form of oath — to be taken reverently — reverently, and there's an end of it. But to talk in a public place about one's most sacred and private sentiments — well, I call it bad taste. (Slight applause.) I call it irreverent. I call it irreverent, and I'm not specially orthodox either."

"I see you are not," said Evan, "but I am."

"We are wandering from the point," said the police magistrate, pulling himself together.

"May I ask why you smashed this worthy citizen's window?"

Evan turned a little pale at the mere memory, but he answered with the same cold and deadly literalism that he showed throughout.

"Because he blasphemed Our Lady."

"I tell you once and for all," cried Mr. Cumberland Vane, rapping his knuckles angrily on the table, "I tell you, once for all, my man, that I will not have you turning on any religious rant or cant here. Don't imagine that it will impress me. The most religious people are not those who talk about it. (Applause.) You answer the questions and do nothing else."

"I did nothing else," said Evan, with a slight smile.

"Eh," cried Vane, glaring through his eye-glass.

"You asked me why I broke his window," said MacIan, with a face of wood. "I answered, 'Because he blasphemed Our Lady.' I had no other reason. So I have no other answer." Vane continued to gaze at him with a sternness not habitual to him.

"You are not going the right way to work, Sir," he said, with severity. "You are not going the right way to work to — a — have your case treated with special consideration. If you had simply expressed regret for what you had done, I should have been strongly inclined to dismiss the matter as an outbreak of temper. Even now, if you say that you are sorry I shall only — "

"But I am not in the least sorry," said Evan, "I am very pleased."

"I really believe you are insane," said the stipendiary, indignantly, for he had really been doing his best as a good-natured man, to compose the dispute. "What conceivable right have you to break other people's windows because their opinions do not agree with yours? This man only gave expression to his sincere belief."

"So did I," said the Highlander.

"And who are you?" exploded Vane. "Are your views necessarily the right ones? Are you necessarily in possession of the truth?"

"Yes," said MacIan.

The magistrate broke into a contemptuous laugh.

"Oh, you want a nurse to look after you," he said. "You must pay £10." Evan MacIan plunged his hands into his loose grey garments and drew out a queer looking leather purse. It contained exactly twelve sovereigns. He paid down the ten, coin by coin, in silence, and equally silently returned the remaining two to the receptacle. Then he said, "May I say a word, your worship?"

Cumberland Vane seemed half hypnotised with the silence and automatic movements of the stranger; he made a movement with his head, which might have been either "yes" or "no." "I only wished to say, your worship," said MacIan, putting back the purse in his trouser pocket, "that smashing that shop window was, I confess, a useless and rather irregular business. It may be excused, however, as a mere preliminary to further proceedings, a sort of preface. Wherever and whenever I meet that man," and he pointed to the editor of "The Atheist," "whether it be outside this door in ten minutes from now, or twenty years hence in some distant country, wherever and whenever I meet that man, I will fight him. Do not be afraid, I will not rush at him like a bully, or bear him down with any brute superiority. I will fight him like a gentleman; I will fight him as our fathers fought. He shall choose how, sword or pistol, horse or foot. But if he refuses, I will write his cowardice on every wall in the world. If he had said of my mother what he said of the Mother of God, there is not a club of clean men in Europe that would deny my right to call him out. If he had said it of my wife, you English would yourselves have pardoned me for beating him like a dog in the market place. Your worship, I have no mother; I have no wife. I have only that which the poor have equally with the rich; which the lonely have equally with the man of many friends. To me this whole strange world is homely, because in the heart of it there is a home; to me this cruel world is kindly, because higher than the heavens there is something more human than humanity. If a man must not fight for this, may he fight for anything? I would fight for my friend, but if I lost my friend, I should still be there. I would fight for my country, but if I lost my country, I should still exist. But if what that devil dreams were true, I should not be — I should burst like a bubble and be gone. I could not live in that imbecile universe. Shall I not fight for my own existence?"

The magistrate recovered his voice and his presence of mind. The first part of the speech, the bombastic and brutally practical challenge, stunned him with surprise; but the rest of Evan's remarks, branching off as they did into theoretic phrases, gave his vague and very English mind (full of memories of the hedging and compromise in English public speaking) an indistinct sensation of relief, as if the man, though mad, were not so dangerous as he had thought. He went into a sort of weary laughter.

"For Heaven's sake, man," he said, "don't talk so much. Let other people have a chance (laughter). I trust all that you said about asking Mr. Turnbull to fight, may be regarded as rubbish. In case of accidents, however, I must bind you over to keep the peace."

"To keep the peace," repeated Evan, "with whom?"

"With Mr. Turnbull," said Vane.

"Certainly not," answered MacIan. "What has he to do with peace?"

"Do you mean to say," began the magistrate, "that you refuse to . . ." The voice of Turnbull himself clove in for the first time.

"Might I suggest," he said, "that I, your worship, can settle to some extent this absurd matter myself. This rather wild gentleman promises that he will not attack me with any ordinary assault—and if he does, you may be sure the police shall hear of it. But he says he will not. He says he will challenge me to a duel; and I cannot say anything stronger about his mental state than to say that I think that it is highly probable that he will. (Laughter.) But it takes two to make a duel, your worship (renewed laughter). I do not in the least mind being described on every wall in the world as the coward who would not fight a man in Fleet Street, about whether the Virgin Mary had a parallel in Mesopotamian mythology. No, your worship. You need not trouble to bind him over to keep the peace. I bind myself over to keep the peace, and you may rest quite satisfied that there will be no duel with me in it."

Mr. Cumberland Vane rolled about, laughing in a sort of relief.

"You're like a breath of April air, sir," he cried. "You're ozone after that fellow. You're perfectly right. Perhaps I have taken the thing too seriously. I should love to see him sending you challenges and to see you smiling. Well, well."

Evan went out of the Court of Justice free, but strangely shaken, like a sick man. Any punishment or suppression he would have felt as natural; but the sudden juncture between the laughter of his judge and the laughter of the man he had wronged, made him feel suddenly small, or at least, defeated. It was really true that the whole modern world regarded his world as a bubble. No cruelty could have shown it, but their kindness showed it with a ghastly clearness. As he was brooding, he suddenly became conscious of a small, stern figure, fronting him in silence. Its eyes were grey and awful, and its beard red. It was Turnbull.

"Well, sir," said the editor of "The Atheist," "where is the fight to be? Name the field, sir."

Evan stood thunderstruck. He stammered out something, he knew not what; he only guessed it by the answer of the other.

"Do I want to fight? Do I want to fight?" cried the furious Free-thinker. "Why, you moonstruck scarecrow of superstition, do you think your dirty saints are the only people who can die? Haven't you hung atheists, and burned them, and boiled them, and did they ever deny their faith? Do you think we don't want to fight? Night and day I have prayed — I have longed — for an atheist revolution — I have longed to see your blood and ours in the streets. Let it be yours or mine?"

"But you said . . ." began MacIan.

"I know," said Turnbull, scornfully. "And what did you say? You damned fool, you said things that might have got us locked up for a year, and shadowed by the coppers for half a decade. If you wanted to fight, why did you tell that ass you wanted to? I got you out, to fight if you want to. Now, fight if you dare."

"I swear to you, then," said MacIan, after a pause. "I swear to you that nothing shall come between us. I swear to you that nothing shall be in my heart or in my head till our swords clash together. I swear it by the God you have denied, by the Blessed Lady you have blasphemed; I swear it by the seven swords in her heart. I swear it by the Holy Island where my fathers are, by the honour of my mother, by the secret of my people, and by the chalice of the Blood of God."

The atheist drew up his head. "And I," he said, "give my word."

CHAPTER III

SOME OLD CURIOSITIES

T HE EVENING SKY, a dome of solid gold, unflaked even by a single
sunset cloud, steeped the meanest sights of London in a strange and
mellow light. It made a little greasy street off St. Martin's Lane look as if
it were paved with gold. It made the pawnbroker's half-way down it shine
as if it were really that Mountain of Piety that the French poetic instinct
has named it; it made the mean pseudo-French bookshop, next but one
to it, a shop packed with dreary indecency, show for a moment a kind of
Parisian colour. And the shop that stood between the pawnshop and the
shop of dreary indecency, showed with quite a blaze of old world beauty,
for it was, by accident, a shop not unbeautiful in itself. The front window
had a glimmer of bronze and blue steel, lit, as by a few stars, by the
sparks of what were alleged to be jewels; for it was in brief, a shop of bric-
a-brac and old curiosities. A row of half burnished seventeenth century
swords ran like an ornate railing along the front of the window; behind
was a darker glimmer of old oak and old armour; and higher up hung
the most extraordinary looking South Sea tools or utensils, whether
designed for killing enemies or merely for cooking them, no mere white
man could possibly conjecture. But the romance of the eye, which
really on this rich evening, clung about the shop, had its main source in
the accident of two doors standing open, the front door that opened on
the street and a back door that opened on an odd green square of garden,
that the sun turned to a square of gold. There is nothing more beautiful
than thus to look as it were through the archway of a house; as if the
open sky were an interior chamber, and the sun a secret lamp of the
place.

I have suggested that the sunset light made everything lovely. To say
that it made the keeper of the curiosity shop lovely would be a tribute to
it perhaps too extreme. It would easily have made him beautiful if he
had been merely squalid; if he had been a Jew of the Fagin type. But he
was a Jew of another and much less admirable type; a Jew with a very
well sounding name. For though there are no hard tests for separating

the tares and wheat of any people; one rude but efficient guide is that the nice Jew is called Moses Solomon, and the nasty Jew is called Thornton Percy. The keeper of the curiosity shop was of the Thornton Percy branch of the chosen people; he belonged to those Lost Ten Tribes whose industrious object is to lose themselves. He was a man still young, but already corpulent, with sleek dark hair, heavy handsome clothes, and a full, fat, permanent smile, which looked at the first glance kindly, and at the second cowardly. The name over his shop was Henry Gordon, but two Scotchmen who were in his shop that evening could come upon no trace of a Scotch accent.

These two Scotchmen in this shop were careful purchasers, but free-handed payers. One of them who seemed to be the principal and the authority (whom, indeed, Mr. Henry Gordon fancied he had seen somewhere before), was a small, sturdy fellow, with fine grey eyes, a square red tie and a square red beard, that he carried aggressively forward as if he defied any one to pull it. The other kept so much in the background in comparison that he looked almost ghostly in his grey cloak or plaid, a tall, sallow, silent young man.

The two Scotchmen were interested in seventeenth century swords. They were fastidious about them. They had a whole armoury of these weapons brought out and rolled clattering about the counter, until they found two of precisely the same length. Presumably they desired the exact symmetry for some decorative trophy. Even then they felt the points, poised the swords for balance and bent them in a circle to see that they sprang straight again; which, for decorative purposes, seems carrying realism rather far.

"These will do," said the strange person with the red beard. "And perhaps I had better pay for them at once. And as you are the challenger, Mr. MacIan, perhaps you had better explain the situation."

The tall Scotchman in grey took a step forward and spoke in a voice quite clear and bold, and yet somehow lifeless, like a man going through an ancient formality.

"The fact is, Mr. Gordon, we have to place our honour in your hands. Words have passed between Mr. Turnbull and myself on a grave and invaluable matter, which can only be atoned for by fighting. Unfortunately, as the police are in some sense pursuing us, we are hurried, and must fight now and without seconds. But if you will be so kind as to take us into your little garden and see fair play, we shall feel how——"

The shopman recovered himself from a stunning surprise and burst out:

"Gentlemen, are you drunk? A duel! A duel in my garden. Go home, gentlemen, go home. Why, what did you quarrel about?"

"We quarrelled," said Evan, in the same dead voice, "about religion." The fat shopkeeper rolled about in his chair with enjoyment.

"Well, this is a funny game," he said. "So you want to commit murder on behalf of religion. Well, well my religion is a little respect for humanity, and——"

"Excuse me," cut in Turnbull, suddenly and fiercely, pointing towards the pawnbroker's next door. "Don't you own that shop?"

"Why—er—yes," said Gordon.

"And don't you own that shop?" repeated the secularist, pointing backward to the pornographic bookseller.

"What if I do?"

"Why, then," cried Turnbull, with grating contempt. "I will leave the religion of humanity confidently in your hands; but I am sorry I troubled you about such a thing as honour. Look here, my man. I do believe in humanity. I do believe in liberty. My father died for it under the swords of the Yeomanry. I am going to die for it, if need be, under that sword on your counter. But if there is one sight that makes me doubt it it is your foul fat face. It is hard to believe you were not meant to be ruled like a dog or killed like a cockroach. Don't try your slave's philosophy on me. We are going to fight, and we are going to fight in your garden, with your swords. Be still! Raise your voice above a whisper, and I run you through the body."

Turnbull put the bright point of the sword against the gay waistcoat of the dealer, who stood choking with rage and fear, and an astonishment so crushing as to be greater than either.

"MacIan," said Turnbull, falling almost into the familiar tone of a business partner, "MacIan, tie up this fellow and put a gag in his mouth. Be still, I say, or I kill you where you stand."

The man was too frightened to scream, but he struggled wildly, while Evan MacIan, whose long, lean hands were unusually powerful, tightened some old curtain cords round him, strapped a rope gag in his mouth and rolled him on his back on the floor.

"There's nothing very strong here," said Evan, looking about him. "I'm afraid he'll work through that gag in half an hour or so."

"Yes," said Turnbull, "but one of us will be killed by that time."

"Well, let's hope so," said the Highlander, glancing doubtfully at the squirming thing on the floor.

"And now," said Turnbull, twirling his fiery moustache and fingering his sword, "let us go into the garden. What an exquisite summer evening!"

MacIan said nothing, but lifting his sword from the counter went out into the sun.

The brilliant light ran along the blades, filling the channels of them with white fire; the combatants stuck their swords in the turf and took off their hats, coats, waistcoats, and boots. Evan said a short Latin prayer to himself, during which Turnbull made something of a parade of lighting a cigarette which he flung away the instant after, when he saw MacIan apparently standing ready. Yet MacIan was not exactly ready. He stood staring like a man stricken with a trance.

"What are you staring at?" asked Turnbull, "Do you see the bobbies?"

"I see Jerusalem," said Evan, "all covered with the shields and standards of the Saracens."

"Jerusalem!" said Turnbull, laughing. "Well, we've taken the only inhabitant into captivity."

And he picked up his sword and made it whistle like a boy's wand.

"I beg your pardon," said MacIan, drily. "Let us begin."

MacIan made a military salute with his weapon, which Turnbull copied or parodied with an impatient contempt; and in the stillness of the garden the swords came together with a clear sound like a bell. The instant the blades touched, each felt them tingle to their very points with a personal vitality, as if they were two naked nerves of steel. Evan had worn throughout an air of apathy, which might have been the stale apathy of one who wants nothing. But it was indeed the more dreadful apathy of one who wants something and will care for nothing else. And this was seen suddenly; for the instant Evan engaged he disengaged and lunged with an infernal violence. His opponent with a desperate promptitude parried and riposted; the parry only just succeeded, the riposte failed. Something big and unbearable seemed to have broken finally out of Evan in that first murderous lunge, leaving him lighter and cooler and quicker upon his feet. He fell to again, fiercely still, but now with a fierce caution. The next moment Turnbull lunged; MacIan seemed to catch the point and throw it away from him, and was thrusting back like a thunderbolt, when a sound paralysed him; another sound beside their ringing weapons. Turnbull, perhaps from an equal astonishment, perhaps from chivalry, stopped also and forbore to send his sword through his exposed enemy.

"What's that?" asked Evan, hoarsely.

A heavy scraping sound, as of a trunk being dragged along a littered floor, came from the dark shop behind them.

"The old Jew has broken one of his strings, and he's crawling about," said Turnbull. "Be quick! We must finish before he gets his gag out."

"Yes, yes, quick! On guard!" cried the Highlander. The blades crossed again with the same sound like song, and the men went to work again with the same white and watchful faces. Evan, in his impatience, went back a little to his wildness. He made windmills, as the French duellists say, and though he was probably a shade the better fencer of the two, he found the other's point pass his face twice so close as almost to graze his cheek. The second time he realised the actual possibility of defeat and pulled himself together under a shock of the sanity of anger. He narrowed, and, so to speak, tightened his operations: he fenced (as the swordman's boast goes), in a wedding ring; he turned Turnbull's thrusts with a maddening and almost mechanical click, like that of a machine. Whenever Turnbull's sword sought to go over that other mere white streak it seemed to be caught in a complex network of steel. He turned one thrust, turned another, turned another. Then suddenly he went forward at the lunge with his whole living weight. Turnbull leaped back, but Evan lunged and lunged and lunged again like a devilish piston rod or battering ram. And high above all the sound of the struggle there broke into the silent evening a bellowing human voice, nasal, raucous, at the highest pitch of pain. "Help! Help! Police! Murder! Murder!" The gag was broken; and the tongue of terror was loose.

"Keep on!" gasped Turnbull. "One may be killed before they come."

The voice of the screaming shopkeeper was loud enough to drown not only the noise of the swords but all other noises around it, but even through its rending din there seemed to be some other stir or scurry. And Evan, in the very act of thrusting at Turnbull, saw something in his eyes that made him drop his sword. The atheist, with his grey eyes at their widest and wildest, was staring straight over his shoulder at the little archway of shop that opened on the street beyond. And he saw the archway blocked and blackened with strange figures.

"We must bolt, MacIan," he said abruptly. "And there isn't a damned second to lose either. Do as I do."

With a bound he was beside the little cluster of his clothes and boots that lay on the lawn; he snatched them up, without waiting to put any of them on; and tucking his sword under his other arm, went wildly at the wall at the bottom of the garden and swung himself over it. Three seconds after he had alighted in his socks on the other side, MacIan alighted beside him, also in his socks and also carrying clothes and sword in a desperate bundle.

They were in a by-street, very lean and lonely itself, but so close to a crowded thoroughfare that they could see the vague masses of vehicles going by, and could even see an individual hansom cab passing the corner at the instant. Turnbull put his fingers to his mouth like a guttersnipe and whistled twice. Even as he did so he could hear the loud voices of the neighbours and the police coming down the garden.

The hansom swung sharply and came tearing down the little lane at his call. When the cabman saw his fares, however, two wild-haired men in their shirts and socks with naked swords under their arms, he not unnaturally brought his readiness to a rigid stop and stared suspiciously.

"You talk to him a minute," whispered Turnbull, and stepped back into the shadow of the wall.

"We want you," said MacIan to the cabman, with a superb Scotch drawl of indifference and assurance, "to drive us to St. Pancras Station — verra quick."

"Very sorry, sir," said the cabman, "but I'd like to know it was all right. Might I arst where you come from, Sir?"

A second after he spoke MacIan heard a heavy voice on the other side of the wall, saying: "I suppose I'd better get over and look for them. Give me a back."

"Cabby," said MacIan, again assuming the most deliberate and lingering lowland Scotch intonation, "if ye're really verra anxious to ken whar a' come fra', I'll tell ye as a verra great secret. A' come from Scotland. And a'm gaein' to St. Pancras Station. Open the doors, cabby."

The cabman stared, but laughed. The heavy voice behind the wall said: "Now then, a better back this time, Mr. Price." And from the shadow of the wall Turnbull crept out. He had struggled wildly into his coat (leaving his waistcoat on the pavement) and he was with a fierce pale face climbing up the cab behind the cabman. MacIan had no glimmering notion of what he was up to, but an instinct of discipline, inherited from a hundred men of war, made him stick to his own part and trust the other man's.

"Open the doors, cabby," he repeated, with something of the obstinate solemnity of a drunkard, "open the doors. Did ye no hear me say St. Pancras Station?"

The top of a policeman's helmet appeared above the garden wall. The cabman did not see it, but he was still suspicious and began:

"Very sorry, sir, but . . ." and with that the catlike Turnbull tore him out of his seat and hurled him into the street below, where he lay suddenly stunned.

"Give me his hat," said Turnbull in a silver voice, that the other obeyed like a bugle. "And get inside with the swords."

And just as the red and raging face of a policeman appeared above the wall, Turnbull struck the horse with a terrible cut of the whip and the two went whirling away like a boomerang.

They had spun through seven streets and three or four squares before anything further happened. Then, in the neighbourhood of Maida Vale, the driver opened the trap and talked through it in a manner not wholly common in conversations through that aperture.

"Mr. MacIan," he said shortly and civilly.

"Mr. Turnbull," replied his motionless fare.

"Under circumstances such as those in which we were both recently placed there was no time for anything but very abrupt action. I trust therefore that you have no cause to complain of me if I have deferred until this moment a consultation with you on our present position or future action. Our present position, Mr. MacIan, I imagine that I am under no special necessity of describing. We have broken the law and we are fleeing from its officers. Our future action is a thing about which I myself entertain sufficiently strong views; but I have no right to assume or to anticipate yours, though I may have formed a decided conception of your character and a decided notion of what they will probably be. Still, by every principle of intellectual justice, I am bound to ask you now and seriously whether you wish to continue our interrupted relations."

MacIan leant his white and rather weary face back upon the cushions in order to speak up through the open door.

"Mr. Turnbull," he said, "I have nothing to add to what I have said before. It is strongly borne in upon me that you and I, the sole occupants of this runaway cab, are at this moment the two most important people in London, possibly in Europe. I have been looking at all the streets as we went past, I have been looking at all the shops as we went past, I have been looking at all the churches as we went past. At first, I felt a little dazed with the vastness of it all. I could not understand what it all meant. But now I know exactly what it all means. It means us. This whole civilisation is only a dream. You and I are the realities."

"Religious symbolism," said Mr. Turnbull, through the trap, "does not, as you are probably aware, appeal ordinarily to thinkers of the school to which I belong. But in symbolism as you use it in this instance, I must, I think, concede a certain truth. We *must* fight this thing out somewhere; because, as you truly say, we have found each other's reality. We *must* kill each other—or convert each other. I used to think all Christians were hypocrites, and I felt quite mildly towards them really. But I know you are sincere—and my soul is mad against you. In the same way you used, I suppose, to think that all atheists thought atheism would leave them free for immorality—and yet in your heart you tolerated them entirely. Now you *know* that I am an honest man, and you are mad against me, as I am against you. Yes, that's it. You can't be angry with bad men. But a good man in the wrong—why one thirsts for his blood. Yes, you open for me a vista of thought."

"Don't run into anything," said Evan, immovably.

"There's something in that view of yours, too," said Turnbull, and shut down the trap.

They sped on through shining streets that shot by them like arrows. Mr. Turnbull had evidently a great deal of unused practical talent which was unrolling itself in this ridiculous adventure. They had got away with such stunning promptitude that the police chase had in all probability not even properly begun. But in case it had, the amateur cabman chose his dizzy course through London with a strange dexterity. He did not do what would have first occurred to any ordinary outsider desiring to destroy his tracks. He did not cut into by-ways or twist his way through mean streets. His amateur common sense told him that it was precisely the poor street, the side street, that would be likely to remember and report the passing of a hansom cab, like the passing of a royal procession. He kept chiefly to the great roads, so full of hansoms that a wilder pair than they might easily have passed in the press. In one of the quieter streets Evan put on his boots.

Towards the top of Albany Street the singular cabman again opened the trap.

"Mr. MacIan," he said, "I understand that we have now definitely settled that in the conventional language honour is not satisfied. Our action must at least go further than it has gone under recent interrupted conditions. That, I believe, is understood."

"Perfectly," replied the other with his bootlace in his teeth.

"Under those conditions," continued Turnbull, his voice coming through the hole with a slight note of trepidation very unusual with him, "I have a suggestion to make, if that can be called a suggestion, which has probably occurred to you as readily as to me. Until the actual event comes off we are practically in the position if not of comrades, at least of business partners. Until the event comes off, therefore, I should suggest that quarrelling would be inconvenient and rather inartistic; while the ordinary exchange of politeness between man and man would be not only elegant but uncommonly practical."

"You are perfectly right," answered MacIan, with his melancholy voice, "in saying that all this has occurred to me. All duellists should behave like gentlemen to each other. But we, by the queerness of our position, are something much more than either duellists or gentlemen. We are, in the oddest and most exact sense of the term, brothers — in arms."

"Mr. MacIan," replied Turnbull, calmly, "no more need be said." And he closed the trap once more.

They had reached Finchley Road before he opened it again.

Then he said, "Mr. MacIan, may I offer you a cigar. It will be a touch of realism."

"Thank you," answered Evan — "You are very kind." And he began to smoke in the cab.

CHAPTER IV

A Discussion at Dawn

THE DUELLISTS HAD from their own point of view escaped or conquered the chief powers of the modern world. They had satisfied the magistrate, they had tied the tradesman neck and heels, and they had left the police behind. As far as their own feelings went they had melted into a monstrous sea; they were but the fare and driver of one of the million hansoms that fill London streets. But they had forgotten something; they had forgotten journalism. They had forgotten that there exists in the modern world, perhaps for the first time in history, a class of people whose interest is not that things should happen well or happen badly, should happen successfully or happen unsuccessfully, should happen to the advantage of this party or the advantage of that party, but whose interest simply is that things should happen.

It is the one great weakness of journalism as a picture of our modern existence, that it must be a picture made up entirely of exceptions. We announce on flaring posters that a man has fallen off a scaffolding. We do not announce on flaring posters that a man has not fallen off a scaffolding. Yet this latter fact is fundamentally more exciting, as indicating that that moving tower of terror and mystery, a man, is still abroad upon the earth. That the man has not fallen off a scaffolding is really more sensational; and it is also some thousand times more common. But journalism cannot reasonably be expected thus to insist upon the permanent miracles. Busy editors cannot be expected to put on their posters, "Mr. Wilkinson Still Safe," or "Mr. Jones, of Worthing, Not Dead Yet." They cannot announce the happiness of mankind at all. They cannot describe all the forks that are not stolen, or all the marriages that are not judiciously dissolved. Hence the complete picture they give of life is of necessity fallacious; they can only represent what is unusual. However democratic they may be, they are only concerned with the minority.

The incident of the religious fanatic who broke a window on Ludgate Hill was alone enough to set them up in good copy for the night. But when the same man was brought before a magistrate and defied his enemy to mortal combat in the open court, then the columns would hardly hold the excruciating information, and the headlines were so large that there was hardly room for any of the text. The "Daily Telegraph" headed a column, "A Duel on Divinity," and there was a correspondence afterwards which lasted for months, about whether police magistrates ought to mention religion. The "Daily Mail," in its dull, sensible way, headed the events, "Wanted to fight for the Virgin." Mr. James Douglas, in "The Star," presuming on his knowledge of philosophical and theological terms, described the Christian's outbreak under the title of "Dualist and Duellist." The "Daily News" inserted a colourless account of the matter, but was pursued and eaten up for some weeks, with letters from outlying ministers, headed "Murder and Mariolatry." But the journalistic temperature was steadily and consistently heated by all these influences; the journalists had tasted blood, prospectively, and were in the mood for more; everything in the matter prepared them for further outbursts of moral indignation. And when a gasping reporter rushed in in the last hours of the evening with the announcement that the two heroes of the Police Court had literally been found fighting in a London back garden, with a shopkeeper bound and gagged in the front of the house, the editors and sub-editors were stricken still as men are by great beatitudes.

The next morning, five or six of the great London dailies burst out simultaneously into great blossoms of eloquent leader-writing. Towards the end all the leaders tended to be the same, but they all began differently. The "Daily Telegraph," for instance began, "There will be little difference among our readers or among all truly English and law-abiding men touching the etc., etc." The "Daily Mail" said, "People must learn, in the modern world, to keep their theological differences to themselves. The fracas, etc., etc." The "Daily News" started, "Nothing could be more inimical to the cause of true religion than etc., etc." The "Times" began with something about Celtic disturbances of the equilibrium of Empire, and the "Daily Express" distinguished itself splendidly by omitting altogether so controversial a matter and substituting a leader about goloshes.

And the morning after that, the editors and the newspapers were in such a state, that, as the phrase is, there was no holding them. Whatever secret and elvish thing it is that broods over editors and suddenly turns their brains, that thing had seized on the story of the broken glass and the duel in the garden. It became monstrous and omnipresent, as do in our time the unimportant doings of the sect of the Agapemonites, or as did at an earlier time the dreary dishonesties of the Rhodesian financiers.

Questions were asked about it, and even answered, in the House of Commons. The Government was solemnly denounced in the papers for not having done something, nobody knew what, to prevent the window being broken. An enormous subscription was started to reimburse Mr. Gordon, the man who had been gagged in the shop. Mr. MacIan, one of the combatants, became for some mysterious reason, singly and hugely popular as a comic figure in the comic papers and on the stage of the music halls. He was always represented (in defiance of fact), with red whiskers, and a very red nose, and in full Highland costume. And a song, consisting of an unimaginable number of verses, in which his name was rhymed with flat iron, the British Lion, sly 'un, dandelion, Spion (with Kop in the next line), was sung to crowded houses every night. The papers developed a devouring thirst for the capture of the fugitives; and when they had not been caught for forty-eight hours, they suddenly turned the whole matter into a detective mystery. Letters under the heading, "Where are They," poured in to every paper, with every conceivable kind of explanation, running them to earth in the Monument, the Twopenny Tube, Epping Forest, Westminster Abbey, rolled up in carpets at Shoolbreds, locked up in safes in Chancery Lane. Yes, the papers were very interesting, and Mr. Turnbull unrolled a whole bundle of them for the amusement of Mr. MacIan as they sat on a high common to the north of London, in the coming of the white dawn.

The darkness in the east had been broken with a bar of grey; the bar of grey was split with a sword of silver and morning lifted itself laboriously over London. From the spot where Turnbull and MacIan were sitting on one of the barren steeps behind Hampstead, they could see the whole of London shaping itself vaguely and largely in the grey and growing light, until the white sun stood over it and it lay at their feet, the splendid monstrosity that it is. Its bewildering squares and parallelograms were compact and perfect as a Chinese puzzle; an enormous hieroglyphic which man must decipher or die. There fell upon both of them, but upon Turnbull more than the other, because he knew more what the scene signified, that quite indescribable sense as of a sublime and passionate and heart-moving futility, which is never evoked by deserts or dead men or men neglected and barbarous, which can only be invoked by the sight of the enormous genius of man applied to anything other than the best. Turnbull, the old idealistic democrat, had so often reviled the democracy and reviled them justly for their supineness, their snobbishness, their evil reverence for idle things. He was right enough; for our democracy has only one great fault; it is not democratic. And after denouncing so justly average modern men for so many years as sophists and as slaves, he looked down from an empty slope in Hampstead and saw what gods they are. Their achievement seemed all the more heroic and divine, because it seemed doubtful whether it was worth doing at all. There seemed to be something greater than mere accuracy in making such a mistake as London. And what was to be the end of it all? what was to be the ultimate transformation of this common and incredible London man, this workman on a tram in Battersea, this clerk on an omnibus in Cheapside? Turnbull, as he stared drearily, murmured to himself the words of the old atheistic and revolutionary Swinburne who had intoxicated his youth:

"And still we ask if God or man
Can loosen thee Lazarus;
Bid thee rise up republican,
And save thyself and all of us.
But no disciple's tongue can say
If thou can'st take our sins away."

Turnbull shivered slightly as if behind the earthly morning he felt the evening of the world, the sunset of so many hopes. Those words were from "Songs before Sunrise." But Turnbull's songs at their best were songs after sunrise, and sunrise had been no such great thing after all. Turnbull shivered again in the sharp morning air. MacIan was also gazing with his face towards the city, but there was that about his blind and mystical stare that told one, so to speak, that his eyes were turned inwards. When Turnbull said something to him about London, they seemed to move as at a summons and come out like two householders coming out into their doorways.

"Yes," he said, with a sort of stupidity. "It's a very big place."

There was a somewhat unmeaning silence, and then MacIan said again:

"It's a very big place. When I first came into it I was frightened of it. Frightened exactly as one would be frightened at the sight of a man forty feet high. I am used to big things where I come from, big mountains that seem to fill God's infinity, and the big sea that goes to the end of the world. But then these things are all shapeless and confused things, not made in any familiar form. But to see the plain, square, human things as large as that, houses so large and streets so large, and the town itself so large, was like having screwed some devil's magnifying glass into one's eye. It was like seeing a porridge bowl as big as a house, or a mouse-trap made to catch elephants."

"Like the land of the Brobdingnagians," said Turnbull, smiling.

"Oh! Where is that?" said MacIan.

Turnbull said bitterly, "In a book," and the silence fell suddenly between them again.

They were sitting in a sort of litter on the hillside; all the things they had hurriedly collected, in various places, for their flight, were strewn indiscriminately round them. The two swords with which they had lately sought each other's lives were flung down on the grass at random, like two idle walking-sticks. Some provisions they had bought last night, at a low public house, in case of undefined contingencies, were tossed about like the materials of an ordinary picnic, here a packet of chocolate, and there a bottle of wine. And to add to the disorder finally, there were strewn on top of everything, the most disorderly of modern things, newspapers, and more newspapers, and yet again newspapers, the ministers of the modern anarchy. Turnbull picked up one of them drearily, and took out a pipe.

"There's a lot about us," he said. "Do you mind if I light up?"

"Why should I mind?" asked MacIan.

Turnbull eyed with a certain studious interest, the man who did not understand any of the verbal courtesies; he lit his pipe and blew great clouds out of it.

"Yes," he resumed. "The matter on which you and I are engaged is at this moment really the best copy in England. I am a journalist, and I know. For the first time, perhaps, for many generations, the English are really more angry about a wrong thing done in England than they are about a wrong thing done in France."

"It is not a wrong thing," said MacIan.

Turnbull laughed. "You seem unable to understand the ordinary use of the human language. If I did not suspect that you were a genius, I should certainly know you were a blockhead. I fancy we had better be getting along and collecting our baggage."

And he jumped up and began shoving the luggage into his pockets, or strapping it on to his back. As he thrust a tin of canned meat, anyhow, into his bursting side pocket, he said, casually:

"I only meant that you and I are the most prominent people in the English papers."

"Well, what did you expect?" asked MacIan, opening his great grave blue eyes.

"The papers are full of us," said Turnbull, stooping to pick up one of the swords.

MacIan stooped and picked up the other.

"Yes," he said, in his simple way. "I have read what they have to say. But they don't seem to understand the point."

"The point of what?" asked Turnbull.

"The point of the sword," said MacIan, violently, and planted the steel point in the soil like a man planting a tree.

"That is a point," said Turnbull, grimly, "that we will discuss later. Come along."

Turnbull tied the last tin of biscuits desperately to himself with string; and then spoke, like a diver girt for plunging, short and sharp.

"Now, Mr. MacIan, you must listen to me. You must listen to me, not merely because I know the country, which you might learn by looking at a map, but because I know the people of the country, whom you could not know by living here thirty years. That infernal city down there is awake; and it is awake against us. All those endless rows of windows and windows are all eyes staring at us. All those forests of chimneys are fingers pointing at us, as we stand here on the hillside. This thing has caught on. For the next six mortal months they will think of nothing but us, as for six mortal months they thought of nothing but the Dreyfus case. Oh, I know it's funny. They let starving children, who don't want to die, drop by the score without looking round. But because two gentlemen, from private feelings of delicacy, do want to die, they will mobilise the army and navy to prevent them. For half a year or more, you and I, Mr. MacIan, will be an obstacle to every reform in the British Empire. We shall prevent the Chinese being sent out of the Transvaal and the blocks being stopped in the Strand. We shall be the conversational substitute when any one recommends Home Rule, or complains of sky signs. Therefore, do not imagine, in your innocence, that we have only to melt away among those English hills as a Highland cateran might into your god-forsaken Highland mountains. We must be eternally on our guard; we must live the hunted life of two distinguished criminals. We must expect to be recognised as much as if we were Napoleon escaping from Elba. We must be prepared for our descriptions being sent to every tiny village, and for our faces being recognised by every ambitious policeman. We must often sleep under the stars as if we were in Africa. Last and most important we must not dream of effecting our — our final settlement, which will be a thing as famous as the Phœnix Park murders, unless we have made real and precise arrangements for our isolation — I will not say our safety. We must not, in short, fight; until we have thrown them off our scent, if only for a moment. For, take my word for it, Mr. MacIan, if the British Public once catches us up, the British Public will prevent the duel, if it is only by locking us both up in asylums for the rest of our days."

MacIan was looking at the horizon with a rather misty look.

"I am not at all surprised," he said, "at the world being against us. It makes me feel I was right to —— "

"Yes?" said Turnbull.

"To smash your window," said MacIan. "I have woken up the world."

"Very well, then," said Turnbull, stolidly. "Let us look at a few final facts. Beyond that hill there is comparatively clear country. Fortunately, I know the part well, and if you will follow me exactly, and, when necessary, on your stomach, we may be able to get ten miles out of London, literally without meeting any one at all, which will be the best possible beginning, at any rate. We have provisions for at least two days and two nights, three days if we do it carefully. We may be able to get fifty or sixty miles away without even walking into an inn door. I have the biscuits and the tinned meat, and the milk. You have the chocolate, I think? And the brandy?"

"Yes," said MacIan, like a soldier taking orders.

"Very well, then, come on. March. We turn under that third bush and so down into the valley." And he set off ahead at a swinging walk.

Then he stopped suddenly; for he realised that the other was not following. Evan MacIan was leaning on his sword with a lowering face, like a man suddenly smitten still with doubt.

"What on earth is the matter?" asked Turnbull, staring in some anger.

Evan made no reply.

"What the deuce is the matter with you?" demanded the leader, again, his face slowly growing as red as his beard; then he said, suddenly, and in a more human voice, "Are you in pain, MacIan?"

"Yes," replied the Highlander, without lifting his face.

"Take some brandy," cried Turnbull, walking forward hurriedly towards him. "You've got it."

"It's not in the body," said MacIan, in his dull, strange way. "The pain has come into my mind. A very dreadful thing has just come into my thoughts."

"What the devil are you talking about?" asked Turnbull.

MacIan broke out with a queer and living voice.

"We must fight now, Turnbull. We must fight now. A frightful thing has come upon me, and I know it must be now and here. I must kill you here," he cried, with a sort of tearful rage impossible to describe. "Here, here, upon this blessed grass."

"Why, you idiot," began Turnbull.

"The hour has come — the black hour God meant for it. Quick, it will soon be gone. Quick!"

And he flung the scabbard from him furiously, and stood with the sunlight sparkling along his sword.

"You confounded fool," repeated Turnbull. "Put that thing up again, you ass; people will come out of that house at the first clash of the steel."

"One of us will be dead before they come," said the other, hoarsely, "for this is the hour God meant."

"Well, I never thought much of God," said the editor of "The Atheist," losing all patience. "And I think less now. Never mind what God meant. Kindly enlighten my pagan darkness as to what the devil *you* mean."

"The hour will soon be gone. In a moment it will be gone," said the madman. "It is now, now, now that I must nail your blaspheming body to the earth — now, now that I must avenge Our Lady on her vile slanderer. Now or never. For the dreadful thought is in my mind."

"And what thought," asked Turnbull, with frantic composure, "occupies what you call your mind?"

"I must kill you now," said the fanatic, "because —— "

"Well, because," said Turnbull, patiently.

"Because I have begun to like you."

Turnbull's face had a sudden spasm in the sunlight, a change so instantaneous that it left no trace behind it; and his features seemed still carved into a cold stare. But when he spoke again he seemed like a man who was placidly pretending to misunderstand something that he understood perfectly well.

"Your affection expresses itself in an abrupt form," he began, but MacIan broke the brittle and frivolous speech to pieces with a violent voice. "Do not trouble to talk like that," he said. "You know what I mean as well as I know it. Come on and fight, I say. Perhaps you are feeling just as I do."

Turnbull's face flinched again in the fierce sunlight, but his attitude kept its contemptuous ease.

"Your Celtic mind really goes too fast for me," he said; "let me be permitted in my heavy Lowland way to understand this new development. My dear Mr. MacIan, what do you really mean?"

MacIan still kept the shining sword-point towards the other's breast.

"You know what I mean. You mean the same yourself. We must fight now or else —— "

"Or else?" repeated Turnbull, staring at him with an almost blinding gravity.

"Or else we may not want to fight at all," answered Evan, and the end of his speech was like a despairing cry.

Turnbull took out his own sword suddenly as if to engage; then planting it point downwards for a moment, he said, "Before we begin, may I ask you a question?"

MacIan bowed patiently, but with burning eyes.

"You said, just now," continued Turnbull, presently, "that if we did not fight now, we might not want to fight at all. How would you feel about the matter if we came not to want to fight at all?"

"I should feel," answered the other, "just as I should feel if you had drawn your sword, and I had run away from it. I should feel that because I had been weak, justice had not been done."

"Justice," answered Turnbull, with a thoughtful smile, "but we are talking about your feelings. And what do you mean by justice, apart from your feelings?"

MacIan made a gesture of weary recognition! "Oh, Nominalism," he said, with a sort of sigh, "we had all that out in the twelfth century."

"I wish we could have it out now," replied the other, firmly. "Do you really mean that if you came to think me right, you would be certainly wrong?"

"If I had a blow on the back of my head, I might come to think you a green elephant," answered MacIan, "but have I not the right to say now, that if I thought that I should think wrong?"

"Then you are quite certain that it would be wrong to like me?" asked Turnbull, with a slight smile.

"No," said Evan, thoughtfully, "I do not say that. It may not be the devil, it may be some part of God I am not meant to know. But I had a work to do, and it is making the work difficult."

"And I suppose," said the atheist, quite gently, "that you and I know all about which part of God we ought to know."

MacIan burst out like a man driven back and explaining everything.

"The Church is not a thing like the Athenæum Club," he cried. "If the Athenæum Club lost all its members, the Athenæum Club would dissolve and cease to exist. But when we belong to the Church we belong to something which is outside all of us; which is outside everything you talk about, outside the Cardinals and the Pope. They belong to it, but it does not belong to them. If we all fell dead suddenly, the Church would still somehow exist in God. Confound it all, don't you see that I am more sure of its existence than I am of my own existence? And yet you ask me to trust my temperament, my own temperament, which can be turned upside down by two bottles of claret or an attack of the jaundice. You ask me to trust that when it softens towards you and not to trust the thing which I believe to be outside myself and more real than the blood in my body."

"Stop a moment," said Turnbull, in the same easy tone, "even in the very act of saying that you believe this or that, you imply that there is a part of yourself that you trust even if there are many parts which you mistrust. If it is only you that like me, surely, also, it is only you that believe in the Catholic Church."

Evan remained in an unmoved and grave attitude.

"There is a part of me which is divine," he answered, "a part that can be trusted, but there are also affections which are entirely animal and idle."

"And you are quite certain, I suppose," continued Turnbull, "that if even you esteem me the esteem would be wholly animal and idle?" For the first time MacIan started as if he had not expected the thing that was said to him. At last he said:

"Whatever in earth or heaven it is that has joined us two together, it seems to be something which makes it impossible to lie. No, I do not think that the movement in me towards you was . . . was that surface sort of thing. It may have been something deeper . . . something strange. I cannot understand the thing at all. But understand this and understand it thoroughly, if I loved you my love might be divine. But in that I hate you, my hatred most certainly is divine. No, it is not some trifle that we are fighting about. It is not some superstition or some symbol. When you wrote those words about Our Lady, you were in that act a wicked man doing a wicked thing. If I hate you it is because you have hated goodness. And if I like you . . . it is because you are good."

Turnbull's face wore an indecipherable expression.

"Well, shall we fight now?" he said.

"Yes," said MacIan, with a sudden contraction of his black brows, "yes, it must be now."

The bright swords crossed, and the first touch of them, travelling down blade and arm, told each combatant that the heart of the other was awakened. It was not in that way that the swords rang together when they had rushed on each other in the little garden behind the dealer's shop.

There was a pause, and then MacIan made a movement as if to thrust, and almost at the same moment Turnbull suddenly and calmly dropped his sword. Evan stared round in an unusual bewilderment, and then realised that a large man in pale clothes and a Panama hat was strolling serenely towards them.

CHAPTER V

THE PEACEMAKER

WHEN THE COMBATANTS, with crossed swords, became suddenly conscious of a third party, they each made the same movement. It was as quick as the snap of a pistol, and they altered it instantaneously and recovered their original pose, but they had both made it, they had both seen it, and they both knew what it was. It was not a movement of anger at being interrupted. Say or think what they would, it was a movement of relief. A force within them, and yet quite beyond them, seemed slowly and pitilessly washing away the adamant of their oath. As mistaken lovers might watch the inevitable sunset of first love, these men watched the sunset of their first hatred.

Their hearts were growing weaker and weaker against each other. When their weapons rang and reposted in the little London garden, they could have been very certain that if a third party had interrupted them something at least would have happened. They would have killed each other or they would have killed him. But now nothing could undo or deny that flash of fact, that for a second they had been glad to be interrupted. Some new and strange thing was rising higher and higher in their hearts like a high sea at night. It was something that seemed all the more merciless, because it might turn out an enormous mercy. Was there, perhaps, some such fatalism in friendship as all lovers talk about in love? Did God make men love each other against their will?

"I'm sure you'll excuse my speaking to you," said the stranger, in a voice at once eager and deprecating.

The voice was too polite for good manners. It was incongruous with the eccentric spectacle of the duellists which ought to have startled a sane and free man. It was also incongruous with the full and healthy, though rather loose physique of the man who spoke. At the first glance he looked a fine animal, with curling gold beard and hair, and blue eyes, unusually bright. It was only at the second glance that the mind felt a sudden and perhaps unmeaning irritation at the way in which the gold beard retreated backwards into the waistcoat, and the way in which the finely shaped nose went forward as if smelling its way. And it was only, perhaps, at the hundredth glance that the bright blue eyes, which normally before and after the instant seemed brilliant with intelligence, seemed as it were to be brilliant with idiocy. He was a heavy, healthy-looking man, who looked all the larger because of the loose, light coloured clothes that he wore, and that had in their extreme lightness and looseness, almost a touch of the tropics. But a closer examination of his attire would have shown that even in the tropics it would have been unique; but it was all woven according to some hygienic texture which no human being had ever heard of before, and which was absolutely necessary even for a day's health. He wore a huge broad-brimmed hat, equally hygienic, very much at the back of his head, and his voice coming out of so heavy and hearty a type of man was, as I have said, startlingly shrill and deferential.

"I'm sure you'll excuse my speaking to you," he said. "Now, I wonder if you are in some little difficulty which, after all, we could settle very comfortably together? Now, you don't mind my saying this, do you?"

The faces of both combatants remained somewhat solid under this appeal. But the stranger, probably taking their silence for a gathering shame, continued with a kind of gaiety:

"So you are the young men I have read about in the papers. Well, of course, when one is young, one is rather romantic. Do you know what I always say to young people?"

A blank silence followed this gay inquiry. Then Turnbull said in a colourless voice:

"As I was forty-seven last birthday, I probably came into the world too soon for the experience."

"Very good, very good," said the friendly person. "Dry Scotch humour. Dry Scotch humour. Well now. I understand that you two people want to fight a duel. I suppose you aren't much up in the modern world. We've quite outgrown duelling, you know. In fact, Tolstoy tells us that we shall soon outgrow war, which he says is simply a duel between nations. A duel between nations. But there is no doubt about our having outgrown duelling."

Waiting for some effect upon his wooden auditors, the stranger stood beaming for a moment and then resumed:

"Now, they tell me in the newspapers that you are really wanting to fight about something connected with Roman Catholicism. Now, do you know what I always say to Roman Catholics?"

"No," said Turnbull, heavily. "Do *they?*" It seemed to be a characteristic of the hearty, hygienic gentleman that he always forgot the speech he had made the moment before. Without enlarging further on the fixed form of his appeal to the Church of Rome, he laughed cordially at Turnbull's answer; then his wandering blue eyes caught the sunlight on the swords, and he assumed a good-humoured gravity.

"But you know this is a serious matter," he said, eyeing Turnbull and MacIan, as if they had just been keeping the table in a roar with their frivolities. "I am sure that if I appealed to your higher natures . . . your higher natures. Every man has a higher nature and a lower nature. Now, let us put the matter very plainly, and without any romantic nonsense about honour or anything of that sort. Is not bloodshed a great sin?"

"No," said MacIan, speaking for the first time.

"Well, really, really!" said the peacemaker.

"Murder is a sin," said the immovable Highlander. "There is no sin of bloodshed."

"Well, we won't quarrel about a word," said the other, pleasantly.

"Why on earth not?" said MacIan, with a sudden asperity. "Why shouldn't we quarrel about a word? What is the good of words if they aren't important enough to quarrel over? Why do we choose one word more than another if there isn't any difference between them? If you called a woman a chimpanzee instead of an angel, wouldn't there be a quarrel about a word? If you're not going to argue about words, what are you going to argue about? Are you going to convey your meaning to me by moving your ears? The Church and the heresies always used to fight about words, because they are the only things worth fighting about. I say that murder is a sin, and bloodshed is not, and that there is as much difference between those words as there is between the word 'yes' and the word 'no'; or rather more difference, for 'yes' and 'no,' at least, belong to the same category. Murder is a spiritual incident. Bloodshed is a physical incident. A surgeon commits bloodshed."

"Ah, you're a casuist!" said the large man, wagging his head. "Now, do you know what I always say to casuists . . . ?"

MacIan made a violent gesture; and Turnbull broke into open laughter. The peacemaker did not seem to be in the least annoyed, but continued in unabated enjoyment.

"Well, well," he said, "let us get back to the point. Now Tolstoy has shown that force is no remedy; so you see the position in which I am placed. I am doing my best to stop what I'm sure you won't mind my calling this really useless violence, this really quite wrong violence of yours. But it's against my principles to call in the police against you, because the police are still on a lower moral plane, so to speak, because, in short, the police undoubtedly sometimes employ force. Tolstoy has shown that violence merely breeds violence in the person towards whom it is used, whereas Love, on the other hand, breeds Love. So you see how I am placed. I am reduced to use Love in order to stop you. I am obliged to use Love."

He gave to the word an indescribable sound of something hard and heavy, as if he were saying "boots." Turnbull suddenly gripped his sword and said, shortly, "I see how you are placed quite well, sir. You will not call the police. Mr. MacIan, shall we engage?" MacIan plucked his sword out of the grass.

"I must and will stop this shocking crime," cried the Tolstoian, crimson in the face. "It is against all modern ideas. It is against the principle of love. How you, sir, who pretend to be a Christian . . ."

MacIan turned upon him with a white face and bitter lip. "Sir," he said, "talk about the principle of love as much as you like. You seem to me colder than a lump of stone; but I am willing to believe that you may at some time have loved a cat, or a dog, or a child. When you were a baby, I suppose you loved your mother. Talk about love, then, till the world is sick of the word. But don't you talk about Christianity. Don't you dare to say one word, white or black, about it. Christianity is, as far as you are concerned, a horrible mystery. Keep clear of it, keep silent upon it, as you would upon an abomination. It is a thing that has made men slay and torture each other; and you will never know why. It is a thing that has made men do evil that good might come; and you will never understand the evil, let alone the good. Christianity is a thing that could only make you vomit, till you are other than you are. I would not justify it to you even if I could. Hate it, in God's name, as Turnbull does, who is a man. It is a monstrous thing, for which men die. And if you will stand here and talk about love for another ten minutes it is very probable that you will see a man die for it."

And he fell on guard. Turnbull was busy settling something loose in his elaborate hilt, and the pause was broken by the stranger.

"Suppose I call the police?" he said, with a heated face.

"And deny your most sacred dogma," said MacIan.

"Dogma!" cried the man, in a sort of dismay. "Oh, we have no *dogmas*, you know!"

There was another silence, and he said again, airily:

"You know, I think, there's something in what Shaw teaches about no moral principles being quite fixed. Have you ever read 'The Quintessence of Ibsenism?' Of course he went very wrong over the war."

Turnbull, with a bent, flushed face, was tying up the loose piece of the pommel with string. With the string in his teeth, he said, "Oh, make up your damned mind and clear out!"

"It's a serious thing," said the philosopher, shaking his head. "I must be alone and consider which is the higher point of view. I rather feel that in a case so extreme as this . . ." and he went slowly away. As he disappeared among the trees, they heard him murmuring in a sing-song voice, "New occasions teach new duties," out of a poem by James Russell Lowell.

"Ah," said MacIan, drawing a deep breath. "Don't you believe in prayer now? I prayed for an angel."

"I am afraid I don't understand," answered Turnbull.

"An hour ago," said the Highlander, in his heavy meditative voice, "I felt the devil weakening my heart and my oath against you, and I prayed that God would send an angel to my aid."

"Well?" inquired the other, finishing his mending and wrapping the rest of the string round his hand to get a firmer grip.

"Well?"

"Well, that man was an angel," said MacIan.

"I didn't know they were as bad as that," answered Turnbull.

"We know that devils sometimes quote Scripture and counterfeit good," replied the mystic. "Why should not angels sometimes come to show us the black abyss of evil on whose brink we stand. If that man had not tried to stop us . . . I might . . . I might have stopped."

"I know what you mean," said Turnbull, grimly.

"But then he came," broke out MacIan, "and my soul said to me: 'Give up fighting, and you will become like That. Give up vows and dogmas, and fixed things, and you may grow like That. You may learn, also, that fog of false philosophy. You may grow fond of that mire of crawling, cowardly morals, and you may come to think a blow bad, because it hurts, and not because it humiliates. You may come to think murder wrong, because it is violent, and not because it is unjust.' Oh, you blasphemer of the good, an hour ago I almost loved you! But do not fear for me now. I have heard the word Love pronounced in *his* intonation; and I know exactly what it means. On guard!"

The swords caught on each other with a dreadful clang and jar, full of the old energy and hate; and at once plunged and replunged. Once more each man's heart had become the magnet of a mad sword. Suddenly, furious as they were, they were frozen for a moment motionless.

"What noise is that?" asked the Highlander, hoarsely.

"I think I know," replied Turnbull.

"What? . . . What?" cried the other.

"The student of Shaw and Tolstoy has made up his remarkable mind," said Turnbull, quietly. "The police are coming up the hill."

CHAPTER VI

THE OTHER PHILOSOPHER

B ETWEEN HIGH HEDGES in Hertfordshire, hedges so high as to create a kind of grove, two men were running. They did not run in a scampering or feverish manner, but in the steady swing of the pendulum. Across the great plains and uplands to the right and left of the lane, a long tide of sunset light rolled like a sea of ruby, lighting up the long terraces of the hills and picking out the few windows of the scattered hamlets in startling blood-red sparks. But the lane was cut deep in the hill and remained in an abrupt shadow. The two men running in it had an impression not uncommonly experienced between those wild green English walls; a sense of being led between the walls of a maze.

Though their pace was steady it was vigorous; their faces were heated and their eyes fixed and bright. There was, indeed, something a little mad in the contrast between the evening's stillness over the empty country-side, and these two figures fleeing wildly from nothing. They had the look of two lunatics, possibly they were.

"Are you all right?" said Turnbull, with civility. "Can you keep this up?"

"Quite easily, thank you," replied MacIan. "I run very well."

"Is that a qualification in a family of warriors?" asked Turnbull.

"Undoubtedly. Rapid movement is essential," answered MacIan, who never saw a joke in his life.

Turnbull broke out into a short laugh, and silence fell between them, the panting silence of runners.

Then MacIan said: "We run better than any of those policemen. They are too fat. Why do you make your policemen so fat?"

"I didn't do much towards making them fat myself," replied Turnbull, genially, "but I flatter myself that I am now doing something towards making them thin. You'll see they will be as lean as rakes by the time they catch us. They will look like your friend, Cardinal Manning."

"But they won't catch us," said MacIan, in his literal way.

45

"No, we beat them in the great military art of running away," returned the other. "They won't catch us unless —— "

MacIan turned his long equine face inquiringly. "Unless what?" he said, for Turnbull had gone silent suddenly, and seemed to be listening intently as he ran as a horse does with his ears turned back.

"Unless what?" repeated the Highlander.

"Unless they do — what they have done. Listen." MacIan slackened his trot, and turned his head to the trail they had left behind them. Across two or three billows of the up and down lane came along the ground the unmistakable throbbing of horses' hoofs.

"They have put the mounted police on us," said Turnbull, shortly. "Good Lord, one would think we were a Revolution."

"So we are," said MacIan, calmly. "What shall we do? Shall we turn on them with our points?"

"It may come to that," answered Turnbull, "though if it does, I reckon that will be the last act. We must put it off if we can." And he stared and peered about him between the bushes. "If we could hide somewhere the beasts might go by us," he said. "The police have their faults, but thank God they're inefficient. Why, here's the very thing. Be quick and quiet. Follow me."

He suddenly swung himself up the high bank on one side of the lane. It was almost as high and smooth as a wall, and on the top of it the black hedge stood out over them at an angle, almost like a thatched roof of the lane. And the burning evening sky looked down at them through the tangle with red eyes as of an army of goblins.

Turnbull hoisted himself up and broke the hedge with his body. As his head and shoulders rose above it they turned to flame in the full glow as if lit up by an immense firelight. His red hair and beard looked almost scarlet, and his pale face as bright as a boy's. Something violent, something that was at once love and hatred, surged in the strange heart of the Gael below him. He had an unutterable sense of epic importance, as if he were somehow lifting all humanity into a prouder and more passionate region of the air. As he swung himself up also into the evening light he felt as if he were rising on enormous wings.

Legends of the morning of the world which he had heard in childhood or read in youth came back upon him in a cloudy splendour, purple tales of wrath and friendship, like Roland and Oliver, or Balin and Balan, reminding him of emotional entanglements. Men who had loved each other and then fought each other; men who had fought each other and then loved each other, together made a mixed but monstrous sense of momentousness. The crimson seas of the sunset seemed to him like a bursting out of some sacred blood, as if the heart of the world had broken.

Turnbull was wholly unaffected by any written or spoken poetry; his was a powerful and prosaic mind. But even upon him there came for the moment something out of the earth and the passionate ends of the sky. The only evidence was in his voice, which was still practical but a shade more quiet.

"Do you see that summer-house-looking thing over there?" he asked shortly. "That will do for us very well."

Keeping himself free from the tangle of the hedge he strolled across a triangle of obscure kitchen garden, and approached a dismal shed or lodge a yard or two beyond it. It was a weather-stained hut of grey wood, which with all its desolation retained a tag or two of trivial ornament, which suggested that the thing had once been a sort of summer-house, and the place probably a sort of garden.

"That is quite invisible from the road," said Turnbull, as he entered it, "and it will cover us up for the night."

MacIan looked at him gravely for a few moments. "Sir," he said, "I ought to say something to you. I ought to say——"

"Hush," said Turnbull, suddenly lifting his hand; "be still, man."

In the sudden silence, the drumming of the distant horses grew louder and louder with inconceivable rapidity, and the cavalcade of police rushed by below them in the lane, almost with the roar and rattle of an express train.

"I ought to tell you," continued MacIan, still staring stolidly at the other, "that you are a great chief, and it is good to go to war behind you."

Turnbull said nothing, but turned and looked out of the foolish lattice of the little windows, then he said, "We must have food and sleep first."

When the last echo of their eluded pursuers had died in the distant uplands, Turnbull began to unpack the provisions with the easy air of a man at a picnic. He had just laid out the last items, put a bottle of wine on the floor, and a tin of salmon on the window-ledge, when the bottomless silence of that forgotten place was broken. And it was broken by three heavy blows of a stick delivered upon the door.

Turnbull looked up in the act of opening a tin and stared silently at his companion. MacIan's long, lean mouth had shut hard.

"Who the devil can that be?" said Turnbull.

"God knows," said the other. "It might be God."

Again the sound of the wooden stick reverberated on the wooden door. It was a curious sound, and on consideration did not resemble the ordinary effects of knocking on a door for admittance. It was rather as if the point of a stick were plunged again and again at the panels in an absurd attempt to make a hole in them.

A wild look sprang into MacIan's eyes and he got up half stupidly, with a kind of stagger, put his hand out and caught one of the swords. "Let us fight at once," he cried, "it is the end of the world."

"You're overdone, MacIan," said Turnbull, putting him on one side. "It's only some one playing the goat. Let me open the door."

But he also picked up a sword as he stepped to open it.

He paused one moment with his hand on the handle and then flung the door open. Almost as he did so the ferrule of an ordinary bamboo cane came at his eyes, so that he had actually to parry it with the naked weapon in his hands. As the two touched, the point of the stick was dropped very abruptly, and the man with the stick stepped hurriedly back.

Against the heraldic background of sprawling crimson and gold offered him by the expiring sunset, the figure of the man with the stick showed at first merely black and fantastic. He was a small man with two wisps of long hair that curled up on each side, and seen in silhouette, looked like horns. He had a bow tie so big that the two ends showed on each side of his neck like unnatural stunted wings. He had his long black cane still tilted in his hand like a fencing foil and half presented at the open door. His large straw hat had fallen behind him as he leapt backwards.

"With reference to your suggestion, MacIan," said Turnbull, placidly, "I think it looks more like the Devil."

"Who on earth are you?" cried the stranger in a high shrill voice, brandishing his cane defensively.

"Let me see," said Turnbull, looking round to MacIan with the same blandness. "Who are we?"

"Come out," screamed the little man with the stick.

"Certainly," said Turnbull, and went outside with the sword, MacIan following.

Seen more fully, with the evening light on his face, the strange man looked a little less like a goblin. He wore a square pale-grey jacket suit, on which the grey butterfly tie was the only indisputable touch of affectation. Against the great sunset his figure had looked merely small: seen in a more equal light it looked tolerably compact and shapely. His reddish-brown hair, combed into two great curls, looked like the long, slow curling hair of the women in some pre-Raphaelite pictures. But within this feminine frame of hair his face was unexpectedly impudent, like a monkey's.

"What are you doing here?" he said, in a sharp small voice.

"Well," said MacIan, in his grave childish way, "what are *you* doing here?"

"I," said the man, indignantly, "I'm in my own garden."

"Oh," said MacIan, simply, "I apologise."

Turnbull was coolly curling his red moustache, and the stranger stared from one to the other, temporarily stunned by their innocent assurance.

"But, may I ask," he said at last, "what the devil you are doing in my summer-house?"

"Certainly," said MacIan. "We were just going to fight."

"To fight!" repeated the man.

"We had better tell this gentleman the whole business," broke in Turnbull. Then turning to the stranger he said firmly, "I am sorry, sir, but we have something to do that must be done. And I may as well tell you at the beginning and to avoid waste of time or language, that we cannot admit any interference."

"We were just going to take some slight refreshment when you interrupted us . . ."

The little man had a dawning expression of understanding and stooped and picked up the unused bottle of wine, eyeing it curiously.

Turnbull continued: —

"But that refreshment was preparatory to something which I fear you will find less comprehensible, but on which our minds are entirely fixed, sir. We are forced to fight a duel. We are forced by honour and an internal intellectual need. Do not, for your own sake, attempt to stop us. I know all the excellent and ethical things that you will want to say to us. I know all about the essential requirements of civil order: I have written leading articles about them all my life. I know all about the sacredness of human life; I have bored all my friends with it. Try and understand our position. This man and I are alone in the modern world in that we think that God is essentially important. I think He does not exist; that is where the importance comes in for me. But this man thinks that He does exist, and thinking that very properly thinks Him more important than anything else. Now we wish to make a great demonstration and assertion — something that will set the world on fire like the first Christian persecutions. If you like, we are attempting a mutual martyrdom. The papers have posted up every town against us. Scotland Yard has fortified every police station with our enemies; we are driven therefore to the edge of a lonely lane, and indirectly to taking liberties with your summer-house in order to arrange our . . ."

"Stop!" roared the little man in the butterfly necktie. "Put me out of my intellectual misery. Are you really the two tomfools I have read of in all the papers? Are you the two people who wanted to spit each other in the Police Court? Are you? Are you?"

"Yes," said MacIan, "it began in a Police Court."

The little man slung the bottle of wine twenty yards away like a stone.

"Come up to my place," he said. "I've got better stuff than that. I've got the best Beaune within fifty miles of here. Come up. You're the very men I wanted to see."

Even Turnbull, with his typical invulnerability, was a little taken aback by this boisterous and almost brutal hospitality.

"Why . . . sir . . ." he began.

"Come up! Come in!" howled the little man, dancing with delight. "I'll give you a dinner. I'll give you a bed! I'll give you a green smooth lawn and your choice of swords and pistols. Why, you fools, I adore fighting! It's the only good thing in God's world! I've walked about these damned fields and longed to see somebody cut up and killed and the blood running. Ha! Ha!"

And he made sudden lunges with his stick at the trunk of a neighbouring tree so that the ferrule made fierce prints and punctures in the bark.

"Excuse me," said MacIan suddenly with the wide-eyed curiosity of a child, "excuse me, but . . ."

"Well?" said the small fighter, brandishing his wooden weapon.

"Excuse me," repeated MacIan, "but was that what you were doing at the door?"

The little man stared an instant and then said: "Yes," and Turnbull broke into a guffaw.

"Come on!" cried the little man, tucking his stick under his arm and taking quite suddenly to his heels. "Come on! Confound me, I'll see both of you eat and then I'll see one of you die. Lord bless me, the gods must exist after all — they have sent me one of my day-dreams! Lord! A duel!"

He had gone flying along a winding path between the borders of the kitchen garden, and in the increasing twilight he was as hard to follow as a flying hare. But at length the path after many twists betrayed its purpose and led abruptly up two or three steps to the door of a tiny but very clean cottage. There was nothing about the outside to distinguish it from other cottages, except indeed its ominous cleanliness and one thing that was out of all the custom and tradition of all cottages under the sun. In the middle of the little garden among the stocks and marigolds there surged up in shapeless stone a South Sea Island idol. There was something gross and even evil in that eyeless and alien god among the most innocent of the English flowers.

"Come in!" cried the creature again. "Come in! it's better inside!"

Whether or no it was better inside it was at least a surprise. The moment the two duellists had pushed open the door of that inoffensive, whitewashed cottage they found that its interior was lined with fiery gold. It was like stepping into a chamber in the Arabian Nights. The door that closed behind them shut out England and all the energies of the West. The ornaments that shone and shimmered on every side of

them were subtly mixed from many periods and lands, but were all
oriental. Cruel Assyrian bas-reliefs ran along the sides of the passage;
cruel Turkish swords and daggers glinted above and below them; the
two were separated by ages and fallen civilisations. Yet they seemed to
sympathise since they were both harmonious and both merciless. The
house seemed to consist of chamber within chamber and created that
impression as of a dream which belongs also to the Arabian Nights
themselves. The innermost room of all was like the inside of a jewel.
The little man who owned it all threw himself on a heap of scarlet and
golden cushions and struck his hands together. A negro in a white robe
and turban appeared suddenly and silently behind them.

"Selim," said the host, "these two gentlemen are staying with me tonight. Send up the very best wine and dinner at once. And Selim, one of
these gentlemen will probably die to-morrow. Make arrangements,
please."

The negro bowed and withdrew.

Evan MacIan came out the next morning into the little garden to a
fresh silver day, his long face looking more austere than ever in that cold
light, his eyelids a little heavy. He carried one of the swords. Turnbull
was in the little house behind him, demolishing the end of an early
breakfast and humming a tune to himself, which could be heard
through the open window. A moment or two later he leapt to his feet and
came out into the sunlight, still munching toast, his own sword stuck
under his arm like a walking-stick.

Their eccentric host had vanished from sight, with a polite gesture,
some twenty minutes before. They imagined him to be occupied on
some concerns in the interior of the house, and they waited for his
emergence, stamping the garden in silence — the garden of tall, fresh
country flowers, in the midst of which the monstrous South Sea idol
lifted itself as abruptly as the prow of a ship riding on a sea of red and
white and gold.

It was with a start, therefore, that they came upon the man himself
already in the garden. They were all the more startled because of the still
posture in which they found him. He was on his knees in front of the
stone idol, rigid and motionless, like a saint in a trance or ecstasy. Yet
when Turnbull's tread broke a twig, he was on his feet in a flash.

"Excuse me," he said with an irradiation of smiles, but yet with a kind
of bewilderment. "So sorry . . . family prayers . . . old fashioned . . .
mother's knee. Let us go on to the lawn behind."

And he ducked rapidly round the statue to an open space of grass on
the other side of it.

"This will do us best, Mr. MacIan," said he. Then he made a gesture
toward the heavy stone figure on the pedestal which had now its blank

and shapeless back turned toward them. "Don't you be afraid," he added, "he can still see us."

MacIan turned his blue, blinking eyes, which seemed still misty with sleep (or sleeplessness), towards the idol, but his brows drew together.

The little man with the long hair also had his eyes on the back view of the god. His eyes were at once liquid and burning, and he rubbed his hands slowly against each other.

"Do you know," he said, "I think he can see us better this way. I often think that this blank thing is his real face, watching, though it cannot be watched. He! he! Yes, I think he looks nice from behind. He looks more cruel from behind, don't you think?"

"What the devil is the thing?" asked Turnbull gruffly.

"It is the only Thing there is," answered the other. "It is Force."

"Oh!" said Turnbull shortly.

"Yes, my friends," said the little man, with an animated countenance, fluttering his fingers in the air, "it was no chance that led you to this garden; surely it was the caprice of some old god, some happy, pitiless god. Perhaps it was his will, for he loves blood; and on that stone in front of him men have been butchered by hundreds in the fierce, feasting islands of the South. In this cursed, craven place I have not been permitted to kill men on his altar. Only rabbits and cats, sometimes."

In the stillness MacIan made a sudden movement, unmeaning apparently, and then remained rigid.

"But to-day, to-day," continued the small man in a shrill voice. "To-day his hour is come. To-day his will is done on earth as it is in heaven. Men, men, men will bleed before him to-day." And he bit his forefinger in a kind of fever.

Still, the two duellists stood with their swords as heavily as statues, and the silence seemed to cool the eccentric and call him back to more rational speech.

"Perhaps I express myself a little too lyrically," he said with an amicable abruptness. "My philosophy has its higher ecstasies, but perhaps you are hardly worked up to them yet. Let us confine ourselves to the unquestioned. You have found your way, gentlemen, by a beautiful accident, to the house of the only man in England (probably) who will favour and encourage your most reasonable project. From Cornwall to Cape Wrath this country is one horrible, solid block of humanitarianism. You will find men who will defend this or that war in a distant continent. They will defend it on the contemptible ground of commerce or the more contemptible ground of social good. But do not fancy that you will find one other person who will comprehend a strong man taking the sword in his hand and wiping out his enemy. My name is Wimpey, Morrice Wimpey. I had a Fellowship at Magdalen. But I assure you I had to drop it, owing to my having said something in a public lecture infringing the popular prejudice against those great gentlemen, the assassins of the Italian Renascence. They let me say it at dinner and so on, and seemed to like it. But in a public lecture . . . so inconsistent. Well, as I say, here is your only refuge and temple of honour. Here you can fall back on that naked and awful arbitration which is the only thing that balances the stars—a still, continuous violence. *Væ Victis!* Down, down, down with the defeated! Victory is the only ultimate fact. Carthage *was* destroyed, the Red Indians are being exterminated: that is the single certainty. In an hour from now that sun will still be shining and that grass growing, and one of you will be conquered; one of you will be the conqueror. When it has been done, nothing will alter it. Heroes, I give you the hospitality fit for heroes. And I salute the survivor. Fall on!"

The two men took their swords. Then MacIan said steadily: "Mr. Turnbull, lend me your sword a moment."

Turnbull, with a questioning glance, handed him the weapon. MacIan took the second sword in his left hand and, with a violent gesture, hurled it at the feet of little Mr. Wimpey.

"Fight!" he said in a loud, harsh voice. "Fight me now!"

Wimpey took a step backward, and bewildered words bubbled on his lips.

"Pick up that sword and fight me," repeated MacIan, with brows as black as thunder.

The little man turned to Turnbull with a gesture, demanding judgment or protection.

"Really, sir," he began, "this gentleman confuses . . ."

"You stinking little coward," roared Turnbull, suddenly releasing his wrath. "Fight, if you're so fond of fighting! Fight, if you're so fond of all that filthy philosophy! If winning is everything, go in and win! If the weak must go to the wall, go to the wall! Fight, you rat! Fight, or if you won't fight—run!"

And he ran at Wimpey, with blazing eyes.

Wimpey staggered back a few paces like a man struggling with his own limbs. Then he felt the furious Scotchman coming at him like an express-train, doubling his size every second, with eyes as big as windows and a sword as bright as the sun. Something broke inside him, and he found himself running away, tumbling over his own feet in terror, and crying out as he ran.

"Chase him!" shouted Turnbull as MacIan snatched up the sword and joined in the scamper. "Chase him over a county! Chase him into the sea! Shoo! Shoo! Shoo!"

The little man plunged like a rabbit among the tall flowers, the two duellists after him. Turnbull kept at his tail with savage ecstasy, still shooing him like a cat. But MacIan, as he ran past the South Sea idol, paused an instant to spring upon its pedestal. For five seconds he strained against the inert mass. Then it stirred; and he sent it over with a great crash among the flowers, that engulfed it altogether. Then he went bounding after the runaway.

In the energy of his alarm the ex-Fellow of Magdalen managed to leap the paling of his garden. The two pursuers went over it after him like flying birds. He fled frantically down a long lane with his two terrors in his trail till he came to a gap in the hedge and went across a steep meadow like the wind. The two Scotchmen, as they ran, kept up a cheery bellowing and waved their swords. Up three slanting meadows, down four slanting meadows on the other side, across another road, across a heath of snapping bracken, through a wood, across another road, and to the brink of a big pool, they pursued the flying philosopher. But when he came to the pool his pace was so precipitate that he could not stop it, and with a kind of lurching stagger, he fell splash into the greasy water. Getting dripping to his feet, with the water up to his knees, the worshipper of force and victory waded disconsolately to the other side and drew himself on to the bank. And Turnbull sat down on the grass and went off into reverberations of laughter. A second afterward the most extraordinary grimaces were seen to distort the stiff face of MacIan, and unholy sounds came from within. He had never practised laughing, and it hurt him very much.

CHAPTER VII

THE VILLAGE OF GRASSLEY-IN-THE-HOLE

A T ABOUT HALF-PAST one, under a strong blue sky, Turnbull got up out of the grass and fern in which he had been lying, and his still intermittent laughter ended in a kind of yawn.

"I'm hungry," he said shortly. "Are you?"

"I have not noticed," answered MacIan. "What are you going to do?"

"There's a village down the road, past the pool," answered Turnbull. "I can see it from here. I can see the whitewashed walls of some cottages and a kind of corner of the church. How jolly it all looks. It looks so — I don't know what the word is — so sensible. Don't fancy I'm under any illusions about Arcadian virtue and the innocent villagers. Men make beasts of themselves there with drink, but they don't deliberately make devils of themselves with mere talking. They kill wild animals in the wild woods, but they don't kill cats to the God of Victory. They don't —" He broke off and suddenly spat on the ground.

"Excuse me," he said; "it was ceremonial. One has to get the taste out of one's mouth."

"The taste of what?" asked MacIan.

"I don't know the exact name for it," replied Turnbull. "Perhaps it is the South Sea Islands, or it may be Magdalen College."

There was a long pause, and MacIan also lifted his large limbs off the ground — his eyes particularly dreamy.

"I know what you mean, Turnbull," he said, "but . . . I always thought you people agreed with all that."

"Agreed with all what?" asked the other.

"With all that about doing as one likes, and the individual, and Nature loving the strongest, and all the things which that cockroach talked about."

Turnbull's big blue-gray eyes stood open with a grave astonishment.

"Do you really mean to say, MacIan," he said, "that you fancied that we, the Free-thinkers, that Bradlaugh, or Holyoake, or Ingersoll, believe all that dirty, immoral mysticism about Nature? Damn Nature!"

"I supposed you did," said MacIan calmly. "It seems to me your most conclusive position."

"And you mean to tell me," rejoined the other, "that you broke my window, and challenged me to mortal combat, and tied a tradesman up with ropes, and chased an Oxford Fellow across five meadows — all under the impression that I am such an illiterate idiot as to believe in Nature!"

"I supposed you did," repeated MacIan with his usual mildness; "but I admit that I know little of the details of your belief — or disbelief."

Turnbull swung round quite suddenly, and set off toward the village.

"Come along," he cried. "Come down to the village. Come down to the nearest decent inhabitable pub. This is a case for beer."

"I do not quite follow you," said the Highlander.

"Yes, you do," answered Turnbull. "You follow me slap into the inn-parlour. I repeat, this is a case for beer. We must have the whole of this matter out thoroughly before we go a step farther. Do you know that an idea has just struck me of great simplicity and of some cogency. Do not by any means let us drop our intentions of settling our differences with two steel swords. But do you not think that with two pewter pots we might do what we really have never thought of doing yet — discover what our difference is?"

"It never occurred to me before," answered MacIan with tranquillity. "It is a good suggestion."

And they set out at an easy swing down the steep road to the village of Grassley-in-the-Hole.

Grassley-in-the-Hole was a rude parallelogram of buildings, with two thoroughfares which might have been called two high streets if it had been possible to call them streets. One of these ways was higher on the slope than the other, the whole parallelogram lying aslant, so to speak, on the side of the hill. The upper of these two roads was decorated with a big public-house, a butcher's shop, a small public-house, a sweetstuff shop, a very small public-house, and an illegible sign-post. The lower of the two roads boasted a horse-pond, a post-office, a gentleman's garden with very high hedges, a microscopically small public-house, and two cottages. Where all the people lived who supported all the public-houses was in this, as in many other English villages, a silent and smiling mystery. The church lay a little above and beyond the village, with a square gray tower dominating it decisively.

But even the church was scarcely so central and solemn an institution as the large public-house, the Valencourt Arms. It was named after some splendid family that had long gone bankrupt, and whose seat was occupied by a man who had invented an hygienic bootjack; but the unfathomable sentimentalism of the English people insisted on regarding the Inn, the seat and the sitter in it, as alike parts of a pure and marmoreal antiquity. And in the Valencourt Arms festivity itself had some solemnity and decorum; and beer was drunk with reverence, as it ought to be. Into the principal parlour of this place entered two strangers, who found themselves, as is always the case in such hostels, the object, not of fluttered curiosity or pert inquiry, but of steady, ceaseless, devouring ocular study. They had long coats down to their heels, and carried under each coat something that looked like a stick. One was tall and dark, the other short and red-haired. They ordered a pot of ale each.

"MacIan," said Turnbull, lifting his tankard, "the fool who wanted us to be friends made us want to go on fighting. It is only natural that the fool who wanted us to fight should make us friendly. MacIan, your health!"

Dusk was already dropping, the rustics in the tavern were already lurching and lumbering out of it by twos and threes, crying clamorous good-nights to a solitary old toper that remained, before MacIan and Turnbull had reached the really important part of their discussion.

MacIan wore an expression of sad bewilderment not uncommon with him. "I am to understand, then," he said, "that you don't believe in nature."

"You may say so in a very special and emphatic sense," said Turnbull. "I do not believe in nature, just as I do not believe in Odin. She is a myth. It is not merely that I do not believe that nature can guide us. It is that I do not believe that nature exists."

"Exists?" said MacIan in his monotonous way, settling his pewter-pot on the table.

"Yes, in a real sense nature does not exist. I mean that nobody can discover what the original nature of things would have been if things had not interfered with it. The first blade of grass began to tear up the earth and eat it; it was interfering with nature, if there is any nature. The first wild ox began to tear up the grass and eat it; he was interfering with nature, if there is any nature. In the same way," continued Turnbull, "the human when it asserts its dominance over nature is just as natural as the thing which it destroys."

"And in the same way," said MacIan almost dreamily, "the superhuman, the supernatural is just as natural as the nature which it destroys."

Turnbull took his head out of his pewter-pot in some anger.

"The supernatural, of course," he said, "is quite another thing; the case of the supernatural is simple. The supernatural does not exist."

"Quite so," said MacIan in a rather dull voice; "you said the same about the natural. If the natural does not exist the supernatural obviously can't." And he yawned a little over his ale.

Turnbull turned for some reason a little red and remarked quickly, "That may be jolly clever, for all I know. But every one does know that there is a division between the things that as a matter of fact do commonly happen and the things that don't. Things that break the evident laws of nature ——"

"Which does not exist," put in MacIan sleepily. Turnbull struck the table with a sudden hand.

"Good Lord in heaven!" he cried ——

"Who does not exist," murmured MacIan.

"Good Lord in heaven!" thundered Turnbull, without regarding the interruption. "Do you really mean to sit there and say that you, like anybody else, would not recognise the difference between a natural occurrence and a supernatural one — if there could be such a thing? If I flew up to the ceiling ——"

"You would bump your head badly," cried MacIan, suddenly starting up. "One can't talk of this kind of thing under a ceiling at all. Come outside! Come outside and ascend into heaven!"

He burst the door open on a blue abyss of evening and they stepped out into it: it was suddenly and strangely cool.

"Turnbull," said MacIan, "you have said some things so true and some so false that I want to talk; and I will try to talk so that you understand. For at present you do not understand at all. We don't seem to mean the same things by the same words."

He stood silent for a second or two and then resumed.

"A minute or two ago I caught you out in a real contradiction. At that moment logically I was right. And at that moment I knew I was wrong. Yes, there is a real difference between the natural and the supernatural: if you flew up into that blue sky this instant, I should think that you were moved by God — or the devil. But if you want to know what I really think . . . I must explain."

He stopped again, abstractedly boring the point of his sword into the earth, and went on:

"I was born and bred and taught in a complete universe. The supernatural was not natural, but it was perfectly reasonable. Nay, the supernatural to me is more reasonable than the natural; for the supernatural is a direct message from God, who is reason. I was taught that some things are natural and some things divine. I mean that some things are mechanical and some things divine. But there is the great difficulty, Turnbull. The great difficulty is that, according to my teaching, you are divine."

"Me! Divine?" said Turnbull truculently. "What do you mean?"

"That is just the difficulty," continued MacIan thoughtfully. "I was told that there was a difference between the grass and a man's will; and the difference was that a man's will was special and divine. A man's free will, I heard, was supernatural."

"Rubbish!" said Turnbull.

"Oh," said MacIan patiently, "then if a man's free will isn't supernatural, why do your materialists deny that it exists?"

Turnbull was silent for a moment. Then he began to speak, but MacIan continued with the same steady voice and sad eyes:

"So what I feel is this: Here is the great divine creation I was taught to believe in. I can understand your disbelieving in it, but why disbelieve in a part of it? It was all one thing to me. God had authority because he was God. Man had authority because he was man. You cannot prove that God is better than a man; nor can you prove that a man is better than a horse. Why permit any ordinary thing? Why do you let a horse be saddled?"

"Some modern thinkers disapprove of it," said Turnbull a little doubtfully.

"I know," said MacIan grimly; "that man who talked about love, for instance."

Turnbull made a humorous grimace; then he said: "We seem to be talking in a kind of shorthand; but I won't pretend not to understand you. What you mean is this: that you learnt about all your saints and angels at the same time as you learnt about common morality, from the same people, in the same way. And you mean to say that if one may be disputed, so may the other. Well, let that pass for the moment. But let me ask you a question in turn. Did not this system of yours, which you swallowed whole, contain all sorts of things that were merely local, the respect for the chief of your clan, or such things; the village ghost, the family feud, or what not? Did you not take in those things, too, along with your theology?"

MacIan stared along the dim village road, down which the last straggler from the inn was trailing his way.

"What you say is not unreasonable," he said. "But it is not quite true. The distinction between the chief and us did exist; but it was never anything like the distinction between the human and the divine, or the human and the animal. It was more like the distinction between one animal and another. But——"

"Well?" said Turnbull.

MacIan was silent.

"Go on," repeated Turnbull; "what's the matter with you? What are you staring at?"

"I am staring," said MacIan at last, "at that which shall judge us both."

"Oh, yes," said Turnbull in a tired way, "I suppose you mean God."

"No, I don't," said MacIan, shaking his head. "I mean him."

And he pointed to the half-tipsy yokel who was ploughing down the road.

"What do you mean?" asked the atheist.

"I mean him," repeated MacIan with emphasis. "He goes out in the early dawn; he digs or he ploughs a field. Then he comes back and drinks ale, and then he sings a song. All your philosophies and political systems are young compared to him. All your hoary cathedrals, yes, even the Eternal Church on earth is new compared to him. The most mouldering gods in the British Museum are new facts beside him. It is he who in the end shall judge us all."

And MacIan rose to his feet with a vague excitement.

"What are you going to do?"

"I am going to ask him," cried MacIan, "which of us is right."

Turnbull broke into a kind of laugh. "Ask that intoxicated turnip-eater ——" he began.

"Yes — which of us is right," cried MacIan violently. "Oh, you have long words and I have long words; and I talk of every man being the image of God; and you talk of every man being a citizen and enlightened enough to govern. But if every man typifies God, there is God. If every man is an enlightened citizen, there is your enlightened citizen. The first man one meets is always man. Let us catch him up."

And in gigantic strides the long, lean Highlander whirled away into the gray twilight, Turnbull following with a good-humoured oath.

The track of the rustic was easy to follow, even in the faltering dark; for he was enlivening his wavering walk with song. It was an interminable poem, beginning with some unspecified King William, who (it appeared) lived in London town and who after the second rise vanished rather abruptly from the train of thought. The rest was almost entirely about beer and was thick with local topography of a quite unrecognisable kind. The singer's step was neither very rapid nor, indeed, exceptionally secure; so the song grew louder and louder and the two soon overtook him.

He was a man elderly or rather of any age, with lean gray hair and a lean red face, but with that remarkable rustic physiognomy in which it seems that all the features stand out independently from the face; the rugged red nose going out like a limb; the bleared blue eyes standing out like signals.

He gave them greeting with the elaborate urbanity of the slightly intoxicated. MacIan, who was vibrating with one of his silent, violent decisions, opened the question without delay. He explained the philosophic position in words as short and simple as possible. But the singular old man with the lank red face seemed to think uncommonly little of the short words. He fixed with a fierce affection upon one or two of the long ones.

"Atheists!" he repeated with luxurious scorn. "Atheists! I know their sort, master. Atheists! Don't talk to me about 'un. Atheists!"

The grounds of his disdain seemed a little dark and confused; but they were evidently sufficient. MacIan resumed in some encouragement:

"You think as I do, I hope; you think that a man should be connected with the Church; with the common Christian ——"

The old man extended a quivering stick in the direction of a distant hill.

"There's the church," he said thickly. "Grassley old church that is. Pulled down it was, in the old squire's time, and ——"

"I mean," explained MacIan elaborately, "that you think that there should be some one typifying religion, a priest ——"

"Priests!" said the old man with sudden passion. "Priests! I know 'un. What they want in England? That's what I say. What they want in England?"

"They want you," said MacIan.

"Quite so," said Turnbull, "and me; but they won't get us. MacIan, your attempt on the primitive innocence does not seem very successful. Let me try. What you want, my friend, is your rights. You don't want any priests or churches. A vote, a right to speak is what you ——"

"Who says I a'n't got a right to speak?" said the old man, facing round in an irrational frenzy. "I got a right to speak. I'm a man, I am. I don't want no votin' nor priests. I say a man's a man; that's what I say. If a man a'n't a man, what is he? That's what I say, if a man a'n't a man, what is he? When I sees a man, I sez 'e's a man."

"Quite so," said Turnbull, "a citizen."

"I say he's a man," said the rustic furiously, stopping and striking his stick on the ground. "Not a city or owt else. He's a man."

"You're perfectly right," said the sudden voice of MacIan, falling like a sword. "And you have kept close to something the whole world of to-day tries to forget."

"Good-night."

And the old man went on wildly singing into the night.

"A jolly old creature," said Turnbull; "he didn't seem able to get much beyond that fact that a man is a man."

"Has anybody got beyond it?" asked MacIan.

Turnbull looked at him curiously. "Are you turning an agnostic?" he asked.

"Oh, you do not understand!" cried out MacIan. "We Catholics are all agnostics. We Catholics have only in that sense got as far as realising that a man is a man. But your Ibsens and your Zolas and your Shaws and your Tolstoys have not even got so far."

CHAPTER VIII

AN INTERLUDE OF ARGUMENT

MORNING BROKE IN bitter silver along the gray and level plain; and almost as it did so Turnbull and MacIan came out of a low, scrubby wood on to the empty and desolate flats. They had walked all night.

They had walked all night and talked all night also, and if the subject had been capable of being exhausted they would have exhausted it. Their long and changing argument had taken them through districts and landscapes equally changing. They had discussed Haeckel upon hills so high and steep that in spite of the coldness of the night it seemed as if the stars might burn them. They had explained and re-explained the Massacre of St. Bartholomew in little white lanes walled in with standing corn as with walls of gold. They had talked about Mr. Kensit in dim and twinkling pine woods, amid the bewildering monotony of the pines. And it was with the end of a long speech from MacIan, passionately defending the practical achievements and the solid prosperity of the Catholic tradition, that they came out upon the open land.

MacIan had learnt much and thought more since he came out of the cloudy hills of Arisaig. He had met many typical modern figures under circumstances which were sharply symbolic; and, moreover, he had absorbed the main modern atmosphere from the mere presence and chance phrases of Turnbull, as such atmospheres can always be absorbed from the presence and the phrases of any man of great mental vitality. He had at last begun thoroughly to understand what are the grounds upon which the mass of the modern world solidly disapprove of her creed; and he threw himself into replying to them with a hot intellectual enjoyment.

"I begin to understand one or two of your dogmas, Mr. Turnbull," he had said emphatically as they ploughed heavily up a wooded hill. "And every one that I understand I deny. Take any one of them you like. You hold that your heretics and sceptics have helped the world forward and handed on a lamp of progress. I deny it. Nothing is plainer from real history than that each of your heretics invented a complete cosmos of his own which the next heretic smashed entirely to pieces. Who knows now exactly what Nestorius taught? Who cares? There are only two things that we know for certain about it. The first is that Nestorius, as a heretic, taught something quite opposite to the teaching of Arius, the heretic who came before him, and something quite useless to James Turnbull, the heretic who comes after. I defy you to go back to the Freethinkers of the past and find any habitation for yourself at all. I defy you to read Godwin or Shelley or the deists of the eighteenth century or the nature-worshipping humanists of the Renaissance, without discovering that you differ from them twice as much as you differ from the Pope. You are a nineteenth-century sceptic, and you are always telling me that I ignore the cruelty of nature. If you had been an eighteenth-century sceptic you would have told me that I ignore the kindness and benevolence of nature. You are an atheist, and you praise the deists of the eighteenth century. Read them instead of praising them, and you will find that their whole universe stands or falls with the deity. You are a materialist, and you think Bruno a scientific hero. See what he said and you will think him an insane mystic. No, the great Freethinker, with his genuine ability and honesty, does not in practice destroy Christianity. What he does destroy is the Freethinker who went before. Freethought may be suggestive, it may be inspiriting, it may have as much as you please of the merits that come from vivacity and variety. But there is one thing Freethought can never be by any possibility — Freethought can never be progressive. It can never be progressive because it will accept nothing from the past; it begins every time again from the beginning; and it goes every time in a different direction. All the rational philosophers have gone along different roads, so it is impossible to say which has gone furthest. Who can discuss whether Emerson was a better optimist than Schopenhauer was pessimist? It is like asking if this corn is as yellow as that hill is steep. No; there are only two things that really progress; and they both accept accumulations of authority. They may be progressing uphill or down; they may be growing steadily better or steadily worse; but they have steadily increased in certain definable matters; they have steadily advanced in a certain definable direction; they are the only two things, it seems, that ever *can* progress. The first is strictly physical science. The second is the Catholic Church."

"Physical science and the Catholic Church!" said Turnbull sarcastically; "and no doubt the first owes a great deal to the second."

"If you pressed that point I might reply that it was very probable," answered MacIan calmly. "I often fancy that your historical generalisations rest frequently on random instances; I should not be surprised if your vague notions of the Church as the persecutor of science were a generalisation from Galileo. I should not be at all surprised if, when you counted the scientific investigations and discoveries since the fall of Rome, you found that a great mass of them had been made by monks. But the matter is irrelevant to my meaning. I say that if you want an example of anything which has progressed in the moral world by the same method as science in the material world, by continually adding to without unsettling what was there before, then I say that there *is* only one example of it. And that is Us."

"With this enormous difference," said Turnbull, "that however elaborate be the calculations of physical science, their net result can be tested. Granted that it took millions of books I never read and millions of men I never heard of to discover the electric light. Still I can see the electric light. But I cannot see the supreme virtue which is the result of all your theologies and sacraments."

"Catholic virtue is often invisible because it is the normal," answered MacIan. "Christianity is always out of fashion because it is always sane; and all fashions are mild insanities. When Italy is mad on art the Church seems too Puritanical; when England is mad on Puritanism the Church seems too artistic. When you quarrel with us now you class us with kingship and despotism; but when you quarrelled with us first it was because we would not accept the divine despotism of Henry VIII. The Church always seems to be behind the times, when it is really beyond the times; it is waiting till the last fad shall have seen its last summer. It keeps the key of a permanent virtue."

"Oh, I have heard all that!" said Turnbull with genial contempt. "I have heard that Christianity keeps the key of virtue, and that if you read Tom Paine you will cut your throat at Monte Carlo. It is such rubbish that I am not even angry at it. You say that Christianity is the prop of morals; but what more do you do? When a doctor attends you and could poison you with a pinch of salt, do you ask whether he is a Christian? You ask whether he is a gentleman, whether he is an M.D. — anything but that. When a soldier enlists to die for his country or disgrace it, do you ask whether he is a Christian? You are more likely to ask whether he is Oxford or Cambridge at the Boat Race. If you think your creed essential to morals why do you not make it a test for these things?"

"We once did make it a test for these things," said MacIan smiling, "and then you told us that we were imposing by force a faith unsupported by argument. It seems rather hard that having first been told that our creed must be false because we did use tests, we should now be told that it must be false because we don't. But I notice that most anti-Christian arguments are in the same inconsistent style."

"That is all very well as a debating-club answer," replied Turnbull good-humouredly, "but the question still remains: Why don't you confine yourself more to Christians if Christians are the only really good men?"

"Who talked of such folly?" asked MacIan disdainfully. "Do you suppose that the Catholic Church ever held that Christians were the only good men? Why, the Catholics of the Catholic Middle Ages talked about the virtues of all the virtuous Pagans until humanity was sick of the subject. No, if you really want to know what we mean when we say that Christianity has a special power of virtue, I will tell you. The Church is the only thing on earth that can perpetuate a type of virtue and make it something more than a fashion. The thing is so plain and historical that I hardly think you will ever deny it. You cannot deny that it is perfectly possible that to-morrow morning, in Ireland or in Italy, there might appear a man not only as good but good in exactly the same way as St. Francis of Assisi. Very well, now take the other types of human virtue; many of them splendid. The English gentleman of Elizabeth was chivalrous and idealistic. But can you stand still here in this meadow and *be* an English gentleman of Elizabeth? The austere republican of the eighteenth century, with his stern patriotism and his simple life, was a fine fellow. But have you ever seen him? have you ever seen an austere republican? Only a hundred years have passed and that volcano of revolutionary truth and valour is as cold as the mountains of the moon. And so it is and so it will be with the ethics which are buzzing down Fleet Street at this instant as I speak. What phrase would inspire the London clerk or workman just now? Perhaps that he is a son of the British Empire on which the sun never sets; perhaps that he is a prop of his Trades Union, or a class-conscious proletarian something or other; perhaps merely that he is a gentleman when he obviously is not. Those names and notions are all honourable; but how long will they last? Empires break; industrial conditions change; the suburbs will not last for ever. What will remain? I will tell you. The Catholic Saint will remain."

"And suppose I don't like him," said Turnbull.

"On my theory the question is rather whether he will like you: or more probably whether he will ever have heard of you. But I grant the reasonableness of your query. You have a right, if you speak as the ordinary man, to ask if you will like the saint. But as the ordinary man you do like him. You revel in him. If you dislike him it is not because you are a nice ordinary man, but because you are (if you will excuse me) a sophisticated prig of a Fleet Street editor. That is just the funny part of it. The human race has always admired the Catholic virtues, however little it can practise them; and oddly enough it has admired most those of them that the modern world most sharply disputes. You complain of Catholicism for setting up an ideal of virginity; it did nothing of the kind.

The whole human race set up an ideal of virginity; the Greeks in Athene, the Romans in the Vestal fire, set up an ideal of virginity. What then is your real quarrel with Catholicism? Your quarrel can only be, your quarrel really only is, that Catholicism has *achieved* an ideal of virginity; that it is no longer a mere piece of floating poetry. But if you, and a few feverish men, in top hats, running about in a street in London, choose to differ as to the ideal itself, not only from the Church, but from the Parthenon whose name means virginity, from the Roman Empire which went outwards from the virgin flame, from the whole legend and tradition of Europe, from the lion who will not touch virgins, from the unicorn who respects them, and who make up together the bearers of your own national shield, from the most living and lawless of your own poets, from Massinger, who wrote the 'Virgin Martyr,' from Shakespeare, who wrote 'Measure for Measure' — if you in Fleet Street differ from all this human experience, does it never strike you that it may be Fleet Street that is wrong?"

"No," answered Turnbull; "I trust that I am sufficiently fair-minded to canvass and consider the idea; but having considered it, I think Fleet Street is right, yes — even if the Parthenon is wrong. I think that as the world goes on new psychological atmospheres are generated, and in these atmospheres it is possible to find delicacies and combinations which in other times would have to be represented by some ruder symbol. Every man feels the need of some element of purity in sex; perhaps they can only typify purity as the absence of sex. You will laugh if I suggest that we may have made in Fleet Street an atmosphere in which a man can be so passionate as Sir Lancelot and as pure as Sir Galahad. But, after all, we have in the modern world erected many such atmospheres. We have, for instance, a new and imaginative appreciation of children."

"Quite so," replied MacIan with a singular smile. "It has been very well put by one of the brightest of your young authors, who said: 'Unless you become as little children ye shall in no wise enter the kingdom of heaven.' But you are quite right; there is a modern worship of children. And what, I ask you, is this modern worship of children? What, in the name of all the angels and devils, is it except the worship of virginity? Why should any one worship a thing merely because it is small or immature? No; you have tried to escape from this thing, and the very thing you point to as the goal of your escape is only the thing again. Am I wrong in saying that these things seem to be eternal?"

And it was with these words that they came in sight of the great plains. They went a little way in silence, and then James Turnbull said suddenly, "But I *cannot* believe in the thing." MacIan answered nothing to the speech; perhaps it is unanswerable. And indeed they scarcely spoke another word to each other all that day.

CHAPTER IX

THE STRANGE LADY

M OONRISE WITH A great and growing moon opened over all those flats, making them seem flatter and larger than they were, turning them to a lake of blue light. The two companions trudged across the moonlit plain for half an hour in full silence. Then MacIan stopped suddenly and planted his sword-point in the ground like one who plants his tent-pole for the night. Leaving it standing there, he clutched his black-haired skull with his great claws of hands, as was his custom when forcing the pace of his brain. Then his hands dropped again and he spoke.

"I'm sure you're thinking the same as I am," he said; "how long are we to be on this damned seesaw?"

The other did not answer, but his silence seemed somehow solid as assent; and MacIan went on conversationally. Neither noticed that both had instinctively stood still before the sign of the fixed and standing sword.

"It is hard to guess what God means in this business. But He means something—or the other thing, or both. Whenever we have tried to fight each other something has stopped us. Whenever we have tried to be reconciled to each other, something has stopped us again. By the run of our luck we have never had time to be either friends or enemies. Something always jumped out of the bushes."

Turnbull nodded gravely and glanced round at the huge and hedge-less meadow which fell away toward the horizon into a glimmering high road.

"Nothing will jump out of bushes here anyhow," he said.

"That is what I meant," said MacIan, and stared steadily at the heavy hilt of his standing sword, which in the slight wind swayed on its tempered steel like some huge thistle on its stalk.

"That is what I meant; we are quite alone here. I have not heard a horse-hoof or a footstep or the hoot of a train for miles. So I think we might stop here and ask for a miracle."

"Oh! Might we?" said the atheistic editor with a sort of gusto of disgust.

"I beg your pardon," said MacIan, meekly. "I forgot your prejudices." He eyed the wind-swung sword-hilt in sad meditation and resumed: "What I mean is, we might find out in this quiet place whether there really is any fate or any commandment against our enterprise. I will engage on my side, like Elijah, to accept a test from heaven. Turnbull, let us draw swords here in this moonlight and this monstrous solitude. And if here in this moonlight and solitude there happens anything to interrupt us — if it be lightning striking our sword-blades or a rabbit running under our legs — I will take it as a sign from God and we will shake hands for ever."

Turnbull's mouth twitched in angry humour under his red moustache. He said: "I will wait for signs from God until I have any signs of His existence; but God — or Fate — forbid that a man of scientific culture should refuse any kind of experiment."

"Very well, then," said MacIan, shortly. "We are more quiet here than anywhere else; let us engage." And he plucked his sword-point out of the turf.

Turnbull regarded him for a second and a half with a baffling visage almost black against the moonrise; then his hand made a sharp movement to his hip and his sword shone in the moon.

As old chess-players open every game with established gambits, they opened with a thrust and parry, orthodox and even frankly ineffectual. But in MacIan's soul more formless storms were gathering, and he made a lunge or two so savage as first to surprise and then to enrage his opponent. Turnbull ground his teeth, kept his temper, and waiting for the third lunge, and the worst, had almost spitted the lunger when a shrill, small cry came from behind him, a cry such as is not made by any of the beasts that perish.

Turnbull must have been more superstitious than he knew, for he stopped in the act of going forward. MacIan was brazenly superstitious, and he dropped his sword. After all, he had challenged the universe to send an interruption; and this was an interruption, whatever else it was. An instant afterward the sharp, weak cry was repeated. This time it was certain that it was human and that it was female.

MacIan stood rolling those great blue Gaelic eyes that contrasted with his dark hair. "It is the voice of God," he said again and again.

"God hasn't got much of a voice," said Turnbull, who snatched at every chance of cheap profanity. "As a matter of fact, MacIan, it isn't the voice of God, but it's something a jolly sight more important — it is the voice of man — or rather of woman. So I think we'd better scoot in its direction."

MacIan snatched up his fallen weapon without a word, and the two raced away toward that part of the distant road from which the cry was now constantly renewed.

They had to run over a curve of country that looked smooth but was very rough; a neglected field which they soon found to be full of the tallest grasses and the deepest rabbit holes. Moreover, that great curve of the countryside which looked so slow and gentle when you glanced over it, proved to be highly precipitous when you scampered over it; and Turnbull was twice nearly flung on his face. MacIan, though much heavier, avoided such an overthrow only by having the quick and incalculable feet of the mountaineer; but both of them may be said to have leapt off a low cliff when they leapt into the road.

The moonlight lay on the white road with a more naked and electric glare than on the grey-green upland, and though the scene which it revealed was complicated, it was not difficult to get its first features at a glance.

A small but very neat black-and-yellow motor-car was standing stolidly, slightly to the left of the road. A somewhat larger light-green motor-car was tipped half way into a ditch on the same side, and four flushed and staggering men in evening dress were tipped out of it. Three of them were standing about the road, giving their opinions to the moon with vague but echoing violence. The fourth, however, had already advanced on the chauffeur of the black-and-yellow car, and was threatening him with a stick. The chauffeur had risen to defend himself. By his side sat a young lady.

She was sitting bolt upright, a slender and rigid figure gripping the sides of her seat, and her first few cries had ceased. She was clad in close-fitting dark costume, a mass of warm brown hair went out in two wings or waves on each side of her forehead; and even at that distance it could be seen that her profile was of the aquiline and eager sort, like a young falcon hardly free of the nest.

Turnbull had concealed in him somewhere a fund of common-sense and knowledge of the world of which he himself and his best friends were hardly aware. He was one of those who take in much of the shows of things absentmindedly, and in an irrelevant reverie. As he stood at the door of his editorial shop on Ludgate Hill and meditated on the non-existence of God, he silently absorbed a good deal of varied knowledge about the existence of men. He had come to know types by instinct and dilemmas with a glance; he saw the crux of the situation in the road, and what he saw made him redouble his pace.

He knew that the men were rich; he knew that they were drunk; and he knew, what was worst of all, that they were fundamentally frightened. And he knew this also, that no common ruffian (such as attacks ladies in novels) is ever so savage and ruthless as a coarse kind of gentleman when he is really alarmed. The reason is not recondite; it is simply because the police-court is not such a menacing novelty to the poor ruffian as it is to the rich. When they came within hail and heard the voices, they confirmed all Turnbull's anticipations. The man in the middle of the road was shouting in a hoarse and groggy voice that the chauffeur had smashed their car on purpose; that they must get to the Cri that evening, and that he would jolly well have to take them there. The chauffeur had mildly objected that he was driving a lady. "Oh! we'll take care of the lady," said the red-faced young man, and went off into gurgling and almost senile laughter.

By the time the two champions came up, things had grown more serious. The intoxication of the man talking to the chauffeur had taken one of its perverse and catlike jumps into mere screaming spite and rage. He lifted his stick and struck at the chauffeur, who caught hold of it, and the drunkard fell backward, dragging him out of his seat on the car. Another of the rowdies rushed forward booing in idiot excitement, fell over the chauffeur, and, either by accident or design, kicked him as he lay. The drunkard got to his feet again; but the chauffeur did not.

The man who had kicked kept a kind of half-witted conscience or cowardice, for he stood staring at the senseless body and murmuring words of inconsequent self-justification, making gestures with his hands as if he were arguing with somebody. But the other three, with a mere whoop and howl of victory, were boarding the car on three sides at once. It was exactly at this moment that Turnbull fell among them like one fallen from the sky. He tore one of the climbers backward by the collar, and with a hearty push sent him staggering over into the ditch upon his nose. One of the remaining two, who was too far gone to notice anything, continued to clamber ineffectually over the high back of the car, kicking and pouring forth a rivulet of soliloquy. But the other dropped at the interruption, turned upon Turnbull and began a battering bout of fisticuffs. At the same moment the man crawled out of the ditch in a masquerade of mud and rushed at his old enemy from behind. The whole had not taken a second; and an instant after MacIan was in the midst of them.

Turnbull had tossed away his sheathed sword, greatly preferring his hands, except in the avowed etiquette of the duel; for he had learnt to use his hands in the old street-battles of Bradlaugh. But to MacIan the sword even sheathed was a more natural weapon, and he laid about him on all sides with it as with a stick. The man who had the walking-stick found his blows parried with promptitude; and a second after, to his great astonishment, found his own stick fly up in the air as by a conjuring trick, with a turn of the swordsman's wrist. Another of the revellers picked the stick out of the ditch and ran in upon MacIan, calling to his companion to assist him.

"I haven't got a stick," grumbled the disarmed man, and looked vaguely about the ditch.

"Perhaps," said MacIan, politely, "you would like this one." With the word the drunkard found his hand that had grasped the stick suddenly twisted and empty; and the stick lay at the feet of his companion on the other side of the road. MacIan felt a faint stir behind him; the girl had risen to her feet and was leaning forward to stare at the fighters. Turnbull was still engaged in countering and pommelling with the third young man. The fourth young man was still engaged with himself, kicking his legs in helpless rotation on the back of the car and talking with melodious rationality.

At length Turnbull's opponent began to back before the battery of his heavy hands, still fighting, for he was the soberest and boldest of the four. If these are annals of military glory, it is due to him to say that he need not have abandoned the conflict; only that as he backed to the edge of the ditch his foot caught in a loop of grass and he went over in a flat and comfortable position from which it took him a considerable time to rise. By the time he had risen, Turnbull had come to the rescue of MacIan, who was at bay but belabouring his two enemies handsomely. The sight of the liberated reserve was to them like that of Blucher at Waterloo; the two set off at a sullen trot down the road, leaving even the walking-stick lying behind them in the moonlight. MacIan plucked the struggling and aspiring idiot off the back of the car like a stray cat, and left him swaying unsteadily in the moon. Then he approached the front part of the car in a somewhat embarrassed manner and pulled off his cap.

For some solid seconds the lady and he merely looked at each other, and MacIan had an irrational feeling of being in a picture hung on a wall. That is, he was motionless, even lifeless, and yet staringly significant, like a picture. The white moonlight on the road, when he was not looking at it, gave him a vision of the road being white with snow. The motor-car, when he was not looking at it, gave him a rude impression of a captured coach in the old days of highwaymen. And he whose whole soul was with the swords and stately manners of the eighteenth century, he who was a Jacobite risen from the dead, had an overwhelming sense of being once more in the picture, when he had so long been out of the picture.

In that short and strong silence he absorbed the lady from head to foot. He had never really looked at a human being before in his life. He saw her face and hair first, then that she had long suède gloves; then that there was a fur cap at the back of her brown hair. He might, perhaps, be excused for this hungry attention. He had prayed that some sign might come from heaven; and after an almost savage scrutiny he came to the conclusion that this one did. The lady's instantaneous arrest of speech might need more explaining; but she may well have been stunned with the squalid attack and the abrupt rescue. Yet it was she who remembered herself first and suddenly called out with self-accusing horror:

"Oh, that poor, poor man!"

They both swung round abruptly and saw that Turnbull, with his recovered sword under his arm-pit, was already lifting the fallen chauffeur into the car. He was only stunned and was slowly awakening, feebly waving his left arm.

The lady in the long gloves and the fur cap leapt out and ran rapidly toward them, only to be reassured by Turnbull, who (unlike many of his school) really knew a little science when he invoked it to redeem the world. "He's all right," said he; "he's quite safe. But I'm afraid he won't be able to drive the car for half an hour or so."

"I can drive the car," said the young woman in the fur cap with stony practicability.

"Oh, in that case," began MacIan, uneasily; and that paralysing shyness which is a part of romance induced him to make a backward movement as if leaving her to herself. But Turnbull was more rational than he, being more indifferent.

"I don't think you ought to drive home alone, ma'am," he said, gruffly. "There seem to be a lot of rowdy parties along this road, and the man will be no use for an hour. If you will tell us where you are going, we will see you safely there and say good-night."

The young lady exhibited all the abrupt disturbance of a person who is not commonly disturbed. She said almost sharply and yet with evident sincerity: "Of course I am awfully grateful to you for all you've done — and there's plenty of room if you'll come in."

Turnbull, with the complete innocence of an absolutely sound motive, immediately jumped into the car; but the girl cast an eye at MacIan, who stood in the road for an instant as if rooted like a tree. Then he also tumbled his long legs into the tonneau, having that sense of degradedly diving into heaven which so many have known in so many human houses when they consented to stop to tea or were allowed to stop to supper. The slowly reviving chauffeur was set in the back seat; Turnbull and MacIan had fallen into the middle one; the lady with a steely coolness had taken the driver's seat and all the handles of that headlong machine. A moment afterward the engine started, with a throb and leap unfamiliar to Turnbull, who had only once been in a motor during a general election, and utterly unknown to MacIan, who in his present mood thought it was the end of the world. Almost at the same instant that the car plucked itself out of the mud and whipped away up the road, the man who had been flung into the ditch rose waveringly to his feet. When he saw the car escaping he ran after it and shouted something which, owing to the increasing distance, could not be heard. It is awful to reflect that, if his remark was valuable, it is quite lost to the world.

The car shot on up and down the shining moonlit lanes, and there was no sound in it except the occasional click or catch of its machinery; for through some cause or other no soul inside it could think of a word to say. The lady symbolised her feelings, whatever they were, by urging the machine faster and faster until scattered woodlands went by them in one black blotch and heavy hills and valleys seemed to ripple under the wheels like mere waves. A little while afterward this mood seemed to slacken and she fell into a more ordinary pace; but still she did not speak. Turnbull, who kept a more common and sensible view of the case than any one else, made some remark about the moonlight; but something indescribable made him also relapse into silence.

All this time MacIan had been in a sort of monstrous delirium, like some fabulous hero snatched up into the moon. The difference between this experience and common experiences was analogous to that between waking life and a dream. Yet he did not feel in the least as if he were dreaming; rather the other way; as waking was more actual than dreaming, so this seemed by another degree more actual than waking itself. But it was another life altogether, like a cosmos with a new dimension.

He felt he had been hurled into some new incarnation: into the midst of new relations, wrongs and rights, with towering responsibilities and almost tragic joys which he had as yet had no time to examine. Heaven had not merely sent him a message; Heaven itself had opened around him and given him an hour of its own ancient and star-shattering energy. He had never felt so much alive before; and yet he was like a man in a trance. And if you had asked him on what his throbbing happiness hung, he could only have told you that it hung on four or five visible facts, as a curtain hangs on four or five fixed nails. The fact that the lady had a little fur at her throat; the fact that the curve of her cheek was a low and lean curve and that the moonlight caught the height of her cheekbone; the fact that her hands were small but heavily gloved as they gripped the steering-wheel; the fact that a white witch light was on the road; the fact that the brisk breeze of their passage stirred and fluttered a little not only the brown hair of her head but the black fur on her cap. All these facts were to him certain and incredible, like sacraments.

When they had driven half a mile farther, a big shadow was flung across the path, followed by its bulky owner, who eyed the car critically but let it pass. The silver moonlight picked out a piece or two of pewter ornament on his blue uniform; and as they went by they knew it was a serjeant of police. Three hundred yards farther on another policeman stepped out into the road as if to stop them, then seemed to doubt his own authority and stepped back again. The girl was a daughter of the rich; and this police suspicion (under which all the poor live day and night) stung her for the first time into speech.

"What can they mean?" she cried out in a kind of temper; "this car's going like a snail."

There was a short silence, and then Turnbull said: "It is certainly very odd; you are driving quietly enough."

"You are driving nobly," said MacIan, and his words (which had no meaning whatever) sounded hoarse and ungainly even in his own ears.

They passed the next mile and a half swiftly and smoothly; yet among the many things which they passed in the course of it was a clump of eager policemen standing at a cross-road. As they passed, one of the policemen shouted something to the others; but nothing else happened. Eight hundred yards farther on, Turnbull stood up suddenly in the swaying car.

"My God, MacIan!" he called out, showing his first emotion of that night. "I don't believe it's the pace; it couldn't be the pace. I believe it's us."

MacIan sat motionless for a few moments and then turned up at his companion a face that was as white as the moon above it.

"You may be right," he said at last; "if you are I must tell her."

"I will tell the lady if you like," said Turnbull, with his unconquered good temper.

"You!" said MacIan, with a sort of sincere and instinctive astonishment. "Why should you — no, I must tell her, of course — "

And he leant forward and spoke to the lady in the fur cap.

"I am afraid, madam, that we may have got you into some trouble," he said, and even as he said it it sounded wrong, like everything he said to this particular person in the long gloves. "The fact is," he resumed, desperately, "the fact is, we are being chased by the police." Then the last flattening hammer fell upon poor Evan's embarrassment; for the fluffy brown head with the furry black cap did not turn by a section of the compass.

"We are chased by the police," repeated MacIan, vigorously; then he added, as if beginning an explanation, "You see, I am a Catholic."

The wind whipped back a curl of the brown hair so as to necessitate a new theory of æsthetics touching the line of the cheek-bone; but the head did not turn.

"You see," began MacIan, again blunderingly, "this gentleman wrote in his newspaper that Our Lady was a common woman, a bad woman, and so we agreed to fight; and we were fighting quite a little time ago — but that was before we saw you."

The young lady driving the car had half turned her face to listen; and it was not a reverent or a patient face that she showed him. Her Norman nose was tilted a trifle too high upon the slim stalk of her neck and body.

When MacIan saw that arrogant and uplifted profile pencilled plainly against the moonshine, he accepted an ultimate defeat. He had expected the angels to despise him if he were wrong, but not to despise him so much as this.

"You see," said the stumbling spokesman, "I was angry with him when he insulted the Mother of God, and I asked him to fight a duel with me; but the police are all trying to stop it."

Nothing seemed to waver or flicker in the fair young falcon profile; and it only opened its lips to say, after a silence: "I thought people in our time were supposed to respect each other's religion."

Under the shadow of that arrogant face MacIan could only fall back on the obvious answer: "But what about a man's irreligion?" The face only answered: "Well, you ought to be more broadminded."

If any one else in the world had said the words, MacIan would have snorted with his equine neigh of scorn. But in this case he seemed knocked down by a superior simplicity, as if his eccentric attitude were rebuked by the innocence of a child. He could not dissociate anything that this woman said or did or wore from an idea of spiritual rarity and virtue. Like most others under the same elemental passion, his soul was at present soaked in ethics. He could have applied moral terms to the material objects of her environment. If some one had spoken of "her generous ribbon" or "her chivalrous gloves" or "her merciful shoe-buckle," it would not have seemed to him nonsense.

He was silent, and the girl went on in a lower key as if she were momentarily softened and a little saddened also. "It won't do, you know," she said; "you can't find out the truth in that way. There are such heaps of churches and people thinking different things nowadays, and they all think they are right. My uncle was a Swedenborgian."

MacIan sat with bowed head, listening hungrily to her voice but hardly to her words, and seeing his great world drama grow smaller and smaller before his eyes till it was no bigger than a child's toy theatre.

"The time's gone by for all that," she went on; "you can't find out the real thing like that — if there is really anything to find — " and she sighed rather drearily; for, like many of the women of our wealthy class, she was old and broken in thought, though young and clean enough in her emotions.

"Our object," said Turnbull, shortly, "is to make an effective demonstration"; and after that word, MacIan looked at his vision again and found it smaller than ever.

"It would be in the newspapers, of course," said the girl. "People read the newspapers, but they don't believe them, or anything else, I think." And she sighed again.

She drove in silence a third of a mile before she added, as if completing the sentence: "Anyhow, the whole thing's quite absurd."

"I don't think," began Turnbull, "that you quite realise —— Hullo! hullo — hullo — what's this?"

The amateur chauffeur had been forced to bring the car to a staggering stoppage, for a file of fat, blue policemen made a wall across the way. A serjeant came to the side and touched his peaked cap to the lady.

"Beg your pardon, miss," he said with some embarrassment, for he knew her for a daughter of a dominant house, "but we have reason to believe that the gentlemen in your car are —— " and he hesitated for polite phrase.

"I am Evan MacIan," said that gentleman, and stood up in a sort of gloomy pomp, not wholly without a touch of the sulks of a schoolboy.

"Yes, we will get out, serjeant," said Turnbull, more easily; "my name is James Turnbull. We must not incommode the lady."

"What are you taking them up for?" asked the young woman, looking straight in front of her along the road.

"It's under the new act," said the serjeant, almost apologetically. "Incurable disturbers of the peace."

"What will happen to them?" she asked, with the same frigid clearness.

"Westgate Adult Reformatory," he replied, briefly.

"Until when?"

"Until they are cured," said the official.

"Very well, serjeant," said the young lady, with a sort of tired commonsense. "I am sure I don't want to protect criminals or go against the law; but I must tell you that these gentlemen have done me a considerable service; you won't mind drawing your men a little farther off while I say good-night to them. Men like that always misunderstand."

The serjeant was profoundly disquieted from the beginning at the mere idea of arresting any one in the company of a great lady; to refuse one of her minor requests was quite beyond his courage. The police fell back to a few yards behind the car. Turnbull took up the two swords that were their only luggage; the swords that, after so many half duels, they were now to surrender at last. MacIan, the blood thundering in his brain at the thought of that instant of farewell, bent over, fumbled at the handle and flung open the door to get out.

But he did not get out. He did not get out, because it is dangerous to jump out of a car when it is going at full speed. And the car was going at full speed, because the young lady, without turning her head or so much as saying a syllable, had driven down a handle that made the machine plunge forward like a buffalo and then fly over the landscape like a greyhound. The police made one rush to follow, and then dropped so grotesque and hopeless a chase. Away in the vanishing distance they could see the serjeant furiously making notes.

The open door, still left loose on its hinges, swung and banged quite crazily as they went whizzing up one road and down another. Nor did MacIan sit down; he stood up stunned and yet staring, as he would have stood up at the trumpet of the Last Day. A black dot in the distance sprang up a tall black forest, swallowed them and spat them out again at the other end. A railway bridge grew larger and larger till it leapt upon their backs bellowing, and was in its turn left behind. Avenues of poplars on both sides of the road chased each other like the figures in a zoetrope. Now and then with a shock and rattle they went through sleeping moonlit villages, which must have stirred an instant in their sleep as at the passing of a fugitive earthquake. Sometimes in an outlying house a light in one erratic, unexpected window would give them a nameless hint of the hundred human secrets which they left behind them with their dust. Sometimes even a slouching rustic would be afoot on the road and would look after them, as after a flying phantom. But still MacIan stood up staring at earth and heaven; and still the door he had flung open flapped loose like a flag. Turnbull, after a few minutes of dumb amazement, had yielded to the healthiest element in his nature and gone off into uncontrollable fits of laughter. The girl had not stirred an inch.

After another half mile that seemed a mere flash, Turnbull leant over and locked the door. Evan staggered at last into his seat and hid his throbbing head in his hands; and still the car flew on and its driver sat inflexible and silent. The moon had already gone down, and the whole darkness was faintly troubled with twilight and the first movement of beasts and fowls. It was that mysterious moment when light is coming, as if it were something unknown whose nature one could not guess — a mere alteration in everything. They looked at the sky and it seemed as dark as ever; then they saw the black shape of a tower or tree against it and knew that it was already grey. Save that they were driving southward and had certainly passed the longitude of London, they knew nothing of their direction; but Turnbull, who had spent a year on the Hampshire coast in his youth, began to recognise the unmistakable but quite indescribable villages of the English south. Then a white witch fire began to burn between the black stems of the fir-trees; and, like so many things in nature, though not in books on evolution, the daybreak, when it did come, came much quicker than one would think. The gloomy heavens were ripped up and rolled away like a scroll, revealing splendours, as the car went roaring up the curve of a great hill; and above them and black against the broadening light, there stood one of those crouching and fantastic trees that are first signals of the sea.

CHAPTER X

THE SWORDS REJOINED

A S THEY CAME over the hill and down on the other side of it, it is not too much to say that the whole universe of God opened over them and under them, like a thing unfolding to five times its size. Almost under their feet opened the enormous sea, at the bottom of a steep valley which fell down into a bay; and the sea under their feet blazed at them almost as lustrous and almost as empty as the sky. The sunrise opened above them like some cosmic explosion, shining and shattering and yet silent; as if the world were blown to pieces without a sound. Round the rays of the victorious sun swept a sort of rainbow of confused and conquered colours—brown and blue and green and flaming rose-colour; as though gold were driving before it all the colours of the world. The lines of the landscape down which they sped, were the simple, strict, yet swerving, lines of a rushing river; so that it was almost as if they were being sucked down in a huge still whirlpool. Turnbull had some such feeling, for he spoke for the first time for many hours.

"If we go down at this rate we shall be over the sea cliff," he said.

"How glorious!" said MacIan.

When, however, they had come into the wide hollow at the bottom of that landslide, the car took a calm and graceful curve along the side of the sea, melted into the fringe of a few trees, and quietly, yet astonishingly, stopped. A belated light was burning in the broad morning in the window of a sort of lodge- or gate-keepers' cottage; and the girl stood up in the car and turned her splendid face to the sun.

Evan seemed startled by the stillness, like one who had been born amid sound and speed. He wavered on his long legs as he stood up; he pulled himself together, and the only consequence was that he trembled from head to foot. Turnbull had already opened the door on his side and jumped out.

The moment he had done so the strange young woman had one more mad movement, and deliberately drove the car a few yards farther. Then she got out with an almost cruel coolness and began pulling off her long gloves and almost whistling.

"You can leave me here," she said, quite casually, as if they had met five minutes before. "That is the lodge of my father's place. Please come in, if you like — but I understood that you had some business."

Evan looked at that lifted face and found it merely lovely; he was far too much of a fool to see that it was working with a final fatigue and that its austerity was agony. He was even fool enough to ask it a question. "Why did you save us?" he said, quite humbly.

The girl tore off one of her gloves, as if she were tearing off her hand. "Oh, I don't know," she said, bitterly. "Now I come to think of it, I can't imagine."

Evan's thoughts, that had been piled up to the morning star, abruptly let him down with a crash into the very cellars of the emotional universe. He remained in a stunned silence for a long time; and that, if he had only known, was the wisest thing that he could possibly do at the moment.

Indeed, the silence and the sunrise had their healing effect, for when the extraordinary lady spoke again, her tone was more friendly and apologetic. "I'm not really ungrateful," she said; "it was very good of you to save me from those men."

"But why?" repeated the obstinate and dazed MacIan, "why did you save us from the other men? I mean the policemen?"

The girl's great brown eyes were lit up with a flash that was at once final desperation and the loosening of some private and passionate reserve.

"Oh, God knows!" she cried. "God knows that if there is a God He has turned His big back on everything. God knows I have had no pleasure in my life, though I am pretty and young and father has plenty of money. And then people come and tell me that I ought to do things and I do them and it's all drivel. They want you to do work among the poor; which means reading Ruskin and feeling self-righteous in the best room in a poor tenement. Or to help some cause or other, which always means bundling people out of crooked houses, in which they've always lived, into straight houses, in which they quite as often die. And all the time you have inside only the horrid irony of your own empty head and empty heart. I am to give to the unfortunate, when my whole misfortune is that I have nothing to give. I am to teach, when I believe nothing of all that I was taught. I am to save the children from death, and I am not even certain that I should not be better dead. I suppose if I actually saw a child drowning I should save it. But that would be from the same motive from which I have saved you, or destroyed you, whichever it is that I have done."

"What was the motive?" asked Evan, in a low voice.

"My motive is too big for my mind," answered the girl.

Then, after a pause, as she stared with a rising colour at the glittering sea, she said: "It can't be described, and yet I am trying to describe it. It seems to me not only that I am unhappy, but that there is no way of being happy. Father is not happy, though he is a Member of Parliament —— " She paused a moment and added with the ghost of a smile: "Nor Aunt Mabel, though a man from India has told her the secret of all creeds. But I may be wrong; there may be a way out. And for one stark, insane second, I felt that, after all, you had got the way out and that was why the world hated you. You see, if there were a way out, it would be sure to be something that looked very queer."

Evan put his hand to his forehead and began stumblingly: "Yes, I suppose we do seem —— "

"Oh, yes, you look queer enough," she said, with ringing sincerity. "You'll be all the better for a wash and brush up."

"You forget our business, madam," said Evan, in a shaking voice; "we have no concern but to kill each other."

"Well, I wouldn't be killed looking like that if I were you," she replied, with inhuman honesty.

Evan stood and rolled his eyes in masculine bewilderment. Then came the final change in this Proteus, and she put out both her hands for an instant and said in a low tone on which he lived for days and nights:

"Don't you understand that I did not dare to stop you? What you are doing is so mad that it may be quite true. Somehow one can never really manage to be an atheist."

Turnbull stood staring at the sea; but his shoulders showed that he heard, and after one minute he turned his head. But the girl had only brushed Evan's hand with hers and had fled up the dark alley by the lodge gate.

Evan stood rooted upon the road, literally like some heavy statue hewn there in the age of the Druids. It seemed impossible that he should ever move. Turnbull grew restless with this rigidity, and at last, after calling his companion twice or thrice, went up and clapped him impatiently on one of his big shoulders. Evan winced and leapt away from him with a repulsion which was not the hate of an unclean thing nor the dread of a dangerous one, but was a spasm of awe and separation from something from which he was now sundered as by the sword of God. He did not hate the atheist; it is possible that he loved him. But Turnbull was now something more dreadful than an enemy; he was a thing sealed and devoted — a thing now hopelessly doomed to be either a corpse or an executioner.

"What is the matter with you?" asked Turnbull, with his hearty hand still in the air; and yet he knew more about it than his innocent action would allow.

"James," said Evan, speaking like one under strong bodily pain, "I asked for God's answer and I have got it — got it in my vitals. He knows how weak I am, and that I might forget the peril of the faith, forget the face of Our Lady — yes, even with your blow upon her cheek. But the honour of this earth has just this about it, that it can make a man's heart like iron. I am from the Lords of the Isles and I dare not be a mere deserter. Therefore, God has tied me by the chain of my worldly place and word, and there is nothing but fighting now."

"I think I understand you," said Turnbull, "but you say everything tail foremost."

"She wants us to do it," said Evan, in a voice crushed with passion. "She has hurt herself so that we might do it. She has left her good name and her good sleep and all her habits and dignity flung away on the other side of England in the hope that she may hear of us and that we have broken some hole into heaven."

"I thought I knew what you meant," said Turnbull, biting his beard; "it does seem as if we ought to do something after all she has done this night."

"I never liked you so much before," said MacIan, in bitter sorrow.

As he spoke, three solemn footmen came out of the lodge gate and assembled to assist the chauffeur to his room. The mere sight of them made the two wanderers flee as from a too frightful incongruity, and before they knew where they were, they were well upon the grassy ledge of England that overlooks the Channel. Evan said suddenly: "Will they let me see her in heaven once in a thousand ages?" and addressed the remark to the editor of the "Atheist," as one which he would be likely or qualified to answer. But no answer came; a silence sank between the two.

Turnbull strode sturdily to the edge of the cliff and looked out, his companion following, somewhat more shaken by his recent agitation.

"If that's the view you take," said Turnbull, "and I don't say you are wrong, I think I know where we shall be best off for the business. As it happens, I know this part of the south coast pretty well. And unless I am mistaken there's a way down the cliff just here which will land us on a stretch of firm sand where no one is likely to follow us."

The Highlander made a gesture of assent and came also almost to the edge of the precipice. The sunrise, which was broadening over sea and shore, was one of those rare and splendid ones in which there seems to be no mist or doubt, and nothing but a universal clarification more and more complete. All the colours were transparent. It seemed like a triumphant prophecy of some perfect world where everything being innocent will be intelligible; a world where even our bodies, so to speak, may be as of burning glass. Such a world is faintly though fiercely figured in the coloured windows of Christian architecture. The sea that lay before them was like a pavement of emerald, bright and almost brittle; the sky against which its strict horizon hung was almost absolutely white, except that close to the sky line, like scarlet braids on the hem of a garment, lay strings of flaky cloud of so gleaming and gorgeous a red that they seemed cut out of some strange blood-red celestial metal, of which the mere gold of this earth is but a drab yellow imitation.

"The hand of Heaven is still pointing," muttered the man of superstition to himself. "And now it is a blood-red hand."

The cool voice of his companion cut in upon his monologue, calling to him from a little farther along the cliff, to tell him that he had found the ladder of descent. It began as a steep and somewhat greasy path, which then tumbled down twenty or thirty feet in the form of a fall of rough stone steps. After that, there was a rather awkward drop on to a ledge of stone and then the journey was undertaken easily and even elegantly by the remains of an ornamental staircase, such as might have belonged to some long-disused watering-place. All the time that the two travellers sank from stage to stage of this downward journey, there closed over their heads living bridges and caverns of the most varied foliage, all of which grew greener, redder, or more golden, in the growing sunlight of the morning. Life, too, of the more moving sort rose at the sun on every side of them. Birds whirred and fluttered in the undergrowth, as if imprisoned in green cages. Other birds were shaken up in great clouds from the tree-tops, as if they were blossoms detached and scattered up to heaven. Animals which Turnbull was too much of a Londoner and MacIan too much of a Northerner to know, slipped by among the tangle or ran pattering up the tree-trunks. Both the men, according to their several creeds, felt the full thunder of the psalm of life as they had never heard it before; MacIan felt God the Father, benignant in all His energies, and Turnbull that ultimate anonymous energy, that *Natura Naturans*, which is the whole theme of Lucretius. It was down this clamorous ladder of life that they went down to die.

They broke out upon a brown semicircle of sand, so free from human imprint as to justify Turnbull's profession. They strode out upon it, stuck their swords in the sand, and had a pause too important for speech. Turnbull eyed the coast curiously for a moment, like one awakening memories of childhood; then he said abruptly, like a man remembering somebody's name: "But, of course, we shall be better off still round the corner of Cragness Point; nobody ever comes there at all." And picking up his sword again, he began striding toward a big bluff of the rocks which stood out upon their left. MacIan followed him round the corner and found himself in what was certainly an even finer fencing court, of flat, firm sand, enclosed on three sides by white walls of rock, and on the fourth by the green wall of the advancing sea.

"We are quite safe here," said Turnbull, and, to the other's surprise, flung himself down, sitting on the brown beach.

"You see, I was brought up near here," he explained. "I was sent from Scotland to stop with my aunt. It is highly probable that I may die here. Do you mind if I light a pipe?"

"Of course, do whatever you like," said MacIan, with a choking voice, and he went and walked alone by himself along the wet, glistening sands.

Ten minutes afterward he came back again, white with his own whirlwind of emotions; Turnbull was quite cheerful and was knocking out the end of his pipe.

"You see, we have to do it," said MacIan. "She tied us to it."

"Of course, my dear fellow," said the other, and leapt up as lightly as a monkey.

They took their places gravely in the very centre of the great square of sand, as if they had thousands of spectators. Before saluting, MacIan, who, being a mystic, was one inch nearer to Nature, cast his eye round the huge framework of their heroic folly. The three walls of rock all leant a little outward, though at various angles; but this impression was exaggerated in the direction of the incredible by the heavy load of living trees and thickets which each wall wore on its top like a huge shock of hair. On all that luxurious crest of life the risen and victorious sun was beating, burnishing it all like gold, and every bird that rose with that sunrise caught a light like a star upon it like the dove of the Holy Spirit. Imaginative life had never so much crowded upon MacIan. He felt that he could write whole books about the feelings of a single bird. He felt that for two centuries he would not tire of being a rabbit. He was in the Palace of Life, of which the very tapestries and curtains were alive. Then he recovered himself, and remembered his affairs. Both men saluted, and iron rang upon iron. It was exactly at the same moment that he realised that his enemy's left ankle was encircled with a ring of salt water that had crept up to his feet.

"What is the matter?" said Turnbull, stopping an instant, for he had grown used to every movement of his extraordinary fellow-traveller's face.

MacIan glanced again at that silver anklet of sea water and then looked beyond at the next promontory round which a deep sea was boiling and leaping. Then he turned and looked back and saw heavy foam being shaken up to heaven about the base of Cragness Point.

"The sea has cut us off," he said, curtly.

"I have noticed it," said Turnbull with equal sobriety. "What view do you take of the development?"

Evan threw away his weapon, and, as his custom was, imprisoned his big head in his hands. Then he let them fall and said: "Yes, I know what it means; and I think it is the fairest thing. It is the finger of God — red as blood — still pointing. But now it points to two graves."

There was a space filled with the sound of the sea, and then MacIan spoke again in a voice pathetically reasonable: "You see, we both saved her — and she told us both to fight — and it would not be just that either should fail and fall alone, while the other — "

"You mean," said Turnbull, in a voice surprisingly soft and gentle, "that there is something fine about fighting in a place where even the conqueror must die?"

"Oh, you have got it right, you have got it right!" cried out Evan, in an extraordinary childish ecstasy. "Oh, I'm sure that you really believe in God!"

Turnbull answered not a word, but only took up his fallen sword.

For the third time Evan MacIan looked at those three sides of English cliff hung with their noisy load of life. He had been at a loss to understand the almost ironical magnificence of all those teeming creatures and tropical colours and smells that smoked happily to heaven. But now he knew that he was in the closed court of death and that all the gates were sealed.

He drank in the last green and the last red and the last gold, those unique and indescribable things of God, as a man drains good wine at the bottom of his glass. Then he turned and saluted his enemy once more, and the two stood up and fought till the foam flowed over their knees.

Then MacIan stepped backward suddenly with a splash and held up his hand. "Turnbull!" he cried; "I can't help it — fair fighting is more even than promises. And this is not fair fighting."

"What the deuce do you mean?" asked the other, staring.

"I've only just thought of it," cried Evan, brokenly. "We're very well matched — it may go on a good time — the tide is coming up fast — and I'm a foot and a half taller. You'll be washed away like seaweed before it's above my breeches. I'll not fight foul for all the girls and angels in the universe."

"Will you oblige me," said Turnbull, with staring grey eyes and a voice of distinct and violent politeness; "will you oblige me by jolly well minding your own business? Just you stand up and fight, and we'll see who will be washed away like seaweed. You wanted to finish this fight and you shall finish it, or I'll denounce you as a coward to the whole of that assembled company."

Evan looked very doubtful and offered a somewhat wavering weapon;

but he was quickly brought back to his senses by his opponent's sword-point, which shot past him, shaving his shoulder by a hair. By this time the waves were well up Turnbull's thigh, and what was worse, they were beginning to roll and break heavily around them.

MacIan parried this first lunge perfectly, the next less perfectly; the third in all human probability he would not have parried at all; the Christian champion would have been pinned like a butterfly, and the atheistic champion left to drown like a rat, with such consolation as his view of the cosmos afforded him. But just as Turnbull launched his heaviest stroke, the sea, in which he stood up to his hips, launched a yet heavier one. A wave breaking beyond the others smote him heavily like a hammer of water. One leg gave way, he was swung round and sucked into the retreating sea, still gripping his sword.

MacIan put his sword between his teeth and plunged after his disappearing enemy. He had the sense of having the whole universe on top of him as crest after crest struck him down. It seemed to him quite a cosmic collapse, as if all the seven heavens were falling on him one after the other. But he got hold of the atheist's left leg and he did not let it go.

After some ten minutes of foam and frenzy, in which all the senses at once seemed blasted by the sea, Evan found himself laboriously swimming on a low, green swell, with the sword still in his teeth and the editor of the "Atheist" still under his arm. What he was going to do he had not even the most glimmering idea; so he merely kept his grip and swam somehow with one hand.

He ducked instinctively as there bulked above him a big, black wave, much higher than any that he had seen. Then he saw that it was hardly the shape of any possible wave. Then he saw that it was a fisherman's boat, and, leaping upward, caught hold of the bow. The boat pitched forward with its stern in the air for just as much time as was needed to see that there was nobody in it. After a moment or two of desperate clambering, however, there were two people in it, Mr. Evan MacIan, panting and sweating, and Mr. James Turnbull, uncommonly close to being drowned. After ten minutes' aimless tossing in the empty fishing-boat he recovered, however, stirred, stretched himself, and looked round on the rolling waters. Then, while taking no notice of the streams of salt water that were pouring from his hair, beard, coat, boots, and trousers, he carefully wiped the wet off his sword-blade to preserve it from possibilities of rust.

MacIan found two oars in the bottom of the deserted boat and began somewhat drearily to row.

· · · · ·

A rainy twilight was clearing to cold silver over the moaning sea, when the battered boat that had rolled and drifted almost aimlessly all night, came within sight of land, though of land which looked almost as lost and savage as the waves. All night there had been but little lifting in the leaden sea, only now and then the boat had been heaved up, as on a huge shoulder which slipped from under it; such occasional sea-quakes came probably from the swell of some steamer that had passed it in the dark; otherwise the waves were harmless though restless. But it was piercingly cold, and there was, from time to time, a splutter of rain like the splutter of the spray, which seemed almost to freeze as it fell. MacIan, more at home than his companion in this quite barbarous and elemental sort of adventure, had rowed toilsomely with the heavy oars whenever he saw anything that looked like land; but for the most part had trusted with grim transcendentalism to wind and tide. Among the implements of their first outfit the brandy alone had remained to him, and he gave it to his freezing companion in quantities which greatly alarmed that temperate Londoner; but MacIan came from the cold seas and mists where a man can drink a tumbler of raw whiskey in a boat without it making him wink.

When the Highlander began to pull really hard upon the oars, Turnbull craned his dripping red head out of the boat to see the goal of his exertions. It was a sufficiently uninviting one; nothing so far as could be seen but a steep and shelving bank of shingle, made of loose little pebbles such as children like, but slanting up higher than a house. On the top of the mound, against the sky line, stood up the brown skeleton of some broken fence or break-water. With the grey and watery dawn crawling up behind it, the fence really seemed to say to our philosophic adventurers that they had come at last to the other end of nowhere.

Bent by necessity to his labour, MacIan managed the heavy boat with real power and skill, and when at length he ran it up on a smoother part of the slope it caught and held so that they could clamber out, not sinking farther than their knees into the water and the shingle. A foot or two farther up their feet found the beach firmer, and a few moments afterward they were leaning on the ragged break-water and looking back at the sea they had escaped.

They had a dreary walk across wastes of grey shingle in the grey dawn before they began to come within hail of human fields or roads; nor had they any notion of what fields or roads they would be. Their boots were beginning to break up and the confusion of stones tried them severely, so that they were glad to lean on their swords, as if they were the staves of pilgrims. MacIan thought vaguely of a weird ballad of his own country which describes the soul in Purgatory as walking on a plain full of sharp stones, and only saved by its own charities upon earth.

> If ever thou gavest hosen and shoon
>> Every night and all,
> Sit thee down and put them on,
>> And Christ receive thy soul.

Turnbull had no such lyrical meditations, but he was in an even worse temper.

At length they came to a pale ribbon of road, edged by a shelf of rough and almost colourless turf; and a few feet up the slope there stood grey and weather-stained, one of those big wayside crucifixes which are seldom seen except in Catholic countries.

MacIan put up his hand to his head and found that his bonnet was not there. Turnbull gave one glance at the crucifix—a glance at once sympathetic and bitter, in which was concentrated the whole of Swinburne's poem on the same occasion.

> O hidden face of man, whereover
>> The years have woven a viewless veil,
> If thou wert verily man's lover
>> What did thy love or blood avail?
> Thy blood the priests mix poison of,
> And in gold shekels coin thy love.

Then, leaving MacIan in his attitude of prayer, Turnbull began to look right and left very sharply, like one looking for something. Suddenly, with a little cry, he saw it and ran forward. A few yards from them along the road a lean and starved sort of hedge came pitifully to an end. Caught upon its prickly angle, however, there was a very small and very dirty scrap of paper that might have hung there for months, since it escaped from some one tearing up a letter or making a spill out of a newspaper. Turnbull snatched at it and found it was the corner of a printed page, very coarsely printed, like a cheap novelette, and just large enough to contain the words: "*et c'est elle qui* —"

"Hurrah!" cried Turnbull, waving his fragment; "we are safe at last. We are free at last. We are somewhere better than England or Eden or Paradise. MacIan, we are in the Land of the Duel!"

"Where do you say?" said the other, looking at him heavily and with knitted brows, like one almost dazed with the grey doubts of desolate twilight and drifting sea.

"We are in France!" cried Turnbull, with a voice like a trumpet, "in the land where things really happen — *Tout arrive en France*. We arrive in France. Look at this little message," and he held out the scrap of paper. "There's an omen for you superstitious hill folk. *C'est elle qui* — *Mais oui, mais oui, c'est elle qui sauvera encore le monde.*"

"France!" repeated MacIan, and his eyes awoke again in his head like large lamps lighted.

"Yes, France!" said Turnbull, and all the rhetorical part of him came to the top, his face growing as red as his hair. "France, that has always been in rebellion for liberty and reason. France, that has always assailed superstition with the club of Rabelais or the rapier of Voltaire. France, at whose first council table sits the sublime figure of Julian the Apostate. France, where a man said only the other day those splendid unanswerable words" — with a superb gesture — "'we have extinguished in heaven those lights that men shall never light again.'"

"No," said MacIan, in a voice that shook with a controlled passion, "but France, which was taught by St. Bernard and led to war by Joan of Arc. France that made the crusades. France that saved the Church and scattered the heresies by the mouths of Bossuet and Massillon. France, which shows to-day the conquering march of Catholicism, as brain after brain surrenders to it, Brunetière, Coppée, Hauptmann, Barrès, Bourget, Lemaître."

"France!" asserted Turnbull with a sort of rollicking self-exaggeration, very unusual with him, "France, which is one torrent of splendid scepticism from Abelard to Anatole France."

"France," said MacIan, "which is one cataract of clear faith from St. Louis to Our Lady of Lourdes."

"France at least," cried Turnbull, throwing up his sword in schoolboy triumph, "in which these things are thought about and fought about. France, where reason and religion clash in one continual tournament. France, above all, where men understand the pride and passion which have plucked our blades from their scabbards. Here, at least, we shall not be chased and spied on by sickly parsons and greasy policemen, because we wish to put our lives on the game. Courage, my friend, we have come to the country of honour."

MacIan did not even notice the incongruous phrase "my friend," but nodding again and again, drew his sword and flung the scabbard far behind him in the road.

"Yes," he cried, in a voice of thunder, "we will fight here and He shall look on at it."

Turnbull glanced at the crucifix with a sort of scowling good-humour and then said: "He may look and see His cross defeated."

"The cross cannot be defeated," said MacIan, "for it is Defeat."

A second afterward the two bright, bloodthirsty weapons made the sign of the cross in horrible parody upon each other.

They had not touched each other twice, however, when upon the hill, above the crucifix, there appeared another horrible parody of its shape; the figure of a man who appeared for an instant waving his outspread arms. He had vanished in an instant; but MacIan, whose fighting face was set that way, had seen the shape momentarily but quite photographically. And while it was like a comic repetition of the cross, it was also, in that place and hour, something more incredible. It had been only instantaneously on the retina of his eye; but unless his eye and mind were going mad together, the figure was that of an ordinary London policeman.

He tried to concentrate his senses on the swordplay; but one half of his brain was wrestling with the puzzle; the apocalyptic and almost seraphic apparition of a stout constable out of Clapham on top of a dreary and deserted hill in France. He did not, however, have to puzzle long. Before the duellists had exchanged half a dozen passes, the big, blue policeman appeared once more on the top of the hill, a palpable monstrosity in the eye of heaven. He was waving only one arm now and seemed to be shouting directions. At the same moment a mass of blue blocked the corner of the road behind the small, smart figure of Turnbull, and a small company of policemen in the English uniform came up at a kind of half-military double.

Turnbull saw the stare of consternation in his enemy's face and swung round to share its cause. When he saw it, cool as he was, he staggered back.

"What the devil are you doing here?" he called out in a high, shrill voice of authority, like one who finds a tramp in his own larder.

"Well, sir," said the serjeant in command, with that sort of heavy civility shown only to the evidently guilty, "seems to me we might ask what are you doing here?"

"We are having an affair of honour," said Turnbull, as if it were the most rational thing in the world. "If the French police like to interfere, let them interfere. But why the blue blazes should you interfere, you great blue blundering sausages?"

"I'm afraid, sir," said the serjeant with restraint, "I'm afraid I don't quite follow you."

"I mean, why don't the French police take this up if it's got to be taken up? I always heard that they were spry enough in their own way."

"Well, sir," said the serjeant, reflectively, "you see, sir, the French police don't take this up — well, because you see, sir, this ain't France. This is His Majesty's dominions, same as 'Ampstead 'eath."

"Not France?" repeated Turnbull, with a sort of dull incredulity.

"No, sir," said the serjeant; "though most of the people talk French. This is the island called St. Loup, sir, an island in the Channel. We've been sent down specially from London, as you were such specially distinguished criminals, if you'll allow me to say so. Which reminds me to warn you that anything you say may be used against you at your trial."

"Quite so," said Turnbull, and lurched suddenly against the serjeant, so as to tip him over the edge of the road with a crash into the shingle below. Then leaving MacIan and the policemen equally and instantaneously nailed to the road, he ran a little way along it, leapt off on to a part of the beach, which he had found in his journey to be firmer, and went across it with a clatter of pebbles. His sudden calculation was successful; the police, unacquainted with the various levels of the loose beach, tried to overtake him by the shorter cut and found themselves, being heavy men, almost up to their knees in shoals of slippery shingle. Two who had been slower with their bodies were quicker with their minds, and seeing Turnbull's trick, ran along the edge of the road after him. Then MacIan finally awoke, and leaving half his sleeve in the grip of the only man who tried to hold him, took the two policemen in the small of their backs with the impetus of a cannon-ball and, sending them also flat among the stones, went tearing after his twin defier of the law.

As they were both good runners, the start they had gained was decisive. They dropped over a high break-water farther on upon the beach, turned sharply, and scrambled up a line of ribbed rocks, crowned with a thicket, crawled through it, scratching their hands and faces, and dropped into another road; and there found that they could slacken their speed into a steady trot. In all this desperate dart and scramble, they still kept hold of their drawn swords, which now, indeed, in the vigorous phrase of Bunyan, seemed almost to grow out of their hands.

They had run another half mile or so when it became apparent that they were entering a sort of scattered village. One or two whitewashed cottages and even a shop had appeared along the side of the road. Then, for the first time, Turnbull twisted round his red beard to get a glimpse of his companion, who was a foot or two behind, and remarked abruptly: "Mr. MacIan, we've been going the wrong way to work all along. We're traced everywhere, because everybody knows about us. It's as if one went about with Kruger's beard on Mafeking Night."

"What do you mean?" said MacIan, innocently.

"I mean," said Turnbull, with steady conviction, "that what we want is a little diplomacy, and I am going to buy some in a shop."

CHAPTER XI

A SCANDAL IN THE VILLAGE

IN THE LITTLE hamlet of Haroc, in the Isle of St. Loup, there lived a man who—though living under the English flag—was absolutely typical of the French tradition. He was quite unnoticeable, but that was exactly where he was quite himself. He was not even extraordinarily French; but then it is against the French tradition to be extraordinarily French. Ordinary Englishmen would only have thought him a little old-fashioned; imperialistic Englishmen would really have mistaken him for the old John Bull of the caricatures. He was stout; he was quite undistinguished; and he had side whiskers, worn just a little longer than John Bull's. He was by name Pierre Durand; he was by trade a wine merchant; he was by politics a conservative republican; he had been brought up a Catholic, had always thought and acted as an agnostic, and was very mildly returning to the Church in his later years. He had a genius (if one can even use so wild a word in connection with so tame a person) a genius for saying the conventional thing on every conceivable subject; or rather what we in England would call the conventional thing. For it was not convention with him, but solid and manly conviction. Convention implies cant or affectation, and he had not the faintest smell of either. He was simply an ordinary citizen with ordinary views; and if you had told him so he would have taken it as an ordinary compliment. If you had asked him about women, he would have said that one must preserve their domesticity and decorum; he would have used the stalest words, but he would have in reserve the strongest arguments. If you had asked him about government, he would have said that all citizens were free and equal, but he would have meant what he said. If you had asked him about education, he would have said that the young must be trained up in habits of industry and of respect for their parents. Still he would have set them the example of industry, and he would have been one of the parents whom they could respect. A state of mind so hopelessly central is depressing to the English instinct. But then in England a man announcing these platitudes is generally a fool and a

93

frightened fool, announcing them out of mere social servility. But Durand was anything but a fool; he had read all the eighteenth century, and could have defended his platitudes round every angle of eighteenth-century argument. And certainly he was anything but a coward: swollen and sedentary as he was, he could have hit any man back who touched him with the instant violence of an automatic machine; and dying in a uniform would have seemed to him only the sort of thing that some-times happens. I am afraid it is impossible to explain this monster amid the exaggerative sects and the eccentric clubs of my country. He was merely a man.

He lived in a little villa which was furnished well with comfortable chairs and tables and highly uncomfortable classical pictures and me-dallions. The art in his home contained nothing between the two extremes of hard, meagre designs of Greek heads and Roman togas, and on the other side a few very vulgar Catholic images in the crudest colours; these were mostly in his daughter's room. He had recently lost his wife, whom he had loved heartily and rather heavily in complete silence, and upon whose grave he was constantly in the habit of placing hideous little wreaths, made out of a sort of black-and-white beads. To his only daughter he was equally devoted, though he restricted her a good deal under a sort of theoretic alarm about her innocence; an alarm which was peculiarly unnecessary, first, because she was an excep-tionally reticent and religious girl, and secondly, because there was hardly anybody else in the place.

Madeleine Durand was physically a sleepy young woman, and might easily have been supposed to be morally a lazy one. It is, however, certain that the work of her house was done somehow, and it is even more rapidly ascertainable that nobody else did it. The logician is, therefore, driven back upon the assumption that she did it; and that lends a sort of mysterious interest to her personality at the begin-ning. She had very broad, low, and level brows, which seemed even lower because her warm yellow hair clustered down to her eyebrows; and she had a face just plump enough not to look as powerful as it was. Anything that was heavy in all this was abruptly lightened by two large, light china-blue eyes, lightened all of a sudden as if it had been lifted into the air by two big blue butterflies. The rest of her was less than middle-sized, and was of a casual and comfortable sort; and she had this difference from such girls as the girl in the motor-car, that one did not incline to take in her figure at all, but only her broad and leonine and innocent head.

Both the father and the daughter were of the sort that would normally have avoided all observation; that is, all observation in that extraordinary modern world which calls out everything except strength. Both of them had strength below the surface; they were like quiet peasants owning enormous and unquarried mines. The father with his square face and grey side whiskers, the daughter with her square face and golden fringe of hair, were both stronger than they knew; stronger than any one knew. The father believed in civilisation, in the storied tower we have erected to affront nature; that is, the father believed in Man. The daughter believed in God; and was even stronger. They neither of them believed in themselves; for that is a decadent weakness.

The daughter was called a devotee. She left upon ordinary people the impression — the somewhat irritating impression — produced by such a person; it can only be described as the sense of strong water being perpetually poured into some abyss. She did her housework easily; she achieved her social relations sweetly; she was never neglectful and never unkind. This accounted for all that was soft in her, but not for all that was hard. She trod firmly as if going somewhere; she flung her face back as if defying something; she hardly spoke a cross word, yet there was often battle in her eyes. The modern man asked doubtfully where all this silent energy went to. He would have stared still more doubtfully if he had been told that it all went into her prayers.

The conventions of the Isle of St. Loup were necessarily a compromise or confusion between those of France and England; and it was vaguely possible for a respectable young lady to have half-attached lovers, in a way that would be impossible in the bourgeoisie of France. One man in particular had made himself an unmistakable figure in the track of this girl as she went to church. He was a short, prosperous-looking man, whose long, bushy black beard and clumsy black umbrella made him seem both shorter and older than he really was; but whose big, bold eyes, and step that spurned the ground, gave him an instant character of youth.

His name was Camille Bert, and he was a commercial traveller who had only been in the island an idle week before he began to hover in the tracks of Madeleine Durand. Since every one knows every one in so small a place, Madeleine certainly knew him to speak to; but it is not very evident that she ever spoke. He haunted her, however; especially at church, which was, indeed, one of the few certain places for finding her. In her home she had a habit of being invisible, sometimes through insatiable domesticity, sometimes through an equally insatiable solitude. M. Bert did not give the impression of a pious man, though he did give, especially with his eyes, the impression of an honest one. But he went to Mass with a simple exactitude that could not be mistaken for a pose, or even for a vulgar fascination. It was perhaps this religious regularity which eventually drew Madeleine into recognition of him. At least it is certain that she twice spoke to him with her square and open smile in the porch of the church; and there was human nature enough in the hamlet to turn even that into gossip.

But the real interest arose suddenly as a squall arises with the extraordinary affair that occurred about five days after. There was about a third of a mile beyond the village of Haroc a large but lonely hotel upon the London or Paris model, but commonly almost entirely empty. Among the accidental group of guests who had come to it at this season was a man whose nationality no one could fix and who bore the non-committal name of Count Gregory. He treated everybody with complete civility and almost in complete silence. On the few occasions when he spoke, he spoke either French, English, or once (to the priest) Latin; and the general opinion was that he spoke them all wrong. He was a large, lean man, with the stoop of an aged eagle, and even the eagle's nose to complete it; he had old-fashioned military whiskers and moustache dyed with a garish and highly incredible yellow. He had the dress of a showy gentleman and the manners of a decayed gentleman; he seemed (as with a sort of simplicity) to be trying to be a dandy when he was too old even to know that he was old. Yet he was decidedly a handsome figure with his curled yellow hair and lean fastidious face; and he wore a peculiar frock-coat of bright turquoise blue, with an unknown order pinned to it, and he carried a huge and heavy cane. Despite his silence and his dandified dress and whiskers, the island might never have heard of him but for the extraordinary event of which I have spoken, which fell about in the following way:

In such casual atmospheres only the enthusiastic go to Benediction; and as the warm blue twilight closed over the little candle-lit church and village, the line of worshippers who went home from the former to the latter thinned out until it broke. On one such evening at least no one was in church except the quiet, unconquerable Madeleine, four old women, one fisherman, and, of course, the irrepressible M. Camille Bert. The others seemed to melt away afterward into the peacock colours of the dim green grass and the dark blue sky. Even Durand was invisible instead of being merely reverentially remote; and Madeleine set forth through the patch of black forest alone. She was not in the least afraid of loneliness, because she was not afraid of devils. I think they were afraid of her.

In a clearing of the wood, however, which was lit up with a last patch of the perishing sunlight, there advanced upon her suddenly one who was more startling than a devil. The incomprehensible Count Gregory, with his yellow hair like flame and his face like the white ashes of the flame, was advancing bareheaded toward her, flinging out his arms and his long fingers with a frantic gesture.

"We are alone here," he cried, "and you would be at my mercy, only that I am at yours."

Then his frantic hands fell by his sides and he looked up under his brows with an expression that went well with his hard breathing. Madeleine Durand had come to a halt at first in childish wonder, and now, with more than masculine self-control, "I fancy I know your face, sir," she said, as if to gain time.

"I know I shall not forget yours," said the other, and extended once more his ungainly arms in an unnatural gesture. Then of a sudden there came out of him a spout of wild and yet pompous phrases. "It is as well that you should know the worst and the best. I am a man who knows no limit; I am the most callous of criminals, the most unrepentant of sinners. There is no man in my dominions so vile as I. But my dominions stretch from the olives of Italy to the fir-woods of Denmark, and there is no nook of all of them in which I have not done a sin. But when I bear you away I shall be doing my first sacrilege, and also my first act of virtue." He seized her suddenly by the elbow; and she did not scream but only pulled and tugged. Yet though she had not screamed, some one astray in the woods seemed to have heard the struggle. A short but nimble figure came along the woodland path like a humming bullet and had caught Count Gregory a crack across the face before his own could be recognised. When it was recognised it was that of Camille, with the black elderly beard and the young ardent eyes.

Up to the moment when Camille had hit the Count, Madeleine had entertained no doubt that the Count was merely a madman. Now she was startled with a new sanity; for the tall man in the yellow whiskers and yellow moustache first returned the blow of Bert, as if it were a sort of duty, and then stepped back with a slight bow and an easy smile.

"This need go no further here, M. Bert," he said. "I need not remind you how far it should go elsewhere."

"Certainly, you need remind me of nothing," answered Camille, stolidly. "I am glad that you are just not too much of a scoundrel for a gentleman to fight."

"We are detaining the lady," said Count Gregory, with politeness; and, making a gesture suggesting that he would have taken off his hat if he had had one, he strode away up the avenue of trees and eventually disappeared. He was so complete an aristocrat that he could offer his back to them all the way up that avenue; and his back never once looked uncomfortable.

"You must allow me to see you home," said Bert to the girl, in a gruff and almost stifled voice; "I think we have only a little way to go."

"Only a little way," she said, and smiled once more that night, in spite of fatigue and fear and the world and the flesh and the devil. The glowing and transparent blue of twilight had long been covered by the opaque and slatelike blue of night, when he handed her into the lamplit interior of her home. He went out himself into the darkness, walking sturdily, but tearing at his black beard.

All the French or semi-French gentry of the district considered this a case in which a duel was natural and inevitable, and neither party had any difficulty in finding seconds, strangers as they were in the place. Two small landowners, who were careful, practising Catholics, willingly undertook to represent that strict church-goer Camille Bert; while the profligate but apparently powerful Count Gregory found friends in an energetic local doctor who was ready for social promotion and an accidental Californian tourist who was ready for anything. As no particular purpose could be served by delay, it was arranged that the affair should fall out three days afterward. And when this was settled the whole community, as it were, turned over again in bed and thought no more about the matter. At least there was only one member of it who seemed to be restless, and that was she who was commonly most restful. On the next night Madeleine Durand went to church as usual; and as usual the stricken Camille was there also. What was not so usual was that when they were a bow-shot from the church Madeleine turned round and walked back to him. "Sir," she began, "it is not wrong of me to speak to you," and the very words gave him a jar of unexpected truth; for in all the novels he had ever read she would have begun: "It is wrong of me to speak to you." She went on with wide and serious eyes like an animal's: "It is not wrong of me to speak to you, because your soul, or anybody's soul, matters so much more than what the world says about anybody. I want to talk to you about what you are going to do."

Bert saw in front of him the inevitable heroine of the novels trying to prevent bloodshed; and his pale firm face became implacable.

"I would do anything but that for you," he said; "but no man can be called less than a man."

She looked at him for a moment with a face openly puzzled, and then broke into an odd and beautiful half smile.

"Oh, I don't mean that," she said; "I don't talk about what I don't understand. No one has ever hit me; and if they had I should not feel as a man may. I am sure it is not the best thing to fight. It would be better to forgive—if one could really forgive. But when people dine with my father and say that fighting a duel is mere murder—of course I can see that is not just. It's all so different—having a reason—and letting the other man know—and using the same guns and things—and doing it in front of your friends. I'm awfully stupid, but I know that men like you aren't murderers. But it wasn't that that I meant."

"What did you mean?" asked the other, looking broodingly at the earth.

"Don't you know," she said, "there is only one more celebration? I thought that as you always go to church — I thought you would communicate this morning."

Bert stepped backward with a sort of action she had never seen in him before. It seemed to alter his whole body.

"You may be right or wrong to risk dying," said the girl, simply; "the poor women in our village risk it whenever they have a baby. You men are the other half of the world. I know nothing about when you ought to die. But surely if you are daring to try and find God beyond the grave and appeal to Him — you ought to let Him find you when He comes and stands there every morning in our little church."

And placid as she was, she made a little gesture of argument, of which the pathos wrung the heart.

M. Camille Bert was by no means placid. Before that incomplete gesture and frankly pleading face he retreated as if from the jaws of a dragon. His dark black hair and beard looked utterly unnatural against the startling pallor of his face. When at last he said something it was: "O God! I can't stand this!" He did not say it in French. Nor did he, strictly speaking, say it in English. The truth (interesting only to anthropologists) is that he said it in Scotch.

"There will be another mass in a matter of eight hours," said Madeleine, with a sort of business eagerness and energy, "and you can do it then before the fighting. You must forgive me, but I was so frightened that you would not do it at all."

Bert seemed to crush his teeth together until they broke, and managed to say between them: "And why should you suppose that I shouldn't do as you say — I mean not do it at all?"

"You always go to Mass," answered the girl, opening her wide blue eyes, "and the Mass is very long and tiresome unless one loves God."

Then it was that Bert exploded with a brutality which might have come from Count Gregory, his criminal opponent. He advanced upon Madeleine with flaming eyes, and almost took her by the two shoulders. "I do not love God," he cried, speaking French with the broadest Scotch accent; "I do not want to find Him; I do not think He is there to be found. I must burst up the show; I must and will say everything. You are the happiest and honestest thing I ever saw in this godless universe. And I am the dirtiest and most dishonest."

Madeleine looked at him doubtfully for an instant, and then said with a sudden simplicity and cheerfulness: "Oh, but if you are really sorry it is all right. If you are horribly sorry it is all the better. You have only to go and tell the priest so and he will give you God out of his own hands."

"I hate your priest and I deny your God!" cried the man, "and I tell you God is a lie and a fable and a mask. And for the first time in my life I do not feel superior to God."

"What can it all mean?" said Madeleine, in massive wonder.

"Because I am a fable also and a mask," said the man. He had been plucking fiercely at his black beard and hair all the time; now he suddenly plucked them off and flung them like moulted feathers in the mire. This extraordinary spoliation left in the sunlight the same face, but a much younger head—a head with close chestnut curls and a short chestnut beard.

"Now you know the truth," he answered, with hard eyes. "I am a cad who has played a crooked trick on a quiet village and a decent woman for a private reason of his own. I might have played it successfully on any other woman; I have hit the one woman on whom it cannot be played. It's just like my damned luck. The plain truth is," and here when he came to the plain truth he boggled and blundered, as Evan had done in telling it to the girl in the motor-car.

"The plain truth is," he said at last, "that I am James Turnbull the atheist. The police are after me; not for atheism but for being ready to fight for it."

"I saw something about you in a newspaper," said the girl, with a simplicity which even surprise could never throw off its balance.

"Evan MacIan said there was a God," went on the other, stubbornly, "and I say there isn't. And I have come to fight for the fact that there is no God; it is for that that I have seen this cursed island and your blessed face."

"You want me really to believe," said Madeleine, with parted lips, "that you think——"

"I want you to hate me!" cried Turnbull, in agony. "I want you to be sick when you think of my name. I am sure there is no God."

"But there is," said Madeline, quite quietly, and rather with the air of one telling children about an elephant. "Why, I touched His body only this morning."

"You touched a bit of bread," said Turnbull, biting his knuckles. "Oh, I will say anything that can madden you!"

"You think it is only a bit of bread," said the girl, and her lips tightened ever so little.

"I know it is only a bit of bread," said Turnbull, with violence.

She flung back her open face and smiled. "Then why did you refuse to eat it?" she said.

James Turnbull made a little step backward, and for the first time in his life there seemed to break out and blaze in his head thoughts that were not his own.

"Why, how silly of them," cried out Madeleine, with quite a schoolgirl gaiety, "why, how silly of them to call *you* a blasphemer! Why, you have wrecked your whole business because you would not commit blasphemy."

The man stood, a somewhat comic figure in his tragic bewilderment, with the honest red head of James Turnbull sticking out of the rich and fictitious garments of Camille Bert. But the startled pain of his face was strong enough to obliterate the oddity.

"You come down here," continued the lady, with that female emphasis which is so pulverising in conversation and so feeble at a public meeting, "you and your MacIan come down here and put on false beards or noses in order to fight. You pretend to be a Catholic commercial traveller from France. Poor Mr. MacIan has to pretend to be a dissolute nobleman from nowhere. Your scheme succeeds; you pick a quite convincing quarrel; you arrange a quite respectable duel; the duel you have planned so long will come off to-morrow with absolute certainty and safety. And then you throw off your wig and throw up your scheme and throw over your colleague, because I ask you to go into a building and eat a bit of bread. And *then* you dare to tell me that you are sure there is nothing watching us. Then you say you know there is nothing on the very altar you run away from. You know ⸺ "

"I only know," said Turnbull, "that I must run away from you. This has got beyond any talking." And he plunged along into the village, leaving his black wig and beard lying behind him on the road.

As the market-place opened before him he saw Count Gregory, that distinguished foreigner, standing and smoking in elegant meditation at the corner of the local café. He immediately made his way rapidly toward him, considering that a consultation was urgent. But he had hardly crossed half of that stony quadrangle when a window burst open above him and a head was thrust out, shouting. The man was in his woollen undershirt, but Turnbull knew the energetic, apoplectic head of the serjeant of police. He pointed furiously at Turnbull and shouted his name. A policeman ran excitedly from under an archway and tried to collar him. Two men selling vegetables dropped their baskets and joined in the chase. Turnbull dodged the constable, upset one of the men into his own basket, and bounding toward the distinguished foreign Count, called to him clamorously: "Come on, MacIan, the hunt is up again."

The prompt reply of Count Gregory was to pull off his large yellow whiskers and scatter them on the breeze with an air of considerable relief. Then he joined the flight of Turnbull, and even as he did so, with one wrench of his powerful hands rent and split the strange, thick stick that he carried. Inside it was a naked old-fashioned rapier. The two got a good start up the road before the whole town was awakened behind them; and half way up it a similar transformation was seen to take place in Mr. Turnbull's singular umbrella.

The two had a long race for the harbour; but the English police were heavy and the French inhabitants were indifferent. In any case, they got used to the notion of the road being clear; and just as they had come to the cliffs MacIan banged into another gentleman with unmistakable surprise. How he knew he was another gentleman merely by banging into him, must remain a mystery. MacIan was a very poor and very sober Scotch gentleman. The other was a very drunk and very wealthy English gentleman. But there was something in the staggered and openly embarrassed apologies that made them understand each other as readily and as quickly and as much as two men talking French in the middle of China. The nearest expression of the type is that it either hits or apologises; and in this case both apologised.

"You seem to be in a hurry," said the unknown Englishman, falling back a step or two in order to laugh with an unnatural heartiness. "What's it all about, eh?" Then before MacIan could get past his sprawling and staggering figure he ran forward again and said with a sort of shouting and ear-shattering whisper: "I say, my name is Wilkinson. You know—Wilkinson's Entire was my grandfather. Can't drink beer myself. Liver." And he shook his head with extraordinary sagacity.

"We really are in a hurry, as you say," said MacIan, summoning a sufficiently pleasant smile, "so if you will let us pass —— "

"I'll tell you what, you fellows," said the sprawling gentleman, confidentially, while Evan's agonised ears heard behind him the first paces of the pursuit, "if you really are, as you say, in a hurry, I know what it is to be in a hurry—Lord, what a hurry I was in when we all came out of Cartwright's rooms—if you really are in a hurry—" and he seemed to steady his voice into a sort of solemnity—"if you are in a hurry, there's nothing like a good yacht for a man in a hurry."

"No doubt you're right," said MacIan, and dashed past him in despair. The head of the pursuing host was just showing over the top of the hill behind him. Turnbull had already ducked under the intoxicated gentleman's elbow and fled far in front.

"No, but look here," said Mr. Wilkinson, enthusiastically running after MacIan and catching him by the sleeve of his coat. "If you want to hurry you should take a yacht, and if—" he said, with a burst of rationality, like one leaping to a further point in logic — "if you want a yacht—you can have mine."

Evan pulled up abruptly and looked back at him. "We are really in the devil of a hurry," he said, "and if you really have a yacht, the truth is that we would give our ears for it."

"You'll find it in harbour," said Wilkinson, struggling with his speech.

"Left side of harbour — called *Gibson Girl* — can't think why, old fellow, I never lent it you before."

With these words the benevolent Mr. Wilkinson fell flat on his face in the road, but continued to laugh softly, and turned toward his flying companion a face of peculiar peace and benignity. Evan's mind went through a crisis of instantaneous casuistry, in which it may be that he decided wrongly; but about how he decided his biographer can profess no doubt. Two minutes afterward he had overtaken Turnbull and told the tale; ten minutes afterward he and Turnbull had somehow tumbled into the yacht called the *Gibson Girl* and had somehow pushed off from the Isle of St. Loup.

CHAPTER XII

THE DESERT ISLAND

THOSE WHO HAPPEN to hold the view (and Mr. Evan MacIan, now alive and comfortable, is among the number) that something supernatural, some eccentric kindness from god or fairy had guided our adventurers through all their absurd perils, might have found his strongest argument perhaps in their management or mismanagement of Mr. Wilkinson's yacht. Neither of them had the smallest qualification for managing such a vessel; but MacIan had a practical knowledge of the sea in much smaller and quite different boats, while Turnbull had an abstract knowledge of science and some of its applications to navigation, which was worse. The presence of the god or fairy can only be deduced from the fact that they never definitely ran into anything, either a boat, a rock, a quicksand, or a man-of-war. Apart from this negative description, their voyage would be difficult to describe. It took at least a fortnight, and MacIan, who was certainly the shrewder sailor of the two, realised that they were sailing west into the Atlantic and were probably by this time past the Scilly Isles. How much farther they stood out into the western sea it was impossible to conjecture. But they felt certain, at least, that they were far enough into that awful gulf between us and America to make it unlikely that they would soon see land again. It was therefore with legitimate excitement that one rainy morning after daybreak they saw the distinct shape of a solitary island standing up against that encircling strip of silver which ran round the skyline and separated the gray and green of the billows from the gray and mauve of the morning clouds.

"What can it be?" cried MacIan, in a dry-throated excitement. "I didn't know there were any Atlantic islands so far beyond the Scillies — Good Lord, it can't be Madeira, yet?"

"I thought you were fond of legends and lies and fables," said Turnbull, grimly. "Perhaps it's Atlantis."

"Of course, it might be," answered the other, quite innocently and gravely; "but I never thought the story about Atlantis was very solidly established."

"Whatever it is, we are running on to it," said Turnbull, equably, "and we shall be shipwrecked twice, at any rate."

The naked looking nose of land projecting from the unknown island was, indeed, growing larger and larger, like the trunk of some terrible and advancing elephant. There seemed to be nothing in particular, at least on this side of the island, except shoals of shell-fish lying so thick as almost to make it look like one of those toy grottos that the children make. In one place, however, the coast offered a soft, smooth bay of sand, and even the rudimentary ingenuity of the two amateur mariners managed to run up the little ship with her prow well on shore and her bowsprit pointing upward, as in a sort of idiotic triumph.

They tumbled on shore and began to unload the vessel, setting the stores out in rows upon the sand with something of the solemnity of boys playing at pirates. There were Mr. Wilkinson's cigar-boxes and Mr. Wilkinson's dozen of champagne and Mr. Wilkinson's tinned salmon and Mr. Wilkinson's tinned tongue and Mr. Wilkinson's tinned sardines, and every sort of preserved thing that could be seen at the Army and Navy stores. Then MacIan stopped with a jar of pickles in his hand and said abruptly:

"I don't know why we're doing all this; I suppose we ought really to fall to and get it over."

Then he added more thoughtfully: "Of course this island seems rather bare and the survivor ——"

"The question is," said Turnbull, with cheerful speculation, "whether the survivor will be in a proper frame of mind for potted prawns."

MacIan looked down at the rows of tins and bottles, and the cloud of doubt still lowered upon his face.

"You will permit me two liberties, my dear sir," said Turnbull at last: "The first is to break open this box and light one of Mr. Wilkinson's excellent cigars, which will, I am sure, assist my meditations; the second is to offer a penny for your thoughts; or rather to convulse the already complex finances of this island by betting a penny that I know them."

"What on earth are you talking about?" asked MacIan, listlessly, in the manner of an inattentive child.

"I know what you are really thinking, MacIan," repeated Turnbull, laughing. "I know what I am thinking, anyhow. And I rather fancy it's the same."

"What are you thinking?" asked Evan.

"I am thinking and you are thinking," said Turnbull, "that it is damned silly to waste all that champagne."

Something like the spectre of a smile appeared on the unsmiling visage of the Gael; and he made at least no movement of dissent.

"We could drink all the wine and smoke all the cigars easily in a week," said Turnbull; "and that would be to die feasting like heroes."

"Yes, and there is something else," said MacIan, with slight hesitation. "You see, we are on an almost unknown rock, lost in the Atlantic. The police will never catch us; but then neither may the public ever hear of us; and that was one of the things we wanted." Then, after a pause, he said, drawing in the sand with his sword-point: "She may never hear of it at all."

"Well?" inquired the other, puffing at his cigar.

"Well," said MacIan, "we might occupy a day or two in drawing up a thorough and complete statement of what we did and why we did it, and all about both our points of view. Then we could leave one copy on the island whatever happens to us and put another in an empty bottle and send it out to sea, as they do in the books."

"A good idea," said Turnbull, "and now let us finish unpacking."

As MacIan, a tall, almost ghostly figure, paced along the edge of sand that ran round the islet, the purple but cloudy poetry which was his native element was piled up at its thickest upon his soul. The unique island and the endless sea emphasised the thing solely as an epic. There were no ladies or policemen here to give him a hint either of its farce or its tragedy.

"Perhaps when the morning stars were made," he said to himself, "God built this island up from the bottom of the world to be a tower and a theatre for the fight between yea and nay."

Then he wandered up to the highest level of the rock, where there was a roof or plateau of level stone. Half an hour afterward, Turnbull found him clearing away the loose sand from this table-land and making it smooth and even.

"We will fight up here, Turnbull," said MacIan, "when the time comes. And till the time comes this place shall be sacred."

"I thought of having lunch up here," said Turnbull, who had a bottle of champagne in his hand.

"No, no—not up here," said MacIan, and came down from the height quite hastily. Before he descended, however, he fixed the two swords upright, one at each end of the platform, as if they were human sentinels to guard it under the stars.

Then they came down and lunched plentifully in a nest of loose rocks. In the same place that night they supped more plentifully still. The smoke of Mr. Wilkinson's cigars went up ceaseless and strong smelling, like a pagan sacrifice; the golden glories of Mr. Wilkinson's champagne rose to their heads and poured out of them in fancies and philosophies. And occasionally they would look up at the starlight and the rock and see the space guarded by the two cross-hilted swords, which looked like two black crosses at either end of a grave.

In this primitive and Homeric truce the week passed by; it consisted almost entirely of eating, drinking, smoking, talking, and occasionally singing. They wrote their records and cast loose their bottle. They never ascended to the ominous plateau; they had never stood there save for that single embarrassed minute when they had had no time to take stock of the seascape or the shape of the land. They did not even explore the island; for MacIan was partly concerned in prayer and Turnbull entirely concerned with tobacco; and both these forms of inspiration can be enjoyed by the secluded and even the sedentary. It was on a golden afternoon, the sun sinking over the sea, rayed like the very head of Apollo, when Turnbull tossed off the last half pint from the emptied Wilkinsonian bottle, hurled the bottle into the sea with objectless energy, and went up to where his sword stood waiting for him on the hill. MacIan was already standing heavily by his with bent head and eyes reading the ground. He had not even troubled to throw a glance round the island or the horizon. But Turnbull being of a more active and birdlike type of mind did throw a glance round the scene. The consequence of which was that he nearly fell off the rock.

On three sides of this shelly and sandy islet the sea stretched blue and infinite without a speck of land or sail; the same as Turnbull had first seen it, except that the tide being out it showed a few yards more of slanting sand under the roots of the rocks. But on the fourth side the island exhibited a more extraordinary feature. In fact, it exhibited the extraordinary feature of not being an island at all. A long, curving neck of sand, as smooth and wet as the neck of the sea-serpent, ran out into the sea and joined their rock to a line of low, billowing and glistening sand-hills, which the sinking sea had just bared to the sun. Whether they were firm sand or quicksand it was difficult to guess; but there was at least no doubt that they lay on the edge of some larger land; for colourless hills appeared faintly behind them and no sea could be seen beyond.

"Sakes alive!" cried Turnbull, with rolling eyes; "this ain't an island in the Atlantic. We've butted the bally continent of America."

MacIan turned his head, and his face, already pale, grew a shade paler. He was by this time walking in a world of omens and hiero-glyphics, and he could not read anything but what was baffling or menacing in this brown gigantic arm of the earth stretched out into the sea to seize him.

"MacIan," said Turnbull, in his temperate way, "whatever our eternal interrupted tête-à-têtes have taught us or not taught us, at least we need not fear the charge of fear. If it is essential to your emotions, I will cheerfully finish the fight here and now; but I must confess that if you kill me here I shall die with my curiosity highly excited and unsatisfied upon a minor point of geography."

"I do not want to stop now," said the other, in his elephantine simplicity, "but we must stop for a moment, because it is a sign — perhaps it is a miracle. We must see what is at the end of the road of sand; it may be a bridge built across the gulf by God."

"So long as you gratify my query," said Turnbull, laughing and letting back his blade into the sheath, "I do not care for what reason you choose to stop."

They clambered down the rocky peninsula and trudged along the sandy isthmus with the plodding resolution of men who seemed almost to have made up their minds to be wanderers on the face of the earth. Despite Turnbull's air of scientific eagerness, he was really the less impatient of the two; and the Highlander went on well ahead of him with passionate strides. By the time they had walked for about half an hour in the ups and downs of those dreary sands, the distance between the two had lengthened and MacIan was only a tall figure silhouetted for an instant upon the crest of some sand dune and then disappearing behind it. This rather increased the Robinson Crusoe feeling in Mr. Turnbull, and he looked about almost disconsolately for some sign of life. What sort of life he expected it to be if it appeared, he did not very clearly know. He has since confessed that he thinks that in his sub-consciousness he expected an alligator.

The first sign of life that he did see, however, was something more extraordinary than the largest alligator. It was nothing less than the notorious Mr. Evan MacIan coming bounding back across the sand heaps breathless, without his cap and keeping the sword in his hand only by a habit now quite hardened.

"Take care, Turnbull," he cried out from a good distance as he ran, "I've seen a native."

"A native?" repeated his companion, whose scenery had of late been chiefly of shell-fish, "what the deuce! Do you mean an oyster?"

"No," said MacIan, stopping and breathing hard, "I mean a savage. A black man."

"Why, where did you see him?" asked the staring editor.

"Over there — behind that hill," said the gasping MacIan. "He put up his black head and grinned at me."

Turnbull thrust his hands through his red hair like one who gives up the world as a bad riddle. "Lord love a duck," said he, "can it be Jamaica?"

Then glancing at his companion with a small frown, as of one slightly suspicious, he said: "I say, don't think me rude — but you're a visionary kind of fellow — and then we drank a great deal. Do you mind waiting here while I go and see for myself?"

"Shout if you get into trouble," said the Celt, with composure; "you will find it is as I say."

Turnbull ran off ahead with a rapidity now far greater than his rival's, and soon vanished over the disputed sand-hill. Then five minutes passed, and then seven minutes; and MacIan bit his lip and swung his sword, and the other did not reappear. Finally, with a Gaelic oath, Evan started forward to the rescue, and almost at the same moment the small figure of the missing man appeared on the ridge against the sky.

Even at that distance, however, there was something odd about his attitude; so odd that MacIan continued to make his way in that direction. It looked as if he were wounded; or, still more, as if he were ill. He wavered as he came down the slope and seemed flinging himself into peculiar postures. But it was only when he came within three feet of MacIan's face, that that observer of mankind fully realised that Mr. James Turnbull was roaring with laughter.

"You are quite right," sobbed that wholly demoralised journalist. "He's black, oh, there's no doubt the black's all right — as far as it goes." And he went off again into convulsions of his humourous ailment.

"What ever is the matter with you?" asked MacIan, with stern impatience. "Did you see the nigger——"

"I saw the nigger," gasped Turnbull. "I saw the splendid barbarian Chief. I saw the Emperor of Ethiopia — oh, I saw him all right. The nigger's hands and face are a lovely colour — and the nigger——" And he was overtaken once more.

"Well, well, well," said Evan, stamping each monosyllable on the sand, "what about the nigger?"

"Well, the truth is," said Turnbull, suddenly and startlingly, becoming quite grave and precise, "the truth is, the nigger is a Margate nigger, and we are now on the edge of the Isle of Thanet, a few miles from Margate."

Then he had a momentary return of his hysteria and said: "I say, old boy, I should like to see a chart of our fortnight's cruise in Wilkinson's yacht."

MacIan had no smile in answer, but his eager lips opened as if parched for the truth. "You mean to say," he began——

"Yes, I mean to say," said Turnbull, "and I mean to say something funnier still. I have learnt everything I wanted to know from the partially black musician over there, who has taken a run in his war-paint to meet a friend in a quiet pub along the coast — the noble savage has told me all about it. The bottle containing our declarations, doctrines, and dying sentiments was washed up on Margate beach yesterday in the presence of one alderman, two bathing-machine men, three policemen, seven doctors, and a hundred and thirteen London clerks on a holiday, to all of whom, whether directly or indirectly, our composition gave enormous literary pleasure. Buck up, old man, this story of ours is a switch-back. I have begun to understand the pulse and the time of it; now we are up in a cathedral and then we are down in a theatre, where they only play farces. Come, I am quite reconciled — let us enjoy the farce."

But MacIan said nothing, and an instant afterward Turnbull himself called out in an entirely changed voice: "Oh, this is damnable! This is not to be borne!"

MacIan followed his eye along the sand-hills. He saw what looked like the momentary and waving figure of the nigger minstrel, and then he saw a heavy running policeman take the turn of the sand-hill with the smooth solemnity of a railway train.

CHAPTER XIII

THE GARDEN OF PEACE

U P TO THIS instant Evan MacIan had really understood nothing; but when he saw the policeman he saw everything. He saw his enemies, all the powers and princes of the earth. He was suddenly altered from a staring statue to a leaping man of the mountains.

"We must break away from him here," he cried, briefly, and went like a whirlwind over the sand ridge in a straight line and at a particular angle. When the policeman had finished his admirable railway curve, he found a wall of failing sand between him and the pursued. By the time he had scaled it thrice, slid down twice, and crested it in the third effort, the two flying figures were far in front. They found the sand harder farther on; it began to be crusted with scraps of turf and in a few moments they were flying easily over an open common of rank sea-grass. They had no easy business, however; for the bottle which they had so innocently sent into the chief gate of Thanet had called to life the police of half a county on their trail. From every side across the gray-green common figures could be seen running and closing in; and it was only when MacIan with his big body broke down the tangled barrier of a little wood, as men break down a door with the shoulder; it was only when they vanished crashing into the under world of the black wood, that their hunters were even instantaneously thrown off the scent.

At the risk of struggling a little longer like flies in that black web of twigs and trunks, Evan (who had an instinct of the hunter or the hunted) took an incalculable course through the forest, which let them out at last by a forest opening — quite forgotten by the leaders of the chase. They ran a mile or two farther along the edge of the wood until they reached another and somewhat similar opening. Then MacIan stood utterly still and listened, as animals listen, for every sound in the universe. Then he said: "We are quit of them." And Turnbull said: "Where shall we go now?"

MacIan looked at the silver sunset that was closing in, barred by plumy lines of purple cloud; he looked at the high tree-tops that caught the last light and at the birds going heavily homeward, just as if all these things were bits of written advice that he could read.

Then he said: "The best place we can go to is to bed. If we can get some sleep in this wood, now every one has cleared out of it, it will be worth a handicap of two hundred yards to-morrow."

Turnbull, who was exceptionally lively and laughing in his demeanour, kicked his legs about like a schoolboy and said he did not want to go to sleep. He walked incessantly and talked very brilliantly. And when at last he lay down on the hard earth, sleep struck him senseless like a hammer.

Indeed, he needed the strongest sleep he could get; for the earth was still full of darkness and a kind of morning fog when his fellow-fugitive shook him awake.

"No more sleep, I'm afraid," said Evan, in a heavy, almost submissive, voice of apology. "They've gone on past us right enough for a good thirty miles; but now they've found out their mistake, and they're coming back."

"Are you sure?" said Turnbull, sitting up and rubbing his red eyebrows with his hand.

The next moment, however, he had jumped up alive and leaping like a man struck with a shock of cold water, and he was plunging after MacIan along the woodland path. The shape of their old friend the constable had appeared against the pearl and pink of the sunrise. Somehow, it always looked a very funny shape when seen against the sunrise.

·　　·　　·　　·　　·

A wash of weary daylight was breaking over the country side, and the fields and roads were full of white mist — the kind of white mist that clings in corners like cotton wool. The empty road, along which the chase had taken its turn, was overshadowed on one side by a very high discoloured wall, stained, and streaked green, as with seaweed — evidently the high-shouldered sentinel of some great gentleman's estate. A yard or two from the wall ran parallel to it a linked and tangled line of lime-trees, forming a kind of cloister along the side of the road. It was under this branching colonnade that the two fugitives fled, almost concealed from their pursuers by the twilight, the mist and the leaping zoetrope of shadows. Their feet, though beating the ground furiously, made but a faint noise; for they had kicked away their boots in the wood; their long, antiquated weapons made no jingle or clatter, for they had strapped them across their backs like guitars. They had all the advantages that invisibility and silence can add to speed.

A hundred and fifty yards behind them down the centre of the empty road the first of their pursuers came pounding and panting — a fat but powerful policeman who had distanced all the rest. He came on at a splendid pace for so portly a figure; but, like all heavy bodies in motion, he gave the impression that it would be easier for him to increase his pace than to slacken it suddenly. Nothing short of a brick wall could have abruptly brought him up. Turnbull turned his head slightly and found breath to say something to MacIan. MacIan nodded.

Pursuer and pursued were fixed in their distance as they fled, for some quarter of a mile, when they came to a place where two or three of the trees grew twistedly together, making a special obscurity. Past this place the pursuing policeman went thundering without thought or hesitation. But he was pursuing his shadow or the wind; for Turnbull had put one foot in a crack of the tree and gone up it as quickly and softly as a cat. Somewhat more laboriously but in equal silence the long legs of the Highlander had followed; and crouching in crucial silence in the cloud of leaves, they saw the whole posse of their pursuers go by and die into the dust and mists of the distance.

The white vapour lay, as it often does, in lean and palpable layers; and even the head of the tree was above it in the half daylight, like a green ship swinging on a sea of foam. But higher yet behind them, and readier to catch the first coming of the sun, ran the rampart of the top of the wall, which in their excitement of escape looked at once indispensable and unattainable, like the wall of heaven. Here, however, it was Mac-Ian's turn to have the advantage; for, though less light-limbed and feline, he was longer and stronger in the arms. In two seconds he had tugged up his chin over the wall like a horizontal bar; the next he sat astride of it, like a horse of stone. With his assistance Turnbull vaulted to the same perch, and the two began cautiously to shift along the wall in the direction by which they had come, doubling on their tracks to throw off the last pursuit. MacIan could not rid himself of the fancy of bestriding a steed; the long, gray coping of the wall shot out in front of him, like the long, gray neck of some nightmare Rosinante. He had the quaint thought that he and Turnbull were the two knights on one steed on the old shield of the Templars.

The nightmare of the stone horse was increased by the white fog, which seemed thicker inside the wall than outside. They could make nothing of the enclosure upon which they were partial trespassers, except that the green and crooked branches of a big apple-tree came crawling at them out of the mist, like the tentacles of some green cuttlefish. Anything would serve, however, that was likely to confuse their trail, so they both decided without need of words to use this tree also as a ladder — a ladder of descent. When they dropped from the lowest branch to the ground their stockinged feet felt hard gravel beneath them.

They had alighted in the middle of a very broad garden-path, and the clearing mist permitted them to see the edge of a well-clipped lawn. Though the white vapour was still a veil, it was like the gauzy veil of a transformation scene in a pantomime; for through it there glowed shapeless masses of colour, masses which might be clouds of sunrise or mosaics of gold and crimson, or ladies robed in ruby and emerald draperies. As it thinned yet further they saw that it was only flowers; but flowers in such insolent mass and magnificence as can seldom be seen out of the tropics. Purple and crimson rhododendrons rose arrogantly, like rampant heraldic animals against their burning background of laburnum gold. The roses were red hot; the clematis was, so to speak, blue hot. And yet the mere whiteness of the syringa seemed the most violent colour of all. As the golden sunlight gradually conquered the mists, it had really something of the sensational sweetness of the slow opening of the gates of Eden. MacIan, whose mind was always haunted with such seraphic or titanic parallels, made some such remark to his companion. But Turnbull only cursed and said that it was the back garden of some damnable rich man.

When the last haze had faded from the ordered paths, the open lawns, and the flaming flower-beds, the two realised, not without an abrupt re-examination of their position, that they were not alone in the garden.

Down the centre of the central garden-path, preceded by a blue cloud from a cigarette, was walking a gentleman who evidently understood all the relish of a garden in the very early morning. He was a slim yet satisfied figure, clad in a suit of pale-grey tweed, so subdued that the pattern was imperceptible — a costume that was casual but not by any means careless. His face, which was reflective and somewhat over-refined, was the face of a quite elderly man, though his stringy hair and moustache were still quite yellow. A double eyeglass, with a broad, black ribbon, drooped from his aquiline nose, and he smiled, as he communed with himself, with a self-content which was rare and almost irritating. The straw panama on his head was many shades shabbier than his clothes, as if he had caught it up by accident.

It needed the full shock of the huge shadow of MacIan, falling across his sunlit path, to rouse him from his smiling reverie. When this had fallen on him he lifted his head a little and blinked at the intruders with short-sighted benevolence, but with far less surprise than might have been expected. He was a gentleman; that is, he had social presence of mind, whether for kindness or for insolence.

"Can I do anything for you?" he said, at last.

MacIan bowed. "You can extend to us your pardon," he said, for he also came of a whole race of gentlemen — of gentlemen without shirts to their backs. "I am afraid we are trespassing. We have just come over the wall."

"Over the wall?" repeated the smiling old gentleman, still without letting his surprise come uppermost.

"I suppose I am not wrong, sir," continued MacIan, "in supposing that these grounds inside the wall belong to you?"

The man in the panama looked at the ground and smoked thoughtfully for a few moments, after which he said, with a sort of matured conviction:

"Yes, certainly; the grounds inside the wall really belong to me, and the grounds outside the wall, too."

"A large proprietor, I imagine," said Turnbull, with a truculent eye.

"Yes," answered the old gentleman, looking at him with a steady smile. "A large proprietor."

Turnbull's eye grew even more offensive, and he began biting his red beard; but MacIan seemed to recognise a type with which he could deal and continued quite easily:

"I am sure that a man like you will not need to be told that one sees and does a good many things that do not get into the newspapers. Things which, on the whole, had better not get into the newspapers."

The smile of the large proprietor broadened for a moment under his loose, light moustache, and the other continued with increased confidence:

"One sometimes wants to have it out with another man. The police won't allow it in the streets — and then there's the County Council — and in the fields even nothing's allowed but posters of pills. But in a gentleman's garden, now —"

The strange gentleman smiled again and said, easily enough: "Do you want to fight? What do you want to fight about?"

MacIan had understood his man pretty well up to that point; an instinct common to all men with the aristocratic tradition of Europe had guided him. He knew that the kind of man who in his own back garden wears good clothes and spoils them with a bad hat is not the kind of man who has an abstract horror of illegal actions or violence or the evasion of the police. But a man may understand ragging and yet be very far from understanding religious ragging. This seeming host of theirs might comprehend a quarrel of husband and lover or a difficulty at cards or even escape from a pursuing tailor; but it still remained doubtful whether he would feel the earth fail under him in that earthquake instant when the Virgin is compared to a goddess of Mesopotamia. Even MacIan, therefore (whose tact was far from being his strong point), felt the necessity for some compromise in the mode of approach. At last he said, and even then with hesitation:

"We are fighting about God; there can be nothing so important as that."

The tilted eyeglasses of the old gentleman fell abruptly from his nose, and he thrust his aristocratic chin so far forward that his lean neck seemed to shoot out longer like a telescope.

"About God?" he queried, in a key completely new.

"Look here!" cried Turnbull, taking his turn roughly, "I'll tell you what it's all about. I think that there's no God. I take it that it's nobody's business but mine — or God's, if there is one. This young gentleman from the Highlands happens to think that it's his business. In consequence, he first takes a walking-stick and smashes my shop; then he takes the same walking-stick and tries to smash me. To this I naturally object. I suggest that if it comes to that we should both have sticks. He improves on the suggestion and proposes that we should both have steel-pointed sticks. The police (with characteristic unreasonableness) will not accept either of our proposals; the result is that we run about dodging the police and have jumped over your garden-wall into your magnificent garden to throw ourselves on your magnificent hospitality."

The face of the old gentleman had grown redder and redder during this address, but it was still smiling; and when he broke out it was with a kind of guffaw.

"So you really want to fight with drawn swords in my garden," he asked, "about whether there is really a God?"

"Why not?" said MacIan, with his simple monstrosity of speech; "all man's worship began when the Garden of Eden was founded."

"Yes, by ——!" said Turnbull, with an oath, "and ended when the Zoölogical Gardens were founded."

"In this garden! In my presence!" cried the stranger, stamping up and down the gravel and choking with laughter, "whether there is a God!" And he went stamping up and down the garden, making it echo with his unintelligible laughter. Then he came back to them more composed and wiping his eyes.

"Why, how small the world is!" he cried at last. "I can settle the whole matter. Why, I am God!"

And he suddenly began to kick and wave his well-clad legs about the lawn.

"You are what?" repeated Turnbull, in a tone which is beyond description.

"Why, God, of course!" answered the other, thoroughly amused. "How funny it is to think that you have tumbled over a garden-wall and fallen exactly on the right person! You might have gone floundering about in all sorts of churches and chapels and colleges and schools of philosophy looking for some evidence of the existence of God. Why, there is no evidence, except seeing him. And now you've seen him. You've seen him dance!"

And the obliging old gentleman instantly stood on one leg without relaxing at all the grave and cultured benignity of his expression.

"I understood that this garden —— " began the bewildered MacIan.

"Quite so! Quite so!" said the man on one leg, nodding gravely. "I said this garden belonged to me and the land outside it. So they do. So does the country beyond that and the sea beyond that and all the rest of the earth. So does the moon. So do the sun and stars." And he added, with a smile of apology: "You see, I'm God."

Turnbull and MacIan looked at him for one moment with a sort of notion that perhaps he was not too old to be merely playing the fool. But after staring steadily for an instant Turnbull saw the hard and horrible earnestness in the man's eyes behind all his empty animation. Then Turnbull looked very gravely at the strict gravel walks and the gay flower-beds and the long rectangular red-brick building, which the mist had left evident beyond them. Then he looked at MacIan.

Almost at the same moment another man came walking quickly round the regal clump of rhododendrons. He had the look of a prosperous banker, wore a good tall silk hat, was almost stout enough to burst the buttons of a fine frock-coat; but he was talking to himself, and one of his elbows had a singular outward jerk as he went by.

CHAPTER XIV

A MUSEUM OF SOULS

THE MAN WITH the good hat and the jumping elbow went by very quickly; yet the man with the bad hat, who thought he was God, overtook him. He ran after him and jumped over a bed of geraniums to catch him.

"I beg your Majesty's pardon," he said, with mock humility, "but here is a quarrel which you ought really to judge."

Then as he led the heavy, silk-hatted man back toward the group, he caught MacIan's ear in order to whisper: "This poor gentleman is mad; he thinks he is Edward VII." At this the self-appointed Creator slightly winked. "Of course you won't trust him much; come to me for everything. But in my position one has to meet so many people. One has to be broadminded."

The big banker in the black frock-coat and hat was standing quite grave and dignified on the lawn, save for his slight twitch of one limb, and he did not seem by any means unworthy of the part which the other promptly forced upon him.

"My dear fellow," said the man in the straw hat, "these two gentlemen are going to fight a duel of the utmost importance. Your own royal position and my much humbler one surely indicate us as the proper seconds. Seconds — yes, seconds —— " and here the speaker was once more shaken with his old malady of laughter.

"Yes, you and I are both seconds — and these two gentlemen can obviously fight in front of us. You, he-he, are the king. I am God; really, they could hardly have better supporters. They have come to the right place."

Then Turnbull, who had been staring with a frown at the fresh turf, burst out with a rather bitter laugh and cried, throwing his red head in the air:

"Yes, by God, MacIan, I think we have come to the right place!" And MacIan answered, with an adamantine stupidity:

"Any place is the right place where they will let us do it."

118

There was a long stillness, and their eyes involuntarily took in the landscape, as they had taken in all the landscapes of their everlasting combat; the bright, square garden behind the shop; the whole lift and leaning of the side of Hampstead Heath; the little garden of the decadent choked with flowers; the square of sand beside the sea at sunrise. They both felt at the same moment all the breadth and blossoming beauty of that paradise, the coloured trees, the natural and restful nooks and also the great wall of stone — more awful than the wall of China — from which no flesh could flee.

Turnbull was moodily balancing his sword in his hand as the other spoke; then he started, for a mouth whispered quite close to his ear. With a softness incredible in any cat, the huge, heavy man in the black hat and frock-coat had crept across the lawn from his own side and was saying in his ear: "Don't trust that second of yours. He's mad and not so mad, either; for he's frightfully cunning and sharp. Don't believe the story he tells you about why I hate him. I know the story he'll tell; I overheard it when the housekeeper was talking to the postman. It's too long to talk about now, and I expect we're watched, but——"

Something in Turnbull made him want suddenly to be sick on the grass; the mere healthy and heathen horror of the unclean; the mere inhumane hatred of the inhuman state of madness. He seemed to hear all round him the hateful whispers of that place, innumerable as leaves whispering in the wind, and each of them telling eagerly some evil that had not happened or some terrific secret which was not true. All the rationalist and plain man revolted within him against bowing down for a moment in that forest of deception and egotistical darkness. He wanted to blow up that palace of delusions with dynamite; and in some wild way, which I will not defend, he tried to do it.

He looked across at MacIan and said: "Oh, I can't stand this!"

"Can't stand what?" asked his opponent, eyeing him doubtfully.

"Shall we say the atmosphere?" replied Turnbull; "one can't use uncivil expressions even to a — deity. The fact is, I don't like having God for my second."

"Sir!" said that being in a state of great offence, "in my position I am not used to having my favours refused. Do you know who I am?"

The editor of "The Atheist" turned upon him like one who has lost all patience, and exploded: "Yes, you are God, aren't you?" he said, abruptly, "why do we have two sets of teeth?"

"Teeth?" spluttered the genteel lunatic; "teeth?"

"Yes," cried Turnbull, advancing on him swiftly and with animated gestures, "why does teething hurt? Why do growing pains hurt? Why are measles catching? Why does a rose have thorns? Why do rhinoceroses have horns? Why is the horn on the top of the nose? Why haven't I a horn on the top of my nose, eh?" And he struck the bridge of his nose smartly with his forefinger to indicate the place of the omission and then wagged the finger menacingly at the Creator.

"I've often wanted to meet you," he resumed, sternly, after a pause, "to hold you accountable for all the idiocy and cruelty of this muddled and meaningless world of yours. You make a hundred seeds and only one bears fruit. You make a million worlds and only one seems inhabited. What do you mean by it, eh? What do you mean by it?"

The unhappy lunatic had fallen back before this quite novel form of attack, and lifted his burnt-out cigarette almost like one warding off a blow. Turnbull went on like a torrent.

"A man died yesterday in Ealing. You murdered him. A girl had the toothache in Croydon. You gave it her. Fifty sailors were drowned off Selsey Bill. You scuttled their ship. What have you got to say for yourself, eh?"

The representative of omnipotence looked as if he had left most of these things to his subordinates; he passed a hand over his wrinkling brow and said in a voice much saner than any he had yet used:

"Well, if you dislike my assistance, of course — perhaps the other gentleman — "

"The other gentleman," cried Turnbull, scornfully, "is a submissive and loyal and obedient gentleman. He likes the people who wear crowns, whether of diamonds or of stars. He believes in the divine right of kings, and it is appropriate enough that he should have the king for his second. But it is not appropriate to me that I should have God for my second. God is not good enough. I dislike and I deny the divine right of kings. But I dislike more and I deny more the divine right of divinity."

Then after a pause in which he swallowed his passion, he said to MacIan: "You have got the right second, anyhow."

The Highlander did not answer, but stood as if thunderstruck with one long and heavy thought. Then at last he turned abruptly to his second in the silk hat and said: "Who are you?"

The man in the silk hat blinked and bridled in affected surprise, like one who was in truth accustomed to be doubted.

"I am King Edward VII," he said, with shaky arrogance. "Do you doubt my word?"

"I do not doubt it in the least," answered MacIan.

"Then, why," said the large man in the silk hat, trembling from head to foot, "why do you wear your hat before the king?"

"Why should I take it off," retorted MacIan, with equal heat, "before a usurper?"

Turnbull swung round on his heel. "Well, really," he said, "I thought at least you were a loyal subject."

"I am the only loyal subject," answered the Gael. "For nearly thirty years I have walked these islands and have not found another."

"You are always hard to follow," remarked Turnbull, genially, "and sometimes so much so as to be hardly worth following."

"I alone am loyal," insisted MacIan; "for I alone am in rebellion. I am ready at any instant to restore the Stuarts. I am ready at any instant to defy the Hanoverian brood—and I defy it now even when face to face with the actual ruler of the enormous British Empire!"

And folding his arms and throwing back his lean, hawklike face, he haughtily confronted the man with the formal frock-coat and the eccentric elbow.

"What right had you stunted German squires," he cried, "to interfere in a quarrel between Scotch and English and Irish gentlemen? Who made you, whose fathers could not splutter English while they walked in Whitehall, who made you the judge between the republic of Sidney and the monarchy of Montrose? What had your sires to do with England that they should have the foul offering of the blood of Derwentwater and the heart of Jimmy Dawson? Where are the corpses of Culloden? Where is the blood of Lochiel?" MacIan advanced upon his opponent with a bony and pointed finger, as if indicating the exact pocket in which the blood of that Cameron was probably kept; and Edward VII fell back a few paces in considerable confusion.

"What good have you ever done to us?" he continued in harsher and harsher accents, forcing the other back toward the flower-beds. "What good have you ever done, you race of German sausages? Yards of barbarian etiquette, to throttle the freedom of aristocracy! Gas of northern metaphysics to blow up Broad Church bishops like balloons. Bad pictures and bad manners and pantheism and the Albert Memorial. Go back to Hanover, you humbug! Go to——"

Before the end of this tirade the arrogance of the monarch had entirely given way; he had fairly turned tail and was trundling away down the path. MacIan strode after him still preaching and flourishing his large, lean hands. The other two remained in the centre of the lawn—Turnbull in convulsions of laughter, the lunatic in convulsions of disgust. Almost at the same moment a third figure came stepping swiftly across the lawn.

The advancing figure walked with a stoop, and yet somehow flung his forked and narrow beard forward. That carefully cut and pointed yellow beard was, indeed, the most emphatic thing about him. When he clasped his hands behind him, under the tails of his coat, he would wag his beard at a man like a big forefinger. It performed almost all his gestures; it was more important than the glittering eyeglasses through which he looked or the beautiful bleating voice in which he spoke. His face and neck were of a lusty red, but lean and stringy; he always wore his expensive gold-rim eyeglasses slightly askew upon his aquiline nose; and he always showed two gleaming foreteeth under his moustache, in a smile so perpetual as to earn the reputation of a sneer. But for the crooked glasses his dress was always exquisite; and but for the smile he was perfectly and perennially depressed.

"Don't you think," said the new-comer, with a sort of supercilious entreaty, "that we had better all come in to breakfast? It is such a mistake to wait for breakfast. It spoils one's temper so much."

"Quite so," replied Turnbull, seriously.

"There seems almost to have been a little quarrelling here," said the man with the goatish beard.

"It is rather a long story," said Turnbull, smiling. "Originally it might be called a phase in the quarrel between science and religion."

The new-comer started slightly, and Turnbull replied to the question on his face.

"Oh, yes," he said, "I am science!"

"I congratulate you heartily," answered the other, "I am Doctor Quayle."

Turnbull's eyes did not move, but he realised that the man in the panama hat had lost all his ease of a landed proprietor and had withdrawn to a distance of thirty yards, where he stood glaring with all the contraction of fear and hatred that can stiffen a cat.

·   ·   ·   ·   ·

MacIan was sitting somewhat disconsolately on a stump of tree, his large black head half buried in his large brown hands, when Turnbull strode up to him chewing a cigarette. He did not look up, but his comrade and enemy addressed him like one who must free himself of his feelings.

"Well, I hope, at any rate," he said, "that you like your precious religion now. I hope you like the society of this poor devil whom your damned tracts and hymns and priests have driven out of his wits. Five men in this place, they tell me, five men in this place who might have been fathers of families, and every one of them thinks he is God the Father. Oh! you may talk about the ugliness of science, but there is no one here who thinks he is Protoplasm."

"They naturally prefer a bright part," said MacIan, wearily. "Protoplasm is not worth going mad about."

"At least," said Turnbull, savagely, "it was your Jesus Christ who started all this bosh about being God."

For one instant MacIan opened the eyes of battle; then his tightened lips took a crooked smile and he said, quite calmly:

"No, the idea is older; it was Satan who first said that he was God."

"Then, what," asked Turnbull, very slowly, as he softly picked a flower, "what is the difference between Christ and Satan?"

"It is quite simple," replied the Highlander. "Christ descended into hell; Satan fell into it."

"Does it make much odds?" asked the free-thinker.

"It makes all the odds," said the other. "One of them wanted to go up and went down; the other wanted to go down and went up. A god can be humble, a devil can only be humbled."

"Why are you always wanting to humble a man?" asked Turnbull, knitting his brows. "It affects me as ungenerous."

"Why were you wanting to humble a god when you found him in this garden?" asked MacIan.

"That was an extreme case of impudence," said Turnbull.

"Granting the man his almighty pretensions, I think he was very modest," said MacIan. "It is we who are arrogant, who know we are only men. The ordinary man in the street is more of a monster than that poor fellow; for the man in the street treats himself as God Almighty when he knows he isn't. He expects the universe to turn round him, though he knows he isn't the centre."

"Well," said Turnbull, sitting down on the grass, "this is a digression, anyhow. What I want to point out is, that your faith does end in asylums and my science doesn't."

"Doesn't it, by George!" cried MacIan, scornfully. "There are a few men here who are mad on God and a few who are mad on the Bible. But I bet there are many more who are simply mad on madness."

"Do you really believe it?" asked the other.

"Scores of them, I should say," answered MacIan. "Fellows who have read medical books or fellows whose fathers and uncles had something hereditary in their heads — the whole air they breathe is mad."

"All the same," said Turnbull, shrewdly, "I bet you haven't found a madman of that sort."

"I bet I have!" cried Evan, with unusual animation. "I've been walking about the garden talking to a poor chap all the morning. He's simply been broken down and driven raving by your damned science. Talk about believing one is God — why, it's quite an old, comfortable, fireside fancy compared with the sort of things this fellow believes. He believes that there is a God, but that he is better than God. He says God will be afraid to face him. He says one is always progressing beyond the best. He put his arm in mine and whispered in my ear, as if it were the apocalypse: 'Never trust a God that you can't improve on.'"

"What can he have meant?" said the atheist, with all his logic awake. "Obviously one should not trust any God that one can improve on."

"It is the way he talks," said MacIan, almost indifferently; "but he says rummier things than that. He says that a man's doctor ought to decide what woman he marries; and he says that children ought not to be brought up by their parents, because a physical partiality will then distort the judgment of the educator."

"Oh, dear!" said Turnbull, laughing, "you have certainly come across a pretty bad case, and incidentally proved your own. I suppose some men do lose their wits through science as through love and other good things."

"And he says," went on MacIan, monotonously, "that he cannot see why any one should suppose that a triangle is a three-sided figure. He says that on some higher plane —— "

Turnbull leapt to his feet as by an electric shock. "I never could have believed," he cried, "that you had humour enough to tell a lie. You've gone a bit too far, old man, with your little joke. Even in a lunatic asylum there can't be anybody who, having thought about the matter, thinks that a triangle has not got three sides. If he exists he must be a new era in human psychology. But he doesn't exist."

"I will go and fetch him," said MacIan, calmly; "I left the poor fellow wandering about by the nasturtium bed."

MacIan vanished, and in a few moments returned, trailing with him his own discovery among lunatics, who was a slender man with a fixed smile and an unfixed and rolling head. He had a goatlike beard just long enough to be shaken in a strong wind. Turnbull sprang to his feet and was like one who is speechless through choking a sudden shout of laughter.

"Why, you great donkey," he shouted, in an ear-shattering whisper, "that's not one of the patients at all. That's one of the doctors."

Evan looked back at the leering head with the long-pointed beard and repeated the word inquiringly: "One of the doctors?"

"Oh, you know what I mean," said Turnbull, impatiently. "The medical authorities of the place."

Evan was still staring back curiously at the beaming and bearded creature behind him.

"The mad doctors," said Turnbull, shortly.

"Quite so," said MacIan.

After a rather restless silence Turnbull plucked MacIan by the elbow and pulled him aside.

"For goodness sake," he said, "don't offend this fellow; he may be as mad as ten hatters, if you like, but he has us between his finger and thumb. This is the very time he appointed to talk with us about our — well, our exeat."

"But what can it matter?" asked the wondering MacIan. "He can't keep us in the asylum. We're not mad."

"Jackass!" said Turnbull, heartily, "of course we're not mad. Of course, if we are medically examined and the thing is thrashed out, they will find we are not mad. But don't you see that if the thing is thrashed out it will mean letters to this reference and telegrams to that; and at the first word of who we are, we shall be taken out of a madhouse, where we may smoke, to a gaol, where we mayn't. No, if we manage this very quietly, he may merely let us out at the front door as stray revellers. If there's half an hour of inquiry, we are cooked."

MacIan looked at the grass frowningly for a few seconds, and then said in a new, small and childish voice: "I am awfully stupid, Mr. Turnbull; you must be patient with me."

Turnbull caught Evan's elbow again with quite another gesture. "Come," he cried, with the harsh voice of one who hides emotion, "come and let us be tactful in chorus."

The doctor with the pointed beard was already slanting it forward at a more than usually acute angle, with the smile that expressed expectancy.

"I hope I do not hurry you, gentlemen," he said, with the faintest suggestion of a sneer at their hurried consultation, "but I believe you wanted to see me at half-past eleven."

"I am most awfully sorry, doctor," said Turnbull, with ready amiability; "I never meant to keep you waiting; but the silly accident that has landed us in your garden may have some rather serious consequences to our friends elsewhere, and my friend here was just drawing my attention to some of them."

"Quite so! Quite so!" said the doctor, hurriedly. "If you really want to put anything before me, I can give you a few moments in my consulting room."

He led them rapidly into a small but imposing apartment, which seemed to be built and furnished entirely in red varnished wood. There was one desk occupied with carefully docketed papers; and there were several chairs of the red varnished wood — though of different shape. All along the wall ran something that might have been a bookcase, only that it was not filled with books, but with flat, oblong slabs or cases of the same polished dark-red consistency. What those flat wooden cases were they could form no conception.

The doctor sat down with a polite impatience on his professional perch; MacIan remained standing, but Turnbull threw himself almost with luxury into a hard wooden arm-chair.

"This is a most absurd business, doctor," he said, "and I am ashamed to take up the time of busy professional men with such pranks from outside. The plain fact is, that he and I and a pack of silly men and girls have organised a game across this part of the country — a sort of combination of hare and hounds and hide and seek — I daresay you've heard of it. We are the hares, and, seeing your high wall look so inviting, we tumbled over it, and naturally were a little startled with what we found on the other side."

"Quite so!" said the doctor, mildly. "I can understand that you were startled."

Turnbull had expected him to ask what place was the headquarters of the new exhilarating game, and who were the male and female enthusiasts who had brought it to such perfection; in fact, Turnbull was busy making up these personal and topographical particulars. As the doctor did not ask the question, he grew slightly uneasy, and risked the question: "I hope you will accept my assurance that the thing was an accident and that no intrusion was meant."

"Oh, yes, sir," replied the doctor, smiling, "I accept everything that you say."

"In that case," said Turnbull, rising genially, "we must not further interrupt your important duties. I suppose there will be some one to let us out?"

"No," said the doctor, still smiling steadily and pleasantly, "there will be no one to let you out."

"Can we let ourselves out, then?" asked Turnbull, in some surprise.

"Why, of course not," said the beaming scientist; "think how dangerous that would be in a place like this."

"Then, how the devil are we to get out?" cried Turnbull, losing his manners for the first time.

"It is a question of time, of receptivity, and treatment," said the doctor, arching his eyebrows indifferently. "I do not regard either of your cases as incurable."

And with that the man of the world was struck dumb, and, as in all intolerable moments, the word was with the unworldly.

MacIan took one stride to the table, leant across it, and said: "We can't stop here, we're not mad people!"

"We don't use the crude phrase," said the doctor, smiling at his patent-leather boots.

"But you *can't* think us mad," thundered MacIan. "You never saw us before. You know nothing about us. You haven't even examined us."

The doctor threw back his head and beard. "Oh, yes," he said, "very thoroughly."

"But you can't shut a man up on your mere impressions without documents or certificates or anything?"

The doctor got languidly to his feet. "Quite so," he said. "You certainly ought to see the documents."

He went across to the curious mock bookshelves and took down one of the flat mahogany cases. This he opened with a curious key at his watch-chain, and laying back a flap revealed a quire of foolscap covered with close but quite clear writing. The first three words were in such large copy-book hand that they caught the eye even at a distance. They were: "MacIan, Evan Stuart."

Evan bent his angry eagle face over it; yet something blurred it and he could never swear he saw it distinctly. He saw something that began: "Prenatal influences predisposing to mania. Grandfather believed in return of the Stuarts. Mother carried bone of St. Eulalia with which she touched children in sickness. Marked religious mania at early age ——"

Evan fell back and fought for his speech. "Oh!" he burst out at last. "Oh! if all this world I have walked in had been as sane as my mother was."

Then he compressed his temples with his hands, as if to crush them. And then lifted suddenly a face that looked fresh and young, as if he had dipped and washed it in some holy well.

"Very well," he cried; "I will take the sour with the sweet. I will pay the penalty of having enjoyed God in this monstrous modern earth that cannot enjoy man or beast. I will die happy in your madhouse, only because I know what I know. Let it be granted, then—MacIan is a mystic; MacIan is a maniac. But this honest shopkeeper and editor whom I have dragged on my inhuman escapades, you cannot keep him. He will go free, thank God, he is not down in any damned document. His ancestor, I am certain, did not die at Culloden. His mother, I swear, had no relics. Let my friend out of your front door, and as for me ——"

The doctor had already gone across to the laden shelves, and after a few minutes' shortsighted peering, had pulled down another parallelogram of dark-red wood.

This also he unlocked on the table, and with the same unerring egotistic eye one of the company saw the words, written in large letters: "Turnbull, James."

Hitherto Turnbull himself had somewhat scornfully surrendered his part in the whole business; but he was too honest and unaffected not to start at his own name. After the name, the inscription appeared to run: "Unique case of Eleutheromania. Parentage, as so often in such cases, prosaic and healthy. Eleutheromaniac signs occurred early, however, leading him to attach himself to the individualist Bradlaugh. Recent outbreak of pure anarchy ——"

Turnbull slammed the case to, almost smashing it, and said with a burst of savage laughter: "Oh! come along, MacIan; I don't care so much, even about getting out of the madhouse, if only we get out of this room. You were right enough, MacIan, when you spoke about — about mad doctors."

Somehow they found themselves outside in the cool, green garden, and then, after a stunned silence, Turnbull said: "There is one thing that was puzzling me all the time, and I understand it now."

"What do you mean?" asked Evan.

"No man by will or wit," answered Turnbull, "can get out of this garden; and yet we got into it merely by jumping over a garden-wall. The whole thing explains itself easily enough. That undefended wall was an open trap. It was a trap laid for the two celebrated lunatics. They saw us get in right enough. And they will see that we do not get out."

Evan gazed at the garden-wall, gravely for more than a minute, and then he nodded without a word.

CHAPTER XV

THE DREAM OF MACIAN

THE SYSTEM OF espionage in the asylum was so effective and complete that in practice the patients could often enjoy a sense of almost complete solitude. They could stray up so near to the wall in an apparently unwatched garden as to find it easy to jump over it. They would only have found the error of their calculations if they had tried to jump.

Under this insulting liberty, in this artificial loneliness, Evan MacIan was in the habit of creeping out into the garden after dark — especially upon moonlight nights. The moon, indeed, was for him always a positive magnet in a manner somewhat hard to explain to those of a robuster attitude. Evidently, Apollo is to the full as poetical as Diana; but it is not a question of poetry in the matured and intellectual sense of the word. It is a question of a certain solid and childish fancy. The sun is in the strict and literal sense invisible; that is to say, that by our bodily eyes it cannot properly be seen. But the moon is a much simpler thing; a naked and nursery sort of thing. It hangs in the sky quite solid and quite silver and quite useless; it is one huge celestial snowball. It was at least some such infantile facts and fancies which led Evan again and again during his dehumanised imprisonment to go out as if to shoot the moon.

He was out in the garden on one such luminous and ghostly night, when the steady moonshine toned down all the colours of the garden until almost the strongest tints to be seen were the strong soft blue of the sky and the large lemon moon. He was walking with his face turned up to it in that rather half-witted fashion which might have excused the error of his keepers; and as he gazed he became aware of something little and lustrous flying close to the lustrous orb, like a bright chip knocked off the moon. At first he thought it was a mere sparkle or refraction in his own eyesight; he blinked and cleared his eyes. Then he thought it was a falling star; only it did not fall. It jerked awkwardly up and down in a way unknown among meteors and strangely reminiscent of the works of man. The next moment the thing drove right across the moon, and from being silver upon blue, suddenly became black upon silver; then although it passed the field of light in a flash its outline was unmistakable though eccentric. It was a flying ship.

The vessel took one long and sweeping curve across the sky and came nearer and nearer to MacIan, like a steam-engine coming round a bend. It was of pure white steel, and in the moon it gleamed like the armour of Sir Galahad. The simile of such virginity is not inappropriate; for, as it grew larger and larger and lower and lower, Evan saw that the only figure in it was robed in white from head to foot and crowned with snow-white hair, on which the moonshine lay like a benediction. The figure stood so still that he could easily have supposed it to be a statue. Indeed, he thought it was until it spoke.

"Evan," said the voice, and it spoke with the simple authority of some forgotten father revisiting his children, "you have remained here long enough, and your sword is wanted elsewhere."

"Wanted for what?" asked the young man, accepting the monstrous event with a queer and clumsy naturalness; "what is my sword wanted for?"

"For all that you hold dear," said the man standing in the moonlight; "for the thrones of authority and for all ancient loyalty to law."

Evan looked up at the lunar orb again as if in irrational appeal — a moon calf bleating to his mother the moon. But the face of Luna seemed as witless as his own; there is no help in nature against the supernatural; and he looked again at the tall marble figure that might have been made out of solid moonlight.

Then he said in a loud voice: "Who are you?" and the next moment was seized by a sort of choking terror lest his question should be answered. But the unknown preserved an impenetrable silence for a long space and then only answered: "I must not say who I am until the end of the world; but I may say what I am. I am the law."

And he lifted his head so that the moon smote full upon his beautiful and ancient face.

The face was the face of a Greek god grown old, but not grown either weak or ugly; there was nothing to break its regularity except a rather long chin with a cleft in it, and this rather added distinction than lessened beauty. His strong, well-opened eyes were very brilliant but quite colourless like steel.

MacIan was one of those to whom a reverence and self-submission in ritual come quite easy, and are ordinary things. It was not artificial in him to bend slightly to this solemn apparition or to lower his voice when he said: "Do you bring me some message?"

"I do bring you a message," answered the man of moon and marble. "The king has returned."

Evan did not ask for or require any explanation. "I suppose you can take me to the war," he said, and the silent silver figure only bowed its head again. MacIan clambered into the silver boat, and it rose upward to the stars.

To say that it rose to the stars is no mere metaphor, for the sky had cleared to that occasional and astonishing transparency in which one can see plainly both stars and moon.

As the white-robed figure went upward in his white chariot, he said quite quietly to Evan: "There is an answer to all the folly talked about equality. Some stars are big and some small; some stand still and some circle round them as they stand. They can be orderly, but they cannot be equal."

"They are all very beautiful," said Evan, as if in doubt.

"They are all beautiful," answered the other, "because each is in his place and owns his superior. And now England will be beautiful after the same fashion. The earth will be as beautiful as the heavens, because our kings have come back to us."

"The Stuart —— " began Evan, earnestly.

"Yes," answered the old man, "that which has returned is Stuart and yet older than Stuart. It is Capet and Plantagenet and Pendragon. It is all that good old time of which proverbs tell, that golden reign of Saturn against which gods and men were rebels. It is all that was ever lost by insolence and overwhelmed in rebellion. It is your own forefather, MacIan with the broken sword, bleeding without hope at Culloden. It is Charles refusing to answer the questions of the rebel court. It is Mary of the magic face confronting the gloomy and grasping peers and the boorish moralities of Knox. It is Richard, the last Plantagenet, giving his crown to Bolingbroke as to a common brigand. It is Arthur, overwhelmed in Lyonesse by heathen armies and dying in the mist, doubtful if ever he shall return."

"But now —— " said Evan, in a low voice.

"But now!" said the old man; "he has returned."

"Is the war still raging?" asked MacIan.

"It rages like the pit itself beyond the sea whither I am taking you," answered the other. "But in England the king enjoys his own again. The people are once more taught and ruled as is best; they are happy knights, happy squires, happy servants, happy serfs, if you will; but free at last of that load of vexation and lonely vanity which was called being a citizen."

"Is England, indeed, so secure?" asked Evan.

"Look out and see," said the guide. "I fancy you have seen this place before."

They were driving through the air toward one region of the sky where the hollow of night seemed darkest and which was quite without stars. But against this black background there sprang up, picked out in glittering silver, a dome and a cross. It seemed that it was really newly covered with silver, which in the strong moonlight was like white flame. But, however, covered or painted, Evan had no difficulty in knowing the place again. He saw the great thoroughfare that sloped upward to the base of its huge pedestal of steps. And he wondered whether the little shop was still by the side of it and whether its window had been mended.

As the flying ship swept round the dome he observed other alterations. The dome had been redecorated so as to give it a more solemn and somewhat more ecclesiastical note; the ball was draped or destroyed, and round the gallery, under the cross, ran what looked like a ring of silver statues, like the little leaden images that stood round the hat of Louis XI. Round the second gallery, at the base of the dome, ran a second rank of such images, and Evan thought there was another round the steps below. When they came closer he saw that they were figures in complete armour of steel or silver, each with a naked sword, point upward; and then he saw one of the swords move. These were not statues but an armed order of chivalry thrown in three circles round the cross. MacIan drew in his breath, as children do at anything they think utterly beautiful. For he could imagine nothing that so echoed his own visions of pontifical or chivalric art as this white dome sitting like a vast silver tiara over London, ringed with a triple crown of swords.

As they went sailing down Ludgate Hill, Evan saw that the state of the streets fully answered his companion's claim about the reintroduction of order. All the old black-coated bustle with its cockney vivacity and vulgarity had disappeared. Groups of labourers, quietly but picturesquely clad, were passing up and down in sufficiently large numbers; but it required but a few mounted men to keep the streets in order. The mounted men were not common policemen, but knights with spur and plume whose smooth and splendid armour glittered like diamond rather than steel. Only in one place — at the corner of Bouverie Street — did there appear to be a moment's confusion, and that was due to hurry rather than resistance. But one old grumbling man did not get out of the way quick enough, and the man on horseback struck him, not severely, across the shoulders with the flat of his sword.

"The soldier had no business to do that," said MacIan, sharply. "The old man was moving as quickly as he could."

"We attach great importance to discipline in the streets," said the man in white, with a slight smile.

"Discipline is not so important as justice," said MacIan.

The other did not answer.

Then after a swift silence that took them out across St. James's Park, he said: "The people must be taught to obey; they must learn their own ignorance. And I am not sure," he continued, turning his back on Evan and looking out of the prow of the ship into the darkness, "I am not sure that I agree with your little maxim about justice. Discipline for the whole society is surely more important than justice to an individual."

Evan, who was also leaning over the edge, swung round with startling suddenness and stared at the other's back.

"Discipline for society—" he repeated, very staccato, "more important—justice to individual?"

Then after a long silence he called out: "Who and what are you?"

"I am an angel," said the white-robed figure, without turning round.

"You are not a Catholic," said MacIan.

The other seemed to take no notice, but reverted to the main topic.

"In our armies up in heaven we learn to put a wholesome fear into subordinates."

MacIan sat craning his neck forward with an extraordinary and unaccountable eagerness.

"Go on!" he cried, twisting and untwisting his long, bony fingers, "go on!"

"Besides," continued he, in the prow, "you must allow for a certain high spirit and haughtiness in the superior type."

"Go on!" said Evan, with burning eyes.

"Just as the sight of sin offends God," said the unknown, "so does the sight of ugliness offend Apollo. The beautiful and princely must, of necessity, be impatient with the squalid and——"

"Why, you great fool!" cried MacIan, rising to the top of his tremendous stature, "did you think I would have doubted only for that rap with a sword? I know that noble orders have bad knights, that good knights have bad tempers, that the Church has rough priests and coarse cardinals; I have known it ever since I was born. You fool! you had only to say, 'Yes, it is rather a shame,' and I should have forgotten the affair. But I saw on your mouth the twitch of your infernal sophistry; I knew that something was wrong with you and your cathedrals. Something is wrong; everything is wrong. You are not an angel. That is, not a church. It is not the rightful king who has come home."

"That is unfortunate," said the other, in a quiet but hard voice, "because you are going to see his Majesty."

"No," said MacIan, "I am going to jump over the side."

"Do you desire death?"

"No," said Evan, quite composedly, "I desire a miracle."

"From whom do you ask it? To whom do you appeal?" said his

companion, sternly. "You have betrayed the king, renounced the cross on the cathedral, and insulted an archangel."

"I appeal to God," said Evan, and sprang up and stood upon the edge of the swaying ship.

The being in the prow turned slowly round; he looked at Evan with eyes which were like two suns, and put his hand to his mouth just too late to hide an awful smile.

"And how do you know," he said, "how do you know that I am not God?"

MacIan screamed. "Ah!" he cried. "Now I know who you really are. You are not God. You are not one of God's angels. But you were once."

The being's hand dropped from his mouth and Evan dropped out of the car.

CHAPTER XVI

THE DREAM OF TURNBULL

TURNBULL WAS WALKING rather rampantly up and down the garden on a gusty evening chewing his cigar and in that mood when every man suppresses an instinct to spit. He was not, as a rule, a man much acquainted with moods; and the storms and sunbursts of MacIan's soul passed before him as an impressive but unmeaning panorama, like the anarchy of Highland scenery. Turnbull was one of those men in whom a continuous appetite and industry of the intellect leave the emotions very simple and steady. His heart was in the right place; but he was quite content to leave it there. It was his head that was his hobby. His mornings and evenings were marked not by impulses or thirsty desires, not by hope or by heart-break; they were filled with the fallacies he had detected, the problems he had made plain, the adverse theories he had wrestled with and thrown, the grand generalisations he had justified. But even the cheerful inner life of a logician may be upset by a lunatic asylum, to say nothing of whiffs of memory from a lady in Jersey, and the little red-bearded man on this windy evening was in a dangerous frame of mind.

Plain and positive as he was, the influence of earth and sky may have been greater on him than he imagined; and the weather that walked the world at that moment was as red and angry as Turnbull. Long strips and swirls of tattered and tawny cloud were dragged downward to the west exactly as torn red raiment would be dragged. And so strong and pitiless was the wind that it whipped away fragments of red-flowering bushes or of copper beech, and drove them also across the garden, a drift of red leaves, like the leaves of autumn, as in parody of the red and driven rags of cloud.

There was a sense in earth and heaven as of everything breaking up, and all the revolutionist in Turnbull rejoiced that it was breaking up. The trees were breaking up under the wind, even in the tall strength of their bloom: the clouds were breaking up and losing even their large heraldic shapes. Shards and shreds of copper cloud split off continually

and floated by themselves, and for some reason the truculent eye of
Turnbull was attracted to one of these careering cloudlets, which
seemed to him to career in an exaggerated manner. Also it kept its shape,
which is unusual with clouds shaken off; also its shape was of an odd
sort.

Turnbull continued to stare at it, and in a little time occurred that
crucial instant when a thing, however incredible, is accepted as a fact.
The copper cloud was tumbling down toward the earth, like some
gigantic leaf from the copper beeches. And as it came nearer it was
evident, first, that it was not a cloud, and, second, that it was not itself of
the colour of copper; only, being burnished like a mirror, it had reflected
the red-brown colours of the burning clouds. As the thing whirled like a
wind-swept leaf down toward the wall of the garden it was clear that it
was some sort of air-ship made of metal, and slapping the air with big
broad fins of steel. When it came about a hundred feet above the
garden, a shaggy, lean figure leapt up in it, almost black against the
bronze and scarlet of the west, and, flinging out a kind of hook or
anchor, caught on to the green apple-tree just under the wall; and from
that fixed holding ground the ship swung in the red tempest like a
captive balloon.

While our friend stood frozen for an instant by his astonishment, the
queer figure in the airy car tipped the vehicle almost upside down by
leaping over the side of it, seemed to slide or drop down the rope like a
monkey, and alighted (with impossible precision and placidity) seated
on the edge of the wall, over which he kicked and dangled his legs as he
grinned at Turnbull. The wind roared in the trees yet more ruinous and
desolate, the red tails of the sunset were dragged downward like red
dragons sucked down to death, and still on the top of the asylum wall sat
the sinister figure with the grimace, swinging his feet in tune with the
tempest; while above him, at the end of its tossing or tightened cord, the
enormous iron air-ship floated as light and as little noticed as a baby's
balloon upon its string.

Turnbull's first movement after sixty motionless seconds was to turn
round and look at the large, luxuriant parallelogram of the garden and
the long, low rectangular building beyond. There was not a soul or a stir
of life within sight. And he had a quite meaningless sensation, as if there
never really had been any one else there except he since the foundation
of the world.

Stiffening in himself the masculine but mirthless courage of the
atheist, he drew a little nearer to the wall and, catching the man at a
slightly different angle of the evening light, could see his face and figure
quite plain. Two facts about him stood out in the picked colours of some
piratical schoolboy's story. The first was that his lean brown body was

bare to the belt of his loose white trousers; the other that through hygiene, affectation, or whatever other cause, he had a scarlet hand-kerchief tied tightly but somewhat aslant across his brow. After these two facts had become emphatic, others appeared sufficiently impor-tant. One was that under the scarlet rag the hair was plentiful, but white as with the last snows of mortality. Another was that under the mop of white and senile hair the face was strong, handsome, and smiling, with a well-cut profile and a long cloven chin. The length of this lower part of the face and the strange cleft in it (which gave the man, in quite another sense from the common one, a double chin) faintly spoilt the claim of the face to absolute regularity, but it greatly assisted it in wearing the expression of half-smiling and half-sneering arrogance with which it was staring at all the stones, all the flowers, but especially at the solitary man.

"What do you want?" shouted Turnbull.

"I want you, Jimmy," said the eccentric man on the wall, and with the very word he had let himself down with a leap on to the centre of the lawn, where he bounded once literally like an India-rubber ball and then stood grinning with his legs astride. The only three facts that Turnbull could now add to his inventory were that the man had an ugly-looking knife swinging at his trousers belt, that his brown feet were as bare as his bronzed trunk and arms, and that his eyes had a singular bleak brilliancy which was of no particular colour.

"Excuse my not being in evening dress," said the new-comer with an urbane smile. "We scientific men, you know— I have to work my own engines— Electrical engineer—very hot work."

"Look here," said Turnbull, sturdily clenching his fists in his trousers pockets, "I am bound to expect lunatics inside these four walls; but I do bar their coming from outside, bang out of the sunset clouds."

"And yet you came from the outside, too, Jim," said the stranger in a voice almost affectionate.

"What do you want?" asked Turnbull, with an explosion of temper as sudden as a pistol shot.

"I have already told you," said the man, lowering his voice and speaking with evident sincerity; "I want you."

"What do you want with me?"

"I want exactly what you want," said the new-comer with a new gravity. "I want the Revolution."

Turnbull looked at the fire-swept sky and the wind-stricken wood-lands, and kept on repeating the word voicelessly to himself—the word that did indeed so thoroughly express his mood of rage as it had been among those red clouds and rocking tree-tops. "Revolution!" he said to himself. "The Revolution — Yes, that is what I want right enough — anything, so long as it is a Revolution."

To some cause he could never explain he found himself completing the sentence on the top of the wall, having automatically followed the stranger so far. But when the stranger silently indicated the rope that led to the machine, he found himself pausing and saying: "I can't leave MacIan behind in this den."

"We are going to destroy the Pope and all the kings," said the newcomer. "Would it be wiser to take him with us?"

Somehow the muttering Turnbull found himself in the flying ship also, and it swung up into the sunset.

"All the great rebels have been very little rebels," said the man with the red scarf. "They have been like fourth-form boys who sometimes venture to hit a fifth-form boy. That was all the worth of their French Revolution and regicide. The boys never really dared to defy the schoolmaster."

"Whom do you mean by the schoolmaster?" asked Turnbull.

"You know whom I mean," answered the strange man, as he lay back on cushions and looked up into the angry sky.

They seemed rising into stronger and stronger sunlight, as if it were sunrise rather than sunset. But when they looked down at the earth they saw it growing darker and darker. The lunatic asylum in its large rectangular grounds spread below them in a foreshortened and infantile plan, and looked for the first time the grotesque thing that it was. But the clear colours of the plan were growing darker every moment. The masses of rose or rhododendron deepened from crimson to violet. The maze of gravel pathways faded from gold to brown. By the time they had risen a few hundred feet higher nothing could be seen of that darkening landscape except the lines of lighted windows, each one of which, at least, was the light of one lost intelligence. But on them as they swept upward better and braver winds seemed to blow, and on them the ruby light of evening seemed struck, and splashed like red spurts from the grapes of Dionysus. Below them the fallen lights were literally the fallen stars of servitude. And above them all the red and raging clouds were like the leaping flags of liberty.

The man with the cloven chin seemed to have a singular power of understanding thoughts; for, as Turnbull felt the whole universe tilt and turn over his head, the stranger said exactly the right thing.

"Doesn't it seem as if everything were being upset?" said he; "and if once everything is upset, He will be upset on top of it."

Then, as Turnbull made no answer, his host continued:

"That is the really fine thing about space. It is topsy-turvy. You have only to climb far enough toward the morning star to feel that you are coming down to it. You have only to dive deep enough into the abyss to feel that you are rising. That is the only glory of this universe — it is a giddy universe."

Then, as Turnbull was still silent, he added:

"The heavens are full of revolution — of the real sort of revolution. All the high things sinking low and all the big things looking small. All the people who think they are aspiring find they are falling head foremost. And all the people who think they are condescending find they are climbing up a precipice. That is the intoxication of space. That is the only joy of eternity — doubt. There is only one pleasure the angels can possibly have in flying, and that is, that they do not know whether they are on their head or their heels."

Then, finding his companion still mute, he fell himself into a smiling and motionless meditation, at the end of which he said suddenly:

"So MacIan converted you?"

Turnbull sprang up as if spurning the steel car from under his feet. "Converted me!" he cried. "What the devil do you mean? I have known him for a month, and I have not retracted a single —— "

"This Catholicism is a curious thing," said the man of the cloven chin in uninterrupted reflectiveness, leaning his elegant elbows over the edge of the vessel; "it soaks and weakens men without their knowing it, just as I fear it has soaked and weakened you."

Turnbull stood in an attitude which might well have meant pitching the other man out of the flying ship.

"I am an atheist," he said, in a stifled voice. "I have always been an atheist. I am still an atheist." Then, addressing the other's indolent and indifferent back, he cried: "In God's name what do you mean?"

And the other answered without turning round:

"I mean nothing in God's name."

Turnbull spat over the edge of the car and fell back furiously into his seat.

The other continued still unruffled, and staring over the edge idly as an angler stares down at a stream.

"The truth is that we never thought that you could have been caught," he said; "we counted on you as the one red-hot revolutionary left in the world. But, of course, these men like MacIan are awfully clever, especially when they pretend to be stupid."

Turnbull leapt up again in a living fury and cried: "What have I got to do with MacIan? I believe all I ever believed, and disbelieve all I ever disbelieved. What does all this mean, and what do you want with me here?"

Then for the first time the other lifted himself from the edge of the car and faced him.

"I have brought you here," he answered, "to take part in the last war of the world."

"The last war!" repeated Turnbull, even in his dazed state a little touchy about such a dogma; "how do you know it will be the last?"

The man laid himself back in his reposeful attitude, and said:

"It is the last war, because if it does not cure the world forever, it will destroy it."

"What do you mean?"

"I only mean what you mean," answered the unknown in a temperate voice. "What was it that you always meant on those million and one nights when you walked outside your Ludgate Hill shop and shook your hand in the air?"

"Still I do not see," said Turnbull, stubbornly.

"You will soon," said the other, and abruptly bent downward one iron handle of his huge machine. The engine stopped, stooped, and dived almost as deliberately as a man bathing; in their downward rush they swept within fifty yards of a big bulk of stone that Turnbull knew only too well. The last red anger of the sunset was ended; the dome of heaven was dark; the lanes of flaring light in the streets below hardly lit up the base of the building. But he saw that it was St. Paul's Cathedral, and he saw that on the top of it the ball was still standing erect, but the cross was stricken and had fallen sideways. Then only he cared to look down into the streets, and saw that they were inflamed with uproar and tossing passions.

"We arrive at a happy moment," said the man steering the ship. "The insurgents are bombarding the city, and a cannon-ball has just hit the cross. Many of the insurgents are simple people, and they naturally regard it as a happy omen."

"Quite so," said Turnbull, in a rather colourless voice.

"Yes," replied the other. "I thought you would be glad to see your prayer answered. Of course I apologise for the word prayer."

"Don't mention it," said Turnbull.

The flying ship had come down upon a sort of curve, and was now rising again. The higher and higher it rose the broader and broader became the scenes of flame and desolation underneath.

Ludgate Hill indeed had been an uncaptured and comparatively quiet height, altered only by the startling coincidence of the cross fallen awry. All the other thoroughfares on all sides of that hill were full of the pulsation and the pain of battle, full of shaking torches and shouting faces. When at length they had risen high enough to have a bird's-eye view of the whole campaign, Turnbull was already intoxicated. He had smelt gunpowder, which was the incense of his own revolutionary religion.

"Have the people really risen?" he asked, breathlessly. "What are they fighting about?"

"The programme is rather elaborate," said his entertainer with some indifference. "I think Dr. Hertz drew it up."

Turnbull wrinkled his forehead. "Are all the poor people with the Revolution?" he asked.

The other shrugged his shoulders. "All the instructed and class-conscious part of them without exception," he replied. "There were certainly a few districts; in fact, we are passing over them just now——"

Turnbull looked down and saw that the polished car was literally lit up from underneath by the far-flung fires from below. Underneath whole squares and solid districts were in flames, like prairies or forests on fire.

"Dr. Hertz has convinced everybody," said Turnbull's cicerone in a smooth voice, "that nothing can really be done with the real slums. His celebrated maxim has been quite adopted. I mean the three celebrated sentences: 'No man should be unemployed. Employ the employables. Destroy the unemployables.' "

There was a silence, and then Turnbull said in a rather strained voice: "And do I understand that this good work is going on under here?"

"Going on splendidly," replied his companion in the heartiest voice. "You see, these people were much too tired and weak even to join the social war. They were a definite hindrance to it."

"And so you are simply burning them out?"

"It *does* seem absurdly simple," said the man, with a beaming smile, "when one thinks of all the worry and talk about helping a hopeless slave population, when the future obviously was only crying to be rid of them. There are happy babes unborn ready to burst the doors when these drivellers are swept away."

"Will you permit me to say," said Turnbull, after reflection, "that I don't like all this?"

"And will you permit me to say," said the other, with a snap, "that I don't like Mr. Evan MacIan?"

Somewhat to the speaker's surprise this did not inflame the sensitive sceptic; he had the air of thinking thoroughly, and then he said: "No, I don't think it's my friend MacIan that taught me that. I think I should always have said that I don't like this. These people have rights."

"Rights!" repeated the unknown in a tone quite indescribable. Then he added with a more open sneer: "Perhaps they also have souls."

"They have lives!" said Turnbull, sternly; "that is quite enough for me. I understood you to say that you thought life sacred."

"Yes, indeed!" cried his mentor with a sort of idealistic animation. "Yes, indeed! Life is sacred—but lives are not sacred. We are improving Life by removing lives. Can you, as a free-thinker, find any fault in that?"

"Yes," said Turnbull with brevity.

"Yet you applaud tyrannicide," said the stranger with rationalistic gaiety. "How inconsistent! It really comes to this: You approve of taking away life from those to whom it is a triumph and a pleasure. But you will not take away life from those to whom it is a burden and a toil."

Turnbull rose to his feet in the car with considerable deliberation, but his face seemed oddly pale. The other went on with enthusiasm.

"Life, yes, Life is indeed sacred!" he cried; "but new lives for old! Good lives for bad! On that very place where now there sprawls one drunken wastrel of a pavement artist more or less wishing he were dead — on that very spot there shall in the future be living pictures; there shall be golden girls and boys leaping in the sun."

Turnbull, still standing up, opened his lips. "Will you put me down, please?" he said, quite calmly, like one stopping an omnibus.

"Put you down — what do you mean?" cried his leader. "I am taking you to the front of the revolutionary war, where you will be one of the first of the revolutionary leaders."

"Thank you," replied Turnbull with the same painful constraint. "I have heard about your revolutionary war, and I think on the whole that I would rather be anywhere else."

"Do you want to be taken to a monastery," snarled the other, "with MacIan and his winking Madonnas?"

"I want to be taken to a madhouse," said Turnbull distinctly, giving the direction with a sort of precision. "I want to go back to exactly the same lunatic asylum from which I came."

"Why?" asked the unknown.

"Because I want a little sane and wholesome society," answered Turnbull.

There was a long and peculiar silence, and then the man driving the flying machine said quite coolly: "I won't take you back."

And then Turnbull said equally coolly: "Then I'll jump out of the car."

The unknown rose to his full height, and the expression in his eyes seemed to be made of ironies behind ironies, as two mirrors infinitely reflect each other. At last he said, very gravely: "Do you think I am the devil?"

"Yes," said Turnbull, violently. "For I think the devil is a dream, and so are you. I don't believe in you or your flying ship or your last fight of the world. It is all a nightmare. I say as a fact of dogma and faith that it is all a nightmare. And I will be a martyr for my faith as much as St. Catherine, for I will jump out of this ship and risk waking up safe in bed."

After swaying twice with the swaying vessel he dived over the side as one dives into the sea. For some incredible moments stars and space and planets seemed to shoot up past him as the sparks fly upward; and yet in that sickening descent he was full of some unnatural happiness. He could connect it with no idea except one that half escaped him — what Evan had said of the difference between Christ and Satan; that it was by Christ's own choice that He descended into hell.

When he again realised anything, he was lying on his elbow on the lawn of the lunatic asylum, and the last red of the sunset had not yet disappeared.

CHAPTER XVII

THE IDIOT

E VAN MacIAN WAS standing a few yards off looking at him in absolute silence.

He had not the moral courage to ask MacIan if there had been anything astounding in the manner of his coming there, nor did MacIan seem to have any question to ask, or perhaps any need to ask it. The two men came slowly toward each other, and found the same expression on each other's faces. Then, for the first time in all their acquaintance, they shook hands.

Almost as if this were a kind of unconscious signal, it brought Dr. Quayle bounding out of a door and running across the lawn.

"Oh, there you are!" he exclaimed with a relieved giggle. "Will you come inside, please? I want to speak to you both."

They followed him into his shiny wooden office where their damning record was kept. Dr. Quayle sat down on a swivel chair and swung round to face them. His carved smile had suddenly disappeared.

"I will be plain with you gentlemen," he said, abruptly; "you know quite well we do our best for everybody here. Your cases have been under special consideration, and the Master himself has decided that you ought to be treated specially and er—under somewhat simpler conditions."

"You mean treated worse, I suppose," said Turnbull, gruffly.

The doctor did not reply, and MacIan said: "I expected this." His eyes had begun to glow.

The doctor answered, looking at his desk and playing with a key: "Well, in certain cases that give anxiety—it is often better——"

"Give anxiety," said Turnbull, fiercely. "Confound your impudence! What do you mean? You imprison two perfectly sane men in a madhouse because you have made up a long word. They take it in good temper, walk and talk in your garden like monks who have found a vocation, are civil even to you, you damned druggists' hack! Behave not only more sanely than any of your patients, but more sanely than half the sane men outside, and you have the soul-stifling cheek to say that they give anxiety."

"The head of the asylum has settled it all," said Dr. Quayle, still looking down.

MacIan took one of his immense strides forward and stood over the doctor with flaming eyes.

"If the head has settled it let the head announce it," he said. "I won't take it from you. I believe you to be a low, gibbering degenerate. Let us see the head of the asylum."

"See the head of the asylum," repeated Dr. Quayle. "Certainly not."

The tall Highlander, bending over him, put one hand on his shoulder with fatherly interest.

"You don't seem to appreciate the peculiar advantages of my position as a lunatic," he said. "I could kill you with my left hand before such a rat as you could so much as squeak. And I wouldn't be hanged for it."

"I certainly agree with Mr. MacIan," said Turnbull with sobriety and perfect respectfulness, "that you had better let us see the head of the institution."

Dr. Quayle got to his feet in a mixture of sudden hysteria and clumsy presence of mind.

"Oh, certainly," he said with a weak laugh. "You can see the head of the asylum if you particularly want to." He almost ran out of the room, and the two followed swiftly on his flying coat tails. He knocked at an ordinary varnished door in the corridor. When a voice said, "Come in," MacIan's breath went hissing back through his teeth into his chest. Turnbull was more impetuous, and opened the door.

It was a neat and well-appointed room entirely lined with a medical library. At the other end of it was a ponderous and polished desk with an incandescent lamp on it, the light of which was just sufficient to show a slender, well-bred figure in an ordinary medical black frock-coat, whose head, quite silvered with age, was bent over neat piles of notes. This gentleman looked up for an instant as they entered, and the lamplight fell on his glittering spectacles and long, clean-shaven face — a face which would have been simply like an aristocrat's but that a certain lion poise of the head and long cleft in the chin made it look more like a very handsome actor's. It was only for a flash that his face was thus lifted. Then he bent his silver head over his notes once more, and said, without looking up again:

"I told you, Dr. Quayle, that these men were to go to cells B and C."

Turnbull and MacIan looked at each other, and said more than they could ever say with tongues or swords. Among other things they said that to that particular Head of the institution it was waste of time to appeal, and they followed Dr. Quayle out of the room.

The instant they stepped out into the corridor four sturdy figures stepped from four sides, pinioned them, and ran them along the galleries. They might very likely have thrown their captors right and left had they been inclined to resist, but for some nameless reason they were more inclined to laugh. A mixture of mad irony with childish curiosity made them feel quite inclined to see what next twist would be taken by their imbecile luck. They were dragged down countless cold avenues lined with glazed tiles, different only in being of different lengths and set at different angles. They were so many and so monotonous that to escape back by them would have been far harder than fleeing from the Hampton Court maze. Only the fact that windows grew fewer, coming at longer intervals, and the fact that when the windows did come they seemed shadowed and let in less light, showed that they were winding into the core or belly of some enormous building. After a little time the glazed corridors began to be lit by electricity.

At last, when they had walked nearly a mile in those white and polished tunnels, they came with quite a shock to the futile finality of a cul-de-sac. All that white and weary journey ended suddenly in an oblong space and a blank white wall. But in the white wall there were two iron doors painted white on which were written, respectively, in neat black capitals B and C.

"You go in here, sir," said the leader of the officials, quite respectfully, "and you in here."

But before the doors had clanged upon their dazed victims, MacIan had been able to say to Turnbull with a strange drawl of significance: "I wonder who A is."

Turnbull made an automatic struggle before he allowed himself to be thrown into the cell. Hence it happened that he was the last to enter, and was still full of the exhilaration of the adventures for at least five minutes after the echo of the clanging door had died away.

Then, when silence had sunk deep and nothing happened for two and a half hours, it suddenly occurred to him that this was the end of his life. He was hidden and sealed up in this little crack of stone until the flesh should fall off his bones. He was dead, and the world had won.

His cell was of an oblong shape, but very long in comparison with its width. It was just wide enough to permit the arms to be fully extended with the dumb-bells, which were hung up on the left wall, very dusty. It was, however, long enough for a man to walk one thirty-fifth part of a mile if he traversed it entirely. On the same principle a row of fixed holes, quite close together, let in to the cells by pipes what was alleged to be the freshest air. For these great scientific organisers insisted that a man should be healthy even if he was miserable. They provided a walk long enough to give him exercise and holes large enough to give him oxygen. There their interest in human nature suddenly ceased. It seemed never to have occurred to them that the benefit of exercise belongs partly to the benefit of liberty. They had not entertained the suggestion that the open air is only one of the advantages of the open sky. They administered air in secret, but in sufficient doses, as if it were a medicine. They suggested walking, as if no man had ever felt inclined to walk. Above all, the asylum authorities insisted on their own extraordinary cleanliness. Every morning, while Turnbull was still half asleep on his iron bedstead which was lifted half-way up the wall and clamped to it with iron, four sluices or metal mouths opened above him at the four corners of the chamber and washed it white of any defilement. Turnbull's solitary soul surged up against this sickening daily solemnity.

"I am buried alive!" he cried, bitterly; "they have hidden me under mountains. I shall be here till I rot. Why the blazes should it matter to them whether I am dirty or clean."

Every morning and evening an iron hatchway opened in his oblong cell, and a brown hairy hand or two thrust in a plate of perfectly cooked lentils and a big bowl of cocoa. He was not underfed any more than he was underexercised or asphyxiated. He had ample walking space, ample air, ample and even filling food. The only objection was that he had nothing to walk toward, nothing to feast about, and no reason whatever for drawing the breath of life.

Even the shape of his cell especially irritated him. It was a long, narrow parallelogram, which had a flat wall at one end and ought to have had a flat wall at the other; but that end was broken by a wedge or angle of space, like the prow of a ship. After three days of silence and cocoa, this angle at the end began to infuriate Turnbull. It maddened him to think that two lines came together and pointed at nothing. After the fifth day he was reckless, and poked his head into the corner. After twenty-five days he almost broke his head against it. Then he became quite cool and stupid again, and began to examine it like a sort of Robinson Crusoe.

Almost unconsciously it was his instinct to examine outlets, and he found himself paying particular attention to the row of holes which let in the air into his last house of life. He soon discovered that these airholes were all the ends and mouths of long leaden tubes which doubtless carried air from some remote watering-place near Margate. One evening while he was engaged in the fifth investigation he noticed something like twilight in one of these dumb mouths, as compared with the darkness of the others. Thrusting his finger in as far as it would go, he found a hole and flapping edge in the tube. This he rent open and instantly saw a light behind; it was at least certain that he had struck some other cell.

It is a characteristic of all things now called "efficient," which means mechanical and calculated, that if they go wrong at all they go entirely wrong. There is no power of retrieving a defeat, as in simpler and more living organisms. A strong gun can conquer a strong elephant, but a wounded elephant can easily conquer a broken gun. Thus the Prussian monarchy in the eighteenth century, or now, can make a strong army merely by making the men afraid. But it does it with the permanent possibility that the men may some day be more afraid of their enemies than of their officers. Thus the drainage in our cities so long as it is quite solid means a general safety, but if there is one leak it means concentrated poison — an explosion of deathly germs like dynamite, a spirit of stink. Thus, indeed, all that excellent machinery which is the swiftest thing on earth in saving human labour is also the slowest thing on earth in resisting human interference. It may be easier to get chocolate for nothing out of a shopkeeper than out an automatic machine. But if you did manage to steal the chocolate, the automatic machine would be much less likely to run after you.

Turnbull was not long in discovering this truth in connection with the cold and colossal machinery of this great asylum. He had been shaken by many spiritual states since the instant when he was pitched head foremost into that private cell which was to be his private room till death. He had felt a high fit of pride and poetry, which had ebbed away and left him deadly cold. He had known a period of mere scientific curiosity, in the course of which he examined all the tiles of his cell, with the gratifying conclusion that they were all the same shape and size; but was greatly puzzled about the angle in the wall at the end, and also about an iron peg or spike that stood out from the wall, the object of which he does not know to this day. Then he had a period of mere madness not to be written of by decent men, but only by those few dirty novelists hallooed on by the infernal huntsman to hunt down and humiliate human nature. This also passed, but left behind it a feverish distaste for many of the mere objects around him. Long after he had returned to sanity and such hopeless cheerfulness as a man might have on a desert island, he disliked the regular squares of the pattern of wall and floor and the triangle that terminated his corridor. Above all, he had a hatred, deep as the hell he did not believe in, for the objectless iron peg in the wall.

But in all his moods, sane or insane, intolerant or stoical, he never really doubted this: that the machine held him as light and as hopelessly as he had from his birth been held by the hopeless cosmos of his own creed. He knew well the ruthless and inexhaustible resources of our scientific civilisation. He no more expected rescue from a medical certificate than rescue from the solar system. In many of his Robinson Crusoe moods he thought kindly of MacIan as of some quarrelsome school-fellow who had long been dead. He thought of leaving in the cell when he died a rigid record of his opinions, and when he began to write them down on scraps of envelope in his pocket, he was startled to discover how much they had changed. Then he remembered the Beauchamp Tower, and tried to write his blazing scepticism on the wall, and discovered that it was all shiny tiles on which nothing could be either drawn or carved. Then for an instant there hung and broke above him like a high wave the whole horror of scientific imprisonment, which manages to deny a man not only liberty, but every accidental comfort of bondage. In the old filthy dungeons men could carve their prayers or protests in the rock. Here the white and slippery walls escaped even from bearing witness. The old prisoners could make a pet of a mouse or a beetle strayed out of a hole. Here the unpierceable walls were washed every morning by an automatic sluice. There was no natural corruption and no merciful decay by which a living thing could enter in. Then James Turnbull looked up and saw the high invincible hatefulness of the society in which he lived, and saw the hatefulness of something else also, which he told himself again and again was not the cosmos in which he believed. But all the time he had never once doubted that the five sides of his cell were for him the wall of the world henceforward, and it gave him a shock of surprise even to discover the faint light through the aperture in the ventilation tube. But he had forgotten how close efficiency has to pack everything together and how easily, therefore, a pipe here or there may leak.

Turnbull thrust his first finger down the aperture, and at last managed to make a slight further fissure in the piping. The light that came from beyond was very faint, and apparently indirect; it seemed to fall from some hole or window higher up. As he was screwing his eye to peer at this gray and greasy twilight he was astonished to see another human finger very long and lean come down from above toward the broken pipe and hook it up to something higher. The lighted aperture was abruptly blackened and blocked, presumably by a face and mouth, for something human spoke down the tube, though the words were not clear.

"Who is that?" asked Turnbull, trembling with excitement, yet wary and quite resolved not to spoil any chance.

After a few indistinct sounds the voice came down with a strong Argyleshire accent:

"I say, Turnbull, we couldn't fight through this tube, could we?"

Sentiments beyond speech surged up in Turnbull and silenced him for a space just long enough to be painful. Then he said with his old gaiety: "I vote we talk a little first; I don't want to murder the first man I have met for ten million years."

"I know what you mean," answered the other. "It has been awful. For a mortal month I have been alone with God."

Turnbull started, and it was on the tip of his tongue to answer: "Alone with God! Then you do not know what loneliness is."

But he answered, after all, in his old defiant style: "Alone with God, were you? And I suppose you found his Majesty's society rather monotonous?"

"Oh, no," said MacIan, and his voice shuddered; "it was a great deal too exciting."

After a very long silence the voice of MacIan said: "What do you really hate most in your place?"

"You'd think I was really mad if I told you," answered Turnbull, bitterly.

"Then I expect it's the same as mine," said the other voice.

"I am sure it's not the same as anybody's," said Turnbull, "for it has no rhyme or reason. Perhaps my brain really has gone, but I detest that iron spike in the left wall more than the damned desolation or the damned cocoa. Have you got one in your cell?"

"Not now," replied MacIan with serenity. "I've pulled it out."

His fellow-prisoner could only repeat the words.

"I pulled it out the other day when I was off my head," continued the tranquil Highland voice. "It looked so unnecessary."

"You must be ghastly strong," said Turnbull.

"One is, when one is mad," was the careless reply, "and it had worn a little loose in the socket. Even now I've got it out I can't discover what it was for. But I've found out something a long sight funnier."

"What do you mean?" asked Turnbull.

"I have found out where A is," said the other.

Three weeks afterward MacIan had managed to open up communications which made his meaning plain. By that time the two captives had fully discovered and demonstrated that weakness in the very nature of modern machinery to which we have already referred. The very fact that they were isolated from all companions meant that they were free from all spies, and as there were no gaolers to be bribed, so there were none to be baffled. Machinery brought them their cocoa and cleaned their cells; that machinery was as helpless as it was pitiless. A little patient violence, conducted day after day amid constant mutual suggestion, opened an irregular hole in the wall, large enough to let in a small man, in the exact place where there had been before the tiny ventilation holes. Turnbull tumbled somehow into MacIan's apartment, and his first glance found out that the iron spike was indeed plucked from its socket, and left, moreover, another ragged hole into some hollow place behind. But for this MacIan's cell was the duplicate of Turnbull's — a long oblong ending in a wedge and lined with cold and lustrous tiles. The small hole from which the peg had been displaced was in that short oblique wall at the end nearest to Turnbull's. That individual looked at it with a puzzled face.

"What is in there?" he asked.

MacIan answered briefly: "Another cell."

"But where can the door of it be?" said his companion, even more puzzled; "the doors of our cells are at the other end."

"It has no door," said Evan.

In the pause of perplexity that followed, an eerie and sinister feeling crept over Turnbull's stubborn soul in spite of himself. The notion of the doorless room chilled him with that sense of half-witted curiosity which one has when something horrible is half understood.

"James Turnbull," said MacIan, in a low and shaken voice, "these people hate us more than Nero hated Christians, and fear us more than any man feared Nero. They have filled England with frenzy and galloping in order to capture us and wipe us out — in order to kill us. And they have killed us, for you and I have only made a hole in our coffins. But though this hatred that they felt for us is bigger than they felt for Bonaparte, and more plain and practical than they would feel for Jack the Ripper, yet it is not we whom the people of this place hate most."

A cold and quivering impatience continued to crawl up Turnbull's spine; he had never felt so near to superstition and supernaturalism, and it was not a pretty sort of superstition either.

"There is another man more fearful and hateful," went on MacIan, in his low monotone voice, "and they have buried him even deeper. God knows how they did it, for he was let in by neither door nor window, nor lowered through any opening above. I expect these iron handles that we both hate have been part of some damned machinery for walling him up. He is there. I have looked through the hole at him; but I cannot stand looking at him long, because his face is turned away from me and he does not move."

All Turnbull's unnatural and uncompleted feelings found their outlet in rushing to the aperture and looking into the unknown room.

It was a third oblong cell exactly like the other two except that it was doorless, and except that on one of the walls was painted a large black A like the B and C outside their own doors. The letter in this case was not painted outside, because this prison had no outside.

On the same kind of tiled floor, of which the monotonous squares had maddened Turnbull's eye and brain, was sitting a figure which was startlingly short even for the sitting posture. Indeed, it had something of the look of a child, only that the enormous head was ringed with hair of a frosty grey. The figure was draped, both insecurely and insufficiently, in what looked like the remains of a brown flannel dressing-gown; an emptied cup of cocoa stood on the floor beside it, and the creature had his big gray head cocked at a particular angle of inquiry or attention which amid all that gathering gloom and mystery struck one as comic if not cocksure.

After six still seconds Turnbull could stand it no longer, but called out to the dwarfish thing — in what words heaven knows. The thing got up with the promptitude of an animal, and turning round offered the spectacle of two owlish eyes and a huge gray-and-white beard not unlike the plumage of an owl. This extraordinary beard covered him literally to his feet (not that that was very far), and perhaps it was as well that it did, for portions of his remaining clothing seemed to fall off whenever he moved. One talks trivially of a face like parchment, but this old man's face was so wrinkled that it was like a parchment loaded with hiero-glyphics. The lines of his face were so deep and complex that one could see five or ten different faces besides the real one, as one can see them in an elaborate wall-paper. And yet while his face seemed like a scripture older than the gods, his eyes were quite bright, blue, and startled like those of a baby. They looked as if they had only an instant before been fitted into his head.

Everything depended so obviously upon whether this buried monster spoke that Turnbull did not know or care whether he himself had spoken. He said something or nothing. And then he waited for this dwarfish voice that had been hidden under the mountains of the world. At last it did speak, and spoke in English, with a foreign accent that was neither Latin nor Teutonic. He suddenly stretched out a long and very dirty forefinger, and cried in a voice of clear recognition, like a child's: "That's a hole."

He digested the discovery for some seconds, sucking his finger, and then he cried, with a crow of laughter: "And that's a head come through it."

The hilarious energy in this idiot attitude gave Turnbull another sick turn. He had grown to tolerate those dreary and mumbling madmen who trailed themselves about the beautiful asylum gardens. But there was something new and subversive of the universe in the combination of so much cheerful decision with a body without a brain.

"Why did they put you in such a place?" he asked at last with embarrassment.

"Good place. Yes," said the old man, nodding a great many times and beaming like a flattered landlord. "Good shape. Long and narrow, with a point. Like this," and he made lovingly with his hands a map of the room in the air.

"But that's not the best," he added, confidentially. "Squares very good; I have a nice long holiday, and can count them. But that not the best."

"What is the best?" asked Turnbull in great distress.

"Spike is the best," said the old man, opening his blue eyes blazing; "it sticks out."

The words Turnbull spoke broke out of him in pure pity. "Can't we do anything for you?" he said.

"I am very happy," said the other, alphabetically. "You are a good man. Can I help you?"

"No, I don't think you can, sir," said Turnbull with rough pathos; "I am glad you are contented at least."

The weird old person opened his broad blue eyes and fixed Turnbull with a stare extraordinarily severe. "You are quite sure," he said, "I cannot help you?"

"Quite sure, thank you," said Turnbull with broken brevity. "Good-day."

Then he turned to MacIan who was standing close behind him, and whose face, now familiar in all its moods, told him easily that Evan had heard the whole of the strange dialogue.

"Curse those cruel beasts!" cried Turnbull. "They've turned him to an imbecile just by burying him alive. His brain's like a pin-point now."

"You are sure he is a lunatic?" said Evan, slowly.

"Not a lunatic," said Turnbull, "an idiot. He just points to things and says that they stick out."

"He had a notion that he could help us," said MacIan, moodily, and began to pace toward the other end of his cell.

"Yes, it was a bit pathetic," assented Turnbull; "such a Thing offering help, and besides—Hallo! Hallo! What's the matter?"

"God Almighty guide us all!" said MacIan.

He was standing heavy and still at the other end of the room and staring quietly at the door which for thirty days had sealed them up from the sun. Turnbull, following the other's eye, stared at the door likewise, and then he also uttered an exclamation. The iron door was standing about an inch and a half open.

"He said—" began Evan, in a trembling voice—"he offered——"

"Come along, you fool!" shouted Turnbull with a sudden and furious energy. "I see it all now, and it's the best stroke of luck in the world. You pulled out that iron handle that had screwed up his cell, and it somehow altered the machinery and opened all the doors."

Seizing MacIan by the elbow he bundled him bodily out into the open corridor and ran him on till they saw daylight through a half-darkened window.

"All the same," said Evan, like one answering in an ordinary conversation, "he did ask you whether he could help you."

All this wilderness of windowless passages was so built into the heart of that fortress of fear that it seemed more than an hour before the fugitives had any good glimpse of the outer world. They did not even know what hour of the day it was; and when, turning a corner, they saw the bare tunnel of the corridor end abruptly in a shining square of garden, the grass burning in that strong evening sunshine which makes it burnished gold rather than green, the abrupt opening on to the earth seemed like a hole knocked in the wall of heaven. Only once or twice in life is it permitted to a man thus to see the very universe from outside, and feel existence itself as an adorable adventure not yet begun. As they found this shining escape out of that hellish labyrinth they both had simultaneously the sensation of being babes unborn, of being asked by God if they would like to live upon the earth. They were looking in at one of the seven gates of Eden.

Turnbull was the first to leap into the garden, with an earth-spurning leap like that of one who could really spread his wings and fly. MacIan, who came an instant after, was less full of mere animal gusto and fuller of a more fearful and quivering pleasure in the clear and innocent flower colours and the high and holy trees. With one bound they were in that cool and cleared landscape, and they found just outside the door the black-clad gentleman with the cloven chin smilingly regarding them; and his chin seemed to grow longer and longer as he smiled.

CHAPTER XVIII

A RIDDLE OF FACES

JUST BEHIND HIM stood two other doctors: one, the familiar Dr. Quayle, of the blinking eyes and bleating voice; the other, a more commonplace but much more forcible figure, a stout young doctor with short, well-brushed hair and a round but resolute face. At the sight of the escape these two subordinates uttered a cry and sprang forward, but their superior remained motionless and smiling, and somehow the lack of his support seemed to arrest and freeze them in the very gesture of pursuit.

"Let them be," he cried in a voice that cut like a blade of ice; and not only of ice, but of some awful primordial ice that had never been water.

"I want no devoted champions," said the cutting voice; "even the folly of one's friends bores one at last. You don't suppose I should have let these lunatics out of their cells without good reason. I have the best and fullest reason. They can be let out of their cell to-day, because to-day the whole world has become their cell. I will have no more mediæval mummery of chains and doors. Let them wander about the earth as they wandered about this garden, and I shall still be their easy master. Let them take the wings of the morning and abide in the uttermost parts of the sea — I am there. Whither shall they go from my presence and whither shall they flee from my spirit? Courage, Dr. Quayle, and do not be downhearted; the real days of tyranny are only beginning on this earth."

And with that the Master laughed and swung away from them, almost as if his laugh was a bad thing for people to see.

"Might I speak to you a moment?" said Turnbull, stepping forward with a respectful resolution. But the shoulders of the Master only seemed to take on a new and unexpected angle of mockery as he strode away.

Turnbull swung round with great abruptness to the other two doctors, and said, harshly: "What in snakes does he mean — and who are you?"

"My name is Hutton," said the short, stout man, "and I am — well, one of those whose business it is to uphold this establishment."

"My name is Turnbull," said the other; "I am one of those whose business it is to tear it to the ground."

The small doctor smiled, and Turnbull's anger seemed suddenly to steady him.

"But I don't want to talk about that," he said, calmly; "I only want to know what the master of this asylum really means."

Dr. Hutton's smile broke into a laugh which, short as it was, had the suspicion of a shake in it. "I suppose you think that quite a simple question," he said.

"I think it a plain question," said Turnbull, "and one that deserves a plain answer. Why did the Master lock us up in a couple of cupboards like jars of pickles for a mortal month, and why does he now let us walk free in the garden again?"

"I understand," said Hutton, with arched eyebrows, "that your complaint is that you are now free to walk in the garden."

"My complaint is," said Turnbull, stubbornly, "that if I am fit to walk freely now, I have been as fit for the last month. No one has examined me, no one has come near me. Your chief says that I am only free because he has made other arrangements. What are those arrangements?"

The young man with the round face looked down for a little while and smoked reflectively. The other and elder doctor had gone pacing nervously by himself upon the lawn. At length the round face was lifted again, and showed two round blue eyes with a certain frankness in them.

"Well, I don't see that it can do any harm to tell you now," he said. "You were shut up just then because it was just during that month that the Master was bringing off his big scheme. He was getting his bill through Parliament, and organising the new medical police. But of course you haven't heard of all that; in fact, you weren't meant to."

"Heard of all what?" asked the impatient inquirer.

"There's a new law now, and the asylum powers are greatly extended. Even if you did escape now, any policeman would take you up in the next town if you couldn't show a certificate of sanity from us."

"Well," continued Dr. Hutton, "the Master described before both Houses of Parliament the real scientific objection to all existing legislation about lunacy. As he very truly said, the mistake was in supposing insanity to be merely an exception or an extreme. Insanity, like forgetfulness, is simply a quality which enters more or less into all human beings; and for practical purposes it is more necessary to know whose mind is really trustworthy than whose has some accidental taint. We have therefore reversed the existing method, and people now have to prove that they are sane. In the first village you entered, the village constable would notice that you were not wearing on the left lapel of your coat the small pewter S which is now necessary to any one who walks about beyond asylum bounds or outside asylum hours."

"You mean to say," said Turnbull, "that this was what the Master of the asylum urged before the House of Commons?"

Dr. Hutton nodded with gravity.

"And you mean to say," cried Turnbull, with a vibrant snort, "that that proposal was passed in an assembly that calls itself democratic?"

The doctor showed his whole row of teeth in a smile. "Oh, the assembly calls itself Socialist now," he said, "but we explained to them that this was a question for men of science."

Turnbull gave one stamp upon the gravel, then pulled himself together, and resumed: "But why should your infernal head medicine-man lock us up in separate cells while he was turning England into a madhouse? I'm not the Prime Minister; we're not the House of Lords."

"He wasn't afraid of the Prime Minister," replied Dr. Hutton; "he isn't afraid of the House of Lords. But——"

"Well?" inquired Turnbull, stamping again.

"He is afraid of you," said Hutton, simply. "Why, didn't you know?"

MacIan, who had not spoken yet, made one stride forward and stood with shaking limbs and shining eyes.

"He was afraid!" began Evan, thickly. "You mean to say that we——"

"I mean to say the plain truth now that the danger is over," said Hutton, calmly; "most certainly you two were the only people he ever was afraid of." Then he added in a low but not inaudible voice: "Except one—whom he feared worse, and has buried deeper."

"Come away," cried MacIan, "this has to be thought about."

Turnbull followed him in silence as he strode away, but just before he vanished, turned and spoke again to the doctors.

"But what has got hold of people?" he asked, abruptly. "Why should all England have gone dotty on the mere subject of dottiness?"

Dr. Hutton smiled his open smile once more and bowed slightly. "As to that also," he replied, "I don't want to make you vain."

Turnbull swung round without a word, and he and his companion were lost in the lustrous leafage of the garden. They noticed nothing special about the scene, except that the garden seemed more exquisite than ever in the deepening sunset, and that there seemed to be many more people, whether patients or attendants, walking about in it.

From behind the two black-coated doctors as they stood on the lawn another figure somewhat similarly dressed strode hurriedly past them, having also grizzled hair and an open flapping frock-coat. Both his decisive step and dapper black array marked him out as another medical

man, or at least a man in authority, and as he passed Turnbull the latter
was aroused by a strong impression of having seen the man somewhere
before. It was no one that he knew well, yet he was certain that it was
some one at whom he had at some time or other looked steadily. It was
neither the face of a friend nor of an enemy; it aroused neither irritation
nor tenderness, yet it was a face which had for some reason been of great
importance in his life. Turning and returning, and making detours
about the garden, he managed to study the man's face again and
again—a moustached, somewhat military face with a monocle, the sort
of face that is aristocratic without being distinguished. Turnbull could
not remember any particular doctors in his decidedly healthy existence.
Was the man a long-lost uncle, or was he only somebody who had sat
opposite him regularly in a railway train? At that moment the man
knocked down his own eye-glass with a gesture of annoyance; Turnbull
remembered the gesture, and the truth sprang up solid in front of him.
The man with the moustaches was Cumberland Vane, the London
police magistrate before whom he and MacIan had once stood on their
trial. The magistrate must have been transferred to some other official
duties—to something connected with the inspection of asylums.

Turnbull's heart gave a leap of excitement which was half hope. As a
magistrate Mr. Cumberland Vane had been somewhat careless and
shallow, but certainly kindly, and not inaccessible to common-sense so
long as it was put to him in strictly conventional language. He was at
least an authority of a more human and refreshing sort than the crank
with the wagging beard or the fiend with the forked chin.

He went straight up to the magistrate, and said: "Good-evening, Mr.
Vane; I doubt if you remember me."

Cumberland Vane screwed the eye-glass into his scowling face for an
instant, and then said curtly but not uncivilly: "Yes, I remember you, sir;
assault or battery, wasn't it?—a fellow broke your window. A tall
fellow—McSomething—case made rather a noise afterward."

"MacIan is the name, sir," said Turnbull, respectfully; "I have him
here with me."

"Eh!" said Vane very sharply. "Confound him! Has he got anything to
do with this game?"

"Mr. Vane," said Turnbull, pacifically, "I will not pretend that either
he or I acted quite decorously on that occasion. You were very lenient
with us, and did not treat us as criminals when you very well might. So I
am sure you will give us your testimony that, even if we were criminals,
we are not lunatics in any legal or medical sense whatever. I am sure you
will use your influence for us."

"My influence!" repeated the magistrate, with a slight start. "I don't
quite understand you."

"I don't know in what capacity you are here," continued Turnbull, gravely, "but a legal authority of your distinction must certainly be here in an important one. Whether you are visiting and inspecting the place, or attached to it as some kind of permanent legal adviser, your opinion must still——"

Cumberland Vane exploded with a detonation of oaths; his face was transfigured with fury and contempt, and yet in some odd way he did not seem specially angry with Turnbull.

"But Lord bless us and save us!" he gasped, at length; "I'm not here as an official at all. I'm here as a patient. The cursed pack of rat-catching chemists all say that I've lost my wits."

"You!" cried Turnbull with terrible emphasis. "You! Lost your wits!"

In the rush of his real astonishment at this towering unreality Turnbull almost added: "Why, you haven't got any to lose." But he fortunately remembered the remains of his desperate diplomacy.

"This can't go on," he said, positively. "Men like MacIan and I may suffer unjustly all our lives, but a man like you must have influence."

"There is only one man who has any influence in England now," said Vane, and his high voice fell to a sudden and convincing quietude.

"Whom do you mean?" asked Turnbull.

"I mean that cursed fellow with the long split chin," said the other.

"Is it really true," asked Turnbull, "that he has been allowed to buy up and control such a lot? What put the country into such a state?"

Mr. Cumberland Vane laughed outright. "What put the country into such a state?" he asked. "Why, you did. When you were fool enough to agree to fight MacIan, after all, everybody was ready to believe that the Bank of England might paint itself pink with white spots."

"I don't understand," answered Turnbull. "Why should you be surprised at my fighting? I hope I have always fought."

"Well," said Cumberland Vane, airily, "you didn't believe in religion, you see—so we thought you were safe at any rate. You went further in your language than most of us wanted to go; no good in just hurting one's mother's feelings, I think. But of course we all knew you were right, and, really, we relied on you."

"Did you?" said the editor of the "Atheist" with a bursting heart. "I am sorry you did not tell me so at the time."

He walked away very rapidly and flung himself on a garden-seat, and for some six minutes his own wrongs hid from him the huge and hilarious fact that Cumberland Vane had been locked up as a lunatic.

The garden of the madhouse was so perfectly planned, and answered so exquisitely to every hour of daylight, that one could almost fancy that the sunlight was caught there tangled in its tinted trees, as the wise men of Gotham tried to chain the spring to a bush. Or it seemed as if this ironic paradise still kept its unique dawn or its special sunset while the rest of the earthly globe rolled through its ordinary hours. There was one evening, or late afternoon, in particular, which Evan MacIan will remember in the last moments of death. It was what artists call a daffodil sky, but it is coarsened even by reference to a daffodil. It was of that innocent lonely yellow which has never heard of orange, though it might turn quite unconsciously into green. Against it the tops, one might say the turrets, of the clipt and ordered trees were outlined in that shade of veiled violet which tints the tops of lavender. A white early moon was hardly traceable upon that delicate yellow. MacIan, I say, will remember this tender and transparent evening, partly because of its virgin gold and silver, and partly because he passed beneath it through the most horrible instant of his life.

Turnbull was sitting on his seat on the lawn, and the golden evening impressed even his positive nature, as indeed it might have impressed the oxen in a field. He was shocked out of his idle mood of awe by seeing MacIan break from behind the bushes and run across the lawn with an action he had never seen in the man before, with all his experience of the eccentric humours of this Celt. MacIan fell on the bench, shaking it so that it rattled, and gripped it with his knees like one in dreadful pain of body. That particular run and tumble is typical only of a man who has been hit by some sudden and incurable evil, who is bitten by a viper or condemned to be hung. Turnbull looked up in the white face of his friend and enemy, and almost turned cold at what he saw there. He had seen the blue but gloomy eyes of the western Highlander troubled by as many tempests as his own west Highland seas, but there had always been a fixed star of faith behind the storms. Now the star had gone out, and there was only misery.

Yet MacIan had the strength to answer the question where Turnbull, taken by surprise, had not the strength to ask it.

"They are right, they are right!" he cried. "O my God! they are right, Turnbull. I ought to be here!"

He went on with shapeless fluency as if he no longer had the heart to choose or check his speech. "I suppose I ought to have guessed long ago—all my big dreams and schemes—and every one being against us—but I was stuck up, you know."

"Do tell me about it, really," cried the atheist, and, faced with the furnace of the other's pain, he did not notice that he spoke with the affection of a father.

"I am mad, Turnbull," said Evan, with a dead clearness of speech, and leant back against the garden-seat.

"Nonsense," said the other, clutching at the obvious cue of benevolent brutality, "this is one of your silly moods."

MacIan shook his head. "I know enough about myself," he said, "to allow for any mood, though it opened heaven or hell. But to see things — to see them walking solid in the sun — things that can't be there — real mystics never do that, Turnbull."

"What things?" asked the other, incredulously.

MacIan lowered his voice. "I saw *her*," he said, "three minutes ago — walking here in this hell yard."

Between trying to look scornful and really looking startled, Turnbull's face was confused enough to emit no speech, and Evan went on in monotonous sincerity:

"I saw her walk behind those blessed trees against that holy sky of gold as plain as I can see her whenever I shut my eyes. I did shut them, and opened them again, and she was still there — that is, of course, she wasn't— She still had a little fur round her neck, but her dress was a shade brighter than when I really saw her."

"My dear fellow," cried Turnbull, rallying a hearty laugh, "the fancies have really got hold of you. You mistook some other poor girl here for her."

"Mistook some other—" said MacIan, and words failed him altogether.

They sat for some moments in the mellow silence of the evening garden, a silence that was stifling for the sceptic, but utterly empty and final for the man of faith. At last he broke out again with the words: "Well, anyhow, if I'm mad, I'm glad I'm mad on that."

Turnbull murmured some clumsy deprecation, and sat stolidly smoking to collect his thoughts; the next instant he had all his nerves engaged in the mere effort to sit still.

Across the clear space of cold silver and a pale lemon sky which was left by the gap in the ilex-trees there passed a slim, dark figure, a profile and the poise of a dark head like a bird's, which really pinned him to his seat with the point of coincidence. With an effort he got to his feet, and said with a voice of affected insouciance: "By George! MacIan, she is uncommonly like——"

"What!" cried MacIan, with a leap of eagerness that was heartbreaking, "do you see her, too?" And the blaze came back into the centre of his eyes.

Turnbull's tawny eyebrows were pulled together with a peculiar frown of curiosity, and all at once he walked quickly across the lawn. MacIan sat rigid, but peered after him with open and parched lips. He saw the sight which either proved him sane or proved the whole universe half-witted; he saw the man of flesh approach that beautiful phantom, saw their gestures of recognition, and saw them against the sunset joining hands.

He could stand it no longer, but ran across to the path, turned the corner and saw standing quite palpable in the evening sunlight, talking with a casual grace to Turnbull, the face and figure which had filled his midnights with frightfully vivid or desperately half-forgotten features. She advanced quite pleasantly and coolly, and put out her hand. The moment that he touched it he knew that he was sane even if the solar system was crazy.

She was entirely elegant and unembarrassed. That is the awful thing about women — they refuse to be emotional at emotional moments, upon some such ludicrous pretext as there being some one else there. But MacIan was in a condition of criticism much less than the average masculine one, being in fact merely overturned by the rushing riddle of the events.

Evan does not know to this day of what particular question he asked, but he vividly remembers that she answered, and every line or fluctuation of her face as she said it.

"Oh, don't you know?" she said, smiling, and suddenly lifting her level brown eyebrows. "Haven't you heard the news? I'm a lunatic."

Then she added after a short pause, and with a sort of pride: "I've got a certificate."

Her manner, by the matchless social stoicism of her sex, was entirely suited to a drawing-room, but Evan's reply fell somewhat far short of such a standard, as he only said: "What the devil in hell does all this nonsense mean?"

"Really," said the young lady, and laughed.

"I beg your pardon," said the unhappy young man, rather wildly, "but what I mean is, why are you here in an asylum?"

The young woman broke again into one of the maddening and mysterious laughs of femininity. Then she composed her features, and replied with equal dignity: "Well, if it comes to that, why are you?"

The fact that Turnbull had strolled away and was investigating rhododendrons may have been due to Evan's successful prayers to the other world, or possibly to his own pretty successful experience of this one. But though they two were as isolated as a new Adam and Eve in a pretty ornamental Eden, the lady did not relax by an inch the rigour of her badinage.

"I am locked up in the madhouse," said Evan, with a sort of stiff pride, "because I tried to keep my promise to you."

"Quite so," answered the inexplicable lady, nodding with a perfectly blazing smile, "and I am locked up because it was to me you promised."

"It is outrageous!" cried Evan; "it is impossible!"

"Oh, you can see my certificate if you like," she replied with some hauteur.

MacIan stared at her and then at his boots, and then at the sky and then at her again. He was quite sure now that he himself was not mad, and the fact rather added to his perplexity.

Then he drew nearer to her, and said in a dry and dreadful voice: "Oh, don't condescend to play the fool with such a fool as me. Are you really locked up here as a patient—because you helped us to escape?"

"Yes," said she, still smiling, but her steady voice had a shake in it. Evan flung his big elbow across his forehead and burst into tears.

The pure lemon of the sky faded into purer white as the great sunset silently collapsed. The birds settled back into the trees; the moon began to glow with its own light. Mr. James Turnbull continued his botanical researches into the structure of the rhododendron. But the lady did not move an inch until Evan had flung up his face again; and when he did he saw by the last gleam of sunlight that it was not only his face that was wet.

Mr. James Turnbull had all his life professed a profound interest in physical science, and the phenomena of a good garden were really a pleasure to him; but after three-quarters of an hour or so even the apostle of science began to find rhododendrus a bore, and was somewhat relieved when an unexpected development of events obliged him to transfer his researches to the equally interesting subject of hollyhocks, which grew some fifty feet farther along the path. The ostensible cause of his removal was the unexpected reappearance of his two other acquaintances walking and talking laboriously along the way, with the black head bent close to the brown one. Even hollyhocks detained Turnbull but a short time. Having rapidly absorbed all the important principles affecting the growth of those vegetables, he jumped over a flower-bed and walked back into the building. The other two came up along the slow course of the path talking and talking. No one but God knows what they said (for they certainly have forgotten), and if I remembered it I would not repeat it. When they parted at the head of the walk she put out her hand again in the same well-bred way, although it trembled; he seemed to restrain a gesture as he let it fall.

"If it is really always to be like this," he said, thickly, "it would not matter if we were here for ever."

"You tried to kill yourself four times for me," she said, unsteadily, "and I have been chained up as a madwoman for you. I really think that after that——"

"Yes, I know," said Evan in a low voice, looking down. "After that we belong to each other. We are sort of sold to each other—until the stars fall." Then he looked up suddenly, and said: "By the way, what is your name?"

"My name is Beatrice Drake," she replied with complete gravity. "You can see it on my certificate of lunacy."

CHAPTER XIX

THE LAST PARLEY

TURNBULL WALKED AWAY, wildly trying to explain to himself the presence of two personal acquaintances so different as Vane and the girl. As he skirted a low hedge of laurel, an enormously tall young man leapt over it, stood in front of him, and almost fell on his neck as if seeking to embrace him.

"Don't you know me?" almost sobbed the young man, who was in the highest spirits. "Ain't I written on your heart, old boy? I say, what did you do with my yacht?"

"Take your arms off my neck," said Turnbull, irritably. "Are you mad?"

The young man sat down on the gravel-path and went into ecstasies of laughter. "No, that's just the fun of it — I'm not mad," he replied. "They've shut me up in this place, and I'm not mad." And he went off again into mirth as innocent as wedding-bells.

Turnbull, whose powers of surprise were exhausted, rolled his round grey eyes and said, "Mr. Wilkinson, I think," because he could not think of anything else to say.

The tall man sitting on the gravel bowed with urbanity, and said: "Quite at your service. Not to be confused with the Wilkinsons of Cumberland; and as I say, old boy, what have you done with my yacht? You see, they've locked me up here — in this garden — and a yacht would be a sort of occupation for an unmarried man."

"I am really horribly sorry," began Turnbull, in the last stage of bated bewilderment and exasperation, "but really ——"

"Oh, I can see you can't have it on you at the moment," said Mr. Wilkinson with much intellectual magnanimity.

"Well, the fact is — " began Turnbull again, and then the phrase was frozen on his mouth, for round the corner came the goatlike face and gleaming eye-glasses of Dr. Quayle.

"Ah, my dear Mr. Wilkinson," said the doctor, as if delighted at a coincidence; "and Mr. Turnbull, too. Why, I want to speak to Mr. Turnbull."

164

Mr. Turnbull made some movement rather of surrender than assent, and the doctor caught it up exquisitely, showing even more of his two front teeth. "I am sure Mr. Wilkinson will excuse us a moment." And with flying frock-coat he led Turnbull rapidly round the corner of a path.

"My dear sir," he said, in a quite affectionate manner, "I do not mind telling you — you are such a very hopeful case — you understand so well the scientific point of view; and I don't like to see you bothered by the really hopeless cases. They are monotonous and maddening. The man you have just been talking to, poor fellow, is one of the strongest cases of pure *idée fixe* that we have. It's very sad, and I'm afraid utterly incurable. He keeps on telling everybody" — and the doctor lowered his voice confidentially — "he tells everybody that two people have taken his yacht. His account of how he lost it is quite incoherent."

Turnbull stamped his foot on the gravel-path, and called out: "Oh, I can't stand this. Really——"

"I know, I know," said the psychologist, mournfully; "it is a most melancholy case, and also fortunately a very rare one. It is so rare, in fact, that in one classification of these maladies it is entered under a heading by itself — Perdinavititis, mental inflammation creating the impression that one has lost a ship. Really," he added, with a kind of half-embarrassed guilt, "it's rather a feather in my cap. I discovered the only existing case of perdinavititis."

"But this won't do, doctor," said Turnbull, almost tearing his hair, "this really won't do. The man really did lose a ship. Indeed, not to put too fine a point on it, I took his ship."

Dr. Quayle swung round for an instant so that his silk-lined overcoat rustled, and stared singularly at Turnbull. Then he said with hurried amiability: "Why, of course you did. Quite so, quite so," and with courteous gestures went striding up the garden-path. Under the first laburnum-tree he stopped, however, and pulling out his pencil and note-book wrote down feverishly: "Singular development in the Eleutheromaniac, Turnbull. Sudden manifestation of Rapinavititis — the delusion that one has stolen a ship. First case ever recorded."

Turnbull stood for an instant staggered into stillness. Then he ran raging round the garden to find MacIan, just as a husband, even a bad husband, will run raging to find his wife if he is full of a furious query. He found MacIan stalking moodily about the half-lit garden, after his extraordinary meeting with Beatrice. No one who saw his slouching stride and sunken head could have known that his soul was in the seventh heaven of ecstasy. He did not think; he did not even very definitely desire. He merely wallowed in memories, chiefly in material

memories; words said with a certain cadence or trivial turns of the neck
or wrist. Into the middle of his stationary and senseless enjoyment were
thrust abruptly the projecting elbow and the projecting red beard of
Turnbull. MacIan stepped back a little, and the soul in his eyes came
very slowly to its windows. When James Turnbull had the glittering
sword-point planted upon his breast he was in far less danger. For three
pulsating seconds after the interruption MacIan was in a mood to have
murdered his father.

And yet his whole emotional anger fell from him when he saw
Turnbull's face, in which the eyes seemed to be bursting from the head
like bullets. All the fire and fragrance even of young and honourable
love faded for a moment before that stiff agony of interrogation.

"Are you hurt, Turnbull?" he asked, anxiously.

"I am dying," answered the other quite calmly. "I am in the quite
literal sense of the words dying to know something. I want to know what
all this can possibly mean."

MacIan did not answer, and he continued with asperity: "You are still
thinking about that girl, but I tell you the whole thing is incredible. She's
not the only person here. I've met that fellow Wilkinson, whose yacht we
lost. I've met the very magistrate you were hauled up to when you broke
my window. What can it mean — meeting all these old people again?
One never meets such old friends again except in a dream."

Then after a silence he cried with a rending sincerity: "Are you really
there, Evan? Have you ever been really there? Am I simply dreaming?"

MacIan had been listening with a living silence to every word, and
now his face flamed with one of his rare revelations of life.

"No, you good atheist," he cried; "no, you clean, courteous, reverent,
pious old blasphemer. No, you are not dreaming — you are waking up."

"What do you mean?"

"There are two states where one meets so many old friends," said
MacIan; "one is a dream, the other is the end of the world."

"And you say —"

"I say this is not a dream," said Evan in a ringing voice.

"You really mean to suggest —" began Turnbull.

"Be silent! or I shall say it all wrong," said MacIan, breathing hard.
"It's hard to explain, anyhow. An apocalypse is the opposite of a dream. A
dream is falser than the outer life. But the end of the world is more
actual than the world it ends. I don't say this is really the end of the
world, but it's something like that — it's the end of something. All the
people are crowding into one corner. Everything is coming to a point."

"What is the point?" asked Turnbull.

"I can't see it," said Evan; "it is too large and plain."

Then after a silence he said: "I can't see it — and yet I will try to describe it. Turnbull, three days ago I saw quite suddenly that our duel was not right, after all."

"Three days ago!" repeated Turnbull. "When and why did this illumination occur?"

"I knew I was not quite right," answered Evan, "the moment I saw the round eyes of that old man in the cell."

"Old man in the cell!" repeated his wondering companion. "Do you mean the poor old idiot who likes spikes to stick out?"

"Yes," said MacIan, after a slight pause, "I mean the poor old idiot who likes spikes to stick out. When I saw his eyes and heard his old croaking accent, I knew that it would not really have been right to kill you. It would have been a venial sin."

"I am much obliged," said Turnbull, gruffly.

"You must give me time," said MacIan, quite patiently, "for I am trying to tell the whole truth. I am trying to tell more of it than I know.

"So you see I confess" — he went on with laborious distinctness — "I confess that all the people who called our duel mad were right in a way. I would confess it to old Cumberland Vane and his eye-glass. I would confess it even to that old ass in brown flannel who talked to us about Love. Yes, they are right in a way. I am a little mad."

He stopped and wiped his brow as if he were literally doing heavy labour. Then he went on:

"I am a little mad; but, after all, it is only a little madness. When hundreds of high-minded men had fought duels about a jostle with the elbow or the ace of spades, the whole world need not have gone wild over my one little wildness. Plenty of other people have killed themselves between then and now. But all England has gone into captivity in order to take us captive. All England has turned into a lunatic asylum in order to prove us lunatics. Compared with the general public, I might positively be called sane."

He stopped again, and went on with the same air of travailing with the truth:

"When I saw that, I saw everything; I saw the Church and the world. The Church in its earthly action has really touched morbid things — tortures and bleeding visions and blasts of extermination. The Church has had her madnesses, and I am one of them. I am the massacre of St. Bartholomew. I am the Inquisition of Spain. I do not say that we have never gone mad, but I say that we are fit to act as keepers to our enemies. Massacre is wicked even with a provocation, as in the Bartholomew. But your modern Nietzsche will tell you that massacre would be glorious without a provocation. Torture should be violently stopped, though the Church is doing it. But your modern Tolstoy will tell you that it ought not to be violently stopped whoever is doing it. In the long run, which is most mad — the Church or the world? Which is madder, the Spanish priest who permitted tyranny, or the Prussian sophist who admired it? Which is madder, the Russian priest who discourages righteous rebellion, or the Russian novelist who forbids it? That is the final and the blasting test. The world left to itself grows wilder than any creed. A few days ago you and I were the maddest people in England. Now, by God! I believe we are the sanest. That is the only real question — whether the Church is really madder than the world. Let the rationalists run their own race, and let us see where *they* end. If the world has some healthy balance other than God, let the world find it. Does the world find it? Cut the world loose," he cried with a savage gesture. "Does the world stand on its own end? Does it stand, or does it stagger?"

Turnbull remained silent, and MacIan said to him, looking once more at the earth: "It staggers, Turnbull. It cannot stand by itself; you know it cannot. It has been the sorrow of your life. Turnbull, this garden is not a dream, but an apocalyptic fulfilment. This garden is the world gone mad."

Turnbull did not move his head, and he had been listening all the time; yet, somehow, the other knew that for the first time he was listening seriously.

"The world has gone mad," said MacIan, "and it has gone mad about Us. The world takes the trouble to make a big mistake about every little mistake made by the Church. That is why they have turned ten counties to a madhouse; that is why crowds of kindly people are poured into this filthy melting-pot. Now is the judgment of this world. The Prince of this World is judged, and he is judged exactly because he is judging. There is at last one simple solution to the quarrel between the ball and the cross — "

Turnbull for the first time started.

"The ball and — " he repeated.

"What is the matter with you?" asked MacIan.

"I had a dream," said Turnbull, thickly and obscurely, "in which I saw the cross struck crooked and the ball secure — "

"I had a dream," said MacIan, "in which I saw the cross erect and the ball invisible. They were both dreams from hell. There must be some round earth to plant the cross upon. But here is the awful difference — that the round world will not consent even to continue round. The astronomers are always telling us that it is shaped like an orange, or like an egg, or like a German sausage. They beat the old world about like a bladder and thump it into a thousand shapeless shapes. Turnbull, we cannot trust the ball to be always a ball; we cannot trust reason to be reasonable. In the end the great terrestrial globe will go quite lop-sided, and only the cross will stand upright."

There was a long silence, and then Turnbull said, hesitatingly: "Has it occurred to you that since — since those two dreams, or whatever they were — "

"Well?" murmured MacIan.

"Since then," went on Turnbull, in the same low voice, "since then we have never even looked for our swords."

"You are right," answered Evan almost inaudibly. "We have found something which we both hate more than we ever hated each other, and I think I know its name."

Turnbull seemed to frown and flinch for a moment. "It does not much matter what you call it," he said, "so long as you keep out of its way."

The bushes broke and snapped abruptly behind them, and a very tall figure towered above Turnbull with an arrogant stoop and a projecting chin, a chin of which the shape showed queerly even in its shadow upon the path.

"You see that is not so easy," said MacIan between his teeth.

They looked up into the eyes of the Master, but looked only for a moment. The eyes were full of a frozen and icy wrath, a kind of utterly heartless hatred. His voice was for the first time devoid of irony. There was no more sarcasm in it than there is in an iron club.

"You will be inside the building in three minutes," he said, with pulverising precision, "or you will be fired on by the artillery at all the windows. There is too much talking in this garden; we intend to close it. You will be accommodated indoors."

"Ah!" said MacIan, with a long and satisfied sigh, "then I was right."

And he turned his back and walked obediently toward the building. Turnbull seemed to canvass for a few minutes the notion of knocking the Master down, and then fell under the same almost fairy fatalism as his companion. In some strange way it did seem that the more smoothly they yielded, the more swiftly would events sweep on to some great collision.

CHAPTER XX

DIES IRÆ

A S THEY ADVANCED toward the asylum they looked up at its rows
on rows of windows, and understood the Master's material threat.
By means of that complex but concealed machinery which ran
like a network of nerves over the whole fabric, there had been shot out
under every window-ledge rows and rows of polished-steel cylinders,
the cold miracles of modern gunnery. They commanded the whole
garden and the whole country side, and could have blown to pieces an
army corps.

This silent declaration of war had evidently had its complete effect.
As MacIan and Turnbull walked steadily but slowly toward the entrance hall of the institution, they could see that most, or at least many,
of the patients had already gathered there as well as the staff of doctors
and the whole regiment of keepers and assistants. But when they
entered the lamp-lit hall, and the high iron door was clashed to and
locked behind them, yet a new amazement leapt into their eyes, and
the stalwart Turnbull almost fell. For he saw a sight which was indeed,
as MacIan had said — either the Day of Judgment or a dream.

Within a few feet of him at one corner of the square of standing
people stood the girl he had known in Jersey, Madeleine Durand. She
looked straight at him with a steady smile which lit up that scene of
darkness and unreason like the light of some honest fireside. Her square
face and throat were thrown back, as her habit was, and there was
something almost sleepy in the geniality of her eyes. He saw her first,
and for a few seconds saw her only; then the outer edge of his eyesight
took in all the other staring faces, and he saw all the faces he had ever
seen for weeks and months past. There was the Tolstoyan in Jaeger
flannel, with the yellow beard that went backward and the foolish nose
and eyes that went forward, with the curiosity of a crank. He was talking
eagerly to Mr. Gordon, the corpulent Jew shopkeeper whom they had
once gagged in his own shop. There was the tipsy old Hertfordshire
rustic; he was talking energetically to himself. There was not only Mr.

Vane the magistrate, but the clerk of Mr. Vane, the magistrate. There was not only Miss Drake of the motor-car, but also Miss Drake's chauffeur. Nothing wild or unfamiliar could have produced upon Turnbull such a nightmare impression as that ring of familiar faces. Yet he had one intellectual shock which was greater than all the others. He stepped impulsively forward toward Madeleine, and then wavered with a kind of wild humility. As he did so he caught sight of another square face behind Madeleine's, a face with long gray whiskers and an austere stare. It was old Durand, the girl's father; and when Turnbull saw him he saw the last and worst marvel of that monstrous night. He remembered Durand; he remembered his monotonous, everlasting lucidity, his stupefyingly sensible views of everything, his colossal contentment with truisms merely because they were true. "Confound it all!" cried Turnbull to himself, "if *he* is in the asylum, there can't be any one outside." He drew nearer to Madeleine, but still doubtfully and all the more so because she still smiled at him. MacIan had already gone across to Beatrice with an air of right.

Then all these bewildered but partly amicable recognitions were cloven by a cruel voice which always made all human blood turn bitter. The Master was standing in the middle of the room surveying the scene like a great artist looking at a completed picture. Handsome as he looked, they had never seen so clearly what was really hateful in his face; and even then they could only express it by saying that the arched brows and the long emphatic chin gave it always a look of being lit from below, like the face of some infernal actor.

"This is indeed a cosy party," he said with glittering eyes.

The Master evidently meant to say more, but before he could say anything M. Durand had stepped right up to him and was speaking.

He was speaking exactly as a French bourgeois speaks to the manager of a restaurant. That is, he spoke with rattling and breathless rapidity, but with no incoherence, and therefore with no emotion. It was a steady, monotonous vivacity, which came not seemingly from passion, but merely from the reason having been sent off at a gallop. He was saying something like this:

"You refuse me my half-bottle of Médoc, the drink the most wholesome and the most customary. You refuse me the company and obedience of my daughter, which Nature herself indicates. You refuse me the beef and mutton, without pretence that it is a fast of the Church. You now forbid me the promenade, a thing necessary to a person of my age. It is useless to tell me that you do all this by law. Law rests upon the social contract. If the citizen finds himself despoiled of such pleasures and powers as he would have had even in the savage state, the social contract is annulled."

"It's no good chattering away, Monsieur," said Hutton, for the Master was silent. "The place is covered with machine guns. We've got to obey our orders, and so have you."

"The machinery is of the most perfect," assented Durand, somewhat irrelevantly; "worked by petroleum, I believe. I only ask you to admit that if such things fall below the comfort of barbarism, the social contract is annulled. It is a pretty little point of theory."

"Oh! I daresay," said Hutton.

Durand bowed quite civilly and withdrew.

"A cosy party," resumed the Master, scornfully, "and yet I believe some of you are in doubt about how we all came together. I will explain it, ladies and gentlemen; I will explain everything. To whom shall I specially address myself? To Mr. James Turnbull. He has a scientific mind."

Turnbull seemed to choke with sudden protest. The Master seemed only to cough out of pure politeness and proceeded: "Mr. Turnbull will agree with me," he said, "when I say that we long felt in scientific circles that great harm was done by such a legend as that of the Crucifixion."

Turnbull growled something which was presumably assent.

The Master went on smoothly: "It was in vain for us to urge that the incident was irrelevant; that there were many such fanatics, many such executions. We were forced to take the thing thoroughly in hand, to investigate it in the spirit of scientific history, and with the assistance of Mr. Turnbull and others we were happy in being able to announce that this alleged Crucifixion never occurred at all."

MacIan lifted his head and looked at the Master steadily, but Turnbull did not look up.

"This, we found, was the only way with all superstitions," continued the speaker; "it was necessary to deny them historically, and we have done it with great success in the case of miracles and such things. Now within our own time there arose an unfortunate fuss which threatened (as Mr. Turnbull would say) to galvanise the corpse of Christianity into a fictitious life — the alleged case of a Highland eccentric who wanted to fight for the Virgin."

MacIan, quite white, made a step forward, but the speaker did not alter his easy attitude or his flow of words. "Again we urged that this duel was not to be admired, that it was a mere brawl, but the people were ignorant and romantic. There were signs of treating this alleged Highlander and his alleged opponent as heroes. We tried all other means of arresting this reactionary hero worship. Working men who betted on the duel were imprisoned for gambling. Working men who drank the health of a duellist were imprisoned for drunkenness. But the popular excitement about the alleged duel continued, and we had to fall back on our old historical method. We investigated, on scientific principles, the story of MacIan's challenge, and we are happy to be able to inform you that the whole story of the attempted duel is a fable. There never was any challenge. There never was any man named MacIan. It is a melodramatic myth, like Calvary."

Not a soul moved save Turnbull, who lifted his head; yet there was the sense of a silent explosion.

"The whole story of the MacIan challenge," went on the Master, beaming at them all with a sinister benignity, "has been found to originate in the obsessions of a few pathological types, who are now all fortunately in our care. There is, for instance, a person here of the name of Gordon, formerly the keeper of a curiosity shop. He is a victim of the disease called Vinculomania — the impression that one has been bound or tied up. We have also a case of Fugacity (Mr. Whimpey), who imagines that he was chased by two men."

The indignant faces of the Jew shopkeeper and the Magdalen Don started out of the crowd in their indignation, but the speaker continued:

"One poor woman we have with us," he said, in a compassionate voice, "believes she was in a motor-car with two such men; this is the well-known illusion of speed on which I need not dwell. Another wretched woman has the simple egotistic mania that she has caused the duel. Madeleine Durand actually professes to have been the subject of the fight between MacIan and his enemy, a fight which, if it occurred at all, certainly began long before. But it never occurred at all. We have taken in hand every person who professed to have seen such a thing, and proved them all to be unbalanced. That is why they are here."

The Master looked round the room, just showing his perfect teeth with the perfection of artistic cruelty, exalted for a moment in the enormous simplicity of his success, and then walked across the hall and vanished through an inner door. His two lieutenants, Quayle and Hutton, were left standing at the head of the great army of servants and keepers.

"I hope we shall have no more trouble," said Dr. Quayle pleasantly enough, and addressing Turnbull, who was leaning heavily upon the back of a chair.

Still looking down, Turnbull lifted the chair an inch or two from the ground. Then he suddenly swung it above his head and sent it at the inquiring doctor with an awful crash which sent one of its wooden legs loose along the floor and crammed the doctor gasping into a corner. MacIan gave a great shout, snatched up the loose chair-leg, and, rushing on the other doctor, felled him with a blow. Twenty attendants rushed to capture the rebels; MacIan flung back three of them and Turnbull went over on top of one, when from behind them all came a shriek as of something quite fresh and frightful.

Two of the three passages leading out of the hall were choked with blue smoke. Another instant and the hall was full of the fog of it, and red sparks began to swarm like scarlet bees.

"The place is on fire!" cried Quayle with a scream of indecent terror. "Oh, who can have done it? How can it have happened?"

A light had come into Turnbull's eyes. "How did the French Revolution happen?" he asked.

"Oh, how should I know!" wailed the other.

"Then I will tell you," said Turnbull; "it happened because some people fancied that a French grocer was as respectable as he looked."

Even as he spoke, as if by confirmation, old Mr. Durand re-entered the smoky room quite placidly, wiping the petroleum from his hands with a handkerchief. He had set fire to the building in accordance with the strict principles of the social contract.

But MacIan had taken a stride forward and stood there shaken and terrible. "Now," he cried, panting, "now is the judgment of this world. The doctors will leave this place; the keepers will leave this place. They will leave us in charge of the machinery and the machine guns at the windows. But we, the lunatics, will wait to be burned alive if only we may see them go."

"How do you know we shall go?" asked Hutton, fiercely.

"You believe nothing," said MacIan, simply, "and you are insupportably afraid of death."

"So this is suicide," sneered the doctor; "a somewhat doubtful sign of sanity."

"Not at all—this is vengeance," answered Turnbull, quite calmly; "a thing which is completely healthy."

"You think the doctors will go," said Hutton, savagely.

"The keepers have gone already," said Turnbull.

Even as they spoke the main doors were burst open in mere brutal panic, and all the officers and subordinates of the asylum rushed away across the garden pursued by the smoke. But among the ticketed maniacs not a man or woman moved.

"We hate dying," said Turnbull, with composure, "but we hate you even more. This is a successful revolution."

In the roof above their heads a panel shot back, showing a strip of starlit sky and a huge thing made of white metal, with the shape and fins of a fish, swinging as if at anchor. At the same moment a steel ladder slid down from the opening and struck the floor, and the cleft chin of the mysterious Master was thrust into the opening. "Quayle, Hutton," he said, "you will escape with me." And they went up the ladder like automata of lead.

Long after they had clambered into the car, the creature with the cloven face continued to leer down upon the smoke-stung crowd below. Then at last he said in a silken voice and with a smile of final satisfaction: "By the way, I fear I am very absent minded. There is one man specially whom, somehow, I always forget. I always leave him lying about. Once I mislaid him on the Cross of St. Paul's. So silly of me; and now I've forgotten him in one of those little cells where your fire is burning. Very unfortunate — especially for him." And nodding genially, he climbed into his flying ship.

MacIan stood motionless for two minutes, and then rushed down one of the suffocating corridors till he found the flames. Turnbull looked once at Madeleine, and followed.

MacIan, with singed hair, smoking garments, and smarting hands and face, had already broken far enough through the first barriers of burning timber to come within cry of the cells he had once known. It was impossible, however, to see the spot where the old man lay dead or alive; not now through darkness, but through scorching and aching light. The site of the old half-wit's cell was now the heart of a standing forest of fire — the flames as thick and yellow as a corn field. Their incessant shrieking and crackling was like a mob shouting against an orator. Yet through all that deafening density MacIan thought he heard a small and separate sound. When he heard it he rushed forward as if to plunge into that furnace, but Turnbull arrested him by an elbow.

"Let me go!" cried Evan, in agony; "it's the poor old beggar's voice — he's still alive, and shouting for help."

"Listen!" said Turnbull, and lifted one finger from his clenched hand.

"Or else he is shrieking with pain," protested MacIan. "I will not endure it."

"Listen!" repeated Turnbull, grimly. "Did you ever hear any one shout for help or shriek with pain in that voice?"

The small shrill sounds which came through the crash of the conflagration were indeed of an odd sort, and MacIan turned a face of puzzled inquiry to his companion.

"He is singing," said Turnbull, simply.

A remaining rampart fell, crushing the fire, and through the diminished din of it the voice of the little old lunatic came clearer. In the heart of that white-hot hell he was singing like a bird. What he was singing it was not very easy to follow, but it seemed to be something about playing in the golden hay.

"Good Lord!" said Turnbull, bitterly, "there seem to be some advantages in really being an idiot." Then advancing to the fringe of the fire he called out on chance to the invisible singer: "Can you come out? Are you cut off?"

"God help us all!" said MacIan, with a shudder; "he's laughing now."

At whatever stage of being burned alive the invisible now found himself, he was now shaking out peals of silvery and hilarious laughter. As he listened, MacIan's two eyes began to glow, as if a strange thought had come into his head.

"Fool, come out and save yourself!" shouted Turnbull.

"No, by Heaven! that is not the way," cried Evan, suddenly. "Father," he shouted, "come out and save us all!"

The fire, though it had dropped in one or two places, was, upon the whole, higher and more unconquerable than ever. Separate tall flames shot up and spread out above them like the fiery cloisters of some infernal cathedral, or like a grove of red tropical trees in the garden of the devil. Higher yet in the purple hollow of the night the topmost flames leapt again and again fruitlessly at the stars, like golden dragons chained but struggling. The towers and domes of the oppressive smoke seemed high and far enough to drown distant planets in a London fog. But if we exhausted all frantic similes for that frantic scene, the main impression about the fire would still be its ranked upstanding rigidity and a sort of roaring stillness. It was literally a wall of fire.

"Father," cried MacIan, once more, "come out of it and save us all!" Turnbull was staring at him as he cried.

The tall and steady forest of fire must have been already a portent visible to the whole circle of land and sea. The red flush of it lit up the long sides of white ships far out in the German Ocean, and picked out like piercing rubies the windows in the villages on the distant heights. If any villagers or sailors were looking toward it they must have seen a strange sight as MacIan cried out for the third time.

That forest of fire wavered, and was cloven in the centre; and then the whole of one half of it leaned one way as a corn field leans all one way under the load of the wind. Indeed, it looked as if a great wind had sprung up and driven the great fire aslant. Its smoke was no longer sent up to choke the stars, but was trailed and dragged across county after county like one dreadful banner of defeat.

But it was not the wind; or, if it was the wind, it was two winds blowing in opposite directions. For while one half of the huge fire sloped one way toward the inland heights, the other half, at exactly the same angle, sloped out eastward toward the sea. So that earth and ocean could behold, where there had been a mere fiery mass, a thing divided like a V—a cloven tongue of flame. But if it were a prodigy for those distant, it

was something beyond speech for those quite near. As the echoes of
Evan's last appeal rang and died in the universal uproar, the fiery vault
over his head opened down the middle, and, reeling back in two great
golden billows, hung on each side as huge and harmless as two sloping
hills lie on each side of a valley. Down the centre of this trough, or
chasm, a little path ran, cleared of all but ashes, and down this little path
was walking a little old man singing as if he were alone in a wood in
spring.

When James Turnbull saw this he suddenly put out a hand and
seemed to support himself on the strong shoulder of Madeleine Durand. Then after a moment's hesitation he put his other hand on the
shoulder of MacIan. His blue eyes looked extraordinarily brilliant and
beautiful. In many sceptical papers and magazines afterward he was
sadly or sternly rebuked for having abandoned the certainties of materialism. All his life up to that moment he had been most honestly
certain that materialism was a fact. But he was unlike the writers in the
magazines precisely in this — that he preferred a fact even to materialism.

As the little singing figure came nearer and nearer, Evan fell on his
knees, and after an instant Beatrice followed; then Madeleine fell on her
knees, and after a longer instant Turnbull followed. Then the little old
man went past them singing down that corridor of flames. They had not
looked at his face.

When he had passed they looked up. While the first light of the fire
had shot east and west, painting the sides of ships with fire-light or
striking red sparks out of windowed houses, it had not hitherto struck
upward, for there was above it the ponderous and rococo cavern of its
own monstrous coloured smoke. But now the fire was turned to left and
right like a woman's hair parted in the middle, and now the shafts of its
light could shoot up into empty heavens and strike anything, either bird
or cloud. But it struck something that was neither cloud nor bird. Far, far
away up in those huge hollows of space something was flying swiftly and
shining brightly, something that shone too bright and flew too fast to be
any of the fowls of the air, though the red light lit it from underneath like
the breast of a bird. Every one knew it was a flying ship, and every one
knew whose.

As they stared upward the little speck of light seemed slightly tilted,
and two black dots dropped from the edge of it. All the eager, upturned
faces watched the two dots as they grew bigger and bigger in their
downward rush. Then some one screamed, and no one looked up any
more. For the two bodies, larger every second flying, spread out and
sprawling in the fire-light, were the dead bodies of the two doctors
whom Professor Lucifer had carried with him — the weak and sneering

Quayle, the cold and clumsy Hutton. They went with a crash into the thick of the fire.

"They are gone!" screamed Beatrice, hiding her head. "O God! They are lost!"

Evan put his arm about her, and remembered his own vision.

"No, they are not lost," he said. "They are saved. He has taken away no souls with him, after all."

He looked vaguely about at the fire that was already fading, and there among the ashes lay two shining things that had survived the fire, his sword and Turnbull's, fallen haphazard in the pattern of a cross.

THE END

A CATALOG OF SELECTED DOVER
BOOKS IN ALL FIELDS OF INTEREST

CONCERNING THE SPIRITUAL IN ART, Wassily Kandinsky. Pioneering work by father of abstract art. Thoughts on color theory, nature of art. Analysis of earlier masters. 12 illustrations. 80pp. of text. 5⅜ × 8½. 23411-8 Pa. $3.95

ANIMALS: 1,419 Copyright-Free Illustrations of Mammals, Birds, Fish, Insects, etc., Jim Harter (ed.). Clear wood engravings present, in extremely lifelike poses, over 1,000 species of animals. One of the most extensive pictorial sourcebooks of its kind. Captions. Index. 284pp. 9 × 12. 23766-4 Pa. $11.95

CELTIC ART: The Methods of Construction, George Bain. Simple geometric techniques for making Celtic interlacements, spirals, Kells-type initials, animals, humans, etc. Over 500 illustrations. 160pp. 9 × 12. (USO) 22923-8 Pa. $9.95

AN ATLAS OF ANATOMY FOR ARTISTS, Fritz Schider. Most thorough reference work on art anatomy in the world. Hundreds of illustrations, including selections from works by Vesalius, Leonardo, Goya, Ingres, Michelangelo, others. 593 illustrations. 192pp. 7⅛ × 10¼. 20241-0 Pa. $8.95

CELTIC HAND STROKE-BY-STROKE (Irish Half-Uncial from "The Book of Kells"): An Arthur Baker Calligraphy Manual, Arthur Baker. Complete guide to creating each letter of the alphabet in distinctive Celtic manner. Covers hand position, strokes, pens, inks, paper, more. Illustrated. 48pp. 8¼ × 11.
24336-2 Pa. $3.95

EASY ORIGAMI, John Montroll. Charming collection of 32 projects (hat, cup, pelican, piano, swan, many more) specially designed for the novice origami hobbyist. Clearly illustrated easy-to-follow instructions insure that even beginning papercrafters will achieve successful results. 48pp. 8¼ × 11. 27298-2 Pa. $2.95

THE COMPLETE BOOK OF BIRDHOUSE CONSTRUCTION FOR WOOD-WORKERS, Scott D. Campbell. Detailed instructions, illustrations, tables. Also data on bird habitat and instinct patterns. Bibliography. 3 tables. 63 illustrations in 15 figures. 48pp. 5¼ × 8½. 24407-5 Pa. $1.95

BLOOMINGDALE'S ILLUSTRATED 1886 CATALOG: Fashions, Dry Goods and Housewares, Bloomingdale Brothers. Famed merchants' extremely rare catalog depicting about 1,700 products: clothing, housewares, firearms, dry goods, jewelry, more. Invaluable for dating, identifying vintage items. Also, copyright-free graphics for artists, designers. Co-published with Henry Ford Museum & Green-field Village. 160pp. 8¼ × 11. 25780-0 Pa. $9.95

HISTORIC COSTUME IN PICTURES, Braun & Schneider. Over 1,450 costumed figures in clearly detailed engravings—from dawn of civilization to end of 19th century. Captions. Many folk costumes. 256pp. 8⅜ × 11¾. 23150-X Pa. $11.95

STICKLEY CRAFTSMAN FURNITURE CATALOGS, Gustav Stickley and L. & J. G. Stickley. Beautiful, functional furniture in two authentic catalogs from 1910. 594 illustrations, including 277 photos, show settles, rockers, armchairs, reclining chairs, bookcases, desks, tables. 183pp. 6½ × 9¼.   23838-5 Pa. $8.95

AMERICAN LOCOMOTIVES IN HISTORIC PHOTOGRAPHS: 1858 to 1949, Ron Ziel (ed.). A rare collection of 126 meticulously detailed official photographs, called "builder portraits," of American locomotives that majestically chronicle the rise of steam locomotive power in America. Introduction. Detailed captions. xi + 129pp. 9 × 12.   27393-8 Pa. $12.95

AMERICA'S LIGHTHOUSES: An Illustrated History, Francis Ross Holland, Jr. Delightfully written, profusely illustrated fact-filled survey of over 200 American lighthouses since 1716. History, anecdotes, technological advances, more. 240pp. 8 × 10¾.   25576-X Pa. $11.95

TOWARDS A NEW ARCHITECTURE, Le Corbusier. Pioneering manifesto by founder of "International School." Technical and aesthetic theories, views of industry, economics, relation of form to function, "mass-production split" and much more. Profusely illustrated. 320pp. 6⅛ × 9¼. (USO)   25023-7 Pa. $8.95

HOW THE OTHER HALF LIVES, Jacob Riis. Famous journalistic record, exposing poverty and degradation of New York slums around 1900, by major social reformer. 100 striking and influential photographs. 233pp. 10 × 7⅞.   22012-5 Pa $10.95

FRUIT KEY AND TWIG KEY TO TREES AND SHRUBS, William M. Harlow. One of the handiest and most widely used identification aids. Fruit key covers 120 deciduous and evergreen species; twig key 160 deciduous species. Easily used. Over 300 photographs. 126pp. 5⅜ × 8½.   20511-8 Pa. $3.95

COMMON BIRD SONGS, Dr. Donald J. Borror. Songs of 60 most common U.S. birds: robins, sparrows, cardinals, bluejays, finches, more—arranged in order of increasing complexity. Up to 9 variations of songs of each species.
                Cassette and manual 99911-4 $8.95

ORCHIDS AS HOUSE PLANTS, Rebecca Tyson Northen. Grow cattleyas and many other kinds of orchids—in a window, in a case, or under artificial light. 63 illustrations. 148pp. 5⅜ × 8½.   23261-1 Pa. $3.95

MONSTER MAZES, Dave Phillips. Masterful mazes at four levels of difficulty. Avoid deadly perils and evil creatures to find magical treasures. Solutions for all 32 exciting illustrated puzzles. 48pp. 8¼ × 11.   26005-4 Pa. $2.95

MOZART'S DON GIOVANNI (DOVER OPERA LIBRETTO SERIES), Wolfgang Amadeus Mozart. Introduced and translated by Ellen H. Bleiler. Standard Italian libretto, with complete English translation. Convenient and thoroughly portable—an ideal companion for reading along with a recording or the performance itself. Introduction. List of characters. Plot summary. 121pp. 5¼ × 8½.
                24944-1 Pa. $2.95

TECHNICAL MANUAL AND DICTIONARY OF CLASSICAL BALLET, Gail Grant. Defines, explains, comments on steps, movements, poses and concepts. 15-page pictorial section. Basic book for student, viewer. 127pp. 5⅜ × 8½.
                21843-0 Pa. $3.95

BRASS INSTRUMENTS: Their History and Development, Anthony Baines. Authoritative, updated survey of the evolution of trumpets, trombones, bugles, cornets, French horns, tubas and other brass wind instruments. Over 140 illustrations and 48 music examples. Corrected and updated by author. New preface. Bibliography. 320pp. 5⅜ × 8½. 27574-4 Pa. $9.95

HOLLYWOOD GLAMOR PORTRAITS, John Kobal (ed.). 145 photos from 1926–49. Harlow, Gable, Bogart, Bacall; 94 stars in all. Full background on photographers, technical aspects. 160pp. 8⅜ × 11¼. 23352-9 Pa. $11.95

MAX AND MORITZ, Wilhelm Busch. Great humor classic in both German and English. Also 10 other works: "Cat and Mouse," "Plisch and Plumm," etc. 216pp. 5⅜ × 8½. 20181-3 Pa. $5.95

THE RAVEN AND OTHER FAVORITE POEMS, Edgar Allan Poe. Over 40 of the author's most memorable poems: "The Bells," "Ulalume," "Israfel," "To Helen," "The Conqueror Worm," "Eldorado," "Annabel Lee," many more. Alphabetic lists of titles and first lines. 64pp. 5³/₁₆ × 8¼. 26685-0 Pa. $1.00

SEVEN SCIENCE FICTION NOVELS, H. G. Wells. The standard collection of the great novels. Complete, unabridged. First Men in the Moon, Island of Dr. Moreau, War of the Worlds, Food of the Gods, Invisible Man, Time Machine, In the Days of the Comet. Total of 1,015pp. 5⅜ × 8½. (USO) 20264-X Clothbd. $29.95

AMULETS AND SUPERSTITIONS, E. A. Wallis Budge. Comprehensive discourse on origin, powers of amulets in many ancient cultures: Arab, Persian, Babylonian, Assyrian, Egyptian, Gnostic, Hebrew, Phoenician, Syriac, etc. Covers cross, swastika, crucifix, seals, rings, stones, etc. 584pp. 5⅜ × 8½. 23573-4 Pa. $12.95

RUSSIAN STORIES/PYCCKNE PACCKA3bl: A Dual-Language Book, edited by Gleb Struve. Twelve tales by such masters as Chekhov, Tolstoy, Dostoevsky, Pushkin, others. Excellent word-for-word English translations on facing pages, plus teaching and study aids, Russian/English vocabulary, biographical/critical introductions, more. 416pp. 5⅜ × 8½. 26244-8 Pa. $8.95

PHILADELPHIA THEN AND NOW: 60 Sites Photographed in the Past and Present, Kenneth Finkel and Susan Oyama. Rare photographs of City Hall, Logan Square, Independence Hall, Betsy Ross House, other landmarks juxtaposed with contemporary views. Captures changing face of historic city. Introduction. Captions. 128pp. 8¼ × 11. 25790-8 Pa. $9.95

AIA ARCHITECTURAL GUIDE TO NASSAU AND SUFFOLK COUNTIES, LONG ISLAND, The American Institute of Architects, Long Island Chapter, and the Society for the Preservation of Long Island Antiquities. Comprehensive, well-researched and generously illustrated volume brings to life over three centuries of Long Island's great architectural heritage. More than 240 photographs with authoritative, extensively detailed captions. 176pp. 8¼ × 11. 26946-9 Pa. $14.95

NORTH AMERICAN INDIAN LIFE: Customs and Traditions of 23 Tribes, Elsie Clews Parsons (ed.). 27 fictionalized essays by noted anthropologists examine religion, customs, government, additional facets of life among the Winnebago, Crow, Zuni, Eskimo, other tribes. 480pp. 6⅛ × 9¼. 27377-6 Pa. $10.95

FRANK LLOYD WRIGHT'S HOLLYHOCK HOUSE, Donald Hoffmann. Lavishly illustrated, carefully documented study of one of Wright's most controversial residential designs. Over 120 photographs, floor plans, elevations, etc. Detailed perceptive text by noted Wright scholar. Index. 128pp. 9¼ × 10¾.
27133-1 Pa. $11.95

THE MALE AND FEMALE FIGURE IN MOTION: 60 Classic Photographic Sequences, Eadweard Muybridge. 60 true-action photographs of men and women walking, running, climbing, bending, turning, etc., reproduced from rare 19th-century masterpiece. vi + 121pp. 9 × 12. 24745-7 Pa. $10.95

1001 QUESTIONS ANSWERED ABOUT THE SEASHORE, N. J. Berrill and Jacquelyn Berrill. Queries answered about dolphins, sea snails, sponges, starfish, fishes, shore birds, many others. Covers appearance, breeding, growth, feeding, much more. 305pp. 5¼ × 8¼. 23366-9 Pa. $7.95

GUIDE TO OWL WATCHING IN NORTH AMERICA, Donald S. Heintzelman. Superb guide offers complete data and descriptions of 19 species: barn owl, screech owl, snowy owl, many more. Expert coverage of owl-watching equipment, conservation, migrations and invasions, etc. Guide to observing sites. 84 illustrations. xiii + 193pp. 5⅜ × 8½. 27344-X Pa. $7.95

MEDICINAL AND OTHER USES OF NORTH AMERICAN PLANTS: A Historical Survey with Special Reference to the Eastern Indian Tribes, Charlotte Erichsen-Brown. Chronological historical citations document 500 years of usage of plants, trees, shrubs native to eastern Canada, northeastern U.S. Also complete identifying information. 343 illustrations. 544pp. 6½ × 9¼. 25951-X Pa. $12.95

STORYBOOK MAZES, Dave Phillips. 23 stories and mazes on two-page spreads: Wizard of Oz, Treasure Island, Robin Hood, etc. Solutions. 64pp. 8¼ × 11.
23628-5 Pa. $2.95

NEGRO FOLK MUSIC, U.S.A., Harold Courlander. Noted folklorist's scholarly yet readable analysis of rich and varied musical tradition. Includes authentic versions of over 40 folk songs. Valuable bibliography and discography. xi + 324pp. 5⅜ × 8½. 27350-4 Pa. $7.95

MOVIE-STAR PORTRAITS OF THE FORTIES, John Kobal (ed.). 163 glamor, studio photos of 106 stars of the 1940s: Rita Hayworth, Ava Gardner, Marlon Brando, Clark Gable, many more. 176pp. 8⅜ × 11¼. 23546-7 Pa. $10.95

BENCHLEY LOST AND FOUND, Robert Benchley. Finest humor from early 30s, about pet peeves, child psychologists, post office and others. Mostly unavailable elsewhere. 73 illustrations by Peter Arno and others. 183pp. 5⅜ × 8½.
22410-4 Pa. $5.95

YEKL and THE IMPORTED BRIDEGROOM AND OTHER STORIES OF YIDDISH NEW YORK, Abraham Cahan. Film Hester Street based on Yekl (1896). Novel, other stories among first about Jewish immigrants on N.Y.'s East Side. 240pp. 5⅜ × 8½. 22427-9 Pa. $6.95

SELECTED POEMS, Walt Whitman. Generous sampling from *Leaves of Grass*. Twenty-four poems include "I Hear America Singing," "Song of the Open Road," "I Sing the Body Electric," "When Lilacs Last in the Dooryard Bloom'd," "O Captain! My Captain!"—all reprinted from an authoritative edition. Lists of titles and first lines. 128pp. 5$\frac{3}{16}$ × 8¼. 26878-0 Pa. $1.00

THE BEST TALES OF HOFFMANN, E. T. A. Hoffmann. 10 of Hoffmann's most important stories: "Nutcracker and the King of Mice," "The Golden Flowerpot," etc. 458pp. 5⅜ × 8½. 21793-0 Pa. $8.95

FROM FETISH TO GOD IN ANCIENT EGYPT, E. A. Wallis Budge. Rich detailed survey of Egyptian conception of "God" and gods, magic, cult of animals, Osiris, more. Also, superb English translations of hymns and legends. 240 illustrations. 545pp. 5⅜ × 8½. 25803-3 Pa. $11.95

FRENCH STORIES/CONTES FRANÇAIS: A Dual-Language Book, Wallace Fowlie. Ten stories by French masters, Voltaire to Camus: "Micromegas" by Voltaire; "The Atheist's Mass" by Balzac; "Minuet" by de Maupassant; "The Guest" by Camus, six more. Excellent English translations on facing pages. Also French-English vocabulary list, exercises, more. 352pp. 5⅜ × 8½. 26443-2 Pa. $8.95

CHICAGO AT THE TURN OF THE CENTURY IN PHOTOGRAPHS: 122 Historic Views from the Collections of the Chicago Historical Society, Larry A. Viskochil. Rare large-format prints offer detailed views of City Hall, State Street, the Loop, Hull House, Union Station, many other landmarks, circa 1904–1913. Introduction. Captions. Maps. 144pp. 9⅜ × 12¼. 24656-6 Pa. $12.95

OLD BROOKLYN IN EARLY PHOTOGRAPHS, 1865–1929, William Lee Younger. Luna Park, Gravesend race track, construction of Grand Army Plaza, moving of Hotel Brighton, etc. 157 previously unpublished photographs. 165pp. 8⅞ × 11¾. 23587-4 Pa. $13.95

THE MYTHS OF THE NORTH AMERICAN INDIANS, Lewis Spence. Rich anthology of the myths and legends of the Algonquins, Iroquois, Pawnees and Sioux, prefaced by an extensive historical and ethnological commentary. 36 illustrations. 480pp. 5⅜ × 8½. 25967-6 Pa. $8.95

AN ENCYCLOPEDIA OF BATTLES: Accounts of Over 1,560 Battles from 1479 B.C. to the Present, David Eggenberger. Essential details of every major battle in recorded history from the first battle of Megiddo in 1479 B.C. to Grenada in 1984. List of Battle Maps. New Appendix covering the years 1967–1984. Index. 99 illustrations. 544pp. 6½ × 9¼. 24913-1 Pa. $14.95

SAILING ALONE AROUND THE WORLD, Captain Joshua Slocum. First man to sail around the world, alone, in small boat. One of great feats of seamanship told in delightful manner. 67 illustrations. 294pp. 5⅜ × 8½. 20326-3 Pa. $5.95

ANARCHISM AND OTHER ESSAYS, Emma Goldman. Powerful, penetrating, prophetic essays on direct action, role of minorities, prison reform, puritan hypocrisy, violence, etc. 271pp. 5⅜ × 8½. 22484-8 Pa. $5.95

MYTHS OF THE HINDUS AND BUDDHISTS, Ananda K. Coomaraswamy and Sister Nivedita. Great stories of the epics; deeds of Krishna, Shiva, taken from puranas, Vedas, folk tales; etc. 32 illustrations. 400pp. 5⅜ × 8½. 21759-0 Pa. $9.95

BEYOND PSYCHOLOGY, Otto Rank. Fear of death, desire of immortality, nature of sexuality, social organization, creativity, according to Rankian system. 291pp. 5⅜ × 8½. 20485-5 Pa. $7.95

A THEOLOGICO-POLITICAL TREATISE, Benedict Spinoza. Also contains unfinished Political Treatise. Great classic on religious liberty, theory of government on common consent. R. Elwes translation. Total of 421pp. 5⅜ × 8½. 20249-6 Pa. $8.95

MY BONDAGE AND MY FREEDOM, Frederick Douglass. Born a slave, Douglass became outspoken force in antislavery movement. The best of Douglass' auto-biographies. Graphic description of slave life. 464pp. 5⅜ × 8½.   22457-0 Pa. $8.95

FOLLOWING THE EQUATOR: A Journey Around the World, Mark Twain. Fascinating humorous account of 1897 voyage to Hawaii, Australia, India, New Zealand, etc. Ironic, bemused reports on peoples, customs, climate, flora and fauna, politics, much more. 197 illustrations. 720pp. 5⅜ × 8½.   26113-1 Pa. $15.95

THE PEOPLE CALLED SHAKERS, Edward D. Andrews. Definitive study of Shakers: origins, beliefs, practices, dances, social organization, furniture and crafts, etc. 33 illustrations. 351pp. 5⅜ × 8½.   21081-2 Pa. $8.95

THE MYTHS OF GREECE AND ROME, H. A. Guerber. A classic of mythology, generously illustrated, long prized for its simple, graphic, accurate retelling of the principal myths of Greece and Rome, and for its commentary on their origins and significance. With 64 illustrations by Michelangelo, Raphael, Titian, Rubens, Canova, Bernini and others. 480pp. 5⅜ × 8½.   27584-1 Pa. $9.95

PSYCHOLOGY OF MUSIC, Carl E. Seashore. Classic work discusses music as a medium from psychological viewpoint. Clear treatment of physical acoustics, auditory apparatus, sound perception, development of musical skills, nature of musical feeling, host of other topics. 88 figures. 408pp. 5⅜ × 8½.   21851-1 Pa. $9.95

THE PHILOSOPHY OF HISTORY, Georg W. Hegel. Great classic of Western thought develops concept that history is not chance but rational process, the evolution of freedom. 457pp. 5⅜ × 8½.   20112-0 Pa. $9.95

THE BOOK OF TEA, Kakuzo Okakura. Minor classic of the Orient: entertaining, charming explanation, interpretation of traditional Japanese culture in terms of tea ceremony. 94pp. 5⅜ × 8½.   20070-1 Pa. $2.95

LIFE IN ANCIENT EGYPT, Adolf Erman. Fullest, most thorough, detailed older account with much not in more recent books, domestic life, religion, magic, medicine, commerce, much more. Many illustrations reproduce tomb paintings, carvings, hieroglyphs, etc. 597pp. 5⅜ × 8½.   22632-8 Pa. $10.95

SUNDIALS, Their Theory and Construction, Albert Waugh. Far and away the best, most thorough coverage of ideas, mathematics concerned, types, construction, adjusting anywhere. Simple, nontechnical treatment allows even children to build several of these dials. Over 100 illustrations. 230pp. 5⅜ × 8½.   22947-5 Pa. $7.95

DYNAMICS OF FLUIDS IN POROUS MEDIA, Jacob Bear. For advanced students of ground water hydrology, soil mechanics and physics, drainage and irrigation engineering, and more. 335 illustrations. Exercises, with answers. 784pp. 6⅛ × 9¼.   65675-6 Pa. $19.95

SONGS OF EXPERIENCE: Facsimile Reproduction with 26 Plates in Full Color, William Blake. 26 full-color plates from a rare 1826 edition. Includes "The Tyger," "London," "Holy Thursday," and other poems. Printed text of poems. 48pp. 5¼ × 7.   24636-1 Pa. $4.95

OLD-TIME VIGNETTES IN FULL COLOR, Carol Belanger Grafton (ed.). Over 390 charming, often sentimental illustrations, selected from archives of Victorian graphics—pretty women posing, children playing, food, flowers, kittens and puppies, smiling cherubs, birds and butterflies, much more. All copyright-free. 48pp. 9¼ × 12¼.   27269-9 Pa. $5.95

PERSPECTIVE FOR ARTISTS, Rex Vicat Cole. Depth, perspective of sky and sea, shadows, much more, not usually covered. 391 diagrams, 81 reproductions of drawings and paintings. 279pp. 5⅜ × 8½. 22487-2 Pa. $6.95

DRAWING THE LIVING FIGURE, Joseph Sheppard. Innovative approach to artistic anatomy focuses on specifics of surface anatomy, rather than muscles and bones. Over 170 drawings of live models in front, back and side views, and in widely varying poses. Accompanying diagrams. 177 illustrations. Introduction. Index. 144pp. 8⅜ × 11¼. 26723-7 Pa. $7.95

GOTHIC AND OLD ENGLISH ALPHABETS: 100 Complete Fonts, Dan X. Solo. Add power, elegance to posters, signs, other graphics with 100 stunning copyright-free alphabets: Blackstone, Dolbey, Germania, 97 more—including many lower-case, numerals, punctuation marks. 104pp. 8⅛ × 11. 24695-7 Pa. $7.95

HOW TO DO BEADWORK, Mary White. Fundamental book on craft from simple projects to five-bead chains and woven works. 106 illustrations. 142pp. 5⅜ × 8. 20697-1 Pa. $4.95

THE BOOK OF WOOD CARVING, Charles Marshall Sayers. Finest book for beginners discusses fundamentals and offers 34 designs. "Absolutely first rate . . . well thought out and well executed."—E. J. Tangerman. 118pp. 7¾ × 10⅝. 23654-4 Pa. $5.95

ILLUSTRATED CATALOG OF CIVIL WAR MILITARY GOODS: Union Army Weapons, Insignia, Uniform Accessories, and Other Equipment, Schuyler, Hartley, and Graham. Rare, profusely illustrated 1846 catalog includes Union Army uniform and dress regulations, arms and ammunition, coats, insignia, flags, swords, rifles, etc. 226 illustrations. 160pp. 9 × 12. 24939-5 Pa. $10.95

WOMEN'S FASHIONS OF THE EARLY 1900s: An Unabridged Republication of "New York Fashions, 1909," National Cloak & Suit Co. Rare catalog of mail-order fashions documents women's and children's clothing styles shortly after the turn of the century. Captions offer full descriptions, prices. Invaluable resource for fashion, costume historians. Approximately 725 illustrations. 128pp. 8⅜ × 11¼. 27276-1 Pa. $11.95

THE 1912 AND 1915 GUSTAV STICKLEY FURNITURE CATALOGS, Gustav Stickley. With over 200 detailed illustrations and descriptions, these two catalogs are essential reading and reference materials and identification guides for Stickley furniture. Captions cite materials, dimensions and prices. 112pp. 6½ × 9¼. 26676-1 Pa. $9.95

EARLY AMERICAN LOCOMOTIVES, John H. White, Jr. Finest locomotive engravings from early 19th century: historical (1804–74), main-line (after 1870), special, foreign, etc. 147 plates. 142pp. 11⅜ × 8¼. 22772-3 Pa. $8.95

THE TALL SHIPS OF TODAY IN PHOTOGRAPHS, Frank O. Braynard. Lavishly illustrated tribute to nearly 100 majestic contemporary sailing vessels: Amerigo Vespucci, Clearwater, Constitution, Eagle, Mayflower, Sea Cloud, Victory, many more. Authoritative captions provide statistics, background on each ship. 190 black-and-white photographs and illustrations. Introduction. 128pp. 8⅞ × 11¾. 27163-3 Pa. $13.95

EARLY NINETEENTH-CENTURY CRAFTS AND TRADES, Peter Stockham (ed.). Extremely rare 1807 volume describes to youngsters the crafts and trades of the day: brickmaker, weaver, dressmaker, bookbinder, ropemaker, saddler, many more. Quaint prose, charming illustrations for each craft. 20 black-and-white line illustrations. 192pp. 4⅝ × 6. 27293-1 Pa. $4.95

VICTORIAN FASHIONS AND COSTUMES FROM HARPER'S BAZAR, 1867–1898, Stella Blum (ed.). Day costumes, evening wear, sports clothes, shoes, hats, other accessories in over 1,000 detailed engravings. 320pp. 9⅜ × 12¼. 22990-4 Pa. $13.95

GUSTAV STICKLEY, THE CRAFTSMAN, Mary Ann Smith. Superb study surveys broad scope of Stickley's achievement, especially in architecture. Design philosophy, rise and fall of the Craftsman empire, descriptions and floor plans for many Craftsman houses, more. 86 black-and-white halftones. 31 line illustrations. Introduction. 208pp. 6½ × 9¼. 27210-9 Pa. $9.95

THE LONG ISLAND RAIL ROAD IN EARLY PHOTOGRAPHS, Ron Ziel. Over 220 rare photos, informative text document origin (1844) and development of rail service on Long Island. Vintage views of early trains, locomotives, stations, passengers, crews, much more. Captions. 8⅞ × 11¾. 26301-0 Pa. $13.95

THE BOOK OF OLD SHIPS: From Egyptian Galleys to Clipper Ships, Henry B. Culver. Superb, authoritative history of sailing vessels, with 80 magnificent line illustrations. Galley, bark, caravel, longship, whaler, many more. Detailed, informative text on each vessel by noted naval historian. Introduction. 256pp. 5⅜ × 8½. 27332-6 Pa. $6.95

TEN BOOKS ON ARCHITECTURE, Vitruvius. The most important book ever written on architecture. Early Roman aesthetics, technology, classical orders, site selection, all other aspects. Morgan translation. 331pp. 5⅜ × 8½. 20645-9 Pa. $8.95

THE HUMAN FIGURE IN MOTION, Eadweard Muybridge. More than 4,500 stopped-action photos, in action series, showing undraped men, women, children jumping, lying down, throwing, sitting, wrestling, carrying, etc. 390pp. 7⅞ × 10⅝. 20204-6 Clothbd. $24.95

TREES OF THE EASTERN AND CENTRAL UNITED STATES AND CANADA, William M. Harlow. Best one-volume guide to 140 trees. Full descriptions, woodlore, range, etc. Over 600 illustrations. Handy size. 288pp. 4½ × 6⅜. 20395-6 Pa. $5.95

SONGS OF WESTERN BIRDS, Dr. Donald J. Borror. Complete song and call repertoire of 60 western species, including flycatchers, juncoes, cactus wrens, many more—includes fully illustrated booklet. Cassette and manual 99913-0 $8.95

GROWING AND USING HERBS AND SPICES, Milo Miloradovich. Versatile handbook provides all the information needed for cultivation and use of all the herbs and spices available in North America. 4 illustrations. Index. Glossary. 236pp. 5⅜ × 8½. 25058-X Pa. $5.95

BIG BOOK OF MAZES AND LABYRINTHS, Walter Shepherd. 50 mazes and labyrinths in all—classical, solid, ripple, and more—in one great volume. Perfect inexpensive puzzler for clever youngsters. Full solutions. 112pp. 8⅛ × 11. 22951-3 Pa. $3.95

PIANO TUNING, J. Cree Fischer. Clearest, best book for beginner, amateur. Simple repairs, raising dropped notes, tuning by easy method of flattened fifths. No previous skills needed. 4 illustrations. 201pp. 5⅜ × 8½. 23267-0 Pa. $5.95

A SOURCE BOOK IN THEATRICAL HISTORY, A. M. Nagler. Contemporary observers on acting, directing, make-up, costuming, stage props, machinery, scene design, from Ancient Greece to Chekhov. 611pp. 5⅜ × 8½. 20515-0 Pa. $11.95

THE COMPLETE NONSENSE OF EDWARD LEAR, Edward Lear. All nonsense limericks, zany alphabets, Owl and Pussycat, songs, nonsense botany, etc., illustrated by Lear. Total of 320pp. 5⅜ × 8½. (USO) 20167-8 Pa. $6.95

VICTORIAN PARLOUR POETRY: An Annotated Anthology, Michael R. Turner. 117 gems by Longfellow, Tennyson, Browning, many lesser-known poets. "The Village Blacksmith," "Curfew Must Not Ring Tonight," "Only a Baby Small," dozens more, often difficult to find elsewhere. Index of poets, titles, first lines. xxiii + 325pp. 5⅜ × 8¼. 27044-0 Pa. $8.95

DUBLINERS, James Joyce. Fifteen stories offer vivid, tightly focused observations of the lives of Dublin's poorer classes. At least one, "The Dead," is considered a masterpiece. Reprinted complete and unabridged from standard edition. 160pp. 5³⁄₁₆ × 8¼. 26870-5 Pa. $1.00

THE HAUNTED MONASTERY and THE CHINESE MAZE MURDERS, Robert van Gulik. Two full novels by van Gulik, set in 7th-century China, continue adventures of Judge Dee and his companions. An evil Taoist monastery, seemingly supernatural events; overgrown topiary maze hides strange crimes. 27 illustrations. 328pp. 5⅜ × 8½. 23502-5 Pa. $7.95

THE BOOK OF THE SACRED MAGIC OF ABRAMELIN THE MAGE, translated by S. MacGregor Mathers. Medieval manuscript of ceremonial magic. Basic document in Aleister Crowley, Golden Dawn groups. 268pp. 5⅜ × 8½. 23211-5 Pa. $8.95

NEW RUSSIAN-ENGLISH AND ENGLISH-RUSSIAN DICTIONARY, M. A. O'Brien. This is a remarkably handy Russian dictionary, containing a surprising amount of information, including over 70,000 entries. 366pp. 4½ × 6⅛. 20208-9 Pa. $9.95

HISTORIC HOMES OF THE AMERICAN PRESIDENTS, Second, Revised Edition, Irvin Haas. A traveler's guide to American Presidential homes, most open to the public, depicting and describing homes occupied by every American President from George Washington to George Bush. With visiting hours, admission charges, travel routes. 175 photographs. Index. 160pp. 8¼ × 11. 26751-2 Pa. $10.95

NEW YORK IN THE FORTIES, Andreas Feininger. 162 brilliant photographs by the well-known photographer, formerly with *Life* magazine. Commuters, shoppers, Times Square at night, much else from city at its peak. Captions by John von Hartz. 181pp. 9¼ × 10¾. 23585-8 Pa. $12.95

INDIAN SIGN LANGUAGE, William Tomkins. Over 525 signs developed by Sioux and other tribes. Written instructions and diagrams. Also 290 pictographs. 111pp. 6⅛ × 9¼. 22029-X Pa. $3.50

CATALOG OF DOVER BOOKS

ANATOMY: A Complete Guide for Artists, Joseph Sheppard. A master of figure drawing shows artists how to render human anatomy convincingly. Over 460 illustrations. 224pp. 8⅜ × 11¼. 27279-6 Pa. $9.95

MEDIEVAL CALLIGRAPHY: Its History and Technique, Marc Drogin. Spirited history, comprehensive instruction manual covers 13 styles (ca. 4th century thru 15th). Excellent photographs; directions for duplicating medieval techniques with modern tools. 224pp. 8⅜ × 11¼. 26142-5 Pa. $11.95

DRIED FLOWERS: How to Prepare Them, Sarah Whitlock and Martha Rankin. Complete instructions on how to use silica gel, meal and borax, perlite aggregate, sand and borax, glycerine and water to create attractive permanent flower arrangements. 12 illustrations. 32pp. 5⅜ × 8½. 21802-3 Pa. $1.00

EASY-TO-MAKE BIRD FEEDERS FOR WOODWORKERS, Scott D. Campbell. Detailed, simple-to-use guide for designing, constructing, caring for and using feeders. Text, illustrations for 12 classic and contemporary designs. 96pp. 5⅜ × 8½. 25847-5 Pa. $2.95

OLD-TIME CRAFTS AND TRADES, Peter Stockham. An 1807 book created to teach children about crafts and trades open to them as future careers. It describes in detailed, nontechnical terms 24 different occupations, among them coachmaker, gardener, hairdresser, lacemaker, shoemaker, wheelwright, copper-plate printer, milliner, trunkmaker, merchant and brewer. Finely detailed engravings illustrate each occupation. 192pp. 4⅝ × 6. 27398-9 Pa. $4.95

THE HISTORY OF UNDERCLOTHES, C. Willett Cunnington and Phyllis Cunnington. Fascinating, well-documented survey covering six centuries of English undergarments, enhanced with over 100 illustrations: 12th-century laced-up bodice, footed long drawers (1795), 19th-century bustles, 19th-century corsets for men, Victorian "bust improvers," much more. 272pp. 5⅜ × 8¼. 27124-2 Pa. $9.95

ARTS AND CRAFTS FURNITURE: The Complete Brooks Catalog of 1912, Brooks Manufacturing Co. Photos and detailed descriptions of more than 150 now very collectible furniture designs from the Arts and Crafts movement depict davenports, settees, buffets, desks, tables, chairs, bedsteads, dressers and more, all built of solid, quarter-sawed oak. Invaluable for students and enthusiasts of antiques, Americana and the decorative arts. 80pp. 6½ × 9¼. 27471-3 Pa. $7.95

HOW WE INVENTED THE AIRPLANE: An Illustrated History, Orville Wright. Fascinating firsthand account covers early experiments, construction of planes and motors, first flights, much more. Introduction and commentary by Fred C. Kelly. 76 photographs. 96pp. 8¼ × 11. 25662-6 Pa. $8.95

THE ARTS OF THE SAILOR: Knotting, Splicing and Ropework, Hervey Garrett Smith. Indispensable shipboard reference covers tools, basic knots and useful hitches; handsewing and canvas work, more. Over 100 illustrations. Delightful reading for sea lovers. 256pp. 5⅜ × 8½. 26440-8 Pa. $7.95

FRANK LLOYD WRIGHT'S FALLINGWATER: The House and Its History, Second, Revised Edition, Donald Hoffmann. A total revision—both in text and illustrations—of the standard document on Fallingwater, the boldest, most personal architectural statement of Wright's mature years, updated with valuable new material from the recently opened Frank Lloyd Wright Archives. "Fascinating"—The New York Times. 116 illustrations. 128pp. 9¼ × 10¾. 27430-6 Pa. $10.95

CATALOG OF DOVER BOOKS

PHOTOGRAPHIC SKETCHBOOK OF THE CIVIL WAR, Alexander Gardner. 100 photos taken on field during the Civil War. Famous shots of Manassas, Harper's Ferry, Lincoln, Richmond, slave pens, etc. 244pp. 10⅝ × 8¼.
22731-6 Pa. $9.95

FIVE ACRES AND INDEPENDENCE, Maurice G. Kains. Great back-to-the-land classic explains basics of self-sufficient farming. The one book to get. 95 illustrations. 397pp. 5⅜ × 8½. 20974-1 Pa. $7.95

SONGS OF EASTERN BIRDS, Dr. Donald J. Borror. Songs and calls of 60 species most common to eastern U.S.: warblers, woodpeckers, flycatchers, thrushes, larks, many more in high-quality recording. Cassette and manual 99912-2 $8.95

A MODERN HERBAL, Margaret Grieve. Much the fullest, most exact, most useful compilation of herbal material. Gigantic alphabetical encyclopedia, from aconite to zedoary, gives botanical information, medical properties, folklore, economic uses, much else. Indispensable to serious reader. 161 illustrations. 888pp. 6½ × 9¼. 2-vol. set. (USO) Vol. I: 22798-7 Pa. $9.95
Vol. II: 22799-5 Pa. $9.95

HIDDEN TREASURE MAZE BOOK, Dave Phillips. Solve 34 challenging mazes accompanied by heroic tales of adventure. Evil dragons, people-eating plants, bloodthirsty giants, many more dangerous adversaries lurk at every twist and turn. 34 mazes, stories, solutions. 48pp. 8¼ × 11. 24566-7 Pa. $2.95

LETTERS OF W. A. MOZART, Wolfgang A. Mozart. Remarkable letters show bawdy wit, humor, imagination, musical insights, contemporary musical world; includes some letters from Leopold Mozart. 276pp. 5⅜ × 8½. 22859-2 Pa. $6.95

BASIC PRINCIPLES OF CLASSICAL BALLET, Agrippina Vaganova. Great Russian theoretician, teacher explains methods for teaching classical ballet. 118 illustrations. 175pp. 5⅜ × 8½. 22036-2 Pa. $4.95

THE JUMPING FROG, Mark Twain. Revenge edition. The original story of The Celebrated Jumping Frog of Calaveras County, a hapless French translation, and Twain's hilarious "retranslation" from the French. 12 illustrations. 66pp. 5⅜ × 8½. 22686-7 Pa. $3.95

BEST REMEMBERED POEMS, Martin Gardner (ed.). The 126 poems in this superb collection of 19th- and 20th-century British and American verse range from Shelley's "To a Skylark" to the impassioned "Renascence" of Edna St. Vincent Millay and to Edward Lear's whimsical "The Owl and the Pussycat." 224pp. 5⅜ × 8½. 27165-X Pa. $4.95

COMPLETE SONNETS, William Shakespeare. Over 150 exquisite poems deal with love, friendship, the tyranny of time, beauty's evanescence, death and other themes in language of remarkable power, precision and beauty. Glossary of archaic terms. 80pp. 5³⁄₁₆ × 8¼. 26686-9 Pa. $1.00

BODIES IN A BOOKSHOP, R. T. Campbell. Challenging mystery of blackmail and murder with ingenious plot and superbly drawn characters. In the best tradition of British suspense fiction. 192pp. 5⅜ × 8½. 24720-1 Pa. $5.95

THE WIT AND HUMOR OF OSCAR WILDE, Alvin Redman (ed.). More than 1,000 ripostes, paradoxes, wisecracks: Work is the curse of the drinking classes; I can resist everything except temptation; etc. 258pp. 5⅜ × 8½. 20602-5 Pa. $5.95

SHAKESPEARE LEXICON AND QUOTATION DICTIONARY, Alexander Schmidt. Full definitions, locations, shades of meaning in every word in plays and poems. More than 50,000 exact quotations. 1,485pp. 6½ × 9¼. 2-vol. set.
Vol. 1: 22726-X Pa. $15.95
Vol. 2: 22727-8 Pa. $15.95

SELECTED POEMS, Emily Dickinson. Over 100 best-known, best-loved poems by one of America's foremost poets, reprinted from authoritative early editions. No comparable edition at this price. Index of first lines. 64pp. 5³⁄₁₆ × 8¼. 26466-1 Pa. $1.00

CELEBRATED CASES OF JUDGE DEE (DEE GOONG AN), translated by Robert van Gulik. Authentic 18th-century Chinese detective novel; Dee and associates solve three interlocked cases. Led to van Gulik's own stories with same characters. Extensive introduction. 9 illustrations. 237pp. 5⅜ × 8½. 23337-5 Pa. $6.95

THE MALLEUS MALEFICARUM OF KRAMER AND SPRENGER, translated by Montague Summers. Full text of most important witchhunter's "bible," used by both Catholics and Protestants. 278pp. 6⅝ × 10. 22802-9 Pa. $10.95

SPANISH STORIES/CUENTOS ESPAÑOLES: A Dual-Language Book, Angel Flores (ed.). Unique format offers 13 great stories in Spanish by Cervantes, Borges, others. Faithful English translations on facing pages. 352pp. 5⅜ × 8½. 25399-6 Pa. $8.95

THE CHICAGO WORLD'S FAIR OF 1893: A Photographic Record, Stanley Appelbaum (ed.). 128 rare photos show 200 buildings, Beaux-Arts architecture, Midway, original Ferris Wheel, Edison's kinetoscope, more. Architectural emphasis; full text. 116pp. 8¼ × 11. 23990-X Pa. $9.95

OLD QUEENS, N.Y., IN EARLY PHOTOGRAPHS, Vincent F. Seyfried and William Asadorian. Over 160 rare photographs of Maspeth, Jamaica, Jackson Heights, and other areas. Vintage views of DeWitt Clinton mansion, 1939 World's Fair and more. Captions. 192pp. 8⅞ × 11. 26358-4 Pa. $12.95

CAPTURED BY THE INDIANS: 15 Firsthand Accounts, 1750–1870, Frederick Drimmer. Astounding true historical accounts of grisly torture, bloody conflicts, relentless pursuits, miraculous escapes and more, by people who lived to tell the tale. 384pp. 5⅜ × 8½. 24901-8 Pa. $8.95

THE WORLD'S GREAT SPEECHES, Lewis Copeland and Lawrence W. Lamm (eds.). Vast collection of 278 speeches of Greeks to 1970. Powerful and effective models; unique look at history. 842pp. 5⅜ × 8½. 20468-5 Pa. $13.95

THE BOOK OF THE SWORD, Sir Richard F. Burton. Great Victorian scholar/adventurer's eloquent, erudite history of the "queen of weapons"—from prehistory to early Roman Empire. Evolution and development of early swords, variations (sabre, broadsword, cutlass, scimitar, etc.), much more. 336pp. 6⅛ × 9¼. 25434-8 Pa. $8.95

AUTOBIOGRAPHY: The Story of My Experiments with Truth, Mohandas K. Gandhi. Boyhood, legal studies, purification, the growth of the Satyagraha (nonviolent protest) movement. Critical, inspiring work of the man responsible for the freedom of India. 480pp. 5⅜ × 8½. (USO) 24593-4 Pa. $7.95

CELTIC MYTHS AND LEGENDS, T. W. Rolleston. Masterful retelling of Irish and Welsh stories and tales. Cuchulain, King Arthur, Deirdre, the Grail, many more. First paperback edition. 58 full-page illustrations. 512pp. 5⅜ × 8½. 26507-2 Pa. $9.95

THE PRINCIPLES OF PSYCHOLOGY, William James. Famous long course complete, unabridged. Stream of thought, time perception, memory, experimental methods; great work decades ahead of its time. 94 figures. 1,391pp. 5⅜ × 8½. 2-vol. set.
Vol. I: 20381-6 Pa. $12.95
Vol. II: 20382-4 Pa. $12.95

THE WORLD AS WILL AND REPRESENTATION, Arthur Schopenhauer. Definitive English translation of Schopenhauer's life work, correcting more than 1,000 errors, omissions in earlier translations. Translated by E. F. J. Payne. Total of 1,269pp. 5⅜ × 8½. 2-vol. set.
Vol. 1: 21761-2 Pa. $11.95
Vol. 2: 21762-0 Pa. $11.95

MAGIC AND MYSTERY IN TIBET, Madame Alexandra David-Neel. Experiences among lamas, magicians, sages, sorcerers, Bonpa wizards. A true psychic discovery. 32 illustrations. 321pp. 5⅜ × 8½. (USO) 22682-4 Pa. $8.95

THE EGYPTIAN BOOK OF THE DEAD, E. A. Wallis Budge. Complete reproduction of Ani's papyrus, finest ever found. Full hieroglyphic text, interlinear transliteration, word-for-word translation, smooth translation. 533pp. 6½ × 9¼. 21866-X Pa. $9.95

MATHEMATICS FOR THE NONMATHEMATICIAN, Morris Kline. Detailed, college-level treatment of mathematics in cultural and historical context, with numerous exercises. Recommended Reading Lists. Tables. Numerous figures. 641pp. 5⅜ × 8½. 24823-2 Pa. $11.95

THEORY OF WING SECTIONS: Including a Summary of Airfoil Data, Ira H. Abbott and A. E. von Doenhoff. Concise compilation of subsonic aerodynamic characteristics of NACA wing sections, plus description of theory. 350pp. of tables. 693pp. 5⅜ × 8½. 60586-8 Pa. $13.95

THE RIME OF THE ANCIENT MARINER, Gustave Doré, S. T. Coleridge. Doré's finest work; 34 plates capture moods, subtleties of poem. Flawless full-size reproductions printed on facing pages with authoritative text of poem. "Beautiful. Simply beautiful."—*Publisher's Weekly*. 77pp. 9¼ × 12. 22305-1 Pa. $5.95

NORTH AMERICAN INDIAN DESIGNS FOR ARTISTS AND CRAFTSPEOPLE, Eva Wilson. Over 360 authentic copyright-free designs adapted from Navajo blankets, Hopi pottery, Sioux buffalo hides, more. Geometrics, symbolic figures, plant and animal motifs, etc. 128pp. 8⅜ × 11. (EUK) 25341-4 Pa. $7.95

SCULPTURE: Principles and Practice, Louis Slobodkin. Step-by-step approach to clay, plaster, metals, stone; classical and modern. 253 drawings, photos. 255pp. 8⅛ × 11. 22960-2 Pa. $10.95

CATALOG OF DOVER BOOKS

THE INFLUENCE OF SEA POWER UPON HISTORY, 1660-1783, A. T. Mahan. Influential classic of naval history and tactics still used as text in war colleges. First paperback edition. 4 maps. 24 battle plans. 640pp. 5⅜ × 8½.
25509-3 Pa. $12.95

THE STORY OF THE TITANIC AS TOLD BY ITS SURVIVORS, Jack Winocour (ed.). What it was really like. Panic, despair, shocking inefficiency, and a little heroism. More thrilling than any fictional account. 26 illustrations. 320pp. 5⅜ × 8½.
20610-6 Pa. $7.95

FAIRY AND FOLK TALES OF THE IRISH PEASANTRY, William Butler Yeats (ed.). Treasury of 64 tales from the twilight world of Celtic myth and legend: "The Soul Cages," "The Kildare Pooka," "King O'Toole and his Goose," many more. Introduction and Notes by W. B. Yeats. 352pp. 5⅜ × 8½.
26941-8 Pa. $8.95

BUDDHIST MAHAYANA TEXTS, E. B. Cowell and Others (eds.). Superb, accurate translations of basic documents in Mahayana Buddhism, highly important in history of religions. The Buddha-karita of Asvaghosha, Larger Sukhavativyuha, more. 448pp. 5⅜ × 8½. ,
25552-2 Pa. $9.95

ONE TWO THREE . . . INFINITY: Facts and Speculations of Science, George Gamow. Great physicist's fascinating, readable overview of contemporary science: number theory, relativity, fourth dimension, entropy, genes, atomic structure, much more. 128 illustrations. Index. 352pp. 5⅜ × 8½.
25664-2 Pa. $8.95

ENGINEERING IN HISTORY, Richard Shelton Kirby, et al. Broad, nontechnical survey of history's major technological advances: birth of Greek science, industrial revolution, electricity and applied science, 20th-century automation, much more. 181 illustrations. ". . . excellent . . ."—Isis. Bibliography. vii + 530pp. 5⅜ × 8¼.
26412-2 Pa. $14.95

Prices subject to change without notice.
Available at your book dealer or write for free catalog to Dept. GI, Dover Publications, Inc., 31 East 2nd St., Mineola, N.Y. 11501. Dover publishes more than 500 books each year on science, elementary and advanced mathematics, biology, music, art, literary history, social sciences and other areas.